THE DEVIL'S RANSOM

The Devil's Ransom

A PIKE LOGAN NOVEL

Brad Taylor

WM

WILLIAM MORROW
An Imprint of HarperCollins*Publishers*

THE DEVIL'S RANSOM. Copyright © 2023 by Brad Taylor. All rights reserved. Printed in the United States of America. No part of this book may be used or reproduced in any manner whatsoever without written permission except in the case of brief quotations embodied in critical articles and reviews. For information, address HarperCollins Publishers, 195 Broadway, New York, NY 10007.

HarperCollins books may be purchased for educational, business, or sales promotional use. For information, please email the Special Markets Department at SPsales@harpercollins.com.

FIRST EDITION

Library of Congress Cataloging-in-Publication Data has been applied for.

ISBN 978-0-06-322198-7

23 24 25 26 27 LBC 5 4 3 2 1

To my editor, David Highfill, who's decided to take a different road in life. May you have the same wind at your back that you've always given me.

We live at a time when every government, every business, every person must focus on the threat of ransomware and take action to mitigate the risk of becoming a victim.

—Jen Easterly, Director, Cybersecurity
and Infrastructure Security Agency

When critical infrastructure is held at risk by foreign hackers operating from a safe haven in an adversary country, that's a national security problem.

—Rob Joyce, NSA Cybersecurity Director

Ransomware remains one of the most disruptive cyber threats to organizations and individuals. This global problem requires a global solution.

—Abigail Bradshaw CSC, Head of the
Australian Cyber Security Centre

THE DEVIL'S RANSOM

CHAPTER 1

August 15, 2021

The Arg presidential palace, Kabul, Afghanistan

Ahmad Khan heard the scurrying of footsteps, a scrum of people storming down the hallway outside of his office. Opening the door, he was startled to see the president of Afghanistan, Ashraf Ghani, walking rapidly past with his wife and a clutch of top advisors. Incongruously, the president was wearing plastic sandals and a thin coat.

Ahmad exited the office and scurried to catch up to the group, wondering what was happening. As the president's national security advisor, he had reason to be concerned. Jalalabad had been taken by the Taliban last night, and Mazar-e Sharif—once the bastion of anti-Taliban resistance—had fallen without a fight the day before. Kabul was surrounded, and even as Ghani's top advisors continued to proclaim all was well, Khan knew the barbarians were at the gate.

Others in the city apparently did as well, as the sky above the Arg—the nineteenth-century presidential palace that had been home to the rulers of Afghanistan for generations—radiated a constant thumping of rotor blades from helicopters of all nations, flying about like someone had smacked a beehive with a stick.

Khan caught up to the entourage and snagged the sleeve of

the man at the rear, saying, "What's going on? The president has a meeting in thirty minutes about the security of the main avenues of approach into Kabul."

The man turned, recognized him, and gave Khan a small shake of his head. Another man said, "He'll be there. Something's just come up. We're going to meet the Americans. They're leaving their embassy and relocating to the airport."

Matching the group's pace, Khan said, "Shouldn't I be there as well?" He nodded toward the older advisor who'd given the small shake, saying, "I mean, along with the foreign minister?"

The foreign minister said, "Not necessary. We're just coordinating. You need to prepare for the security meeting. We'll be back in plenty of time."

Khan stopped and they sped away, exiting into the palace gardens. He saw two Mi-17 helicopters land, and the entire group split up, boarding the aircraft. Within seconds, they were gone, the leaves and branches of the garden whipped about as if a small hurricane had come and gone.

He went back to his office, thinking, *Why is the president not dressed more formally? And why would Ghani's wife attend a meeting with the Americans?*

He opened the door to his office and found a man sitting in a chair in front of his desk. A small girl who appeared to be a tween was playing on the floor in front of his feet. It took a split second, but then he recognized the man. A friend Khan had known since childhood, and someone who had proven fearless over twenty years of war.

Only now, for the first time in Khan's life, he saw fear in the man's eyes.

Khan said, "Jahn, what are you doing here? And who's the child?"

Khan knew Jahn's wife had died from cancer a few years ago, and his son was now in the fight himself, a second-generation war.

Jahn said, "My son was killed in Jalalabad last night. This is my sister's child. She asked me to take her to America. She fears for her future."

Taken aback, Khan said, "Jahn, I'm so sorry." They'd both lost friends in the war, but Khan had never lost a relative. He said, "We'll turn this around. His loss won't be in vain. President Ghani has a plan. I'm working on it now."

Jahn stood up, and Khan saw the pressure mounting behind his eyes. He said, "Ghani is gone. He's not coming back. This is done. And my sister asked me to take her daughter to America. This is not going to be a place for her in two days."

Incredulous, Khan said, "I just saw him. He's going to talk to the Americans. He'll be here in thirty minutes for the security discussion."

Jahn looked him in the eye and said, "Ghani is fleeing. The Taliban are inside the city. We have hours, not days. We need to leave, and you have the ability to do so."

"What are you talking about?"

Jahn closed in on him and said, "I know what's happening, even if you government sops don't want to believe it. They're here. They'll be in control by nightfall."

Khan understood like few others the abilities of Jahn and was taken aback by the statement. Ghani's aide had just told him he was returning for a security briefing. How would Jahn know more than the president of Afghanistan?

But he knew how. Jahn had been at the forefront of the war since the twin towers had fallen in America. They'd been unlikely friends all their lives, Khan a little plump, short guy with no athletic skills, and Jahn the raw-boned, towering kid who excelled at everything. Khan never understood what Jahn saw in him, but they'd bonded, with Jahn beating back the bullies in the school and Khan helping him with his homework.

Then 9/11 had happened. After living under Taliban rule, the Americans had shattered the Taliban, and Khan had gone into the government after a stint at Oxford. Jahn had gone to war.

At six feet, he was tall for an Afghan, and he radiated energy. He'd started out in the Counterterrorism Pursuit Teams funded by the CIA, chasing Al Qaida into Pakistan, and then had gravitated to the Commando *Kandaks*, fighting all the way. Eventually, because of his skill, he'd returned to the CIA and become a deep-cover operative, penetrating Taliban operations. He was, to say the least, a most wanted man. And one who had the pulse of what was happening much more than anyone else in the country.

Khan, remembering what he'd just seen, said, "Are you sure?"

"Yes. It's done. Kabul has fallen, but they just don't know it yet. We need to leave, and you have the means to do it. Call a helicopter. Get us out of the country."

"You and the child?"

"Yes. I promised my sister. She won't become some Taliban wife wearing a burka."

Still not wanting to believe, Khan said, "But the Americans have the visa system. We can use that. We're not talking about this going to pieces in hours. I can't just call someone to fly us away."

Jahn stood up, and Khan saw the fear again. He said, "Ghani is gone. You saw the helicopters. This is done. The Americans mean well, but this is going to pieces much faster than they're aware. We need to go. Now."

Khan stuttered, walked in a tight circle, then said, "How can we just fly out? Where will be go? Even if I can get a helicopter?"

"Dushanbe, Tajikistan. The window is closing. We cannot go to the airport. It's absolute chaos. We need to fly from here. If you wait much longer, all the helicopter pilots will have gone without passengers, fleeing the death. They know what's coming."

Khan remained still. Jahn said, "Ahmad, please. If not for yourself, do it for the child. This country is gone, and she will endure a life of pain. They also know my name. They want me worse than they want the country. I have killed many, many of them. They'll skin me alive when they find me. They know you as well. They *might* just put you in jail."

Khan said, "I need to go home. To pack. To get my things. I can't just fly out. I have nothing."

Jahn said, "You will have nothing but your life. If you go home, we will lose the window. And be stuck here."

Khan said, "The Americans . . ."

"They are no help. They can't even get their own people out."

Khan nodded, and went to his phone. He dialed, then began speaking, eventually shouting into the handset. He hung up, turned to Jahn, and said, "A helicopter is on the way. What will we do when we land in Tajikistan?"

"We'll figure that out when we get there. The first step is just getting out."

Khan nodded, thinking. He turned a circle and Jahn said, "What?"

"The Bactrian Treasure. It's here, in the palace."

"What? You want to steal it?"

"Yes. I do. We need something when we land."

"It's huge. How are we going to get that out of here, under the noses of the guards protecting it?"

"I'll say I've been ordered to move it for its own protection. Take it to a hiding place, just like the last president did with the Soviets."

"They eviscerated him and hung his ass from a streetlight."

"That's my point. If he'd have taken the gold instead of burying it under the central bank, he might have been able to escape his fate."

The Bactrian Treasure was a trove of over twenty thousand gold artifacts from all over the world. Roman coins, Serbian jewel-encrusted daggers, gold belts from India, it was a horde that delineated the history of the famed Silk Road during the time of Alexander the Great. Found by a Soviet archeologist in 1978 in six royal tombs in northern Afghanistan, the persons buried there remained a mystery, but the treasure was most definitely real. During the time of the Soviet occupation, it had been housed in the Arg. When the Soviets left, and the Taliban came knocking much like they would decades later, the final communist president had ordered the horde hidden in a secret vault under the central bank, with only five persons knowing of its existence.

There it had remained, hidden, during the entire rule of the first Taliban regime. The leader of the Taliban, Mullah Omar, had tried mightily to find it, to no avail. It had become a sticking point of embarrassment, with many, many men killed trying to recover it.

The conventional wisdom was that the Soviet troops had taken it on their way out the door fleeing Afghanistan, and it was forgotten. In 2003, after the Taliban had fallen, a retired museum worker revealed the truth: it was buried in a secret vault under the central bank. Now it was displayed in the Arg, just as it had been before.

Jahn said, "Even if they give you access to the treasure, it's too big for you to move. It's not fitting into a single suitcase."

"I'll get them to move it for me. There are special cases built for travel, used when it went on its world tour. It'll fit into three, but I'll take only one with the best pieces. We can leverage it when we land. We'll need some ability to get money. I have a man I know. A Russian. He'll be willing to give us cash for the treasure."

"A Russian? They support the damn Taliban, and make no mistake, when this comes up missing, they're going to hunt it down."

"This isn't like that. He's a computer guy. Made a fortune doing networking in Russia."

Jahn squinted his eyes and said, "What kind of 'networking'?"

"I don't know, and really don't care. He loves collecting things. He was here for a conference last year and asked me to contact him if I came across anything unique. You know, outside of my job."

Jahn grimaced and said, "Yeah, I get it. 'Outside of your job.' Like every other bureaucrat in this damn palace. It's why we're about to lose the country to a bunch of savages. You fucks couldn't keep your hands out of the pig trough."

Khan recoiled and said, "I have never taken a bribe or other graft. I have the means to secure our future. That's all. Those savages will melt the gold down into bars if we leave it."

Jahn stood, took the hand of the girl, and said, "Whatever lets you sleep at night. Just get me to Tajikistan. I want no part of the treasure. That's all you."

CHAPTER 2

Sirajuddin Haqqani studied a single sheet of paper, the double row of names and offenses against the Taliban printed out, some with convenient biometric data left behind by the Americans. Now the "interior minister" of the new Islamic Emirate of Afghanistan, he meant to cleanse the country of those who were apostates to Taliban rule. Officially, the Taliban had offered amnesty to any who had opposed their onslaught. Unofficially, it was Haqqani's job to bring select people to justice. The rank and file of the armed forces and police would be given amnesty, but some would feel his wrath, if he could find them in time.

Currently, the Taliban leadership were taking pictures in the president's office, vacated hours before, proving they were in charge, but the Americans were evacuating traitors at an incredible rate. If he wanted to catch the men on the list, it had to be swift.

And there was one name that he wanted more than any other. Jahn Azimi.

That single man had done more damage to the Haqqani network than any American platoon of commandos. In fact, he'd led the commandos to his doorstep time and time again, killing his men with impunity. Whether a drone strike or an outright assault, Jahn Azimi was at the heart of death. And Sirajuddin was determined to make him pay. It wasn't personal. It was Afghanistan.

Two men burst into the room, dragging another man in uniform on his knees. The first said, "Jahn was on a helicopter! He took the Bactrian Treasure! This man helped him."

Sirajuddin stood up and said, "What are you talking about?"

The first man cuffed the guard in the head, knocking him to the ground. The second said, "Jahn was here, hours ago. He left with the national security advisor. Both of them took the Bactrian Treasure. This pig actually loaded it onto the helicopter."

The guard began blubbering, saying, "He told me he was protecting it. He told me it was sanctioned. I did what they said. I wasn't trying to harm anything."

Sirajuddin circled his newfound desk and said, "You saw the treasure leaving?"

Fearful for his life, the guard said, "Yes. I'm sorry. I didn't mean anything by helping. I just did my job."

Sirajuddin said, "Stand up."

He did. Sirajuddin said, "We gave amnesty to all who fought against us. You have nothing to fear."

The man nodded, not believing the words, but hoping.

Sirajuddin pulled a picture from the stack on his desk and said, "Did you see this man today?"

The guard nodded, saying, "He was with the national security advisor. Ahmad Khan. They had us load the Bactrian Treasure into a helicopter. And then they left."

While he knew the Taliban hierarchy would care a great deal about the treasure, Sirajuddin did not. He said, "This man was the one? He was there?"

"Yes, sir. He was there. He flew away."

"Where? Where did he go?"

"I don't know. I think Tajikistan. Dushanbe. But I don't know for sure."

One of the men cursed him, then smacked him in the head again, slamming him to the floor.

Sirajuddin held his hand up and said, "Stop. He is not the enemy."

The guard looked at him with dread, saying, "I was just doing my job."

Sirajuddin said, "I know. And now you'll continue your job. You are free to go."

The man looked at the two others, waiting on the axe to fall. When it didn't, he scurried out of the room, running as if he were escaping a fire.

Sirajuddin let him go, then said, "Get me Shakor. Right now."

Four minutes later a man entered. Unlike the others in the room, Shakor was dressed like a Western soldier, with a camouflage uniform that included body armor and an M4 rifle with optics instead of a beat-up AK-47. If one didn't know better, he could have been one of the elite Afghan Commandos trained by the United States Special Forces.

But he wasn't. He was the commander of the Badr 313 Battalion. Named after the Battle of Badr, where the prophet Muhammed led 313 men to victory in the first century, the battalion was the elite of the Taliban. At the forefront of the fighting, using both special operations tactics and suicide missions, it was not an exaggeration to say that the battalion was the reason the Taliban were sitting in the Arg. And if imitation was the sincerest form of flattery, the men of the battalion were outfitted and clothed just like the Western Special Forces they had fought for more than twenty long years.

Removing his helmet and Peltor headset, Shakor said, "The airport is held by the Americans. They're trying to get everyone out. We can't penetrate without a fight. Do you want to do that? I can take the airfield right now, but I can't in three hours."

"Why?

"They're flooding in the 82nd Airborne and Marines. I can't fight them. Well, I can, but if I do, I'll lose. Those men are not something to trifle with."

Sirajuddin scoffed and said, "You can't take them out? We've taken out their entire military machine."

Shakor said, "We have, but never in a straight-up fight. We now have the tiger by the tail. You want me to attack them, and I will lose. And you will, too. The Americans are dumb. They have no idea of our culture or society, but if you push them, they *will* win in a fight. Right now they're scared. They're worried. Let them leave."

Sirajuddin waved his hand and said, "That's not my concern. My job is internal security, and we've lost two things I want you to get back."

He explained the stealing of the Bactrian Treasure and then showed him the picture of Jahn, saying, "This man has killed many, many of your soldiers. He flew out with the national security advisor, who took the treasure."

He placed another picture on the desk, saying, "And this is Ahmad Khan, the national security advisor. I want the treasure back, and I want Jahn. You can kill Ahmad Khan to get the treasure back, but Jahn returns here."

Shakor nodded and said, "Where is he?"

"Best guess is Dushanbe. They took a helicopter. We don't have that capability, but we do own all the border crossings by road. You need to leave immediately. Split up into two teams. One is for Jahn, the other is for the treasure. I'm sure by the time you get there it'll be gone. You'll have to hunt it."

Shakor said, "I'm needed here. This place could devolve into a maelstrom of looting in the next thirty-six hours. My men are the only ones who can stop that."

"This is more important. Pick ten of your best men. Only English speakers who have worked or gone to school in the West. No farmers you've trained. You lead them. You go after the treasure, another team goes after Jahn. I want him back, alive. Don't kill him."

"That's an impossible challenge. How am I going to find the treasure or the man a day after it was flown out?"

"They took a helicopter. I'm sure that made a stir in Dushanbe. I'll contact our men there and give you a lead. Jahn will try to hide, but Ahmad will be touting his credentials. It'll be just as big a stir as Ghani flying into Uzbekistan."

"But that asshole is already on a flight to the UAE. If the treasure leads there, you want me to follow to another Muslim country? I can create a team of men who can work in the West, but I can't do the same if it leads to Saudi Arabia, Qatar, or the UAE. We won't survive."

Sirajuddin turned back to his desk, looked at a map, and said, "He's not going there with the treasure. He has the same problem you do. He's going to sell it, and it won't be to a Muslim. It'll be to someone in Europe."

Shakor nodded, grabbing his helmet. "The one good thing is the entire city is chaos. I can form the teams and leave in the next two hours because of the complete breakdown in security. I can be across the border by tomorrow morning, but I'll need your contacts in Dushanbe, and I'll need some support once I'm there."

Sirajuddin said, "That will not be a problem. You still have your satellite phone?"

"Yes, but I'm not using that. It's a magnet for American bombs."

"Not in Dushanbe. Call me once you cross the border. I'll give you the contact information."

Shakor nodded again, then picked up the pictures, saying, "I don't know about this treasure, but I'll definitely find Jahn. For a little payback."

CHAPTER 3

I rolled over in my sleeping bag and bumped into Jennifer, now contorted like a circus act within her mummy bag. I raised up on an elbow, seeing her splayed like she'd been thrown out of the back of a pickup truck, her head leaning over the opening of the bag, her hair draped all over the place. I was amazed. *How could someone sleep like that?* She routinely took over any bed we shared, but now she was trying to take over a sleeping bag she was the sole owner of. It was like she wanted to spread out and deprive me of the bed, but she couldn't, because she was in a mummy bag.

I grinned, checked my watch, then felt the tightness in my back from what I was using as a mattress. You can't sleep on the ground for any length of time before it takes a toll. In this case, we'd been living like animals for close to two weeks, but unlike the past, I didn't have to worry about someone shooting at me, so at least I could take off my boots before going to bed. Even so, sleeping on the ground was miserable. Sometimes, like today, it was a good miserable, but miserable, nonetheless.

I studied her for a moment, content. I didn't want to wake her, because the sun was just cresting the horizon, and even though it was August, it was a little crisp here in Tajikistan. And I knew that if I did, I'd be back to helping her dig up pottery shards, her like her life depended on it, and me just wanting to quit and have a beer.

No, I'd let her sleep until she woke up on her own. I lay back down and then saw the zipper of our tent begin moving. I groaned, because I knew who it was.

The zipper split, and I saw Amena staring at me, her hazel eyes focusing first on my face, then on Jennifer's contorted body. She was our adopted daughter, and Jennifer had decided to bring her on this dig, which I thought was a mistake—not the least of which because she routinely woke us up at the crack of dawn. These artifacts had waited centuries to be found, and yet she seemed to think another hour was a tragedy.

Or she just knew I hated it.

Olive skin, black hair, and eyes with a color that were piercing, at fourteen years old she was turning into quite the beauty, but she still had a little bit of a rebellious streak in her from her time in Syria. Which is to say, she could hold her own with anyone she faced, no matter the age. Including me.

She said, "What on earth is Jennifer doing? Were you guys . . ."

I sat up and hissed, "No! Stop that. She's sleeping. She's in her own bag."

"It looks like you two were wrestling."

Jennifer stirred, rubbed her eyes, and said, "What's up?"

I said, "Nothing. The little devil is here to wake us up."

Amena said, "Only two more days left. We need to get to work."

We were at a place called Ajina Tepa, about a hundred kilometers from Dushanbe, the capital of Tajikistan. Known as the Devil's Hill in Tajik, it was an eighth-century Buddhist monastery and temple that had been on the UNESCO world heritage tentative list since 1999, and was the biggest archeological site in the entire country.

Our company, Grolier Recovery Services, had asked permission to camp out and explore it for a couple of weeks, and the country of Tajikistan had obliged—mainly because they thought we could get them a leg up on the UNESCO decision, but since the designation had been sitting dormant for more than two decades, I seriously doubted it.

That, and because our company really had nothing to do with archeology or UNESCO, but that was a secret I wasn't going to tell anyone in Tajikistan.

GRS was what we called a front company. Ostensibly, we facilitated archeological work around the world, helping real archeologists on their way in areas that were not that conducive to the work. Meaning, we could assist them both with the government in question and the bad man outside the gates. Jennifer had a degree in anthropology, and I had a degree in killing people, which worked out for our little company.

We spent our off days helping universities and other organizations with government permits, doing security assessments, and generally greasing the skids, and it was a good living, but while Jennifer loved these excursions, I thought of them as work. I wanted to hunt, but I understood the reason for this trip. We needed to make sure our cover was solid if anyone came looking.

In the end, using that façade, our real purpose was hunting terrorists in both nonpermissive and permissive environments, cloaking our actions with the company's name. It was ingenious, if I do say so myself, because there were very few places on earth that didn't have some sort of archeological site we could leverage.

Jennifer was my partner in the company, and she truly loved this end of the work. She had developed into a little bit of a killer herself over the years for the other side of our job, even if she wouldn't admit it. She didn't like looking in the mirror and seeing what came back, but she *was* a killer. At her core, she wanted to explore, digging up pottery shards and pieces of skulls, because that's what made her whole. But I'd seen her on the other end of a barrel, and she was a predator just like I was. I, on the other hand, could fully admit that digging up bones in the middle of nowhere was about as much fun as sticking a fork in my eye.

This excursion was really nothing more than a vacation designed to increase the believability of the company. Called a "cover development" trip, it was paid by the U.S. taxpayer, and solely designed to show that Grolier really did do archeological work. Don't believe me? Just take a look at this work we did in Tajikistan!

We had to execute about two cover development trips for every one where we put somebody's head on a spike just to make sure we could bullshit our way around anyone investigating us—be that a friendly government or a hostile sub-state group—and this was one such trip, only this time Jennifer had brought Amena with us.

For the life of me, I don't know why. We'd brought her on our honeymoon a couple of months ago, and that had turned into an absolute shit show.

Jennifer sat up, her blond hair looking like she'd plugged her finger into a socket, and smiled, saying, "Well, at least two of us enjoy the work."

Amena fully unzipped the tent and scampered inside, saying, "There's room in here for me. Can I stay with you guys at least one night?"

I let her flop on top of me and said, "You have a tent. Why cram three people into one?"

She said, "Nick snores. I mean bad."

I laughed, knowing she was just making excuses. I had three other team members with me on the "dig," all there simply to solidify their "employment" with the company. We needed to have ironclad backstopping when we did clandestine work on the off chance we were compromised, so I could "prove" they were who they said they were.

Given that, it meant three tents total for the excursion, which left one tent with only a single person. Nicholas Seacrest—callsign Veep—had been chosen as the outlier, 1) because he was the junior team member, but 2) because his girlfriend was actually Amena's nanny when we were away.

Given that the sun had barely crested the horizon, I was regretting she wasn't watching Amena right now.

Jennifer tousled her hair and said, "Yeah, maybe you can stay for one night."

Amena looked at me to see if I agreed, and I smiled. I literally couldn't tell her no. In truth, Jennifer was the disciplinarian of this relationship, but Amena and I had a little bit of a personal connection that went beyond adoption. Meaning when we'd first met, I'd slaughtered several men to keep her alive. Those actions hadn't been pretty, but the end result had been. She was now my daughter, not by birth, but by a shared experience.

I heard a scuffling outside the tent, then my second-in-command poked his head in. I rolled my eyes and said, "Come on in, Knuckles. Let's get everyone inside here."

Knuckles looked every bit like some wandering Birkenstock-wearing backpacker, complete with shaggy black hair, a T-shirt espousing some ironic saying, and puka beads around his neck. If you looked closely, you'd see that shirt stretched over ropes of muscle, and if you reached his eyes, you'd see that he wasn't being ironic. He was wanting you to test him for wearing it. And if you did, you'd be the worse for it.

Knuckles was a Navy SEAL, but I didn't hold that against him, because he was one of the finest operators I had ever served with. He'd just picked the wrong service to start with, his wardrobe notwithstanding.

He chuckled and said, "No, that's okay. Jennifer looks like she's been in a dogfight. Not sure what you guys do in here at night."

Amena laughed, and Knuckles grew serious. "Pike, the sat phone went off in the night. I think you should check it."

I sat up, moving Amena to the side, and, while putting on my boots, said, "What's up?"

He stepped back, letting me exit the tent, then said, "I don't know, but it's Taskforce. They called while we were asleep."

CHAPTER 4

Istumbled out of the tent saying, "Why would the Taskforce call us here? They know we're doing cover development."

Knuckles said, "I have no idea, but we don't get voice mails on that system, and all I saw was the number. It's George Wolffe. Something's gone bad."

I nodded, saying, "What, though? We're in Tajikistan. What could have gone so wrong that we need to be pulled in?"

He just shook his head.

We worked for a government organization called Project Prometheus, which was the classified code name for our unit. Since we couldn't say the name out loud, we'd just taken to calling ourselves the Taskforce. Simple. A name that meant nothing. But really meant everything—especially if I was getting a call in Tajikistan on a cover development trip.

I picked up the sat phone, saw the last called number, and looked at Knuckles. He nodded, saying, "I think we're going to get some high adventure here."

I shook my head, not wanting to dial, but did so. The phone rang out to a voice mail for a cover organization called Blaisdell Consulting. Which was the headquarters for the Taskforce.

I left a message and hung up. "This had better not be some bullshit that the CIA or SOCOM couldn't handle."

Project Prometheus—the Taskforce—was a unique unit designed to solve unique problems. Issues that the traditional intelligence or military architecture couldn't solve. We were only pulled into play when all other options were exhausted, and that was for a reason—namely, that we operated outside the bounds of the U.S. Constitution. We had free rein to stop a threat, but in so doing, we also had free rein to ignore any rights ensconced in the very thing we were protecting. It was something I took very, very seriously, as did the man I'd just called.

When the unit had been formed after 9/11, we'd all cheered about how we were going to take it to the enemy, but some had realized that what we'd created had the potential to go bad. I say "some," but it was really my mentor, the first commander of the Taskforce, Colonel Kurt Hale. He'd been killed by a car bomb in my front yard and I'd proven the risks of the organization when I'd gone off the reservation to avenge him, slaughtering anyone who'd had anything to do with his death. That had caused some consternation within the chain of command, to say the least, but in my heart, I held his views.

Most of the time.

We weren't hired guns. We were problem solvers who could shoot. Give me a problem you couldn't solve, and I would do it. If I had to shoot to get it done, I would, but it had to be for the right reasons.

I saw Knuckles' tent open and my third team member appear, Brett Thorpe. A short fireplug of muscle, he was out of place as an African American here in Tajikistan—but then again, so were we, I suppose. Didn't really matter, because like everyone else, he was ostensibly an employee of GRS. It wasn't like we were trying to pretend we were Tajiks. He was also a prior Force Recon Marine and currently a paramilitary officer with the Special Activities

Center of the CIA, with a little bit of a wicked sense of humor. Which is to say, I wouldn't do a mission without him.

He approached, looked at Knuckles, then at me, saying, "So what's up?"

I said, "Left a message. No idea."

Knuckles said, "What do you think this is about? We're here in the middle of nowhere."

I took a breath and said, "I don't know, but it's not going to be good. Wolffe would never interrupt this trip for something mundane."

He chuckled and said, "Well, if it's something bad here in the barren wildlands, all I've got is my ZEV Tech Glock. I only brought two magazines for someone trying to harm us here. I didn't think about getting into a gunfight. You got more?"

I said, "Not here. I have the same. Two mags. Thank God I demanded the Rock Star bird come with a package."

Surprised, Knuckles said, "You got permission for a loadout in the Rock Star bird for a signature reduction trip? How did you manage that?"

I smiled. "I'm very persuasive when I want to be." I shook my head, stared at the phone, and said, "What the hell is going on?"

This was supposed to be a simple cover development mission, and I was now glad my insistence on the package for the Rock Star bird had been approved.

Then the phone rang.

I answered, saying, "This is Pike."

I heard, "Stand by for Wolffe. We've been trying to get you for hours."

Knuckles gave me a look and I said, "On hold. Wolffe is coming on the line."

I waited, then heard, "Is this Pike?"

I said, "Yes, sir, this is Pike. What's up?"

"Have you been watching the news?"

A little incensed, I said, "No, sir. I'm in Tajikistan. I have no ability to watch the news. Did Kim Kardashian do something I missed?"

"Pike, Afghanistan is lost. The Taliban just took over Kabul. It's done."

It took a second to process. We'd only been here a week, and when I'd left, there were peace discussions going on in Doha, Qatar. *We've lost the country?*

I said, "Say again? What do you mean Kabul is lost? You mean it's coming to a close and Kabul is in danger?"

"No. Kabul is lost. It's over. I don't have time to get into it, but Kabul has fallen, and we're doing everything we can to evacuate AMCITS from the county. It's a mess. The 82nd is in right now controlling the Kabul airfield. But that's not why I'm calling."

I said, "Wait, wait, are you saying we've folded up the flag?"

"Yes. But that's not why I'm calling—"

The statement was a body blow to me. I'd spent more than a few years in Afghanistan after 9/11 and his words were like blistering acid. Not that I didn't know it was coming. I knew we were leaving, but that was when the Afghan government had a least a year to succeed against the Taliban. According to our own Taskforce intel guys.

I snarled, "We've lost the whole damn country? What about Maser or Jalalabad?"

"Pike, it's done. They're gone. The president fled the country. The Taliban are running amok. Haven't you been watching the news?"

"Sir, I told you, we don't have news out here in the wild lands. I'm living in a tent talking to you on a sat phone. I have seen nothing on this."

I couldn't believe it. *We* were the eight-hundred-pound gorilla. How could those fucks have taken over the entire country? But I knew how, in my heart. Like a lightning strike going from pole to pole, I thought about the Afghan men I'd served with who were now at the hands of savages.

I said, "What about the *Kandaks*? The Commandos? What are we doing for them?"

"The 82nd is evacuating as many as they can, but that's why I'm calling. We have a special request from the CIA."

I looked at the sky, then at Knuckles. He squinted his eyes and I said, "What is it?"

"There's a man who worked both for the CIA counter pursuit teams, then for the Commandos, then went deep cover penetrating Taliban infrastructure. He managed to make it to Tajikistan and he's on the run."

I nodded, even as I knew Wolffe couldn't see it, saying, "Okay, go on."

"He's in Dushanbe. He fled with the national security advisor, but they split up. We have intel that the Badr 313 Battalion is hunting him. We want to bring him home. The CIA doesn't have the assets to do it, but you do. Kerry Bostwick asked for you."

Kerry was the head of the CIA, and a good man. While I had my issues with the organization, I didn't with the man running it. He wouldn't have delegated it to us if he had any ability to extract this asset. But I asked anyway.

"Why isn't he pulling the guy out? What do I have that he doesn't? I'm here as a private company. He owns the entire CIA."

I heard heat from the phone, the distance not diluting the anger. "I can't believe you're even asking that question. I don't *know* why he can't do it. What I know is that the asset is going to be dead in twenty-four hours or less and the CIA asked for our help."

Chagrined, I said, "Sorry, sir. Just trying to get the state of play here. Of course we'll pull him out. Where is he?"

"Dushanbe. That's all I know. Start moving, and I'll give you a lock-on. We have a case officer working it right now. He contacted his CO in Afghanistan, but that guy had already gone home to DC. He passed the contact to us. We have Carly in Dushanbe. She's setting up the meet. It should just be a quick in-and-out."

I said, "Carly? What's she doing here? She speaks Spanish and Portuguese."

"All we could get on short notice. She's in Dushanbe coordinating with the CIA station chief. She's in charge of the meet. All you need to do is get him, take him to the bird, and let him fly. Then you can return to digging up pottery shards."

I said, "No issues. Is the Oversight Council aware, in case I have to go kinetic here?"

The Oversight Council was the body of men and women who oversaw all Taskforce actions. Comprised of thirteen members drawn from both the government and civilian world, they were the ones I'd aggravated in my quest to avenge Kurt Hale, but they still oversaw my operations. Since we were—to say the least—a little illegal, nothing we did happened without their approval, and I wanted to know, if I was forced into lethal action, that I was approved.

Wolffe said, "Yeah, they're all read on. Kerry was pretty forceful, and as a member of the Council his words held weight. This guy was apparently one of their best operatives, and the president himself approved the mission. The ROE is hostile force."

That made me smile. Hostile force rules of engagement meant I could kill whomever I wanted. I said, "Hostile force? Seriously? This man is worth upsetting our relationships inside another country?"

George Wolffe said, "According to Kerry, he did more for the military mission than most of the U.S. folks in uniform. We're getting him to the United States. That's from the president himself."

My smile grew larger. I said, "Perfect. Give me the lock-on, and I'll get him out."

Wolffe said, "I'm working it now, but Pike, this still needs to be clandestine. We can't compromise your company or the Taskforce."

I laughed and said, "I can't promise that, sir, and you know it. I'll do what I can, but when you grab the tiger by the tail, you still get the tiger."

"The Oversight Council doesn't want the tiger. They want a seamless extraction."

I said, "And Kerry? What's he want?"

"He wants his man out. Period."

And I realized why I liked Kerry Bostwick. He cared more about the men than whatever bullshit was going on in Washington, DC.

I said, "Then fuck the Oversight Council. I'll get his man home, but it may be behind a wrecking ball."

CHAPTER 5

Sitting in the fetid alley, water dripping from the roof above, his niece next to him, Jahn wondered about his next move. He was free from Afghanistan, as far as that went, but he was a long way from any help, and he was sure they were being hunted. He would be Target Number One on the Taliban hit list, and the exit from the Dushanbe airport hadn't been very smooth.

As soon as their helicopter had set down, Ahmad saw a bunch of people running toward it across the tarmac. With the rotors still turning, the whine of the Mi-17 loud in the cabin, the pilot looked to the rear and said, "This is it. I'm surprised they let us land. We are done."

Wearing a headset, Ahmad said, "Are you talking to the tower?"

The pilot pointed at the men jogging across the field and said, "Yes, but they are not happy."

Ahmad looked at Jahn and shouted, "It's not good. They're coming for us."

For the first time, Jahn pulled a pistol from his waist. He moved the small girl behind him and said, "We have to fight, we fight."

The pilot looked like he was going to throw up. Ahmad said, "Go. Get out. The price of your flight is this helicopter. They can have it. You're good. Get out."

He nodded, ripped off his helmet, and took off running across the tarmac. Ahmad saw him tackled at the edge of the fence, turned around to Jahn, and said, "Follow my lead. We have more than they know. We'll get out."

Jahn said, "That's not good enough. These men can be as bad as the Taliban. They don't care about us. They care about whoever is controlling the strings, and it's not us."

"The Americans are controlling the strings. That's who we trust."

Jahn said, "I've trusted them before. They won't come. This is in the Russian sphere of influence."

Even as he said it, he was thinking about an American he could call. Someone who could possibly save him and his niece.

Ahmad said, "That's true, and that's why we'll be okay. I have a Russian who wants what's in this helicopter."

He pulled up his phone and started talking, keeping his eyes on the men advancing. By the time he was done, the Tajiks had surrounded the helicopter.

Jahn saw the men and raised his hands. In short order, they were searched and evacuated, with Ahmad protesting the entire way. They were taken to a hangar and allowed to sit alone, with a single guard. Jahn wondered what would happen next. What he needed to do was get out of the airport. Get into the city, with his niece.

Eventually, a man entered the room. A Caucasian with a scar that leaked into his left eye. He was someone who had seen war, and not from a television screen. He said, "Who is the leader here?" He spoke English, but his accent was Russian. He was not from Tajikistan. Ahmad raised his hand. The man said, "You have something my boss wants, correct?"

Ahmad smiled, looked at Jahn, and said, "Yes, yes I do."

The man said, "Where is it?"

"In the helicopter we flew in on."

"Let's go get it."

Ahmad said, "Wait, before we do that, we need some assurances." He pointed at Jahn and said, "I have a friend here. We need some help."

The man looked at Jahn, then at the small girl. He said, "You'll get nothing from me. I have my orders. Get me what you say you have and you might live to see another sunrise. I can't promise anything else."

Jahn stood up, ready to fight, and the man said, "You are free to go. Nobody here will interfere. I'm sorry, but I can't help you, other than letting you leave here on your own accord."

Jahn stood still for a moment, then took the hand of his niece, saying, "Let's go."

She said, "Where? Where are we going?"

"Away from here."

Ahmad said, "Wait a minute. We have what your boss wants. That is our ticket out of here."

The man flipped back his jacket, showing a pistol. He said, "It's *your* ticket out. Nobody else. I don't own this airport, but I own the security for the next sixty seconds. If you want to push this, I'll leave, and you'll be on your own. My boss will help you, but he doesn't care about refugees."

Ahmad looked at Jahn, and Jahn smiled, saying, "You did what you said you would. I'll get out on my own. Can I have your cell phone?"

Ahmad passed it over, a look of pain on his face. Jahn took it and, in Pashto, Ahmad said, "One thing about that phone. It's loaded with spyware. Ghani made all cabinet members download a program that allowed him to see what you did with the phone. His way to stamp out corruption."

"Who can see it?"

"Ghani's men. And they're all gone."

"Give me your other phone."

"I don't have another phone."

"Yes, you do. Otherwise, you wouldn't have this contact that's here right now. You didn't use this phone for your side projects."

Ahmad smiled and said, "You were always ahead of everyone else. But I'm sorry, I'm not giving you my other phone. It's my lifeline out of here. It's where all of my contacts are stored."

Jahn glanced at the Russian, continuing in Pashto, "You got me here. It's okay. Good luck with the devil's ransom on this."

Jahn left the terminal, the girl in tow. He passed by several armed guards, but they showed him no interest. He was allowed to leave the building, entering the streets of southern Dushanbe. He'd never been to the city, but knew he needed to get off the streets immediately. He had no doubt the Taliban or Haqqani network would find out he'd fled, and Tajikistan was not exactly a safe haven.

He dragged his niece into a fetid alley and called a man whom he'd risked his life for on multiple occasions. He got some panicked flunky on the other end, someone who didn't know him and seemed to be shouting at others in the room as much as talking to into the phone. The man said, "Look, I understand you want to leave Afghanistan. Everyone wants to leave Afghanistan, but we can only take so many. You'll have to make your way to the airport gate like everyone else."

Jahn said, "Let me speak to Bill Akers, please."

"He's not here."

"When will he be back?"

"Never. He's gone to the United States, and trust me, nobody's coming back here."

He was disgusted. He knew what was happening in Kabul, and he knew nobody cared about him or his niece here in Tajikistan.

Jahn said, "Can someone pass him a message for me? Please?"

"Yeah, yeah, I can do that I guess."

Jahn said, "Just tell him Cowboy is in trouble in Dushanbe and give him this number."

The man agreed, but Jahn didn't believe him. He sat down on a trash heap, pulling the girl into his lap, thinking about options. He was on his own, but he wasn't without skills. Skills he'd learned from the very United States government that had abandoned him.

They remained in the alley for four hours, Jahn afraid to leave until he'd determined the best course of action. Once he did, he planned on executing it on the run, with plenty of fallback options. He was using the mapping function of his phone, planning a route out of the city, then out of the country, when it rang, surprising him. He answered, unsure if he was creating a geolocation target for whoever was on the other end.

He heard a woman's voice say, "Jahn? Jahn Azimi?"

He said, "Yes. This is Jahn. Who is this?"

"It's a friend. We understand you're in Tajikistan. Dushanbe. Is that correct?"

He felt the relief flow over him, embarrassed at his earlier chastisement of the United States. He said, "Yes. I'm on the run. I have a small child with me."

She said, "No problem. I'm going to set up a meeting with you, and we're going to get you out."

"I'm being hunted. I know it. There are people here who will kill me and her for what I've done."

She said, "I understand. Listen to me closely. I'm going to give you information to get you out. It has to happen quickly. Do you have the ability to write something down?"

"No. I'm in an alley. I can't write anything down."

Soothingly, she said, "That's okay. Do you know the Victory Park?"

"Yes. I've seen it on maps."

"That's where we're going to meet. You bring the girl, and you will get out clean."

"I don't think you understand. There are dangerous people hunting me. I can't show my face. I can't go to a park."

She chuckled and said, "I don't think *you* understand. I work with dangerous people. I'm bringing a wrecking crew. You get there, and you're good."

CHAPTER 6

I parked on a side alley, circling around until I was right at the intersection of Bekhzod street, the road that ran in front of the Dushanbe Mall entrance, with a clear view of anyone exiting. It had taken a little over three hours to pack our stuff up and drive from the dig to the capital city, with a detour to the Bokhtar airport just outside the site, but we'd made it in time for the meet.

We could have flown into Dushanbe on our plane, but given that the Mi-17 helicopter that had brought the man we were tasked with exfiling was now guarded by about a hundred goons, and that the security apparatus was grilling everyone who came and went because of the stink involved, I'd decided to do the two-hour drive to the city instead of attempting to smuggle the Afghan past immigration and security at the Dushanbe airport. But that didn't mean we couldn't take a little bit of what was hidden within the bird.

Leased to Grolier Recovery Services through about four hundred different shell companies to hide its provenance, it was a Gulfstream 650. We called it the Rock Star bird because it's the same model that drug-addled musicians used to travel the world, the difference being that instead of hot tubs and a king-sized bed, ours held a wealth of lethal instruments hidden in compartments throughout the interior.

Outfitting everyone with long guns, ammunition, surveillance gear, and anything else I thought would be necessary, I told the pilots to remain on alert, because I wasn't sure if I'd be coming back here, or calling them to come to us somewhere else. They took it in stride, because that's what always happened to them. As the men were unloading the kit, I pulled Jennifer aside.

She said, "What's up?"

"What about Amena? We should leave her here with the pilots. We don't know what's going to happen. She'll be safer here."

Jennifer said, "I don't know about that. You want to leave her in the care of these guys? They don't have any way to take care of her, and probably have no idea how. Is she going to stay in a tent next to the plane?"

Taking a look at the pilots, both in their thirties, she had a point. Still, I said, "She can go to their hotel. We'll get her a room at the same place. She can order room service. It's not like I'm asking them to babysit, and we're only going to be gone for a day."

Amena saw us talking and came up to our little tête-à-tête.

Jennifer saw her coming and sighed, saying, "Yeah, okay. I guess we can't take her on the mission itself."

Amena reached us and I explained the situation, to which, as expected, she immediately balked. Things began to grow heated, with me sternly saying, "You can't come. We have a mission. Be thankful we brought you to Tajikistan at all. We could have left you with Kylie."

Kylie was Veep's girlfriend and sort of our go-to nanny in Charleston. She was supposed to watch Amena while we were gone, but Amena had insisted on coming with us, and I'd relented.

Amena said, "I've done missions with you before! Remember Zurich? Remember Geneva? Remember Nice? That was me!"

Which was actually true, but that had been because of the knowledge in her head about a terrorist we were tracking, not because I thought my team needed her limited skills.

I saw the rest of my team loading up the Land Rovers and surreptitiously glancing our way. I said, "Amena, it's not going to happen."

She wound up into what I recognized as an Amena temper tantrum, and Jennifer took her arm, leading her away. They spoke for a few minutes, and I saw a tear in Amena's eye. I knew Jennifer had won, but it sure didn't feel like victory.

She came running back to me and wrapped her arms around my waist, saying, "You'd better come back."

I hugged her and laughed, saying, "Of course I'm coming back. If I don't, you can have the airplane." After all this time, she was still worried about being abandoned.

She looked up to me and said, "I mean it. Don't let the bad man get you."

And with her words I realized she wasn't afraid of being abandoned. She was afraid of Jennifer and me getting killed. She'd lived through a remarkable amount of death in her young life, and I knew she wasn't speaking out of some imaginative fear. She had lost her family first in Syria and then in France as an illegal refugee, and had seen more death as I tracked the men who'd done it. Remarkably, she seemed to think she could prevent any harm coming to me or Jennifer if she came along.

I broke the hug and held her shoulders, saying, "We'll be back in a day. All we're doing is picking up a guy who needs a ride."

She sniffled, looked at the men loading up the Land Rovers, and said, "Yeah, that's why you need all those guns."

I smiled and said, "Just being cautious. Go let Jennifer introduce you to the pilots. They'll take care of you. You can eat whatever you want, stay up late watching TV, whatever you want to do. We'll be back tomorrow."

She hugged me again and said, "I'll bet the TV has three channels in Tajik."

She started walking away, then said over her shoulder, "If the hotel room has a minibar, I'm cleaning it out. The pilots can have the booze. I'm eating all the candy and drinking the Cokes."

I shouted, "They don't get any booze! They're on alert for us!"

I watched her take Jennifer's hand and go to the cockpit. I went to the trucks to finish loadout and Knuckles said, "How'd that go?"

"Not as good as I would have liked."

He laughed and said, "The joys of parenting. Only instead of telling your kid she's too short for the roller coaster, you're telling her she can't go on a top-secret mission with us."

I grimaced, helping Brett with a Pelican case full of surveillance gear, and he said, "You have one tangled mess on your hands with her."

I closed the hatch to the Rover and said, "Tell me about it."

Jennifer arrived and I said, "Okay, she going to live?"

Jennifer said, "She's fine. Just a little miffed. The pilots actually took a shine to her. I think they're bored and like the idea of some responsibility."

I said, "Or her minibar."

"What's that mean?"

"Nothing." I turned to the team, saying, "Okay, it's about a two-hour drive, which puts us close to the contact time with Carly. Knuckles and Brett, rear Rover. Jennifer and Veep, here with me. We'll do the initial contact, then bring her to the hotel. You guys will get that hotel so we have some place to show up to."

People started moving, doors slamming, and I turned to get behind the wheel, finding Knuckles blocking my way. He said, "Hey, man, come on. I'm doing the meet."

Jennifer was already in the passenger seat, Veep in the back. I glanced at them and said, "Come on, Knuckles. I can't afford some bullshit here. Just get the hotel."

He leaned into me and said, "I'm doing the meet, Pike. This is *my* mission."

The case officer we were meeting was Carly Ramirez, a covert operative for the Taskforce and an old flame of Knuckles'. They'd met on an operation when she was working for the CIA and he was with the Taskforce. He'd recruited her for our organization with an idea that she would be the second female operator in the Taskforce—after Jennifer—and he'd started training her while he dated her.

It had ended up in the usual Knuckles fashion, which is to say, they were no longer dating. She'd quit Assessment and Selection, he'd been embarrassed about it, and they'd broken up. There was no shame in it, because she'd never wanted it and Knuckles had forced the issue, but I was worried about him conducting this meet. I knew he still cared for her, and I didn't need another problem.

I said, "You sure about this? The mission comes first, and I don't want her getting skittish because you show up."

He laughed and said, "We're good, Pike. Really good. I'm happy for her, and we made up on that last mission in Brazil. She's happy doing what she's doing, and I'm happy she's doing it."

I thought about it for a second, then leaned into the vehicle, saying, "Veep, you're with Brett. Get the hotel."

He nodded and left without a word. Knuckles smiled and squeezed into the back of the vehicle. Two hours later, we were sitting in an alley right outside the Dushanbe Mall, waiting on Carly to show.

CHAPTER 7

George Wolffe slapped his keyboard in disgust, his computer not responding to any commands at all. He moved the mouse around on its pad and got nothing. He assumed it was simply the pain of working in a classified organization with a byzantine path of internet protocols to protect the fact that he actually was a cover organization for the National Command Authority. The pipe running through the building was T1, but the layers of TOR cutouts and other things routinely made simple tasks, like checking his email, as slow as a nineties dial-up network.

Headquartered in a nondescript office building in Clarendon, Virginia, just across the Potomac from Washington, DC, the only indication of what was inside the brick and glass structure was a sign proclaiming Blaisdell Consulting. To the uninitiated, it was just one more firm circling like a shark for the scraps coming out of DC, but inside it housed everything from an indoor range to a minor surgical suite to team rooms used by the various Taskforce elements for planning prior to executing a mission.

A lean, wiry man with a salt-and-pepper mustache, Wolffe was an old-school paramilitary officer from the Special Activities Division's Ground Branch, now renamed the Special Activities Center. He was well versed in the black arts of covert operations but had little tolerance for the technology required to maintain cover in the modern world.

He hollered outside his open office door, "Blaine! Get in here!"

A younger man with the body of a linebacker appeared, saying, "What's up, boss?"

"You get the SITREP from Pike? I can't get my damn email to work, and he should have linked up with Carly by now."

"Nope. Mine's working slow as well, but it'll be in the comm center. Their distribution is firewalled from ours and works without all the cutouts."

"You mind checking?"

"Sure. Be right back." He reached the door and turned around. Wolffe said, "What?"

"Am I going forward if this gets hot? As the Omega Team Chief?"

Every Taskforce operation proceeded through various gates, each phase following the Greek alphabet, with Alpha being phase one—the introduction of forces for exploratory purposes. Omega was the kinetic end of putting some terrorist's head on a spike. Each phase had to be approved by the Oversight Council, and prior to the previous commander's death, Blaine Alexander's job was the leader of all Omega operations, regardless of the team executing. When it came time for direct action, the Oversight Council wanted a semblance of control, and he was it. Right up until Kurt Hale had been killed two years ago. Since then, George Wolffe had been "acting commander" and Lieutenant Colonel Blaine Alexander had become "acting" DCO, or deputy commander, Wolffe's old role.

Wolffe leaned back in his chair and said, "I don't know. The Oversight Council has been dragging its feet on appointing a new commander. Since COVID hit, they don't seem to have any urgency on solving the problem. Or maybe it's just easier to ignore."

"COVID's pretty much gone now. They no longer have any

excuses. Surely they'll make you the official commander, right? Then all they'll need to do is find a new DCO."

Wolffe laughed and said, "That just may well be you. Who else knows how this circus runs?"

"I don't want the job. Too political. I want to go back to the sharp end of the spear. Omega operations."

"I know. Trust me, I know, but we don't always get what we want. You don't like it, you can always go back to the Special Mission Unit. Or even a regular Special Forces Group. I'll help the transfer. You've given enough here anyway. It's going to affect your career if you don't get back into the regular world of special operations."

"I don't want to go back, and I don't care about my career. I just don't want to deal with all the political bullshit you do. Omega would be fine with me."

Wolffe looked at him for a moment, thinking he sounded just like Kurt Hale when he'd been alive.

He said, "One step at a time. Just see if you can track down that SITREP."

Before Blaine could leave the office, Bartholomew Creedwater came running into the room, his face sweating and red. He exclaimed, "We've been hit with a ransomware attack, and it's spreading. I can't shut it down."

Incredulous, Wolffe said, "What? Ransomware? You mean like that Colonial Pipeline attack?"

"Yes. Blaisdell Consulting has been hit just like them, but it's much worse for us. I don't know how it got into our systems, but because we're interconnected with all of our other cover companies, it's spreading like wildfire. It's going to shut us down completely."

"Creed, we pay you to do this sort of thing. Tell me you can stop it."

Bartholomew Creedwater—Creed—was what was known in polite society as a "network engineer," meaning he was a master at cyberattacks. A hacker, and one of the best in the world.

"Sir, I could have if I'd caught it in time, but it infiltrated somehow through our network of cutouts, probably through one of those piece-of-shit government service providers we have to use to interface with the National Command Authority. They never patch anything, and once it got into the system, it started shutting everything down. And I mean everything."

The first thing Wolffe thought about was compromise. "Do you think they hit us on purpose? That they know what this organization represents? Is it a nation-state?"

"I don't think so. If it was a nation-state, like Russia, they'd just hide and exploit, like the SolarWinds hack a couple of years ago, or the Chinese hack of our Office of Personnel Management. Ransomware is for profit. They hit hospitals and corporations for cash. I don't think they had any idea of the number of connections they were going to affect, but they do now."

Wolffe turned to his screen and saw that his web mail was gone. In its place was a large banner saying:

YOUR COMPUTER HAS BEEN INFECTED

All of your data is now encrypted. To decrypt, you will need our software. You have four days to pay four bitcoin. After four days, the price will double to eight bitcoin. Follow the instructions at the bottom of the screen.

There was a link to another address, and a clock counting down.

Wolffe stared at the screen for a moment, then turned back to Creed, saying, "Surely we can do something. We have the best hackers in the world."

"Sir, this is no longer a hacking problem. It's an encryption one. I can't do anything with this."

"Can you find out where it came from?"

"Possibly. That might be something in the doable category, but it'll end up in some country where we have no reach. And I could use some help to do it. Someone with skill at this."

"Skill at ransomware?"

"Exactly. There's a company called Second Day Solutions. The guy who runs it has government contracts and a top-secret clearance. He does this for a living."

"Second Day Solutions? Why that name?"

Creed gave a small smile and said, "It's a play on Zero Day vulnerabilities. When someone gets hacked, they always first try to solve the problem with in-house IT people to spare the embarrassment or loss of confidence in their business. By day two, they give up and call him."

"Who is he?"

"His name is Dylan Hobbes. He was a coder for the NSA for twenty years, worked in TAO, helped stand up Cyber Command, then went out to the private sector. He's very, very good. But we need to get on this quickly. Every minute is causing problems."

"Can we stop it from spreading?"

"Yeah, if you get all of our cover organizations to shut down their systems. They can't turn them back on until this is resolved."

Wolffe turned to Blaine and said, "Call Alexander Palmer. Tell him we have an emergency and need the principals of the Oversight Council at the White House in the next hour."

"Sir, I'll try, but there's no guarantee I can get them on short notice."

The principals of the Oversight Council were the meat of the thirteen members, comprising the secretary of state, the secretary of defense, the director of the CIA, the national security advisor, and the president of the United States.

Wolffe said, "It's a Sunday. We should be able to get most of them. Hell, half of them will be blabbing on the Sunday talk shows." He went back to Creed and said, "Get to the comms center and start the chain of shutting everything down. Use a landline and explain what's going on. Tell them to shut it all down. Then get me a status report of how much has been affected in the organization and how much we prevented."

Creed nodded and started to leave. Wolffe said, "And get this Dylan Hobbes's number. He needs to be at the Oversight Council meeting. Is he in DC?"

"Yes, he is. But a word of warning on him. He's a little bit quirky. He doesn't like politics at all. I mean he hates the political divide we have right now. He's a little bit crazy about it, because he was routinely beat up by both parties for his work, solely for political points depending on who was in power at the time. He was the punching bag to tar and feather someone else. It's why he left government service, so when dealing with him, don't bring up any political stuff. It'll just set him off."

Wolffe nodded and said, "I got it. Nobody's going to beat him up for doing this, no matter what happens. You two get on it."

CHAPTER 8

Wolffe pulled into the visitors' checkpoint for the entrance to the West Wing, showing the Capitol policeman his driver's license. The policeman checked his clipboard, ran through the names, stared at him like he was a criminal, and let him through. Wolffe parked outside the Rotunda and entered the vaunted West Wing of the White House, walking to a desk that monitored all who entered. He gave his name to the man and in return was given a neck badge with a ton of script and a large *V* superimposed over the writing.

V for visitor, meaning an escort was required. Something that Wolffe had to endure every time he entered. It would have been very easy for President Hannister to give him a permanent White House badge, but in so doing, it would be recorded, and that, in and of itself, would be a seam the press or someone else could exploit.

Why does this guy from a supposed company called Blaisdell Consulting have a permanent White House badge? What's he doing as a permanent White House person? Let's start digging!

Because of it, he had to act like a visitor every time he entered the West Wing. It was a small price to pay to keep what he did secret, but it still got under his skin when he was treated like a lobbyist who was only out for profit.

He saw the national security advisor, Alexander Palmer, coming down the hallway and knew he was about to get grilled. Palmer was the gateway to the president, and as such, he didn't like surprises, which this most certainly was. On top of that, Palmer didn't really like Wolffe, and the feeling was mutual.

Wolffe shook his hand and started walking toward the Oval Office, saying, "How many did we get to show up?"

"You got them all. You're lucky it's a slow Sunday. What's the fire?"

"What about Dylan Hobbes? Is he here?"

"Not yet, but he's on the way; now what's up?"

They passed the secretary's desk for the Oval and reached the door. Wolffe said, "We've been hacked."

Palmer's mouth opened, and Wolffe entered the room, seeing Amanda Croft, the secretary of state, Mark Oglethorpe, the secretary of defense, and Kerry Bostwick, the director of the CIA. Behind the Resolute Desk was President Philip Hannister, who looked more like an accountant than a president—which is what he used to be before he'd assumed the mantle of the most powerful leadership post on earth.

They all turned at his entrance and he said, "I'm sorry to cause everyone to come here on a Sunday, but we have a significant problem."

He went between the two couches where the principals sat and talked to President Hannister, saying, "Blaisdell Consulting has been hit with a ransomware attack, and because we're linked via the internet to our myriad of cover organizations, they're being hit as well. It's shutting us down."

From the couch, the D/CIA Bostwick said, "A targeted attack? They know who you are?"

Wolffe shook his head and said, "Creed doesn't think so. If it was targeted, they'd just root around and see what they could find in the background. They wouldn't announce themselves. But the damage is pretty complete. We can't operate right now because my cover organizations are either locked out, or are shut down to prevent being locked out."

President Hannister said, "What are they asking for?"

"Four bitcoin—but we don't know if that's four bitcoin just for Blaisdell Consulting or four bitcoin for every different company they've infected. We don't think they knew they were going to hit all of these different companies because they had no idea they were connected. We don't know the final ransom at this point, and I don't think they do, either."

"What's four bitcoin worth? Maybe we just pay them off and keep this quiet."

Amanda Croft said, "Sir, you've made it a policy not to pay ransomware attacks because it just encourages more."

President Hannister rolled his eyes and said, "Yeah, I get that, but this is a little different. We're not talking about some embarrassment here. We're talking about national security. It needs to be kept quiet."

Wolffe said, "Four bitcoin—at today's prices—is about a hundred and sixty thousand dollars. But the price of bitcoin shifts dramatically on a daily basis. Either way, it's not cheap."

Kerry said, "I'm sick of this crap. Is it the Russians again?"

"We don't know. We're trying to find out. That's why I asked for Dylan Hobbes. He's apparently an expert on this stuff."

President Hannister said, "We requested his appearance, and he's on the way. He's apparently doing a lot of contract work for the U.S. government, but I've never heard of him. Who is he?"

"Someone Creed recommended. Spent a career in the NSA

working with TAO and the new Cyber Command, then went private sector. He has a clearance, but he's going to need to be read on to Project Prometheus. I know that's not optimal, but we need to do this quickly."

The secretary of state, Amanda Croft asked, "I know NSA, but what's TAO?"

The secretary of defense said, "Tailored Access Operations. Most of what the NSA does is passive listening to various methods of communication, but sometimes they need entry first. TAO does the penetration. It's the most highly classified stuff inside the NSA. They're basically the best hackers in the world."

Palmer's phone buzzed and he said, "He's here. Be right back." A minute later, he returned with a slender man in tow, another visitor's badge around his neck. Tall, more than six feet, with gray hair and round glasses that made him look a little like John Lennon, he walked like a stork, all gangly legs and arms. He entered the room and waited for someone to speak.

President Hannister said, "Dylan, thank you for coming. We hear you're the best at a problem we have."

"Oh? And what's that?"

Wolffe brought him up to speed on the problem set, ending with, "Can you help with this?"

Hobbes nodded, saying, "I'm assuming we're at Day Two here?"

Wolffe laughed and said, "No. We're smarter than that. We're at Zero Day, plus about four hours."

Wolffe explained what they were doing to mitigate the damage and Hobbes said, "Good. Very good. But you also need to isolate the boxes that are infected for me to inspect. Take them off the network to prevent them from altering anything. I want to see what happened when they struck, because they'll be messing with your systems every single minute. I want to see what they saw the minute they hit, not what they're now doing to camouflage their actions."

Wolffe nodded and got on his phone, calling Creed.

President Hannister said, "Can you locate them? Even if you can't solve the ransomware problem? Can you thread it back to where they are?"

Hobbes said, "Yes, usually we can. When REvil hit Kaseya we were able to locate them virtually and take back their ransom. When SolarWinds was hit we could trace it back to Russia, but if you're asking for an actual address, I don't know. It depends on the clues they left behind in the code."

Amanda Croft said, "What's that mean?"

Hobbes held out his hands and said, "Sometimes these guys are stupid, and sometimes they're a nation-state trying to cause havoc. I can't predict what I'll find until I do a deep dive into your systems."

Wolffe hung up and said, "We have a couple of systems isolated right now for you to check out. Can you do this today?"

Hobbes nodded slowly, then said, "Why am I being asked to do this, if I may? You guys have Cyber Command. You have the NSA. You have the heart of the United States offensive capability. Why are you asking me?"

President Hannister said, "Because we heard you were the best. That's why."

Hobbes shook his head and said, "That doesn't make any sense. I dealt in your world for twenty years, and I'm not about to make my company cannon fodder because you're afraid of using government assets on this problem. I'm not going to be a scapegoat like before."

The people in the room let that comment settle like a turd in a punch bowl, then Wolffe spoke.

"It's because what we're dealing with is very, very delicate. We need someone discreet. We can't use the usual architecture for this."

"What's that mean?"

Wolffe smiled and said, "It's like *Mission: Impossible*. I can't tell you unless you decide to accept the mission. If you do, I'll read you on. If you don't, you're free to go, but I promise, it's not because we're looking for a scapegoat."

Hobbes slowly nodded, thinking. He said, "Okay. I can help. But it won't be just me. I need a team to do this."

"Can they work with the code without knowing who or why?"

"Yes, as long as I'm directing them."

"That's not a problem. As far as they know, they'll be working for a consulting business in Clarendon."

President Hannister said, "Good, good. That will work. I want you to see if you can crack the ransomware code without paying the penalty, but your primary objective is to find out where this crew is located."

Hobbes said, "Okay, but why? I'll be wasting time on geolocation when I could be working on evidence for the FBI. Worst case, if we have to pay, they can recover the bitcoin like they did with the ransomware group REvil. You aren't going to reach these guys in the physical world, but you can virtually."

"Why is that?"

"They're always in some place where the United States has no law enforcement reach. They aren't doing these hacks from the United Kingdom."

President Hannister glanced around the room, then said,

"You're about to be read onto a specific program that has a world-wide reach, and I'm a little sick of just stealing back the bitcoin and calling that success. I want to know where these guys are."

Hobbes chuckled and said, "You're not going to be able to arrest them. I can give you everything I find, but you won't have enough to stand up in a court of law. These guys change names every month, from REvil to BlackMatter to DarkSide to who knows what. You won't be able to arrest them or even connect whatever name they use now to what they did in the past."

President Hannister said, "I think it's time we made a statement here. I'm not going to arrest or sanction them. I'm going to hammer them."

CHAPTER 9

The sun began to dip lower in the sky, and I saw a Caucasian woman exit the mall, about five-six, wearing jeans and a loose shirt. She was lithe, with long muscles like a swimmer, and had a bob haircut, freckles on her face, and a cute little upturned nose. She hit the street, looking left and right.

Knuckles said, "She's still a heartbreaker."

I laughed and said, "Go get her."

We were at what constituted a modern shopping center in Dushanbe, with multiple stores crammed into a four-story building of burnished metal and glass, selling everything from washing machines to work clothes. It was not unlike anything you'd see in the States, with the exception that every store had a purpose designed to satisfy the basest level of existence. There were no frivolous shops selling pet rocks or expensive designer shirts. It was all business.

Knuckles exited the vehicle at a trot, and Jennifer said, "I knew he still cared for her."

I said, "He does. But Knuckles cares for them all. He just can't not care. He'd take her back in a heartbeat, because he's a romantic, but she knows better, because she's a realist. She's done with him, but he's not done with her."

Jennifer turned from the windshield and looked at me. I said, "What?"

"That's probably the most introspective thing I've ever heard you say."

"What do you mean? Knuckles is a man-whore. That's all I meant."

She shook her head and said, "That's not what you meant. You're just too big of a coward to admit to having feelings."

Jesus Christ. What the hell did I say?

Before I could respond, we saw them walking back toward us. I looked at her and said, "Therapy night is over. Do we actually have a hotel room? Where are we going?"

Jennifer looked at me, squinted, then said, "We're going to talk about you sooner or later. You bottle up too much stuff."

I knew where she was going, and also knew she was right. She was convinced that the things I'd done in the name of national security were eating at my soul—and they were. But tonight was not the night for that discussion. I said, "Hotel?"

Jennifer pursed her lips, knowing I was changing the subject, and looked at her phone, saying, "Yeah, we have a few rooms at a place called the Serena. It's about five minutes from here. Veep and Brett are there now. They picked it for the robust Wi-Fi, which is apparently hard to find here in Dushanbe."

Knuckles reached the Rover and I opened the door, stepping out and giving Carly a hug. "Not sure why a Spanish speaker is running the show here in Tajikistan."

She laughed and said, "Not sure why they got you two to do anything about it. Wouldn't be my first choice."

I opened the passenger door and said, "You take what you can get. Like getting you."

She gave me a fake frown, then sat down, seeing Jennifer in the front seat. I saw her face light up, and she leaned forward, giving her a hug. She said something, and Jennifer laughed, then she leaned back again. I really wanted to know what she'd said, but those two had been through hell together, and I wasn't going to interrupt the reunion.

I sat behind the wheel and said, "Okay, Jane Bond, what's going on here?"

"They didn't tell you? You just drove up here in a lather because they asked?"

I started driving and said, "No. I know there's a guy to get out, but that's about it. What's your cover for status here? We're running around as a bunch of archeologists to get them a UNESCO rating. Why are you here?"

She looked at Knuckles and said, "I'm here under diplomatic cover. Under the State Department, with the cover coming from the chief of station. I came in two days ago as an agricultural expert, and that's what I'm doing, as far as the government here knows."

"So you have official creds? You're not here as a NOC?" Meaning she had backstopping from the embassy as opposed to operating like us—nonofficial cover.

"Definitely official. I'm backstopped all the way through the embassy. But that's why we need you. The embassy can't be involved in this. It's a clean in-and-out. We get this done, and nobody will even know."

Knuckles said, "Yeah, well, we'd kind of like to know what the 'in-and-out' is all about. What's going on?"

She held out a thumb drive and said, "At the hotel. Let's get everyone together, because we're going to need the entire team."

CHAPTER 10

Twenty minutes later, we were in our suite at the Serena. After living on the ground for two weeks, I was hoping the place was like the Ritz-Carlton, but it wasn't. It was utilitarian to the extreme, meaning that the room was serviceable, but was definitely built for some Soviet Union officers. There were no amenities, outside of a few pictures on the walls that looked as if they'd been painted by the maids. If it served a purpose, they had included it, but if it didn't, it was gone. The toilet paper was like a roll of brown restaurant hand wipes and the bed was apparently built on a plywood stage without a mattress.

It did have a desk with a power outlet, though, and that's where I found Brett, furiously working a computer, but having no luck.

He turned when I entered, saying, "None of the Taskforce shit works here. It's like the government has a firewall against us connecting."

I said, "Okay, okay. We need to get the SITREP in to Wolffe. I'm sure the Oversight Council is wetting their pants because we haven't contacted them. Keep trying, but I'm not holding up the mission for a report just saying we've made linkup with Carly."

I turned to the room and said, "Nobody use a Taskforce cell phone unless I say. Use the burner phones we purchased. I want nothing from the Taskforce touching cell infrastructure here."

I got a bunch of nods, then turned to Carly and said, "So, good to be working together again. Now tell me what the hell we're doing here."

She said, "There's a man on the run who's done more for the United States than any man penetrating the Iron Curtain during the Cold War. I mean this guy helped us more than Jack Strong in Poland. He is the singular reason for most of our strategic successes against the Haqqani network and the Taliban."

I smiled and said, "Well, from what I'm hearing, that amounted to jack shit. The country is falling apart, and all we're doing is holding on to the airport."

Carly scowled and said, "That's not his fault. He risked his life for us, and we're going to bring him home. That's the mission."

"Why him? Why should I risk my team and my company to get *him* home? When there are a thousand others to save? Where's the CIA on this? He's their guy. I've seen the news now. The airport is a shit show. Why does he rate 'favored nation status'?"

Jennifer saw my anger and stood up, as if she was going to say something. I held out my hand, telling her to keep her mouth shut, because I was a little aggravated at the secrecy. And a little aggravated at how Afghanistan had ended. I wanted some payback, and if sweating Carly was the only way to get it, I would.

She said, "The CIA is doing what they can for the men they recruited. He is just one of them, but *we* have the ability to get him out of here."

"Out of what? He's *out* of Afghanistan. And you haven't answered why he can't just walk to a personal meet with some James Bond from the CIA and get free. Why am I here?"

She said, "Pike, I don't know. I think it's because the station here doesn't have the assets needed on short notice, and you do. Kerry Bostwick asked for you specifically. We know for a fact he's being hunted. He has no money and nowhere to go. He'll last about a day on the street."

I said, "Just like every other Kandak we abandoned, only they're *inside* Afghanistan, getting hunted on home turf. So I'm the white knight, saving the one guy to give the CIA some sort of credibility because of the ones they left behind? Makes me sick."

"Yeah. But you can save this one."

I knew I was doing the mission, because the guy deserved it, but it aggravated me to no end that the CIA was going to call on me when they could have pulled this guy out months before. I said, "And if I say I'm not doing it? What then?"

Carly said, "He has his niece with him. A small girl. The mother gave her to him to save because she was afraid of what the Taliban would do. He was supposed to take her away. Take her somewhere safe. And now they're both on the run, here, in Dushanbe."

I closed my eyes at the words. *That's not fair.*

Jennifer saw how her information had affected me, and knew what I was going to do next. I blew out a sigh and said, "Okay, where is he?"

Carly smiled and said, "You really make this hard."

She pulled out a cell phone and showed me the text messages between her and someone named Jahn Azimi, dictating a meeting tonight at 8 P.M.

I said, "The texts are in blue. This guy has an iPhone?"

"Yes. We don't know why, but it's a number in our database. It belongs to the former national security advisor to Afghanistan. We have no idea why he has the phone, but he does."

I shook my head and said, "That doesn't sound good. Something else is in play here."

She ignored my statement, saying, "I found a gazebo on the

outskirts of the war memorial at Victory Park. It's a wide-open space that the people here routinely use for picnics. A lot of teenagers drinking vodka and families enjoying the open air. Perfect for a meet because nobody will try to interfere there."

I looked at the map, seeing the location was at the top of a hill, a long flight of stairs leading up to it, right next to a cable car system that would save you the steps. I said, "So what's the mission? You go meet the guy and we take him to our bird down south?"

"Basically, yes. But I need eyes on the meet site before I go in. I'm his contact. I'm who he's expecting. You guys will be the early warning. I don't need security per se, because he's an unknown here, but I want eyes on the site before I go in."

I nodded, knowing exactly what she was asking. I said, "Okay. Two up top. One at the bottom for countersurveillance. But we can only track one approach. If someone goes to the stairs, we can do that, but if someone uses the cable car, we can't watch both."

"The cable car has been defunct for about fifteen years. That's not an issue. They'll use the stairs."

I looked at the map, seeing a road running by the gazebo. I said, "So you meet him and want us to extract via the road? You don't want to walk him all the way back down, right?"

"Exactly right. The road is blocked with a chain down at the bottom, in the parking lot for the broken cable car. When we make the meet, someone cuts the chain and drives up, and then we drive out the back of the park."

Brett said, "Why don't we just drive in from the back of the park?"

"Because it's a spaghetti road. It'll take you thirty minutes to get to our location from the back of the park. It'll take three from the front. I don't mind the exfil being long, but I really want the initial contact to be quick."

Which made sense to me. I said, "Okay, here are the team assignments. Me and Knuckles up top for atmospherics. Brett at the bottom for countersurveillance. Veep and Jenn with the vehicles. Jenn, you have the job of defeating the chain for the road. Take some bolt cutters and when I call, cut the chain and come up as fast as possible. Questions?"

Jennifer said, "Do I need to use bolt cutters? What's the lock like?"

Carly said, "It's just a padlock. Why?"

"Because if I walk out with a four-foot skeleton key and cut that lock, I'm going to draw attention. Attention we don't want. We want to look like we belong there, on that road. What's the lock like?"

Carly said, "I don't really know. I didn't look at it." And I saw the embarrassment form on her face. She was supposed to be planning the perfect mission, but she'd missed a key ingredient.

Jennifer saw it, too, and said, "No worries. I can pick any padlock they have. It'll look like I have a key and am supposed to be there. I'll take the bolt cutters just in case."

She flicked a glance at me, wondering if she had overstepped her bounds, and I winked. She was spot-on, as usual.

Brett said, "If I see someone tracking you, what's the call? Blow off the meeting, or continue? Do you want me to interdict them?"

Carly said, "No. Definitely not. If you spot something, let me know, and I'll wave off the meeting. We'll reengage at a later time. But I don't think that will happen. He's only been here for a day."

I said, "And us? If we pinpoint the site, call it clear and you enter, and then we see a threat approaching, what do you want from us? What's the ROE?"

"If Jahn has not shown up yet, I'll wave him off. If we're in the meet together, just keep eyes on. But you need to make sure it's actually a threat. There are a lot of people who wander around the memorial for picnics, and it's also apparently a little bit of a lover's lane for the Tajiks. Don't go calling a threat just because you see some MAMs wandering about. They're probably just drinking."

MAM was an acronym for Military Age Male, and she was letting me know there would be plenty running around.

She saw my face, not liking that answer, and she said, "Look, your primary role here is getting him exfiled on the Rock Star bird. The meet itself is secondary. Don't get in a gunfight because you think a couple of teenagers are a threat. Once I have him in the box, you call for exfil and we all leave as a happy family. The only thing I want from you is early warning of anyone spoiling the meet site. I picked the gazebo because it's off the beaten path, but if someone's coming up to it, just give me a call. When they pass, let me know and I'll enter the kill zone."

"Kill zone?"

"Sorry. I'll enter the meet site."

I looked at her hard, then said, "Why'd you call it that?"

"Pike, no reason. It was just a slip of the tongue from dealing with you knuckle draggers."

I said, "Yeah, well, don't use that phrase. It makes me skittish."

She laughed and said, "Sorry, but this is going to be a walk in the park, literally. I promise."

CHAPTER 11

Shakor dialed the phone and waited, hearing it ring endlessly. He thought for a spastic second that the split team had been arrested. And then someone answered, saying, "Who is this?"

"It's Shakor, you idiot. Couldn't you see that from the number?"

And then the backpedaling began: "Sorry, sir. I wasn't sure if I should answer. What's up?"

"We've had to move my team to Uzbekistan. The treasure left on a plane from Tajikistan to parts unknown, but wherever it went, we can't get there by driving cars without passports. Haqqani is making us some documents from Turkey with a Schengen visa, so we should be able to travel at will, but it will take a day or two."

"So you'll travel as Turkish citizens?"

"Yes, that will be the easy part. The hard part will be finding out where that plane landed. We have the tail number of the aircraft that left with the treasure and the national security advisor, but we haven't tracked its flight path as of yet. We were simply going to track his phone, but we can't, because your man has it."

"Jahn Azimi has a government phone? How does that help us? Because I'll be honest, we have no leads. They didn't detain him at the airport, and he's either somewhere in the city, or he's trying to find a way overland to get out."

"He's not getting out overland. He has help from the CIA."

"How do you know this?"

"Through some light interrogation of the Ghani people who didn't make it out. They're doing anything they can to keep their head attached to their neck. It turns out that President Ghani infected every phone on his staff with tracking software in an effort to slow the corruption of his inner circle. Jahn's phone has something called Pegasus, from Israel, of all places."

"What's that mean?"

"It means his phone is literally a geolocation recording device. Whoever uses that handset can be tracked. We were stalking the phone through that app because it would lead us to the treasure, but Ahmad Khan gave the phone to Jahn. He's been communicating with a CIA case officer, and we saw it all. He's got a meet tonight to flee the city."

"How sure are you that this is correct?"

"It's ironclad. We have his phone because Ghani didn't trust anyone. He installed the spyware, and now we get to see what it's doing. We have the meet site location. All you have to do is roll him up."

"Send me the meeting location."

"I will. But don't make a grand show out of this. Just take him and be done. The meet site they've chosen is away from where the usual tourist crowds hang out. You need to get in and get out."

"If he's meeting a CIA controller, it won't be that easy. They'll have protocols in place precisely to prevent what you want me to do. What about them?"

"They'll have overwatch for sure, but I don't think they'll treat this like a meeting at a hostile site. The CIA man will be the first to arrive, so it would be better if you could take Jahn before the meeting, but if you can't, eliminate the threat and then get out."

"Why can't I just kill both of them? Be done with this?"

"Haqqani wants Jahn Azimi alive. He wants to administer justice personally. That is your mission. If he is killed, don't bother coming back, because Haqqani will do to you what he wanted to do to Jahn."

CHAPTER 12

Jennifer circled the cable car parking lot, letting us get a quick shot of the atmospherics of the area. The sun was beginning to set, throwing shadows everywhere, but I could still see about twenty cars in the lot, meaning it was going to be crowded up top. Hopefully, the gazebo was as off the beaten path as Carly seemed to think it was. I most definitely would have liked an earlier trip just to conduct a reconnaissance of the area, but the time was too short, so I'd be seeing it for the first time like everyone else.

Jennifer parked, and Carly pointed to an alley leading up the hillside, blocked by a simple length of chain on two steel poles. Carly said, "That's the road. You can go get a visual of the lock once the team is set and I leave."

Driving the Rover behind us, Veep pulled into the parking slot to the right. I exited the vehicle and waved him and the rest of the team over to the hood of Jennifer's vehicle. I said, "Okay, nothing in the plan has changed. Knuckles and I will go up top and get eyes on the gazebo. Veep and Jennifer stay down here to conduct exfil. Brett, you head to the restaurant at the old cable car terminal. Keep eyes on until you see the target take the stairs and give us a call."

I turned to Carly and said, "I'll give you a call once I've cleared the area and see no threats. You're the stationary element, right?"

"Yes."

"What's the wave-off?"

She held up a hat, saying, "This on my head. No hat, and meeting is a go."

Every meet had a stationary element that set up the site— usually the one who'd called the meeting, in this case, Carly— and a moving element, the source or asset that was coming to talk. Once the site was set up, an intricate dance would play out, with a far signal indicating whether the meet site was secure or dangerous. In this case, it was a simple hat. Carly bareheaded meant the man could approach. The hat on her head would tell him to keep moving and reestablish contact because there was a threat, which was my job to determine.

His far-side recognition was simply a male with a child. He'd approach, and then the near-side dance would commence. A give-and-take of verbal phrases that would ensure both were who they said they were. Once that was done, Carly would signal me on the radio, and I'd call Jennifer. Twenty minutes later, we'd all be happy campers headed back to our aircraft at the dig. Two hours after that, we'd be in the air, mission complete.

At least that was how it was supposed to work, but the enemy always got a vote, no matter how hard you planned.

I looked at my watch and said, "Guess we'd better get going. Comms check."

Individually, one by one, each team member called me, ending with Carly. I said, "Good to go." I turned to Knuckles and said, "Ready?"

"Yeah. Let's roll."

Knuckles and I left the vehicles and went toward the cable station. We passed the rusting ticket room, going up some concrete stairs past the defunct cable car, still hanging on its steel towline, stoically waiting on someone to board. Something that wasn't going to happen anytime soon.

Knuckles pointed to a second staircase, one that was much wider, with flagstones of granite instead of concrete. It snaked up the hill less steeply than the one next to the cable car, a landing after every tenth step or so. We started up it, seeing at every level a marble monument to the left and right, the pictures of soldiers embedded into the rock like a tombstone. Knuckles said, "What do you suppose that is?"

I said, "I think it's the pictures of Tajikistan soldiers that received the Soviet Union's version of the Medal of Honor. But I could be wrong. Either way, it's dead guys from the war."

Fifteen minutes later we reached the top, seeing the World War II monument spilled out in front of us, the area having a large amphitheater with the monument itself a long dark granite wall running down the length, gold Cyrillic lettering under a hammer and sickle describing what I assumed was the valiant fight during the war. The amphitheater had a little bit of a crowd, with families eating picnics on blankets and packs of teenagers sitting around like stray cats, smoking cigarettes and sneaking nips from bottles.

I pointed at a path leading away from the memorial, the single track disappearing into the foliage, saying, "Gazebo is supposed to be down that way."

Knuckles and I took the path and entered the woods, the sounds from the amphitheater becoming muted by the vegetation. Eventually, we reached a small open area on a cliff, the gazebo right on the edge.

Small, maybe fifteen feet across, it was made of black iron with a wooden bench running around the circumference inside. To the left of it was a one-lane blacktop road, running to the back of the memorial itself. To the right the path continued on deeper into the woods, the setting sun causing shadows that made it hard to see. Which was good for us.

I pointed at the road and said, "That's exfil. Let's find a place to set up." We left the path, went behind a patch of scrub, and Knuckles got in the prone, looking under the foliage toward the gazebo. He said, "This'll work."

I got down next to him, looking not at the gazebo, but at any avenues of approach behind us. I didn't want a surprise lurking here in the bushes. The wooded area became much denser behind our position, to the point that we'd definitely hear someone coming from the rear.

The path to the right of the gazebo gave me some concern, but we could see down it a fairly long way, about fifty meters, and it was coming from the bottom of the hill, which meant it wouldn't be in play. Any threat coming up from the bottom would be pre-planned, which wasn't in the cards. The only threat we had to worry about was someone following our target into the meet site because they knew who he was. Anyone using that path would be a pack of teenagers sneaking around after sunset, and we were only early warning. All I'd have to do is call off the meet if someone came up.

I got on the net and said, "Meet site is clear. Nobody in the gazebo, and nobody around."

Carly came back and said, "Thirty minutes until linkup."

"Then you need to start moving. It took a good fifteen minutes to get up here."

We settled down behind the copse of bushes and began to wait. I heard Brett call that he saw Carly on the stairs, then after a few minutes saw her coming down the path. By now the sun was below the horizon, but there was enough nautical twilight to see clearly. She sauntered down the dirt track not looking around, not trying to find us, which was expected.

Once she was in the gazebo, she wouldn't be able to see anything. We were her eyes.

She took a seat on the bench, pulled out a paperback, and began reading. She looked a little out of place—a single female in the gazebo—but not unduly so.

Ten minutes later, Brett called again, saying, "I've got the target. Male, about five-ten, with a preteen girl holding his hand. He's looking around like he's trying to find the bad man. It's him."

Carly said, "Roger that. Pike, status?"

"You're still good. Nobody on the road or the path. All activity is at the memorial. Brett, any trailers?"

"None so far. He's leading the child alone. Nobody's shown any interest."

Good.

Eventually I made out a man and a child walking down the path in the darkening gloom. I keyed the radio and said, "Target inbound. Walking slow."

The man stopped short of the gazebo, and Carly stood up, running her hand through her hair, telling him it was okay. He approached, entered, and sat the girl on the bench. He turned to Carly and said a few words. She responded, and I saw him smile in relief.

Knuckles kicked my leg, saying, "Someone coming up the path."

I focused there and saw three males walking up the trail and talking. Not trying to hide their appearance.

I keyed the radio and said, "Three MAMs inbound. Dressed like locals, talking and laughing. Don't think they're a threat."

The age was a concern. If it had been two males and a ninety-year-old female I'd feel more comfortable.

Carly put the target on the inside of the gazebo bench, then sat next to him, her body the closest to the opening of the iron gazebo. She called the girl forward and began to pretend she was engaging her in conversation.

I got on the net and said, "Koko, Koko, ready for exfil. Start your move. We've got activity here."

Jennifer came back, saying, "We're on the way. Lock is already defeated. Five minutes out."

Knuckles said, "MAMs are slowing down outside the gazebo."

I looked at them and saw the lead man pull something out of his pants. It was long, like a section of pipe, and I recognized it immediately. A suppressed pistol. On the net, I shouted, "Gun, gun, gun!" and saw him put the barrel right between Carly's eyes.

He pulled the trigger and I saw her beautiful face crater open, the bullet splitting her eyes left and right like someone had driven a spike into her skull. Then her head jerked back, hitting the grating of the gazebo, and I saw her hands fly up.

She flopped over and I stood up, Knuckles right behind me. I heard a car screaming up the hill and yelled into my radio, "Hostile force! Hostile force! Koko, Veep, take them down!"

I burst out of the bushes, Knuckles tearing through to my right, both of us drawing our Glocks from a holster.

Jennifer came back, saying, "We're not there. Still a minute out."

I realized the vehicle wasn't Jennifer just as the window of the car came down. It was the enemy. I felt the wasp-snap of rounds coming by my head. I dove behind a tree, rolled to the right around the trunk, and saw the target and his child being crammed into the back seat. In seconds, it was heading back the way it had come.

Knuckles stood up, running flat out behind the vehicle, blazing away with his pistol in the night, eventually taking a knee and continuing to fire, to no avail. I ran to the gazebo and saw Carly's shattered body. She was slumped over as if she'd had too much to drink, her head leaking blood in a slow stream like a faucet that hadn't been turned off all the way.

I heard Knuckles behind me and turned, pushing him away. He tore at my arms and I slammed him like he was a blocking dummy, getting him away from the gazebo, saying, "No, no, no. You don't want to see it. She's gone."

He screamed in my face, a visceral, lethal wail, and I put my leg behind his and flipped him on his back. He hit the ground and began to fight me. I trapped his arms and leaned above him, saying, "Stop. Stop. Stop. We have to get out of here."

He gained control of his rage and said, "Carly."

I said, "She's gone. She's under diplomatic cover. The CIA is going to have to sort this out."

I saw headlights, then Jennifer was out of her car, running to me. She saw the body in the dusk of the gazebo and said, "Is that . . . ?"

I hoisted Knuckles to his feet and said, "Yeah, it is. Let's go."

CHAPTER 13

Ahmad Khan shivered on the marble bench, not used to the chill in the room. Sitting in a large foyer of a mountain chalet the size of a castle, there was one other person seated across from him on a duplicate marble bench, the hallway large enough to drive a car through. A younger man of about twenty-five, he didn't fit the décor—but then neither did Ahmad, his rumpled suit showing the stains from his flight out of Afghanistan.

The guy was dressed in a denim jacket, jeans, and a T-shirt proclaiming some rock band's tour, with greasy black hair that came down to his shoulders and a pockmarked face from childhood acne. The man never looked up, simply staring at his cell phone as he scrolled through one app after another.

The same Russian with the scar who'd transported him from Tajikistan had brought him here, and like he'd told him when he dropped Ahmad off at the hotel after the final flight, he was simply instructed to wait. Ahmad had plopped down on a bench, and had been sitting ever since.

At this point, Ahmad was willing to give up any claim or payment for the treasure. All he wanted now was to be let go, but he was worried the men he'd crawled into bed with would consider that option to be permanent. Outside of Jahn, he was the only one who knew he'd left Afghanistan with the treasure. And he was sure his friend was dead.

After Jahn had left them in the airport, the Russian with the scar had transported the treasure to a private Learjet, a small team of men appearing out of nowhere to conduct the manual labor, all of them hard, with scars like the leader.

The Russian had forced him to board the aircraft, ignoring all questions about where they were going. Eventually they'd landed at an airport somewhere, hopefully in Europe. All Ahmad could see were mountains covered in snow in the distance. As they taxied to the hardstand for private aircraft, he'd seen signs for the Zurich airport in Switzerland, giving him some relief. For a minute, he'd thought they'd landed in Russia.

They'd transferred from the jet to a helicopter, and then had taken off again. Thirty minutes later, they'd landed at a helipad, and Ahmad was taken to a fancy hotel called the Park Sonnenhof. He was told to simply wait until someone came to get him.

It was a full day and a half before he even learned he was no longer in Switzerland, but instead in Liechtenstein, a small microstate sandwiched between Switzerland and Austria and known as much for its loose tax laws and a preponderance of expat billionaires as its spectacular alpine views.

Eating breakfast at the included buffet, he asked the man cooking omelets how far it was to the airport in Zurich, and was told it was "fairly close, just across the border." Seeing the confusion on his face, the chef had said, "The border to Liechtenstein. To us."

Acting like it had all become clear, Ahmad had smiled and nodded his head, now completely confused. A day later, the Russian with the scar had returned, putting him in a fancy Mercedes SUV and driving him on a winding road into the foothills. They stopped at a spectacular chalet that looked as if it were built into the mountain itself. Led into the foyer, he'd been seated on a marble bench across from the younger man. The pockmarked, greasy-haired man showed no fear, like he belonged in the palatial estate.

Ahmad wished he could generate the same feelings.

The guy finally looked up from his phone and seemed to notice Ahmad for the first time. In English, he said, "You look a little worn out."

His accent was Eastern European, and Ahmad assumed he was from Russia. He let out a tired smile and said, "Yeah, it's been a little bit of a trip."

"Where'd you come from?"

"Afghanistan."

"No kidding? I didn't know Andrei was working in Afghanistan. What were you doing?"

Ahmad didn't want to continue the conversation, not knowing who he was or what he had to do with Andrei. And then he thought the opposite; this man could be useful. It might help if Ahmad learned why *he* was here.

He said, "I was doing this and that. Came here on the jet from Tajikistan. You?"

The man smiled and said, "Yeah, same. From Zagreb. That's a pretty good perk, but he'll make you pay for it in the end." He chuckled, then said, "Are you one of those refugees I see on the news?"

"Sort of. Not really. Not with Andrei."

The man nodded, interested in the story. He said, "That's true, that's true. So you do computer work?"

Ahmad chuckled and said, "No. I wish I had that skill. You do?"

The man nodded and said, "It pays the bills, no doubt. But you left Afghanistan for good, huh?"

"Yes, unfortunately, it was time."

"No kidding." He said, "I've had my share of not being wanted, trust me. But that was just my parents." He laughed again at his joke and said, "My name's Branko. If you get to Zagreb, look me up. I'll show you a good time, courtesy of Andrei."

He theatrically looked left and right, then whispered, "Don't tell him I said that."

Ahmad smiled and said, "I'm not sure where I'm going next."

He held up his phone and said, "Let me pass you my number. Call me if you get to Zagreb. I'll show you the town."

Embarrassed, Ahmad said, "I don't have a phone. I lost it."

Branko said, "Wow. That must have been some trip." He dug into his jacket, pulled out a piece of paper, and wrote something down, saying, "This is my email. I'm not kidding. You give me a ring and I'll show you the town."

He passed across the slip of paper, and they both heard the clacking of heels down the hall, the sound reverberating against the colossal walls, growing louder. Branko put a finger to his lips, then leaned back and played with his phone. The Russian with the scar appeared and pointed to Ahmad, then waved him forward. Branko looked up for a second, but immediately returned to his screen.

Ahmad followed the Russian down the hallway, passing through an enormous great room with a fireplace the size of a Volkswagen Beetle, and into a smaller study. Behind an ornate desk, the view through the window beyond something from a postcard, sat Andrei Obrenovic. He was a little older, but the same man Ahmad had met in Kabul years before.

If Ahmad could describe Andrei in one word, it would be "oligarch," one of the famed Russians who seemed to have absolute power without needing a government position, and he looked the part. A balding head of gray hair, corpulent cheeks saddled with a graying goatee, and a waistline that stretched out enough to make his legs look sticklike, he'd made his money in the burgeoning tech sector just as the Soviet Union was collapsing. Granted multiple licenses by President Putin in 1999, he'd expanded his empire just as other Russians had in the oil, construction, or defense sectors, until the term *oligarch* had become almost a definition in and of itself to describe a Russian man of significant means.

At the time, Ahmad knew Andrei was intimately wedded to the infamous Russian Internet Research Agency and its "troll farms" under the sway of the GRU, but that hadn't stopped President Ghani from asking him for digital support in Afghanistan.

Andrei had offered a suite of banking software solutions that would streamline the payroll for all personnel working within the Afghanistan government, and President Ghani had pushed hard to implement the software in an effort to stem the massive graft of the Afghanistan system. Because of Andrei's connection to Russian GRU, Ahmad, as the national security advisor, had been tasked as the intermediary.

The deal had never been consummated, primarily because of a little bit of a bait and switch on the oligarch's part. It turned out Andrei wanted more than simply money. He had plenty of that. A collector of antiques, he wanted some pieces from the Bactrian Treasure, a request that was clearly off the table for President Ghani.

But not for Ahmad, now that Afghanistan had fallen and Ghani had fled.

Andrei stood when Ahmad entered the room, holding his arms wide and saying, "Welcome, welcome."

The scar-faced Russian took a position next to the door, hands clasped in front of his waist in a position of attention. Ahmad hesitantly circled the chair in front of the desk and was embraced in a bear hug for a moment, then Andrei placed his hands on his shoulders and looked him up and down, saying, "That must have been some trip out of Afghanistan. You look a little worse for wear."

Ahmad was still wearing the suit he'd worn on his last day of work. The tie was gone, and the shirt and jacket were becoming threadbare, with glaring sweat stains on his back and under his arms.

He smiled weakly and said, "It was a quick trip, as you can imagine."

"We'll get you fixed up. Nikita here will take you into town for some proper clothes."

Ahmad thought, *So he does have a name,* but said nothing, wondering if the conversation was a trick.

Andrei said, "So, besides the clothes, what can I do for you?"

Ahmad wasn't sure how to answer. They already had the treasure, meaning he had no leverage. He decided to broach that very thing, just to see where it would go. "I remembered you wanted pieces of the Bactrian Treasure for your collection. I brought most of it."

"Yes, yes. I appreciate it. It is splendid."

The conversation died into an uncomfortable silence. Ahmad finally managed to splutter, "I was hoping a donation for my efforts would be in order."

"So you don't feel my helping you flee was donation enough? If it weren't for me, you'd still be in Tajikistan, running for your life like that friend you had with you."

Ahmad said nothing. Andrei continued, circling back around

the desk as he spoke, finally sitting again. "But I can see you need a stake to continue on your journey. Clothes alone won't be enough." He held up a finger, saying, "Understand, the price I was offering last year in the form of digital infrastructure is no longer on the table, but I can get you some seed money for a new start. Where is it you'd like to go?"

Ahmad realized that was the best he was going to get, and considered himself lucky that the man didn't simply kill him. He said, "The United States embassy. Take me to the embassy so I can get a visa for onward travel."

Andrei clucked his tongue, blew out a breath, then said, "That may be difficult. Would you be willing instead to travel to Russia?"

Feeling the sweat beginning to flow under his arms, visions of Soviet gulags flitting in his head, he said, "That is very kind, but the Americans will provide me free passage to the United States because of my position."

Andrei laughed and said, "So you want to be an Uber driver or run a McDonald's? Is that it?"

When Ahmad remained silent, Andrei said, "Unfortunately, there is no U.S. embassy here in Liechtenstein, and even if there was, I wouldn't allow you to go there for obvious reasons. In no way can I be connected to you in Liechtenstein. I can, however, take you back to Zurich, where you'll have to do the rest by yourself. I believe there is a U.S. consulate in Zurich."

Ahmad nodded again and said, "That would be fine. Thank you."

Andrei left his seat, came around the desk, and leaned into his face, his expression turning cruel. He was so close that Ahmad smelled the garlic on his breath and saw the red-lined veins in his eyes.

He said, "But you understand that the method you used to get to Europe is a little delicate—along with the payment for that travel. Correct?"

Ahmad nodded his head furiously, saying, "Of course. I don't want anyone to know I stole a cultural treasure from Afghanistan any more than you want anyone to know you have it."

Andrei's visage relaxed again, a false smile appearing. "Good, good. Return to the foyer and wait for Nikita. I have other business to conduct."

CHAPTER 14

Andrei watched the door close behind Ahmad, then looked to Nikita, saying, "What do you think?"

"Sir, I think we make him disappear. My views haven't changed. I should have tossed him out of the helicopter coming here."

Andrei laughed and said, "You might be right, and he still has a helicopter flight left. But I think he might be valuable. He gets to America, and we get to control him. For the rest of his life. Might be useful, even if he ends up as an Uber driver."

"Not if he gives up that you have the treasure. It's sitting here in the garage. One slip out of his mouth, and you and I will be persona non grata here. Liechtenstein will not look kindly on looting treasures when the European Union and America get in the fray, especially because of the debacle that is happening with Afghanistan. America will be looking for a way to be the hero, and this is it. They already don't like us. We'll have to find a new base of operations, and they're getting fewer and fewer for Russians on the European continent."

Andrei pursed his lips, putting a finger to them, thinking. He said, "Yes. That is a risk. But I can't send it back to Russia. It'll end up in Putin's hands within days. Or some other thief working in the government. It's why I'm here instead of in Moscow."

"Then send it somewhere else, just for safekeeping. It'll give us a cutout if it's found. Maybe to a safe in Zurich at a bank, or something like that. Just to get it away from us if this guy talks."

Andrei paced a bit, then said, "Get him his clothes. Give him some loaded credit cards and a sheaf of U.S. dollars. Say, ten thousand. Let him stay at the hotel for a few days until I make an ultimate decision. You'll either take him to Zurich, or lose him out of the helicopter over the border. Not sure yet."

Nikita nodded, saying, "Up to you, boss."

Andrei waved his hand and said, "Bring in Branko. We have more important things to do than collecting antiquities."

Nikita left the room, returning a few moments later with the scraggly twenty-something Ahmad had sat across from. Branko entered the room and plopped down like he belonged, belying his clothing. Andrei saw it as a sign of disrespect, but one he was used to. The kids he employed had a skill in computers that few others possessed, but he was a little sick of the insolence. Well, not insolence, just a lack of understanding of the power he wielded. Which he knew Nikita would solve.

Nikita came up behind him and snatched him out of the chair by his hair.

In Russian, he snarled, "Show some respect."

Branko's eyes flew open as he flailed around. Nikita slapped his hands away and held him upright, his hand still in the hair, Branko's head bent back.

Branko nodded as best he could, shouting, "I meant no disrespect!"

Andrei flicked his eyes, and Nikita released the youth, letting him fall back into the chair.

He rubbed his head, feeling the pull of the hair, and said, "What did I do?"

Andrei said, "You disrespected me. You and your men need to learn respect. I pay you for your services, but I can just as easily kill you. Do you understand?"

Now fully attentive, the slacker attitude from the foyer long gone, Branko nodded, his eyes wide.

Andrei said, "So, where do we stand?"

Branko said, "The test went perfectly. The zero-click penetration worked just as advertised."

The usual penetration of a computer system for ransomware employed social engineering, whereby one enticed someone to click on a malicious link through email or some other communication and inadvertently caused a cascading effect of malware in the system, such as John Podesta had done in 2016 when he'd tried to change a password from a site that wasn't authentic, allowing the Russian state to penetrate his entire system. Zero click meant they'd no longer need such efforts from the far end. They could inject the malware without anyone's help. It was unique, in that it didn't require someone in the targeted organization being dumb enough to click on a link.

"So it will work on the final target?"

"Yes, as long as they're running Windows or Linux. Which they will be. Nobody is going to use the Apple operating system for what we want to hit."

"Good. Who did you attack?"

"We just picked a company out of Washington, DC. Someplace called Blaisdell Consulting. They do work for the government, so we figured it was a good fit, but you wouldn't believe what we found."

"What?"

"We thought Blaisdell Consulting would be just a one-off,

where we'd get some ransom and test the system, but the Trojan horse kept going. Before we knew it, we were embedded in like twenty different companies. It was like that Kaseya hack last year, where the infected operating system was used by a bazillion different companies, and they in turn were infected. We had no idea it would go so far."

"So Blaisdell Consulting is a software firm?"

"No. Not at all. We have no idea how the various companies were connected, but their IT architecture sure was, and we flooded the entire system."

That didn't sound good to Andrei. Having worked at the height of the Russian state doing controlled penetrations of ostensibly secure government systems, he knew there was a fragile line between ransomware attacks by criminal gangs and state-sanctioned penetrations that could be traced. Most of the ransomware attacks against corporations could be denied by Russia, but if they hit the wrong system, it was a very fine line. In no way did he want the U.S. government to start investigating. Especially with what he had planned.

He said, "Did any of those systems turn out to be government? Did you infect a United States government system?"

"No. They were all private." He chuckled and said, "And they have about two more days to pay up. We'll get a good payday for this test."

"Can any of this be tracked back to Russia? To me?"

"Nope. We're working out of Croatia. They don't really like Serbs there, but it's better than working out of Belgrade. The U.S. has already started shutting those farms down through sanctions and arrests. It's why we chose Croatia, because of the scrutiny. We have a little cell set up. It doesn't take much."

"Where in Croatia?"

"Actually, we bounce around. We're like a group of gypsies. All we need is an internet trunk."

"And you can penetrate the final target?"

"Yeah, I'm pretty sure we can after this test. But I need the gateway. And the date. When do I get that?"

"When I get it. Just be ready. It won't be like the test. It'll have to be precise, on a certain date at a certain hour. Understand?"

Andrei didn't tell him he already had the gateway. All he was waiting on was the timing, and he was afraid that Branko would attempt penetration early, which would invite compromise. His target took cybersecurity very seriously, and while the zero click would solve the problem of penetration, remaining in the system for days before initiation was inviting discovery.

"Yes, that won't be a problem if I get the gateway. But . . ."

Branko rubbed his hands on his jeans and Andrei said, "What?"

"Well, we aren't making any money with our usual ransomware attacks because you told us to quit that. So we did. And we haven't gotten any ransom yet from this test. And we're running out of money. Croatia isn't cheap."

"I don't really care about your woes. The contract was payment after resolution. Go pick some pockets and live in a hostel until I call."

Branko took a breath, then pressed ahead. "That's not fair. We've done the test. That should get us some payment. Right?"

"You'll get the payment in two days from the ransomware attack."

"Maybe, but maybe not. If they refuse to pay and just take the punishment, we get nothing, and in any case, we need to eat today. Not in two days. We've worked hard for you on this."

Andrei sat and stared at him, thinking. He finally said, "You said you had assets all over the country, correct?"

"Well, I wouldn't say 'assets,' but we've been up and down the coast."

"Can you hide something there? Put something in a secure location until I ask for it?"

"Like what? A computer? Or jewelry?"

"It's nothing like that. It's a trunk full of printed information that I need protected. Kept well away from any prying eyes. Something from my past that will protect my future. It's worth nothing except to me. Can you do that?"

Branko thought for a moment, then nodded his head, saying, "Yes. If you give me the cash I need, I can find a place. It won't be a vault or anything like that. More like an apartment in a small town, or a cave in the countryside, but it'll be safe. Will that work?"

Andrei said, "That will work, as long as you tell me where you left it, down to the inch of latitude and longitude. You do that, and I'll keep funding your gypsy lifestyle."

Branko smiled and said, "I can do that easy. Just show me the trunk and give me a ride back."

Andrei said, "So we understand each other, I'm putting this case in your care. If it goes missing, so do you. It's locked, of course. If you try to penetrate that lock, I will know."

Nikita came into view from his left, towering over the chair, the punishment implicit.

Andrei said, "Stand by for the gateway information and final timeline. Nikita will arrange transportation for you and the case. He'll also be the one who finds you if you fail me."

Branko nodded slowly, wondering if the deal he'd made was worth it.

CHAPTER 15

We need to go back."

Knuckles' face was stone. No emotion. No crying or wailing. Just pure stone. But I knew that behind it was a lava of molten rage. We'd both lost friends in combat over the years, but rarely was it with either of us watching the execution. He felt responsible for Carly's death, and I knew it was eating at him just like it was eating at me.

Jennifer flicked her eyes to me, and I saw the fear. She had seen me at my worst and knew the horrific violence both Knuckles and I were capable of. She knew where Knuckles was right now. I shook my head, telling her to keep going.

We had failed, but I needed to stay focused on the task at hand. It was terrible to say, but I couldn't allow us to be compromised even with the disaster. Going back for her body was asking for compromise. We'd be questioned by any number of local forces. She had a backstop with the embassy, and, as much as it pained me, I'd let them handle it. We still had a mission. Jahn Azimi had been captured, and if Carly's death would mean anything, I was going to bring him home. But I needed Knuckles to do that.

I said, "We can't go back. We have no way to bring her off that hill and explain what we were doing there."

I saw his eyes snap open, going wild. He jerked forward, his body rigid, and shouted with spittle coming from his lips like a drunk in Times Square. "You're leaving one of our own on the battlefield! You want to do that? I'm not doing it!"

In a calm voice, I said, "I hear you, man. I hear you. But we have a mission. Think about the mission."

Knuckles had been my second-in-command since I'd *had* a command in the Taskforce. I knew him like I knew myself. And Knuckles surprised me, showing how little I knew about myself. He attacked me.

He leapt up from the back and wrapped an arm around my neck, trapping it against the headrest of the passenger seat, shouting, "We're going back! Turn around!"

It happened so fast, I reacted out of instinct. I sensed his arm drape over my face a split second before he could sink the hold, putting my hand in between his arm and my neck, then explosively leapt out of my seat, pushing through his control with my feet against the windshield, now parallel to the floor of the vehicle.

Jennifer shouted, the car swerved, and I launched into the back, hammering Knuckles in the face with my elbow. We fell into the well of the vehicle and started fighting, the only noise the grunting from the effort.

He landed two solid blows, which I took because I was going for a submission, and I got it, circling his head in my arms. But it had been too easy. He was letting me win. I almost didn't want to follow through, but I did. I began to torque, going so far that I thought I'd been wrong and he wasn't going to quit, wanting the punishment I was providing. A split second later, he tapped my arm, and I relaxed. Letting him sag into the seat next to me.

We both sat for a second, huffing. He said, "Is that what you felt when Heather died?"

I looked at him and said, "A small part. You now have some idea of the pain. But fighting me isn't going to cleanse it."

He nodded, his nose running with blood. He said, "Tell me we're going to find them. Tell me we get some vengeance."

I said, "Knuckles, we're going to rescue that man and his niece. *That* is vengeance. If we get to smoke some guys along the way, then so be it. Carly was working to get him home, to us. That's what we're going to do. It's what she would tell you right now. Given the choice between vengeance for her death or saving Jahn, you know what she would say. Can I count on you?"

He looked at me and I saw the pain I'd lived with for years, but had managed to survive. He was now leaning over the edge.

He said, "Yes, I can do that. But there is no mercy here. I'm going to kill all of them to free that man."

I said, "Tilt your head back." And put a wad of tissues to his nose.

In the front, Jennifer said, "We're out of the park. Where am I going?"

I looked at her and saw her face ghost white. She was petrified at what had just happened. Had no ability to assimilate it.

I said, "Go back to the hotel. We need to regroup. We need to find that guy's phone."

Four hours later, Jennifer turned from the computer and said, "That's it. First floor is a garage area for the complex, so the phone's on the second. It's an Airbnb apartment, but that's all we know, because Creed can't do anything from the Taskforce."

I leaned into the screen and saw a narrow metal stairway leading up to a second-floor landing, a balcony trailing away down from the entrance to a sliding door, two chairs out front, and a small table.

I said, "Creed still can't do anything more?"

"Not when I talked to him last."

Shit.

We'd gone straight back to the hotel after Carly's murder, and I'd pulled up our website VPN, contacting the Taskforce on a channel that was reserved for emergencies, and got the second shock of my night. The VPN failed to work. In fact, every link I had for the Taskforce failed.

I gave the Taskforce duty officer a call on an unencrypted sat phone, my last ability, knowing it was not the thing to do, but at least it went straight into space and didn't touch the Tajik cell network. I wanted to get a lock on the number we had for Jahn sooner rather than later, because Knuckles was pacing around the room like a caged tiger, and every second we waited meant Jahn might be killed before we could get him.

I knew that didn't matter to Knuckles, but he also knew that if Jahn was tossed in a dumpster somewhere, it meant he would lose the thread of those who killed Carly. He really wanted that phone lock.

I'd put Brett on him to keep him in check—one of the few men who could—and then dialed the phone. I was given some seriously bad news.

Apparently, Blaisdell Consulting had been hit with some type of ransomware attack, and all of our systems were now shut down and firewalled from the rest of the intelligence community architecture to prevent the spread. It had already infected numerous of our cover organizations, and would have infected my own company, Grolier Recovery Services, except for the fact that we'd been out in the wild with the systems basically turned off.

Knuckles heard the conversation and I saw him getting agitated. I held up a finger and said, "Put George or Blaine on the phone."

I waited a minute, and then Blaine came on, saying, "Sorry about that, Pike, this just happened, and it's a disaster. How is the exfil going? You're conducting exfil tonight, right?"

"No. That's why I'm calling. Take a seat, because things have gone bad."

"What?"

I told him what had transpired, from the moment we'd picked up Carly until right now, and he was suitably shocked. When I was done, because he was a good leader, he didn't question anything I'd said, only driving forward. He said, "Carly? What about her body?"

I said, "The CIA is going to have to deal with that. She was under official cover, right?"

"Yeah, she was. Because of Kerry."

"Well, I hate to give him that situation, but it is what it is. The reason I'm calling is I need a phone tracked. Jahn's phone. I have the number, but Creed is saying you guys are worthless now."

"Jahn's probably dead."

"No. No, he's not. If he was going to be killed, they would have done it when they killed Carly. They wanted him alive, and I'm going to find him."

"Pike, we have no ability to find that phone. If he's captured, they'll have him out of the country in twenty-four hours. He'll be gone before we can inject something into the traditional intelligence architecture. I'm sorry about Carly's loss, but you need to get out of the country, and I need to start the chain to get her covered and extracted. I need to talk to Kerry Bostwick."

I looked at Knuckles and knew that wasn't going to be enough.

I said, "I'm not leaving here without him. And you *do* need to talk to Kerry Bostwick, because the phone Jahn was using is in the CIA database. Carly told me that, and I need its IMEI. I'll find the phone myself with my own assets."

The Rock Star bird had an IMSI grabber built into the nose. Basically, it was a device that pretended to be a cell tower and would suck in every cell phone within range by tricking the phone to establish contact. The IMEI was a select number assigned to every single cell phone on earth, and the grabber would discard all phones until it hit the correct one. Once it was locked, we could triangulate the location, but I needed the IMEI to make it work. A simple phone number wouldn't cut it, as that was tied to the SIM card and not the phone.

"How are you going to do that over the entire city?"

He had a point. The IMSI grabber wasn't strong enough to suck in phones at a distance, because it would be competing with local cell towers. The aircraft would have to fly a grid pattern, basically mowing the lawn in the sky in the hopes that it would register.

"It's all I've got, sir. Please."

He said, "Let me see what I can do. Give me the number."

I did, and then got our aircraft moving to Dushanbe. It was only about a thirty-minute flight, but with the pilots getting scrambled out of bed, more like an hour. I turned to the room and told them the situation, then said, "I need someone who knows how to work the system in the plane. That's you, Knuckles."

I wanted to get him out of the fight, and this was the way to do it. I didn't need him going full crazy on an assault. And he *was* qualified on the system in the plane, having used it on several different missions.

He said, "Nope. Not going to happen. We find that phone, and I'm going on the assault. Don't even ask me that."

I knew we were about to come to a head, dreading the fight. This had become personal, which was bad. Veep came forward and said, "I can work it. Let me do it."

Veep was a combat controller from the Air Force Special Operations Command, meaning his job, outside of shooting, was controlling multiple different aircraft using everything from a Dixie cup and string to the most cutting-edge radio gear on earth. Truthfully, his expertise was exactly this. And I appreciated him defusing the situation. Although all he'd done was kick the can down the road, because I would still have to control Knuckles.

I nodded and told him it was his mission. Three hours later, after flying a pattern in the sky over the city, he got his first lock. Forty-five minutes after that, he had a grid, and transmitted it to us. Jennifer had pulled up the location on her computer, and we were in business. Except we couldn't get any information on the target itself like we could in the past through the Taskforce. It would be a cold hit.

I looked at the surrounding area as Brett and Knuckles came around to the screen, saying, "Okay, Jenn, I want you on the building across the circle. See it? Two-story structure? Can you get to the roof?"

She looked at the building and said, "Yeah, I can get up that."

Jennifer was a little bit of a freak when it came to climbing, and I knew she could use the bricks, copper gutters, and balconies to get to the roof as soon as I saw it, but I wanted to hear her say it, and by the way she did, I could tell she wasn't sure about the mission.

She turned to me and said, "Pike, all we really have is a lock on a phone. We don't know if he's there or not. We don't know anything about the place. You sure you want to go assault a building in a foreign country with this little bit of intel?"

I looked at Knuckles, and saw him nod. I said, "I'll explore. You cover me. If it shows promise, we'll push it. If not, we'll back off."

Then I turned to Knuckles, saying with a little bit of force, "And we *will* back off if it's nothing."

CHAPTER 16

Dylan Hobbes sat in front of his desktop computer and went through his email exchanges on multiple different addresses, using a virtual machine that wasn't tied to his computer and going down to the IP addresses in the messages themselves, trying to determine if there was any indication of his contact with a group of criminals. He was sure he had no proof in his systems, because he did this for a living, but he completed this check at the end of every day, just to be positive, scrubbing the computer with a program that would literally bleach the system when he found anything that could be construed as incriminating.

He finished the task, seeing nothing, and the speaker on his computer came alive, saying, "Hey, boss. You need to come down here. See what I've got. It's not good."

Surprised, he pressed a button on his keyboard and said, "What is it?"

"I don't want to say over the net."

Meaning, it could be saved for posterity. He'd instilled in his staff never, ever to say anything sensitive on the network, be it verbal, text, or chat, because he knew that once it touched the internet, it was there forever, no matter what anyone said. The only way to prevent that was good ol' fashioned paper notes or face-to-face conversations. But in this case, there should be no reason to use such security.

He said again, "What is it?"

"You need to see it."

Exasperated, he said, "Come up here and talk to me. I'm doing other work."

"Roger that. Will do."

The man Hobbes had chosen for the security assessment of the strange government organization called Blaisdell Consulting was a prior member of both the NSA and Cyber Command. Someone who would understand the firewalls, nondisclosure statements, and intricacies of what they were dealing with. Someone who wouldn't talk. The researcher had no idea of the scope of the problem set he had been presented, but would know that no matter what it was, he wasn't allowed to talk. He was a good man.

Seven minutes later, Hobbes heard the footsteps in the utilitarian hallway. While their business earned millions a year, his company worked out of a two-story warehouse in a nondescript area of Tysons Corner, Virginia. Close enough to do the work with the government cyber agencies as required, but far enough away from the players in DC to protect him. Just like the greater intelligence community. A stone's throw from Liberty Crossing, the home of the National Counterterrorism Center and the headquarters of the Director of National Intelligence, it was a convenient location. But it still looked like a warehouse from the outside. Like an old storage unit facility that one wouldn't rent without some references.

His door opened and he saw Kirk in the hallway. He said, "What's the fire? I have my own issues here."

Kirk entered and said, "Yeah, you think you have a flame, but it's nothing like I'm bringing to you."

Hobbes leaned back in his chair and said, "What's that mean?"

"I've poked around the code used for the penetration of that computer at Blaisdell Consulting, and it looks like ours."

Hobbes heard the words, but they didn't assimilate immediately. He thought, *What? That can't be right.*

Kirk said, "Did you hear me?"

Hobbes said, "Yeah, yeah, I heard you, but that can't be accurate. What do you mean, it's similar to what we were doing with Project Speargun?"

"I mean the code is our own. It *is* Project Speargun. The one we developed for the zero click. It's in this ransomware. They have our code. That's how they did the attack, and now I'm worried that it's somehow escaped our lab, but I don't know how."

Feeling the sweat form on his brow, knowing *exactly* how, he said, "Surely you're mistaken. That can't be right. There's no way our code got out into the wild. No way. It's been air-gapped since we started."

Kirk said, "Come downstairs. I'll show you. It's our code. We have a leak somehow. We should have never done the work to develop it."

Last year, Hobbes had created a "Tiger Team" to develop the ability to inject malware with a zero click into Windows computer systems, ostensibly to learn how to deconstruct such penetrations for their business of solving ransomware attacks, much like gain-of-function research into viruses in order to develop effective treatments before they became a threat. But Hobbes had a separate reason for such work. One that was now about to be discovered.

He couldn't believe the zero click in this attack had come from him. How stupid could the people he'd contacted be? Attacking a secret US government organization? One that could wipe them out?

A smart man, he quickly realized that they had no idea what

they'd attacked. All they thought was they'd get a ransom from some bloated consulting firm. After all, *he* had no idea until he'd been read on to the Blaisdell Consulting program.

Kirk said, "Hey, boss, you okay?"

Hobbes snapped out of his thoughts and said, "Yeah, yeah, of course. It's just a little bit of a shock hearing this. Are you sure?"

"Oh, I'm sure. I wrote that code. It's mine. How on earth did it get out in the wild? We had that shit locked up tight."

His head still spinning, Hobbes said, "Show me. Show me the code."

Kirk nodded and said, "Follow me."

They walked down the hallway, Hobbes feeling sick to his stomach. He had agreed to help solve the ransomware problem for some obscure consulting firm, only to find out it was actually a covert agency of the United States government. He'd brought in his best man to penetrate the systems and deconstruct the code, and that man had now told him his very own code was in the ransomware.

Because it was him who'd let it out in the wild. He'd given it to a ransomware gang for a specific hit at a specific time, for a specific reason.

There was no way he could let this covert top-secret killer organization know it was his code involved in the attack. *His* code. Why they'd chosen this target was what he didn't understand.

He walked down the hall panting, his eyes becoming blurry. He was going to be found out. Going to go to jail. Lose everything he'd worked toward.

Lose the mission.

Kirk glanced back at him and said, "You okay, boss? You look a little sick."

Hobbes gave a weak smile and said, "Yeah, yeah, just something I ate."

He had to do something. Had to prevent the leak of his code from getting back to anyone at Blaisdell Consulting. And the only way to do that was to keep Kirk from talking. But how? He was a good man, but not someone who would understand what was at stake here. Kirk would not agree with Hobbes's worldview, of that he was sure.

Since the fateful day of 9/11, Dylan Hobbes had lived in a universe of vitriol that only grew worse after each passing year. He'd worked to defend the United States from fanatical enemies all over the earth, and had been castigated for his efforts by elected leaders when leak after leak occurred. It didn't matter which party was in charge at the moment: He was always the punching bag for cheap political points from pandering windbags who had no idea what it took to defend the United States. Nobody stood up for him or the men around him. Democrats called him a Nazi, Republicans called him the Deep State. None of the people ever said he was needed to defend the nation—right up until a terrorist attack occurred, and then they all called him incompetent.

It was impossible to succeed in such an environment, and the rot extended past his small world. It wasn't about him. It permeated the entire country, extending down through every level from the decision making of the federal government to the kitchen table. Each party was simply looking for an edge in an upcoming election, focusing on the near-term target while ignoring the long-term implications to the country.

What was needed was a union of national pride, as had happened briefly after 9/11. Or after Pearl Harbor. Something to unify the country once and for all. Something that would give the entire population a focus other than partisan politics. He'd seen it happen before, and he was determined to make it happen again.

Only now his plan was about to be short-circuited by a man he'd hired to solve a problem that was one of his own creation.

They reached the top of a stairwell, a metal door held open by a rubber stop, the stairs themselves concrete with a steel plate at each edge, thick utilitarian tubes for railing leading down, the stairwell itself as dark as pitch.

Kirk waved his hand and a motion light came on, saying, "I get the need to control costs, but those lights are creepy."

He smiled at Hobbes, the smile fading when he saw Hobbes's face. He said, "What's wrong?"

And Hobbes shoved him with all his might. Kirk flew off the landing, going about three feet through the air, his arms windmilling before he slammed into the sharp edges of the stairs. He tumbled down to the next landing and then moaned, rolling over.

Hobbes opened and closed his fists, not sure what do to. Surprised he'd even done the shove. He turned to the door, then turned back. Finally, he made a decision, bounding down the stairs to the body below. Kirk looked up at him, pain on his face, saying, "My back. My back. What did you do?"

Hobbes wrapped his hair in his hands and pulled his head off the concrete. Kirk raised his hands and moaned, "No, no, no."

Hobbes paused, and then committed, smashing Kirk's forehead into the steel plate of the stairs. He dropped the head, sank down, and began crying.

Five minutes later, he rubbed his face, then checked Kirk's pulse, finding it gone. He raced back upstairs to a bathroom, looked in the mirror, and saw blood on his face. He leaned forward in astonishment, as if what had happened shouldn't have painted him with the results. He looked at his hands and saw more splatter. He furiously scrubbed his face and arms, then sagged into the corner, wondering what he had done, and what he should do now.

He came to a conclusion. There was nothing to do but continue.

He pulled out his cell phone and called 911.

CHAPTER 17

Jennifer radioed, "In position," then snuggled behind her weapon as gently as if she were wrapping a puppy in her arms, seating the butt into the pocket of her shoulder, shifting it minutely left and right on its bipod until she achieved a natural point of aim on the apartment door.

She took long, slow breaths to calm her pulse after the climb up the wall. While it wasn't that challenging in a technical sense, it did require a significant effort, especially with a rifle strapped to her back, and she needed to lower her heart rate.

She put her eye to the scope, seeing the stairwell ninety meters away, the single bulb at the door providing enough illumination to determine targets. There was one man on the stoop, sitting and smoking a cigarette. She had no idea if he was a threat but had to assume so. She centered the reticle on his chest and waited, breathing in a practiced manner as precise as a metronome.

She thought this entire thing was a bad idea, but Pike had a way of solving a problem, and even when that sometimes involved violence, it was usually correct. So she deferred to her team leader.

She saw a vehicle come around the circle and knew who it was. The car parked and she saw Pike, Knuckles, and Brett exit, but only Pike mounted the stairs. He walked up, the light above him making him look like something out of a horror movie. She tracked him with the scope, praying this was a dead end. They had no way of knowing what was behind that door, and she honestly didn't want to find out.

The man on the stoop stood up, tossed his cigarette over the railing, and said something to Pike. Pike answered, pointing at the door. The man shook his head, waving Pike away. Pike insisted, and the man swung a right cross punch that caught Pike in the left temple, slamming him into the railing. She watched him fall down the stairs end over end and thought, *Oh. My. God.*

Not because of the strike, but what she knew was about to come from it.

Pike sat up, turned to the bottom of the landing, and said something. Then rose like a curtain of death. She saw the rage on his face and knew it was time. He charged up the stairs and the man who'd struck him pulled out a pistol.

Jennifer broke the trigger, splitting his head open.

A second man exited the front door, and Jennifer cracked the trigger again, dropping him. Pike, Knuckles, and Brett didn't even break stride, launching over his body and entering the apartment.

Within seconds they were inside and she was panting, trying to control the adrenaline flowing through her.

I parked the car knowing I had overwatch from Jennifer, but still wasn't sure if the juice was worth the squeeze on this thing. I'd done enough hits on SIGINT intelligence that went nowhere to understand that this was a long shot. But you never knew, so I continued forward.

Knuckles was in the backseat, and he was in a bad way. He wanted to kill anyone who'd had anything to do with Carly, and I understood that, but I couldn't let his beast of vengeance consume what we were trying to accomplish. I turned off the engine and said, "You good here? Or do I just take Brett up there?"

He glared at me and said, "Let me know if it's the place. If it is, I'm in. If not, okay."

I looked at Brett and said, "Don't let him do something stupid. This is probably nothing."

Brett looked at Knuckles and said, "We're good, right?"

Knuckles nodded with little enthusiasm, saying, "Yeah. We're good."

Then his voice turned cold, saying, "If this is it, I'm going in."

I said, "Knuckles, let me sort it out first. Stop if it's not the place. Don't come running up just because you want to kill someone. It might be nothing."

He said, "I'll stop just like you did."

I knew what he was talking about. I'd been where he was, and he'd help pull me out of the brink. I would do the same for him.

I said, "I was wrong then, and we want to be right here."

He nodded and I got face-to-face with him, saying, "You get that, correct?"

His gaze penetrated me, and I saw the bloodlust. I slowly shook my head and said, "Stay in the car. I'll deal with this."

He said, "You don't trust me? After all this time?"

"Not right now. You've got a little bit of an anger issue, and we don't even know if this location has anything to do with Carly."

He said, "This is the place. And I'm going to kill them."

I said, "Stay in the car. I'll be right back. If I see anything that looks bad, we can go up."

I left him with Brett, who looked like he wanted to draw his Glock. Not a good way to run a team.

I walked up the stairs and met a man smoking a cigarette,

with a swarthy complexion and a little bit of an Afghanistan vibe because of his dress. Nothing overt, but he was a little off, like a glitch in a computer game, but because I wasn't an expert on Tajikistan, I let it roll. I said, "I'm trying to find a friend of mine. Came here from Afghanistan. He told me he was here."

The man stood up, and he was big, about six feet two, and none of it was fat. He said, "Get out of here."

Mildly surprised he spoke English, I said, "Okay, but I'm just trying to find my friend. Do you know anything about any Afghan people fleeing here, to Tajikistan?"

Out of nowhere, he swung a right cross that hit my left temple and knocked me into the railing of the stairs, hard enough to almost render me unconscious. I tumbled a few feet down, disbelieving that the guy would do that. I remained still for a second, my head on the stairs, then rose to a sitting position and looked back at him.

He pulled a pistol from his waist, putting the sights on me, but not firing. Just showing me he had it.

I glanced down to my car, feeling the rage build. Feeling the beast wanting to run free.

Knuckles was out and spoiling for a fight. He shouted, "Enough. Let me go."

I stood up, shook my head to clear the fog, then looked at him with the same bloodlust he felt and said, "Bring it the fuck on."

And turned to fight.

I drew my Glock knowing there was no way I could beat the man to his trigger. He would fire as soon as he recognized what I held. But I also knew something he didn't. He was a dead man.

I saw his head explode and then another man exit the door. Jennifer pumped two rounds into him before he could even recognize what was happening.

We raced up the stairs, vaulted over the dead body and bashed into the apartment, facing five guys standing up in a living room, all wondering what the commotion was about. Two of them had weapons in their hands. The rest had none showing, but that meant nothing.

A sixth man to my right hammered my wrist with something rigid, knocking my Glock free.

It clattered to the floor, and at that moment, I knew I was dead. There was no way to beat them all.

But I'd forgotten about Knuckles and his rage.

The first man raised his pistol and I charged forward to the immediate threat, ignoring the guy who'd smacked my arm. I knocked the weapon wide before he could fire, raking his arm over a chair and hammering the joint. He screamed, his arm splintered with the bones showing, and I drove a fist like a sledgehammer into his face, putting him on the ground. My second punch was to his throat, killing him.

The entire universe shrank into this room, and I entered the savage world of survival. It turned into a vortex of violence. Brett entered right behind me and immediately pulled the trigger on the other weapon in the room, punching two bullets into his chest.

A lamp shattered against my skull and I went to my knees. A guy jumped on me, grabbing my hair and raising my head.

Then Knuckles entered the fray. And he was a death dealer with a little bit of a rage issue. He could have just shot the man holding me, but did not.

He snatched the man's throat, ripping him off me, then dropped, one knee out, hammering the base of the man's head on the bony part of his thigh, breaking his neck like a twig. Another man jumped on him and Brett ripped him off, wrapping up his body in a rear naked choke, rolling on the ground. The fifth man yelled and raised his fists. Knuckles stood up from the body below him, turned, and smiled, a predator grin that told me what was going to happen.

I dove into the sixth man, the one that had first hit me, smashing his head into a cabinet. He tried to fight, but had no skill. I punched his leg right next to the femoral artery, in the tangle of nerves there, and he shouted, collapsing on the ground like a tripod with one leg cut away. He rolled on the floor, holding his thigh, and I hammered the base of his skull with a punch that had all of my weight behind it, separating his spine from his head.

While I was pounding my man and Brett was choking out his like a python, the one in front of Knuckles screamed and charged him, whipping out a blade and diving forward, waving it like a magic wand. Knuckles turned and took his attack like a ballerina conducting a dance. He trapped the man's arm, then cinched it tight into his chest while bleeding off his energy by rotating around in a circle. He looked the man in the eye and then pounded him with the bone of his forehead right on the bridge of the man's nose, shattering it, then picked the man up and drove him into the wall like a linebacker sliding a blocking dummy. His body hit the brick wall face-first, the knife dropping away, the carcass falling to the floor.

Brett stood up from his man and Knuckles said, "Is he still alive?"

Brett nodded, and Knuckles advanced on him.

I said, "Knuckles. Don't do it. We don't know he's bad yet. He had no weapons. We don't know what we have here. Could just be a drug den."

He looked at me with the same rage I had held, and said, "They're all dead. All of them."

He wrapped his arms around the neck of Brett's target and sank in his hold. The man was unconscious. Knuckles was going to kill a helpless target.

I said, "Stop. Stop what you're doing."

He looked at me with unbridled rage and said, "They killed Carly. They can now reap what they sowed."

I honestly didn't care about the man on the ground. He was a piece of shit, but this was murder. I knew it wasn't right. We didn't do what they did, no matter how much we wanted to. I'd killed two men in the room, but only in self-defense. We didn't even know if these men were involved with Carly and Jahn.

Knuckles said, "They all die. That's the way it is."

I raised my voice, saying, "Don't. You will never sleep again. Trust me. I know. And we can use his information."

He released the man, snarling.

The body fell to the ground and the man began coming out of the loss of oxygen to his brain, regaining consciousness. He rolled over and tried to sit up, groggy.

Knuckles punched him so hard his head left a dent in the wood of the floor.

We stood for a moment, breathing heavily, surveying the damage.

I retrieved my Glock and said, "Okay, okay, let's check and see if this place is anything other than a fistfight."

In the second room we found our man, with his niece, both chained to a bed. He looked at us in fear.

I said, "Jahn Azimi?"

He nodded slowly, unsure if he should admit his name.

I turned to Brett and said, "Get the bolt cutters."

To Jahn I said, "Hang on for just a second, and you'll be free."

His head sagged back into the pillow and the girl said something in Pashto that I didn't understand. He turned to her, rubbed her head, and I saw a tear form in his eye.

And that was all the thanks in the world.

CHAPTER 18

Shakor heard the robotic voice mail invitation and hung up the phone, wondering why his team leader refused to answer. He had not been able to get in touch with the capture team for close to twenty-four hours, and it worried him. The team leader, Bashir, had called him yesterday, jubilantly bragging about the successful mission against Jahn and the CIA agent. He'd said they were in a safehouse and intending to travel back to Afghanistan after midnight, when any Tajik checkpoints would be laxer.

And now Shakor couldn't get in touch with Bashir at all. Out of the four different calls throughout the night, only one resulted in contact early in the morning, but it wasn't Bashir. It was a lowly team member, who'd told him Bashir had gone out for supplies and would call as soon as he came back, but Bashir had not.

After that one contact, nobody was picking up, leaving him without an answer as to why the team member had Bashir's phone. He'd thought about that question after he'd disconnected, and it made him uneasy.

It might mean nothing. In fact, the lack of contact was probably a good sign, as Shakor knew the cell service dropped to nothing outside of Dushanbe, so the team was probably on the road right now. At any rate, he had little time to dwell on it, as he had his own mission to complete.

He turned to the other man inside their little Airbnb and said, "Any word from the airport?"

"Nothing. A few private aircraft taking off and that same shuttle helicopter coming and going, but nobody's touched our plane."

It had taken them two days to get their passports in order from the Haqqani network in Uzbekistan, and in that time, using the tail number of the aircraft, they'd determined that the plane was owned by a rich Russian and had flown to Zurich.

That was the worst possible case, leaving Shakor with fantasies of the treasure disappearing into a Swiss vault owned by some bloated Russian oligarch. It was the same thing they'd thought had happened the first time the Taliban had taken over, way back in 1989, which had proven false, but now they *knew* Ahmad had taken the treasure, and that he'd taken *this* plane to Zurich. And so, without anything else, he'd flown his team to Zurich and placed surveillance on the aircraft, waiting on someone to show up so they could interdict him. Or surveil him. Or something.

So far, it had not provided any fruit.

Just as he was wondering about becoming more aggressive in his tactics, but unsure of what that would be, his phone rang. He looked at the number, and saw it was Haqqani. Shakor dreaded answering it, but he did anyway.

"Hello, sir."

"I received no status report yesterday. Where do we stand?"

"I had nothing to report yesterday, but I do today. We have Jahn."

"You have Jahn? Seriously? Why wasn't I told?"

"It just happened. We caught him in Tajikistan."

"When will he be here? Back in Kabul?"

"Soon. Bashir is driving now. I'm sorry I didn't call, but I've been busy in Zurich trying to catch that other traitor and find the treasure."

"You mean Ahmad Khan? You don't have him? You've been in Zurich for over a day and a half."

Taken aback, Shakor said, "I know that, sir, but the only lead we have is the aircraft. We're on it twenty-four seven, and so far nobody's gone to it. When they do, we'll get them and find out where he went. Best case, it will be Ahmad himself."

He heard a breath, then some cursing. When Haqqani came back on the phone he said, "Do you not watch the news? *Ahmad* is in Zurich. He's turned himself in to the United States consulate there. He's under the protection of the Americans now. How could you miss that?"

Shakor said nothing, the words bouncing through his head like a cue ball smashing around a billiard table. He put his hand over the phone and snapped his fingers, saying, "Google Ahmad Khan in Zurich."

The team member at the computer said, "What?"

"Do it!"

He returned to the phone and said, "Sir, we knew that, and we have people on the consulate, but we can't snatch him there. We're working on it."

Haqqani said, "I don't like excuses. Get me that treasure. And bring me Jahn."

The phone disconnected and Shakor turned to the team member sitting in front of the computer. Looking chagrined, knowing the answer he gave would reflect on him as much as Shakor, the man said, "Ahmad turned himself in to the consulate. They're working his visa to get him to the States. He's all over the news as a great story for the US evacuation, because that's going so poorly. They're trumpeting his escape. He's going to be on a press conference today at four."

Shakor looked at his watch and said, "That's in two hours. Get the team here. Now."

"All of them? You want to pull off the airport completely?"

He paced for a minute, unsure, then said, "Leave one person watching the plane. Everyone else comes here."

Forty-five minutes later he had a four-man team surrounding a computer, a Google map displaying the location of the United States consulate. All of them were dressed in European clothing, with short hair and no beards. All of them spoke English, with two fluent in German and two in French. They could blend into any European country, and Shakor would use that now.

He said, "Ahmad Khan made it into the U.S. consulate. He's being presented today at a press conference where the United States will blather about protecting the allies they pretend to hold dear. The mission is simple: We wait for it to be over, and then follow him to wherever he's being kept. When we find that, we take him. Understand?"

The men in the room nodded, waiting on their specific assignments. Using Google Street View, Shakor pulled up detailed pictures of the consulate, showing a nondescript five-story office complex with a parking garage underneath, the building itself about four blocks east of Lake Zurich.

He said, "The consulate is on the third floor, and we obviously aren't going to be invited to watch the press conference, but sooner or later, they'll have to leave the building. When that happens, the mission is to simply find out where they take him."

He then dictated positions, saying, "I'll be the control. Each position will have two people, as I have no idea how long it will take for him to leave the building. He could stay there for hours getting debriefed, but sooner or later, he's going to leave. Use the Vespa scooters and relieve each other as necessary. Sooner or later, they'll leave the parking garage and go to wherever they've paid to put him up."

One of the men asked, "What about security? We can't attack them without causing a reaction."

Shakor said, "He's not going to spend the night in the consulate, and the U.S. will feel no threat here in Switzerland. I'm sure there will be security when he leaves, but that's going to just be show. When he gets to the bed-down site, he'll be left alone. That's where we'll take him. Questions?"

Ghulam, one of the more violent members of the crew, said, "When he leaves, why not just take him off the street? Before he gets to the safehouse? Put a bullet in his head?"

Shakor actually had to take a minute to process what the man said. When he did, he fought to control his voice. "This isn't a kill mission. We're here to find the treasure. Anyone who thinks that killing Ahmad is the mission is sorely wrong. He is a link to the treasure. That's all. Do *not* kill him."

The men nodded and, as he'd done on multiple operations with the Badr 313 Battalion, Shakor said one final time, "Any more questions? If there are, ask them now."

Unlike the usual Taliban attack forces, the Badr Battalion had learned from their very enemy, the United States Special Forces, and they'd become better because of it. They had studied. Had learned that each member of the team had something to offer. And after twenty years of war, they were now the equal of the men they were against, if only because their enemy held them in disdain.

Nobody around the computer said anything else. Shakor said, "Okay, remember, this isn't about Ahmad. It's about the treasure. We need him alive. When we find the treasure, then, and only then, can we kill him."

CHAPTER 19

Dylan Hobbes pulled into the checkpoint for the West Wing and showed his driver's license. The man took it, scrolling through a list on a computer, and Hobbes used the opportunity to wipe the sweat from his forehead. Having always had hyperhidrosis, he was used to the moisture under his arms and his hands, but it increased exponentially when he was stressed.

Which he was now.

The 911 call the night before had worked out as best as he could hope, with the police and EMT response deciding it was an accident—a tragic fall down the stairs. The coroner would have the final say, and one man appeared to question the wound on the forehead, saying it was much too deep and precise to be from a random fall, but Hobbes had been told at the scene that it looked pretty cut-and-dried. No foul play.

It was still nerve-racking, and because of it, he couldn't turn off his body's reaction, the beads rolling down him like he was the character in the sweating scene from the comedy movie *Airplane!*

It wasn't just the killing making him sweat, though. It was what he was about to do. He couldn't allow the Serbians to continue the attack he'd planned. The risk was too great that he'd be found out as the source of the code for the attack, and in so doing be branded as a traitor, when that was the absolute opposite of what he was. He was a patriot. The problem was he couldn't simply turn them off. He wasn't in control of their operations—the Russian, Andrei, was.

While he had given them the code with the promise that they use it on a specific target of his choosing, he couldn't stop them from doing whatever else they wanted before that time. He'd had no fear of discovery when he believed they'd simply attack some European airline, but they'd hit something else entirely—and he was sure they had no idea of the trouble they'd caused.

Why did they choose this place to attack? Why?

He'd scrabbled for a solution all night long like a rat gnawing on a piece of gristle, tossing and turning, his bedsheets damp with the sweat rolling off his body. One answer was to simply "admit" failure, telling the secret people at the White House that he couldn't crack the code and had given up. But that would invite questions. Who gives up after two days? These sorts of things took much longer than that, but there was no way he could let anyone else from his team look at the code. They'd recognize it just as Kirk had, and he most certainly couldn't start killing everyone in his company, and so he'd have to engineer another reason he couldn't continue.

But that brought up a second problem. If he quit, the United States government wouldn't. They'd find someone else, and that company would be outside of his control. Eventually they might make the same connection Kirk had, exposing him to the same problem. The Vault 7 leaks from WikiLeaks taught him that. The world was a much smaller place than it used to be. The only way to be clean was to keep the problem set to himself.

After a sleepless night, he'd decided on a different course of action. One that would be executed by the very people those idiots had attacked. He'd been hired for a specific purpose: geolocation of the hackers. He wasn't hired to defeat the ransomware code, but to locate the people doing the extortion. That's what the president had said. He wanted to punish them, and that might be the best way to solve the problem. Let this Project Prometheus loose, killing the Serbians before they could expose their connection with him. It would mean the end of his primary mission in the short term, but he couldn't see any way around that.

The problem with that plan was the Russian, Andrei. In no way could he lead the US team to him, because he was the one person who knew Hobbes personally.

Well, that, and the fact that attempting to attack the Russian was asking for his own demise. The man was much more powerful than Hobbes—more powerful than anyone Hobbes even knew—and he had no illusions of what would happen if what he was planning reached Andrei.

He'd be found dead from some poisoning if he was lucky. Found in pieces if he wasn't. That final thought caused his sweat to spring anew.

The guard waved him through, and Hobbes parked his car in the lot adjacent to the entrance to the West Wing, the lot fairly empty due to the late hour. He turned up the air-conditioning in a futile attempt to dry the moisture, sitting for five minutes with the air flowing over his face, putting his hands up to the vents like he was a professional bowler about to roll for a strike. Eventually he turned off the engine and sat for a minute, gathering his courage.

He was startled when someone knocked on his window. He turned and saw National Security Advisor Alexander Palmer outside his door. He opened it, saying, "You scared me."

Palmer smiled and said, "I saw you pull in, but when you

didn't exit the car, I figured I'd check on you to make sure you knew where to go."

Hobbes exited the vehicle and Palmer said, "You okay?"

"I'm fine. Just a little nervous about this meeting, I guess."

Palmer saw the moisture on his brow and said, "You had a COVID test, right?"

Hobbes smiled and said, "Yes, it's not the dreaded Rona, I promise. I'm vaxxed and boosted, and you guys made me test before the first meeting two days ago. I'm good. Just nervous."

Palmer nodded and handed him a visitor's badge, saying, "Put that on and follow me."

They entered the West Wing, skirting by the security desk and the staff secretary, walking directly to the Oval Office, Palmer saying, "You said on the phone that you had some information, is that right?"

"Yes. I think so. I have a location."

Palmer opened the door to the Oval Office, saying, "Good, good. Go on in."

Hobbes entered, seeing the president and five other people waiting expectantly. He recognized the chairman of the Joint Chiefs of Staff, the director of the CIA, and the secretary of state but was unsure about the others.

President Hannister said, "You have some news?"

"Yes, sir. We haven't been able to crack the encryption, but they left enough fingerprints to tell us who they are. It's not conclusive, of course, but it's pretty damn close."

"Who?"

"It's a ransomware group called Dark Star, and its leader is a Serbian named Branko Markovic."

Amanda Croft, the secretary of state, said, "Serbian? Not Russian?"

Hobbes said, "The actual men working the keyboards are Serbian, but we honestly don't know who's behind them. Maybe Russians, maybe nobody. We've encountered Dark Star multiple times in the past, and they leave certain clues behind in every attack. We've published their digital traces in technical magazines, so there is a bit of caution in this assessment. Someone could be trying to throw authorities off the trail by duplicating them, or it could be a splinter group that left Dark Star and went off on their own. Happens all the time."

The director of the CIA, Kerry Bostwick, said, "So, this isn't definitive?"

"It's as definitive as I can make it. There are no absolutes in this world, like DNA in criminal cases. My forensics are not as clear-cut, but in my professional opinion, this *is* Dark Star."

President Hannister said, "Okay, assuming this is Dark Star, how does this help us? We need a location. Hopefully someplace we can reach. Where is their base of operations?"

Hobbes said, "Honestly, they operate all over the continent, depending on the target, but we've managed to find an association with the attack."

He opened his briefcase and withdrew a tablet, saying, "This one came from Croatia, specifically Zagreb."

He laid the tablet on the table, and everyone gathered around, staring at the map displayed. A bright blue marble highlighted a location inside a four-story building in the upper town of Zagreb, Croatia.

CIA director Bostwick, said, "How can you be this precise? What in the code led to this? I mean, I could see saying it came from Croatia, or even Zagreb, but you're saying it came from this building?"

Hobbes felt the sweat start to build under his arms and on his forehead. He hoped nobody noticed. He certainly couldn't tell them that he had no ability to geolocate the hacking crew to this fidelity, something the D/CIA seemed to suspect. The location was the last known address for the leader of the crew, but he couldn't very well tell them a specific apartment.

He said, "They used an ISP that was tied to a café on the fourth floor. The A'è bar. I don't know if it's accurate, but it's all we have."

"Wait, wait. Are you saying they used an open Wi-Fi network from a bar to conduct the attack? That makes no sense. Anyone on that net could see what they were doing, starting with the ISP provider."

Feeling the sweat start to roll down his face, Hobbes said, "I can't explain it. I can only report what I find. Maybe they're stupid, or maybe they're in an apartment next door using a VPN while piggybacking off the bar. I can't tell you specifically. Maybe the bar has something to hide, I don't know. This is what I found."

In truth, Hobbes had simply used the nearest Wi-Fi node to the apartment he could find.

President Hannister said, "Are you sure of this location?"

"Yes, sir. I'm sure. I can't say they're still at that location, but the attack came from there. I'd look for an apartment in that building associated with Branko Markovic. Why they touched the open Wi-Fi network, I can't say, but it's there, and it's real."

Hobbes wondered if he'd overplayed his hand. If, by his mentioning looking for an apartment, they'd see through his ruse.

Hannister looked at a man on the couch, one who hadn't said a word. Lithe, with a full mustache going gray, he projected an air of quiet competence. Hobbes recognized him as George Wolffe, the man who'd provided him the computer boxes for analysis. Hobbes had assumed from the first meeting that he was simply a bureau-crat, but President Hannister's next words belied that notion.

The president said, "What do you have available in that area?"

Wolffe considered for a moment, then said, "Nothing right now. Johnny's in Africa, but he's tied up on something else. Pike's the closest, but as we were discussing before Dylan arrived, he's committed with that other thing."

President Hannister nodded, saying, "That should be done to-night, right?"

Wolffe looked at his watch and said, "If not already. It's three in the morning his time. I'm just waiting on a SITREP."

Hobbes wondered what Wolffe really did, but was afraid to ask. He should have shown more curiosity, if only for his own protection, because the man on the couch was the catalyst for his own destruction.

President Hannister said, "Don't wait for him to call. Contact him and find out if he's complete. If he is, get Pike on it."

CHAPTER 20

Circling around the Zurich neighborhood of Enge, just west of the lake, Shakor caught two parked scooters in the glare of his headlights. He slowed down and recognized the man standing next to them. He pulled his vehicle into a parking slot fifty meters down the road, adjacent to the southern edge of Rieterpark, the largest greenspace in Zurich. He killed the engine, turned to the men in the back, and said, "Wait here."

He exited the car, ducking his head when another vehicle passed on the thoroughfare running by the park, the headlights silhouetting his body against the tall shrubs marking the edge. The vehicle disappeared in the distance, and he walked back to the scooters, checking for cameras on the houses across the road as he went. He saw none. A man approached out of the darkness, and he recognized his head of surveillance, Din, by the limp from an old war injury. He said, "Any trouble at the consulate?"

"None. They did exactly like you said. We had to wait a long time, but we had the press conference streaming on our phones, so we knew when it ended. It took about four hours after that, and then they tried to sneak him out through the garage, but they didn't really put any effort into it. They drove him out in a two-car motorcade of black SUVs and it was easy to track. They went around the lake to this place."

"Where is he?"

"Just up the street, to the right on Kurfirstenstrasse, in a little bungalow set back off the road, but he has security. Or a butler. Or something."

"What do you mean?"

"One SUV left with most of the security, one remained behind with a single guy. He looked more like a babysitter than security. No hard edges and I saw him use two different cell phones talking to someone."

"Show me."

They went back north, stopping for a moment at Shakor's vehicle. Shakor explained what he knew, then told them to stand by.

Shakor continued to follow Din north, the park to his right and the road to his left. They went slowly, fading close to the shrubbery anytime a vehicle approached. They reached a T intersection, a sign proclaiming KURFIRSTENSTRASSE, the blacktop snaking away from the park to the west, faintly illuminated by house lights on either side.

Din hissed and a man crawled out from the shrubbery of the park, standing up. Shakor recognized the second member of the surveillance team, Karim. He nodded at Shakor but remained silent. Din said, "It's the first house on the northwest corner. You can't see the structure, but you can see the gap for the drive in the bushes."

Shakor saw a line of tall shrubs like sentries running along the road, the vegetation stopping and making a right angle away from the blacktop at the boundary for the next house, a single break in the center, presumably the drive to the target building. Directly across the street was another house, this one not set back, with windows facing the target, but no lights on.

He said, "Any movement from the house across the street?"

Karim said, "Not since we've been watching. The entire street's been quiet. We can probably take him in the house, do the interrogation inside, eliminate Ahmad, and get out without anyone even knowing."

"What about this security man? Is he still there?"

"Yes. Well, at least the vehicle hasn't left. He'll have to be dealt with."

"Is there a gate?"

"No. The house is just set back from the edge about fifty meters. No gate, just the shrubs, which works in our favor. Once we're in, nobody's going to see us."

Pointing up the road next to the park, Din said, "You can see the second level over the shrubs. See that balcony?"

Shakor looked, then nodded. Din said, "That's the target. It's a two-story dwelling, but pretty small as far as footprint. I would say maybe two bedrooms on the second floor, a den and kitchen on the first, with maybe another bedroom in the back. Security will probably be downstairs, with Ahmad upstairs."

Shakor nodded, going through assault options in his mind, then felt his phone buzz. He slapped his hand to his pocket, thinking, *Who could be calling me? Surely not the team at the car. They'd use the radio.*

He thought about ignoring it as spam, then realized it could be the solitary man they'd left on surveillance at the airport. He answered.

"Hello?"

"Shakor, it's Abdul. The helicopter has returned. The pilots are on the private plane and two people have left the helicopter and also boarded. Now some men are unloading a case from the helicopter."

"Case? What kind of case?"

"It's a two-man lift, like a meter and a half long and a meter deep."

Shakor inwardly cursed, wondering if he'd made a mistake in hunting Ahmad. *Should have stayed on the airport.* "You think it's the treasure?"

"I can't tell. It's just a case. There's no indication of what's inside."

"Did you get a picture of the men and the case?"

"Yes. I have that."

"Send them to me, and find out where that plane is going."

He saw a single headlight from a motorcycle coming toward them and said, "I have to go."

He hung up and the three-man team faded into the shrubs, waiting on the motorcycle to pass. Din said, "What was that about?"

Shakor said, "I don't know, but they might be moving the treasure at the airport while we waste time out here."

The motorcycle slowed and Shakor moved deeper in the brush, wondering if they'd been spotted, praying it wasn't a police cycle. He saw it was a scooter, much like the ones his team had used. On the back was a large box with an advertisement emblazoned across it. He thought, *Food delivery.*

The scooter stopped right in front of them, the rider looking at his phone. *Trying to find an address.* The rider glanced up Kurfirstenstrasse, then turned the scooter in that direction, going away from them.

Shakor said, "We'll have to wait until that delivery person is gone, but once he is, we penetrate."

Karim said, "Kurfirstenstrasse is a one-way road. He can't come back. He'll leave going away from us."

Shakor nodded, reached into the pocket of his jacket, and withdrew a cheap handheld radio. He held it up, turned it on, then said to Karim, "Got yours?"

Karim nodded and Shakor said, "Get the others. We do it right now. Din and I are going to take a look."

Shakor and Din slinked across the road in the darkness, trading the shrubs of the park for the landscaping surrounding the target. They reached the gap in the vegetation and Shakor looked across the street, seeing no movement in the windows, the entire façade black. He whispered, "I'm going to walk across like a pedestrian in case someone's looking from the target. You follow one minute behind."

Din nodded, and Shakor stood, walking nonchalantly past the target, glancing up the drive as he went. He saw a small porch with an overhang and a light fixture on either side of a wooden door. To the left of the house was another overhang, like a side door, but he couldn't be sure. He reached the far side of the gap and blended back in with the shrubs, keying his radio and saying, "Din, I'm across. When you come, focus on the left side of the target. See if there's a door there. I couldn't tell."

Din said, "Coming," and Shakor watched him rise and walk forward, briefly silhouetted by the lights from the front of the target, then reenter the gloom. Din took a knee next to him and said, "It's a side door. No light."

Shakor said, "That's our entry. I'll take in Ghulam, you, and Karim. The other two pull security just inside the drive, giving us early warning while we do the work. We eliminate the butler/bodyguard, then interrogate Ahmad."

No sooner had he said the words than a headlight appeared, coming from the west down the street toward the park. They both sank back into the bushes, with Shakor hissing, "I thought you said this was a one-way road?"

"It is. It is."

CHAPTER 21

Shakor and Din waited, finally seeing the same delivery driver puttering down the avenue. He passed them and slowed next to the gap of the drive, looking at his phone. Shakor saw an opening. He said, "Get the men up here," and stood up without waiting on an answer, walking to the scooter.

In English, he said, "You looking for an address?"

Startled, the rider said, "Yes. The address given isn't on this street. At least as far as I can find."

"Who are you looking for? I know everyone on this street."

The rider studied his phone and said, "The charge card is under the U.S. Department of State. The name is someone called Andrew Dumas, and the address is on this road, but I can't find it."

Shakor said, "You found it."

"What?"

Shakor ripped him off the scooter, using his helmet to drag him behind the shrubs, the man's legs kicking, but the chinstrap in his throat preventing him from screaming. He thrashed his arms wildly against the assault and Shakor applied more pressure, using the helmet to cinch the chinstrap deep into his throat. Eventually the rider ceased moving.

Din reached him, agitated, looking around wildly and saying, "What are you doing?"

Shakor began stripping the dead man of the uniform jacket he was wearing, saying, "This is our way in. Get the men up here. I'm going to take this scooter to the door."

Breathing through an open mouth, Din said, "Are you crazy?"

Shakor stood up, now wearing the jacket and holding the helmet, saying, "No. Get them up here."

Din ran back to the park and Shakor went to the scooter, turning on the ignition and steering it boldly up the drive. He parked it like he belonged, hand-checked his weapon underneath the jacket, making sure he could get to it, then opened the case on the back, finding four pizza boxes. He had no idea what the house had ordered, but hoped it wasn't all four, because that would mean there were more men inside than Din had indicated.

Using his radio, he said, "Are you ready?"

Ghulam answered, saying, "We're on the edge of the landscaping."

"I'm going to the door. There might be more in here than we know. If there is, I'm going to deliver the food and back out. If not, I'm taking out whoever answers. When I do, follow quickly."

"Wait. How are you going to determine that?"

"With the pizza."

"What's that mean?"

Shakor simply said, "I'm moving."

Without waiting for an answer, he took all four boxes and went to the stoop, entering the light. He rang the bell and waited. He heard footsteps, then the door opened, a tall man in a business suit behind it. The man said, "About time. We've been waiting for an hour."

Shakor said, "Sorry. Here's your order."

The man said, "We only got a single pizza. Not four."

In a single move Shakor dropped the pizza boxes with his right hand and withdrew his pistol with the left in a cross-draw, hammering the man in the face with a backhanded blow that raked the slide and front sight post against his temple. Shakor saw the blood flow as the man shouted and fell backward into the house. Shakor pushed inside right behind him, tripping up his legs. He hit the floor, desperately trying to draw his own pistol. Shakor slammed his boot into the man's gun hand, pinning it to the ground, and the weapon fired, the sound earsplitting in the small house.

The man tried to roll free and Shakor knew that quiet no longer mattered. He put the barrel of his pistol to the man's face and pulled the trigger, splitting the back of his head open against the hardwood floor, the brain and blood splattering out like a cherry pie thrown against a wall, some parts liquid, some parts lumpy, some parts red, some parts gray.

He heard footsteps pounding behind him and shouted, "Two upstairs, two down! Clear for threats!" and began sprinting to the landing in front of him. They reached the top and he pointed left, two men running that way, and he went right, kicking in a door and seeing Ahmad on the balcony that overlooked the park road, preparing to jump. In Pashto, he shouted, "Ahmad, stop right there, or you're dead."

Ahmad jumped. Shakor ran to the balcony, hearing a scream. He looked below and saw Ahmad on the ground, writhing in pain and holding his leg. Shakor turned back around and sprinted to the lower level, finding Karim coming out of a room. Shakor said, "On me," and ran out the door, circling the house. They found Ahmad trying to crawl to the road through the bushes.

Shakor grabbed a leg and pulled, eliciting another scream. Shakor punched him in the temple, stunning him, then said, "Grab his arms."

Karim did as he was asked, and they huffed back into the

house, laying him on the floor next to the dead man, Ahmad slowly rolling back and forth. Shakor leaned back, panting, and said, "Is the house clear?"

Ghulam appeared from the second floor and said, "Upstairs is clear."

Din said, "Nothing downstairs."

Shakor nodded and said, "Close the front door. Put a man outside to see if the neighbors heard anything. Get the side door unlocked and get everyone ready to run. We have probably five minutes to know if we've been compromised. If we have, we starburst and meet back at the hotel. If you're caught, you're on your own."

The men did as they were told and Shakor turned to Ahmad, lightly tapping his face until he focused. Ahmad saw him and tried to backpedal. Shakor grabbed his injured leg, bringing another scream. Shakor slapped his face, saying, "Shut up and take it like a man."

Ahmad lay down, panting. He said, "Just kill me. Do it. Get it over with."

Shakor said, "Believe it or not, I'm not here to kill you. I don't care about you. I care about what you did with the treasure."

Ahmad looked at him with wild eyes and said, "Treasure?"

Shakor put his hand on Ahmad's knee, drawing a wince, and said, "I don't have time for games. Where is the treasure?"

And Ahmad told him everything. The escape, Jahn, the Russian, Liechtenstein, the helicopter trip, everything.

Inwardly, Shakor believed he was telling the truth, and also that they'd lost the treasure yet again. He pulled out his phone, went to the picture that Abdul had sent, and held it up, saying, "Is this the box the treasure was in?"

Ahmad looked at it, and Shakor didn't even need to hear the answer to know what was coming. "Yes. Yes, that's it."

Shakor heard Ghulam return and said, "Are we good?"

"So far. No new lights, nobody on the street, nothing."

Shakor returned to Ahmad and said, "Where is it going? Where are they flying it to?"

Confused, Ahmad said, "Flying it? It's in Liechtenstein. It's already flown, and I told you where it is. I can't give you any more information, which means you don't need me anymore, right?"

Shakor said, "Right," and put his forearm into Ahmad's throat.

Ahmad thrashed, fighting, but Shakor used the blade of his forearm to cut off his air. Ahmad choked out, "There was a man. A man."

Shakor relaxed his arm and said, "What man?"

Ahmad coughed and rolled over, saying, "There was a man from Croatia with me when I met the Russian. Maybe he has it."

Shakor could see he was grasping for anything to save his life, but it was worth exploring. They had nothing else. "What man?"

"I don't know. Some guy like twenty-five. Does computer work for the Russian. He was leaving after me. If the treasure is gone, maybe it went with him."

"Why would the Russian give the treasure to some twenty-five-year-old?"

"I don't know. I'm just telling you what I saw. I'm trying to help."

"What was his name? Who is he?"

"He said his name is Branko. He lives in Zagreb. I don't know who he is. I only know he was meeting the Russian." Ahmad fumbled in his pocket and pulled out a slip of paper, saying, "This is his email. He told me to contact him if I ever made it to Croatia."

Shakor assumed that Ahmad was simply spinning a story to delay the inevitable, but the slip of paper was just enough to prove what Ahmad was saying was true. He looked at it, seeing a Gmail address for "Branko_420." He said, "Why would this man have the treasure?"

"I don't know that he does. If you say it flew away, he was the only other man there who was leaving."

Shakor flipped through the pictures sent from Abdul and showed him the first man who'd entered the aircraft. "Is this him?"

Ahmad looked and said, "No. That's the Russian's bodyguard. Nikita."

Shakor flipped to another, holding the phone up. Ahmad said, "That's Branko. That's the man who was there. Is that from the airport?"

Shakor put his phone away and said, "You should have stayed in Afghanistan. It would have been better for you."

"I'll go back. I'll go back right now!"

Shakor said, "You made your choice. Maybe your body will return."

He turned to Ghulam and said, "Hold him down."

CHAPTER 22

My little caravan was about an hour outside of the Bokhtar airport near our original dig site, banging along what passed for an interstate in Tajikistan, when my satellite phone rang. I looked to Knuckles in the passenger seat, saying, "Who in the hell could that be?"

He had a laptop in—of course—his lap and was typing away on a situation report to give to our higher headquarters, and was still surly. I didn't blame him, but knew even with his attitude that he'd use the appropriate euphemisms to describe our engagement.

I didn't charge up the stairwell after getting clocked in the head. I'd "assessed the target location and determined it was hostile." Jennifer didn't start splitting heads open with a sniper rifle while we ran helter-skelter up the stairs. Our "planned overwatch eliminated threats to the penetration." And Knuckles hadn't slaughtered everyone he'd encountered. We'd all "used the minimum force necessary to subdue the opposition."

To whit: we had a prisoner in the car behind us being driven by Brett. Nowhere would the SITREP mention the discussion about killing that guy in cold blood.

Even though I'd ordered the plane to displace to Dushanbe, we were executing the original plan of driving back south. It would be much easier transferring our passengers at the Bokhtar airfield than at the only international airport in Tajikistan.

The phone rang again and Knuckles said, "You going to answer?"

I pursed my lips and said, "I guess I have to, but man, I don't want to. I'm sure it's Veep about to tell me something's gone wrong on the flight."

I picked it up, hit the button for the call, and said, "Hello?"

I heard, "Pike? Is this Pike Logan?"

I honestly expected to hear Veep giving me some sort of shit sandwich, but the voice wasn't his. I said, "Yeah, it's Pike. Who's this?"

"It's Blaine. Blaine Alexander."

Great. It's going to be a bigger *shit sandwich.*

Blaine was the designated commander for Omega operations, but since Kurt Hale's death, he'd been acting as the deputy commander of the Taskforce while George Wolffe—the previous DCO—acted as the commander. Him calling could not be good news, unless in his new role he just didn't have the patience to wait for a SITREP.

"What's up, sir? I'm a little busy right now. Driving down a goat trail in Tajikistan. SITREP on the operation is coming your way. I was going to send it when I got to the airfield before we went wheels up."

"Yeah, I know. I'm not pushing, but the National Command Authority has. The president initiated this call. Can you talk?"

I looked in the rearview mirror and saw Jahn staring intently at me. I said, "Hold on, sir. I need to stop and get out."

I flashed my brake lights and then pulled over to the side of the road, saying, "Knuckles, keep typing. Jahn, no offense, but you can't hear this."

He smiled and said, "No offense taken."

I exited the vehicle and held up my hand, showing the trail vehicle the phone. They'd know why I stopped when they saw it. I walked a few feet away into the desert darkness and said, "Okay, sir, what's up?"

"We have a mission, but it's predicated on your last one. Is it complete?"

"Well, if you'd have waited an hour for the SITREP, you'd know that. But I guess now that you're the DCO, it's time to start bugging the guys in the field while they're still running an operation."

Blaine had been my commander on more Omega operations than I could remember, and he was truly a good man that I respected, so I figured I'd give him some grief, since I was sure he was about to return it in spades.

"Pike, you're on speakerphone. George Wolffe is here as well."

Oops.

I heard, "Pike, just give us the bare bones here. Are you complete?"

"Sorry, sir. Yes, we are. Jahn and his niece are recovered. We left five dead bodies at the target, and have one live one with us now. We located the target through airborne assets and then penetrated. We got out clean, but there's a mess that's going to be found in the morning. We're currently headed away from Dushanbe to Bokhtar airfield. I'm going to pack up my kit from the dig site and evacuate in the morning. I'm going to need a transfer location for both Jahn and the Taliban we captured."

Blaine took that in and I could imagine him looking at George incredulously. I heard, "Five dead? Did you say you had five dead?"

"Yes, sir. It'll be in the SITREP, but we had a forced entry. It was their call, not mine. It's not a worry. They're all Afghans.

Nobody's going to come looking for Americans on this thing. It's clean, but there's something else that's not."

George cut in, saying, "How can you be sure you're clean with five dead?"

Getting a little aggravated, I said, "Because we were silent. Everything was silent. Nobody reacted. I left Jennifer on the roof for an hour after we exfilled. Nobody showed any interest. They'll be found in a day or two when the Airbnb contract runs out. Now can I get to the new threat you guys need to worry about, or do you want to keep worrying about what I just told you?"

"Okay, okay. What is it?"

"I told you we had a prisoner, and between him and Jahn, we've learned a few things. The national security advisor gave Jahn his flight out, and he also stole something called the Bactrian Treasure. I don't know what it is, but it's something big for Afghanistan. The Taliban want it back really bad, and they have two teams out. One was to find Jahn and bring him back for torture and propaganda—which, of course, isn't going to happen now because we killed all of those savages. The other was to recover this treasure. And they're on the hunt right now, with the linkage target being the national security advisor. Some guy named Ahmad Khan, who's connected to some Russian."

"Yeah, we know about Ahmad Khan. He's okay. He turned himself in to the consulate in Zurich, Switzerland. He's in the fold."

"In the fold? What about the Russian?"

"I don't know about any Russian. He appeared at the consulate all by himself."

"And this treasure? Where'd it go?"

"Honestly, it's the first I'm hearing about a treasure. And I really don't give a shit. That's some Afghanistan thing that doesn't matter to me. We have another problem, and you're the closest to solve it."

"Wait, I just told you that there's another team looking for Ahmad Khan. They're from the Badr 313 Battalion. They aren't goat herder Taliban guys. They're fluent English speakers and most have spent time in Europe or the United States. They're hunting him, and he's somehow dealing with Russians. It stinks to high heaven. What kind of protection does he have?"

"Pike, he's in Switzerland. They aren't going to find him there. We have another problem."

I gave up, saying, "Okay, okay, what is it?"

"You know we've been hit by ransomware, right?"

"Oh, yeah, I know. I had to solve this last problem all by myself. Why?"

"We have a location for the people who did the attack. A last known location, anyway. It's in Zagreb, Croatia."

Now really confused, I looked at my two Land Rovers, one holding two freed hostages and one holding a terrorist. I slowly said, "Okay . . . I'm in the middle of an operation here. Exfil is not complete."

"We'll deal with that. You need to get to Zagreb, and investigate this."

"Are you serious? What's the mission?"

"The president is sick of these ransomware attacks. Colonial Pipeline, hospitals, schools, it's like we're impotent. He wants to send a signal to people like them."

"And what's that?"

There was a pause, and I said, "Sir?"

"Honestly, I don't know right now. Just investigate this target and use your best judgment. I'll send you a complete package with everything we know. We've done some work on our end and we have a location down to an apartment. We don't know if it's him or not, and that's what you're going to figure out. Right now, it's Alpha. Just explore and see what linkages you can make."

"If I make them?"

"Then it'll probably go to Omega, but not DOA."

While we always had the right of self-defense—like we'd done in Dushanbe—our charter was always to capture the target. DOA meant the threat to national security was so grave the target could be resolved dead or alive. If capture wasn't feasible, but killing was, then we had a green light to kill—but only if capture wasn't feasible. It was rarely given.

On the teams, while the Oversight Council called it "Dead or Alive," like we'd make the choice depending on our ability to capture juxtaposed against the time frame of the threat involved, we colloquially called it "Dead on Arrival," because if you gave me the DOA authority, I was going to kill him with the least threat to my team. Why would I attempt a capture when I could put a bullet in his head from a thousand yards out?

I would never tell the Oversight Council that, because the DOA authority was as controversial as it sounded—way, way outside any tenets of our own Constitution—but when DOA was given, that guy was dead. The Oversight Council could sleep peacefully at night thinking we'd done our best to bring him in alive. The teams knew the truth.

Wolffe said, "This is going very fast, and it's straight from President Hannister. Like I said, he's smoking mad about the ransomware attack and wants to send a signal to these groups. Covertly. There won't be any press on it, but word will spread. I honestly don't know the end result, but I do know the beginning, and that's you exploring the target package."

I said, "Okay, sir. We're headed to the bird right now. We'll be landing at the Zagreb international airport in about seven or eight hours. I'm going to need a complete exfil package to meet us."

"Why? Just hit the ground and roll out, then send the plane on its way to us with Jahn and the Taliban guy."

Were these guys thinking through the problem?

"Sir, if I do that I'll have to leave at least one team member on the bird, more likely two. We have one hostile and two recovered hostages. And I'll need what's inside the Rock Star bird. I can't do this mission with half a team, and I'm going to need the bird. Although I suppose I could leave Amena to watch them. She's pretty switched on."

"Amena? What does she have to do with this?"

"She's here as well. She was helping on the dig until you pulled us off. She's going to need an escort, too. All the way back to Charleston. Kylie's house-sitting, so that's not an issue, but someone's got to get her there."

I heard nothing for a moment, and could almost see their heads billowing smoke.

Wolffe said, "Get going. We'll have an extraction team there waiting. We'll deal with Croatian immigration, but you'd better have the terrorist prepped for onward travel. I'm talking blindfolds and earmuffs."

"And Amena?"

"I'll handle it. Damn it. If I have to fly her back myself, she'll be taken care of."

I knew he meant it. He had a little history with Amena himself. She'd be okay.

I said, "One last thing: What happened with Carly?"

I heard nothing for a moment, then, "The police found her body about an hour ago. The embassy is working it. It's being called a random attack. A mugging."

He said nothing for a moment, then, "I'm sorry, Pike. I know she was one of yours."

I appreciated the sentiment, but I would expect nothing less. We weren't interchangeable robots sent to kill, and Wolffe knew that better than most.

I said, "Thanks. She was doing what we all do. Get Jahn back to the United States to make it right."

"How's Knuckles?"

Wolffe knew what Carly meant to him. I looked at the vehicle, seeing Knuckles typing through the dim glow of the dashboard lights, and said, "He's good. He's in the game. Send me the target package. I'll look at it in the air."

CHAPTER 23

Sitting behind his computer, Branko heard Pushka come out of the bathroom, drying his head with a towel. Branko said, "You still put out? It wasn't that big of a deal, and it was for Andrei."

"Don't give me that shit. Whatever you've got going on as a side gig for Andrei has nothing to do with me. I stroke the keyboards, that's all. Except now I'm also paid to be a porter like I'm in Mumbai or something."

"I'll buy you lunch. Last night was a pain in the ass, I admit, but it was worth it, trust me. It paid the rent."

Pushka was Branko's lead penetrator inside Dark Star, and he felt that's where his work should end. Dark Star itself was designed by Branko as a multilayered system like any other modern-day company, only it was solely designed to find and exploit targets. Even given his youth, Branko was a smart man, and a survivor. One who could gather both the capital needed for operations and the necessary people to execute.

One layer surveyed the marketplace looking for targets, analyzing the income and determining the pain threshold they could manage. Another layer then analyzed the computer network for penetration, and the final one did the work. Pushka was the final dimension. The guy who actually penetrated the network and installed the malware. As such, he hadn't appreciated Branko asking for help.

Branko had come home late at night, driving his car from the airport to his apartment in Zagreb, the trunk from Andrei in the back burning a hole through his thoughts. He knew he had to do something with it, and storing it in his apartment was a nonstarter because of the maintenance people and management constantly coming into his place.

He didn't do any computer work from this apartment, only using it as a sort of headquarters for his operations due to the location. Zagreb was overrun with various foreign intel agencies, and as such it would be the last place he'd use to conduct his attacks, but it was convenient when he had to travel—which he often did—so he kept the apartment as a staging base. It doubled as a place he could let his men, like Pushka, use when they wanted to come up and blow off some steam. It had become sort of a frat house for Dark Star.

He'd felt lucky when he'd shown up and found Pushka there. He had been running through his head where he could hide the trunk—stashing it somewhere secure that had no connection to him—and had kicked around an idea about burying the damn thing in the woods. When he'd seen Pushka at the apartment, he thought it was a sign.

They'd gone up to the A'è bar for some drinks on the terrace, and after he'd lubricated Pushka a little, he'd broached his plan.

"You used to work at Plitvice Lakes National Park, right?"

"Yeah. Worst two years of my life. Picking up the trash from all of the tourists year-round. All I did was walk those paths. Miles and miles, picking up shit that people tossed."

"Was there a place you could hide something? Like a trunk?"

"Oh, yeah. There are caves and hideaways all over that place. It's like the place was created for pirates. Why?"

The waitress came over and Branko ordered two more drinks. When she left, Branko said, "I have a little bit of a problem from Andrei. He's given me something to hide. Something that needs to be kept secret, but because we move around so much, I can't use one of our places. I need someplace secure, where nobody will find it."

Pushka said, "So you want to hide it in the woods? That's insane."

"No, it's smart. Is there a cave you know of?"

"Branko, the national park is blanketed with tourists. They have thousands of people a week go through there."

"But they're only allowed on the paths, right? Surely you know of a place they don't go. That nobody goes."

Pushka thought for a moment, then said, "There's a major cave called Supljara—meaning Silver Lakes. The tourists walk up a shitload of stairs through it, but underneath there are hollows that are unknown. I used to go into them to smoke a joint now and then. As far as I know, nobody even knows they exist. I could sit there for hours hearing the people go by. It was like my special hiding place."

"Can you still find it? Now, at night?"

Wary, Pushka said, "Yeah, I guess, but it's really not that safe at night. It's a long way to the bottom, and the stairs are something out of a medieval castle. I mean like carved out of stone and super steep."

Branko said, "I got the money for us to continue, but it's predicated on hiding this box. I can cover your rent in Korcula and Split, but only if you help me with this. It's the price we pay."

Thirty minutes later they were driving down the A1 highway through the countryside, passing by one small town after another. After two hours of staring at the headlights racing along the blacktop, the woods passing by in a blur, the road went through the entrance to the park, a hotel, restaurant, and parking on the left and the park on the right. Branko began to turn into the parking lot for the tour buses and Pushka said, "No, keep going on the highway. We're going to jump the fence. The park is closed, and there's no way we're going to lug that trunk to where I want to go through the main gate. We'll pull over next to the path, where the road comes right up to the edge."

They crawled down the blacktop another mile, maybe a mile and a half, with Pushka shouting to pull over every hundred meters, then saying he was wrong and to keep going. Eventually he seemed satisfied. Branko pulled as far off the road as he could, snuggling under the trees, and Pushka left the vehicle.

He was gone about twenty minutes, and Branko used the time to stick an Apple AirTag on the base of the trunk. He held his iPhone to it, registered the tag, and named it "Demon Seed." He tested the tag with the Find My feature of the phone, saw the tag was active, and closed the app just as Pushka returned.

Pushka said, "This is it, but I'm telling you, it's going to be rough."

"How rough?"

"Like three stories of stone steps from the Middle Ages. One wrong slip and we're going down."

"Give me a hand."

They wrestled the trunk out of the back of the SUV, setting it on the ground. Pushka said, "That thing is heavy. I'm not sure we can do this at night."

"You brought a headlamp, right?"

"Yeah."

"Then it's the same as daylight. Let's go."

They both turned on their lamps and began walking through the woods, finally coming to a simple wooden fence marking the outer edge of the park. They hoisted the trunk over and began again, finally reaching a footpath with another railing. After crossing it, Branko said, "Which way?"

Pushka pointed to the left and Branko shined his headlamp, seeing a gaping darkness that swallowed his light like the maw of a whale, the blackness overpowering the feeble stab of his lamp. He went forward and saw a set of stairs carved out of the rock, enhanced with slipshod concrete work, the entire thing disappearing into the black hole, an iron railing on the side away from the cave wall. The entire width was just barely smaller than the trunk itself, and the stairs switched back and forth down the rock wall.

It *was* going to be rough.

He returned to Pushka, and they began laboriously dragging the trunk down the incline. Sweating and swearing after the third narrow switchback, Pushka said, "What's in this thing, anyway?"

"I don't know. Some type of papers or something that Andrei wants hidden. I didn't open it. It's locked up tight."

Eventually they reached the bottom, the lake and waterfalls of the park visible in the moonlight outside the entrance, a wooden boardwalk leading in to where they stood. Branko said, "Okay, this is what the tourists do. Where did you go for a smoke?"

Pushka said, "Leave the trunk here. Follow me."

Branko did as he asked, and they crossed the iron railing designed to corral the tourists, entering a tunnel of stone that led away from the main chamber. Pushka ducked his head, the ceiling getting lower and lower, finally entering another chamber that allowed him to stand up. Branko flicked his headlamp around and saw water bottles and cigarette butts.

"This isn't going to work. Clearly, people climb that railing and explore. We can't leave it here. I thought you said it was secret?"

"This isn't it. If I smoked here, I'd have been found either by smell or sight."

He went left, got down on his belly, and crawled through one of the myriad holes in the side of the cave, disappearing into the darkness. Branko followed and eventually found himself in another chamber, this one much smaller, forcing him to crouch, with a natural chimney showing the starlight above.

Pushka said, "Nobody comes here. There are plenty of tunnels like you just crawled through, but all of them end up in a dead end, where getting back out is hard as shit. I know from experience. This is the only one that ends up in an open chamber, and as far as I know, I'm the only one who's found it. Outside of cavemen, I guess."

Branko looked around and saw no signs of human presence. He said, "Does it flood? Like in a heavy rain?"

"No. Some dripping down that chimney, but it's higher than the lake level. Even when the main chamber floods with, like, a foot of water, this one is always dry. Take it from me. I used it plenty of times."

An hour later they'd pushed and pulled the trunk into the small chamber. Branko checked the AirTag, saw it functioning, and then checked the signal all the way out. The tag worked on Bluetooth, and he lost the signal just outside of the main chamber, but—with the location—it was enough for someone from Andrei's organization to find it. The AirTag was crowdsourced with anyone who owned an iPhone with Bluetooth enabled, and every time someone explored the larger chamber with an iPhone, that trunk would register without them even knowing. With a battery that lasted a year, he was comfortable that it was safe.

They'd traveled back to the apartment in Zagreb and had crashed, exhausted. Now, the next morning, Pushka was still surly. In fact, he seemed more aggravated than he had the night before, when he was lugging the trunk to the cave.

Pushka repeated, "I do computer work. I'm not Andrei's personal servant. There are plenty of people who want my skills. My back is killing me, and my knuckles are scraped raw from last night."

Branko bristled, saying, "You won't have to do anything like that again. It's not like I control everything. Maybe next time, you can fly to Liechtenstein for an update. Leave me here to drink beer and do nothing while getting paid."

Pushka backed down, saying, "Buy me lunch and we'll call it even. But I'd really like to know when the next attack is happening. That last one got us zero. I've heard absolutely nothing from the target. I think they're going to suck it up."

"They might, but it's irrelevant. With that trunk, I got us the money to keep working even if they don't pay. I know the next target, I'm just waiting on the gateway. When we get it, we go operational again. I'm thinking the place in Split."

"What's the target?"

Branko gave him a sly look and said, "That's a secret. Andrei's orders. But it's big. Biggest one we've ever hit."

Pushka grinned and said, "You owe me for this."

Branko turned back to the computer, saying, "I told you, I'm paying for lunch." He clicked on his email and brightened, saying, "I'll be damned."

"What?"

"You want to go out tonight? Get someone else to pay for it?"

"Sure. What's up?"

"Remember I told you about that guy from Afghanistan I met in Liechtenstein?"

"Yeah. The one who looked like he'd hiked to the house? That one?"

"Yeah. He was a good dude. I gave him my burner email. He's in town and wants to party."

CHAPTER 24

Brett tapped into the website Creed had provided and we got a blurry mess, like looking at something through glasses smeared with Vaseline. After a second it cleared up, as if the camera were waking from a slumber and shaking its head to focus.

He said, "Looks like Creed's little backup attempt is working out. At least we have a view down the hall."

I leaned over his shoulder and saw the door of one Branko Markovic. Or at least the door that Creed *said* was his. Creed had never let me down before, but then again, he'd never been working with the shoestring computers like he was now due to the ransomware. He'd built an emergency backup out of old tools, and that's all we had.

We'd packed up our dig site tents and tools and met the aircraft at the Bokhtar airfield in the final hours of darkness, everyone happy to be exfiltrating successfully. Amena was ecstatic to see us, and the pilots were ready to get home. I didn't say a word until we were in the air, but I knew my team was suspecting something when I spent about ten minutes in the cockpit giving the flight crew new directions.

We were in the air for about thirty minutes before I gave them the new mission, waiting until we were out of Tajikistan airspace. They were understandably a little confused, since we were also transporting a terrorist with a blindfold across his eyes and sound-canceling earphones on his head, bound and stuffed in the back of the plane, along with Jahn and his niece, who were expecting to land in the United States.

Most took it in stride, as I would expect. Jennifer was the only one who was a little put out, asking what the hell we were going to do with Amena. I glanced at the rear of the plane where she was sitting, staring at me with daggers, and said, "Jenn, she's going home with Jahn and the rest. The Taskforce will escort her to Charleston. Kylie's house-sitting, so she'll be fine."

"We're going to send her home with a terrorist and some guy we just rescued?"

I saw Brett, Veep, and Knuckles looking at me and said, "Could I see you in the galley for a minute?"

We got there and she was spitting mad, like a momma grizzly, but I was having none of that. She started to talk and I held up my finger, saying, "Wait a minute here. *I'm* the one who said we shouldn't bring her on a cover development trip. *You're* the one who said it would be fun to show her the world. And it *was* fun. But the reason I didn't want her here is precisely this. She's going home, and that's it. You need to pull back from the family thing and get your head in the game here."

She looked at me with a little bit of venom and then shook her head, saying, "So that's it, huh. Mission before family. We're going to run off doing something else when Carly is in a box headed to the United States. The mission will always trump anything else."

I leaned back, now knowing what this was about. It wasn't Amena. I said, "That's what you think?"

She slammed a fist into the wall, then felt the pain. She curled up, holding her hand, and I saw the tears. I went to her, wrapping her body. Carly had been one of her best friends, and I should have known this would be hard. I was so worried about Knuckles, I'd forgotten about her. She'd seen a friend and operator called Decoy have his head split open right next to her once, and she'd blamed herself for the death. Now, Carly was gone, and she was wondering if the loss was her fault.

They'd worked many, many missions together, and she was now letting that out, incensed that the Taskforce could simply give us another mission like some mechanical part had broken and it had shifted to another piece of the machine.

She brushed her eyes and said, "Do you think this is right? Leaving like this?"

I cupped her chin and said, "Yes. I do. We fucked up with Carly, and we did what we could to fix it. Now, we have another mission. The guys hitting us with ransomware don't care about Carly. The mission never ends. We can do some good here."

"It doesn't seem right. We should at least have a pause to remember her. Somebody in the Taskforce should give a shit."

"They do. Trust me, they do. We'll celebrate her in time. Remember Guy? Remember that?"

Her hitching stopped and she said, "Yes."

"It's the same way here. Let it go for a while. Dislocate yourself from the death. We have a mission, and we'll execute that mission."

She chuckled without any humor and said, "Like a bunch of robots."

"No, not like robots. Like what you did twenty-four hours ago. Look in the back of this plane and tell me that wasn't just."

She nodded, and I could see her remembering breaking the trigger. She said, "That was just."

I said, "Okay, then, let's get this done. We'll mourn Carly's death, but we have a mission. Are you in?"

She looked at me like she had way back in the day, when I was the only thing standing between her and certain death. When she'd believed in me for the first time. She leaned forward and kissed me on the lips, saying, "I'm always in. As long as you are."

The trust she placed in me was disconcerting, and I hoped to live up to it.

We'd landed the plane in Zagreb, Croatia, at their general aviation terminal, and sure as shit, George Wolffe had executed. We were met by a group of guys who looked like Croatian immigration, but were not. Well, they might have been—I don't know—but they certainly didn't do any immigration work.

We bundled off the terrorist outside of prying eyes, and then escorted Jahn and his niece to the new aircraft. Surprisingly, Amena hadn't put up a fight at all about going home alone. She seemed to know what was happening, spending all of her time with the niece.

I took Jennifer and Knuckles to do the transfer, because I wanted them to see what the loss of Carly was earning. We reached the plane and Jahn looked at me, saying, "Is this for real? We get to leave for good? To the United States?"

I said, "It's for real, but don't let anyone on the far end try to leverage you. You've worked with the CIA, right?"

He said, "Yes, why?"

"Because they might want to use you again. You've done your duty to our country. You've done more for our nation than most of the people *in* my country. They get to enjoy the freedom out of an accident of being born there. You get it now because you earned it. Don't let anyone fuck with you. If they do, use my name."

He laughed and said, "What, just say 'Pike says this isn't right'?"

I said, "Yes. That's *exactly* what you say. When you meet my people, say that. It will hold some weight."

He looked at me with new eyes and said, "Why?"

"Because if they don't do what they say, they know I'll rip off their heads."

He kept my gaze, trying to determine if I was telling the truth. And he saw I was.

Jennifer broke the tension, saying, "Because Pike has a way with people. Let's get on the plane."

Jahn said, "I hope this is the right thing."

I said, "Better than being chained to a bed."

He chuckled and said, "What about my niece? She doesn't have the same pedigree as me, to say the least."

"She's good. Trust me. I have a little experience in that department."

"But I have no proof about her. I have no birth certificate, no identification, no nothing."

Amena came forward at that point, taking the niece's hand and saying, "I'll take her home. Does she speak Arabic? I don't speak Pashto."

Jahn nodded, confused.

Amena spoke a few sentences to the girl and put her arm around her, turning and pointing at me. The girl smiled for the first time ever, and they walked up the stairs.

Jahn said, "Who is that? Why is there a kid here on this?"

I said, "She's with me. She's like your niece, only she's from Syria. She's now my daughter. Trust me, you're in good hands."

He looked at me dumbfounded, then said, "I don't know what to say."

I said, "You don't need to say anything. You helped our country, now you get to enjoy it. Give me a call when you get there. We'll have a beer."

He laughed and said, "I don't drink."

I said, "Well, you'd better learn, because that's going to be a detriment in my world."

He laughed again, and then did what I'd hoped he would. He shook Knuckles' hand and kissed Jennifer on the cheek, saying, "I'm so sorry that saving my life cost the life of your friend. If I could reverse it, I would."

Knuckles heard the words and they seemed to mean something to him. He patted Jahn on the shoulder and said, "You getting out is what she wanted. Don't dwell on the past. Plan for the future."

Jahn nodded, and in five minutes they were gone.

CHAPTER 25

Jennifer waited until the computer screen cleared, showing a long hallway, then said, "It's going to be hard to get down that thing without being seen."

I was glad to see she was thinking about the mission. I was worried about both her and Knuckles, about their ability to continue. I wouldn't tell the Taskforce that, because I trusted them both, but they were still feeling the loss of Carly.

In Hollywood, someone dies and it's just a flash of film. In the real world, it bites deep, in ways that could explode like the *Challenger*, with one small O-ring failure causing a catastrophic event. They could pretend all day long that nothing was wrong, but when the pressure on the O-ring happened, it either held, or it was total destruction.

And I was the NASA scientist who should be calling for a delay of launch. But, like that guy back in 1986, I didn't.

I said, "Yeah, well, Veep got the camera in there with no issue, so it's not like it's impossible."

We'd been given an address for the supposed mastermind in the target package, and it was in the upper town of Zagreb, where all the old shit existed. We were holed up in a hotel in the lower town called Esplanade, right outside the train station. It was a good place to plan because it had robust Wi-Fi that our VPN could access, and it was only a fifteen-minute walk to the upper town.

The difference was really just a function of time: the upper town was the original part of the city, on a plateau, where the parliament and historical sites were located, and where the streets were built before anyone thought about a car. The lower town was where the real world lived, full of hotels and glass buildings that were the engine of Zagreb.

The target in question was a four-story building that was a mix of apartments and businesses. The bar we'd been given as the source of the penetration was deeper in the building on the same floor, with the Wi-Fi extending weakly to this hallway, although even my Cro-Magnon brain thought it was stupid for anyone to attack anything in the United States using their open Wi-Fi network. And Creed agreed with that assessment.

Using the enormous reach of the United States government, he'd found an apartment under Branko's name, but had sent a note in the target package saying it made no sense for Branko to use the bar Wi-Fi. Basically telling me it smelled, but that what Dylan Hobbes had said did, in fact, pan out. The apartment was in the same building as the bar.

Made me wonder.

I'd sent in Knuckles and Veep to penetrate the building, looking for cameras and other surveillance, then plant a small Wi-Fi camera on the wall to surveil the apartment. They'd managed to do so without any high drama, and now we were looking at the feed in our hotel using the very same open Wi-Fi network of the bar upstairs.

We had no idea if anyone was in that apartment, but with enough watching, we'd figure it out. This was only Alpha, so sitting and watching was the whole point. No rush. The plan was to see the guy leave, put someone on him for early warning, then crack the apartment and rip through it for evidence of the ransomware attack.

The president of the United States was screaming for results, but that mattered little with me. Slow and steady wins the race.

I said, "Jennifer's right. That's a long hallway with a lot of doors, so we need to get in without a lot of dicking around. We can't be sitting on the ground working the door when someone else comes out. Did you guys take a look at the locks when you put the camera in?"

Knuckles said, "Yeah, we did. It's old-world crap. If he doesn't use the bolt lock, it's a credit card. If he does use the bolt lock, it's like seven seconds with a pick kit. We can get in."

I said, "Alrighty then, we have a winner. Knuckles and I will get inside, with Knuckles doing the work. Jennifer, you get surveillance right here, watching the computer. Brett and Veep take the follow, giving us early warning. Any questions?"

Jennifer said, "Yeah, why do I get computer surveillance?"

"Because that's the way it is."

"But you've got Brett doing the follow. He sticks out like a sore thumb here. I should do the follow."

"What the hell are you talking about? He's one of the best I've ever seen at that."

She looked at Brett, then back at me, saying nothing. I said, "What?"

She looked at Brett again and said, "He's black. We haven't seen a single black person here. He's going to stand out. He'll be burned with one turn of the target."

She looked at him and said, "I'm sorry."

I didn't know what to say about that. Brett Thorpe was one of the best operators I'd ever served with—a killer with an instinct that was above reproach—but Jennifer had a point. I thought about how to respond, and was saved by Brett himself.

He said, "She's right. I can follow that guy to a single point of entry, but if he moves again, I'm done. Especially if he has some countersurveillance in motion. You guys can put on a different hat or coat, but I can't put on a different skin."

I honestly thought the entire thing was bullshit because I respected his skills greatly, but the real world didn't care about diversity, especially when it came to killing. I said, "You sure about that?"

He laughed and said, "Yeah. The next mission we do will probably be in Soweto. When that happens, you can repay me by staying in the hotel."

I smiled, him reminding me once again about the sacrosanct worth of our team. I said, "Okay, okay. It's Veep and Jennifer on the follow. It's getting late. If they're going out, it'll be soon. Let's go."

We left the hotel after lunchtime, going toward the target, walking down a park that spanned the length between the lower level and the upper level, nobody saying anything. The park itself was crowded with families, most out enjoying the weather. If I hadn't been working a problem, I would have enjoyed it.

The road we were on ended at a large square with a statue of some guy on a horse holding a sword, the front of the square bounded by public trolleys going left and right. This was the beginning of the upper level, and you could readily see the difference. The roads turned into cobblestone alleys, laced with bars and cafés as far as the eye could see, all of the alleys rising to the high ground at the top.

We crossed the square and Jennifer checked her phone, pointing up one narrow thoroughfare lined with umbrellas and tables. We continued on, now walking uphill with me watching the people at the outdoor tables enjoying life, with laughter and the clink of beer mugs permeating the air like some idolized commercial selling a lifestyle. It really made me want to hold up a hand and say, "Hey, I have a better idea. Let's get some lunch and a beer."

Instead of breaking a hundred different laws inside this country based on some vague order from an organization that didn't exist—and clearly didn't understand what my team had just been through—we could enjoy life, like everyone else seemed to do in the real world. We could become the beer commercial on TV. Happy smiles and success just by opening a bottle.

I knew that wasn't going to happen, though. I had a mission, and I would execute. Just like the man I was targeted against was trying to do.

We took another narrow alley running perpendicular to the one we were on, walking by a bar named after J. R. R. Tolkien, then entered a park, a huge mural of Gulliver tied to the ground running the length of the building.

I said, "Jenn, you sure you know where you're going?"

She pointed at an archway spanning a set of steps, appearing to be some city wall from ancient times, saying, "The street is about a hundred meters through that arch."

We started walking again and Brett called, saying, "Two men just exited the apartment. Pictures on the way."

Shit.

I hung up, told the team what had transpired, and said, "Two out. Most we can do is check for a third. That'll be Knuckles and me."

I pointed to a couple of park benches next to the mural of

Gulliver and said, "Let's give them a chance to clear the building before we continue. Don't want to burn ourselves this soon without even knowing our target."

On the one hand, we could probably penetrate the apartment right now and drain it of anything valuable, but that was a risk, and there was no ticking time bomb here. I didn't want to crack that apartment without having eyes on the people who lived there. If that took three days, then it took three days. I saw no reason to push the issue, but seeing if anybody else was inside was something we could do while we waited.

The pictures came in and I saw two twenty-somethings walking down the hallway, caught midstride like a bad police capture you see when they want "anyone with information to call."

One was dressed in torn jeans with acne scars and greasy black hair. The other was taller, with reddish hair and thick glasses. I confirmed that everyone had the photos, then called Brett saying, "Knuckles and I are going to penetrate just to see if the apartment's empty. Radarscope only. Jennifer and Veep are going to find us a place to stage while we play the waiting game."

I hung up and said, "You guys hear that?"

They nodded and I said, "Okay then, let's go check it out. Veep, Jenn, find a place to stage where we can sit for a while. Knuckles, prep the radarscope. Right now, all I want to know is if that place is truly empty."

The radarscope was a small device that looked like a cell phone on steroids, about eight inches long and three inches wide. It was designed to detect movement through walls, even cinder block. It didn't matter if someone was actually walking around; it could detect the rise and fall of a diaphragm from a person just sitting in a chair.

Knuckles dug through his small knapsack as Jennifer led us to a narrow stairwell with a sign proclaiming MLINSKI STAIRS. Why this little footpath had a street name was beyond me, but it was obviously old. We went down it, passing small courtyards and windows, eventually reaching a larger north–south thoroughfare called Radiceva. Jennifer stopped and said, "It's the next building up on the right."

I looked the other way, seeing one of the ubiquitous outdoor cafés down the street. I said, "We'll meet you back there. Be gone about ten minutes."

She nodded and said, "Don't do anything stupid."

I smiled and said, "Not yet. Too early in the game. That'll come later."

We separated, with Knuckles and me going to the next building up, stopping at an arched stone doorway leading into the building, a stair landing on the left inside. I put in my earpiece, Knuckles doing the same, and said, "About to make entry. Commo check. Blood/Koko, you got me?"

Knuckles nodded his head, saying he could hear me. Jennifer came on, still hating her callsign, "This is Koko. I have you, Lima Charlie."

Brett said, "This is Blood. I'll call when you're on camera."

I said, "Okay, breaching now. Give me early warning to anyone coming up."

We entered, the building looking like it had been constructed sometime in the eighteenth century, if not earlier, the hallways seemingly built when the human race was a lot smaller. We skipped up the stairs two at a time, went past the second landing to the third floor, then proceeded down another narrow hallway, doors on the left and right.

Brett said, "I have you. I see you."

I held up a thumb, knowing he could see that and saving me from making any noise. We skipped down to the corner room where the hallway took a sharp left. I went down it for early warning and Knuckles pulled out the radarscope. He employed it along the length of the wall like a doctor using a stethoscope, moving it higher and lower as he went along, holding it steady for a minute before placing it in a new position. He was done in under three minutes. He snapped his finger and I returned. He shook his head.

Two minutes later we were back on the street; thirty seconds after that we were sitting with Veep and Jennifer at an outdoor picnic table with an umbrella.

I said, "Apartment is empty. It's only those two guys."

Veep said, "Now what?"

"Now we wait for them to return."

CHAPTER 26

Jennifer checked her watch, seeing they'd been sitting at the café for a little over two hours. She turned to Pike to suggest they might want to jump to another location when she saw two men walking down the street to the arched entrance of the building. She pointed, and Pike turned around just as the two entered a doorway. The distance was too great to identify them, but Jennifer knew they didn't need to. Four minutes later Brett called and said, "They're back. Both in the nest."

They'd been at the café for about as long as Jennifer thought they logically could without generating questions, so she broached what she was originally going to say: "We should probably find another lily pad. This one is getting hot. Especially since we haven't been drinking beer like everyone else."

Pike said, "Probably right." He looked at his watch and said, "Close to five on a Friday. I'll be willing to bet they're going to clean up and head out. Jenn, where are we going?"

She said, "We reposition on the other side of the buildings, back up that stairwell. That pub right next to the arch looked right up your alley, pun intended."

Pike said, "That Oliver Twist place?"

"Yeah. It's close enough for me and Veep to interdict, but far enough away to keep us from being burned. This time we can get some dinner to stall. I'm starving."

Veep said, "Me, too."

Pike smiled and said, "Sounds good." They retraced their path, then settled in at the new pub, the waitress bringing them menus. When she was gone, Pike clicked into the net. "Blood, Blood, we're repositioning to the other side of the buildings. Getting some chow. Keep eyes on the camera. When they leave again, we're going in."

Brett came back, saying, "When the hell do I get to eat? I have to sit here and stare at the camera feed twenty-four seven."

Pike said, "There's a minibar in the room. I authorize you to eat the Oreos and potato chips."

The table laughed and they ordered their own food, Jennifer surreptitiously checking out the area with her eyes. Pike said, "What are you looking for?"

She flicked her head to the rear and said, "See that balcony up there? With the tables? That's the Café A'è. The bar that they supposedly used for the Wi-Fi. The same one we're using. It's on the backside of the building they live in."

Across the table from her, Pike looked at it intently, then said, "Maybe we should have gone there instead of here."

They had their food delivered, and ten seconds later Brett called, saying, "Targets are on the move. I say again, targets are on the move."

Jennifer said, "Damn it. Figures."

Pike said, "Get moving."

Veep shoved an entire taco in his mouth and stood, saying into his earpiece through the mess in his mouth, "Commo check."

Pike said, "I got you," and Jennifer took off behind Veep, going back down the same little stairwell. They reached Radiceva in time to see the targets exit the building and start heading north.

They kept them in sight, Jennifer clicking on the net and saying, "I've got eyes on. Cleared to breach."

The two only walked to the next doorway, and then disappeared inside. Veep said, "Shit. We're going to lose them."

Jennifer quickened her pace and said, "That's the entrance to the bar with the Wi-Fi. The balcony I talked about is in the back, on the second floor."

They reached the door and saw a sign hanging in the entrance proclaiming the A'è bar. Jennifer took Veep's hand as if they were on a date and they entered a darkened hallway, a runner on the floor and plants hanging from the ceiling. They followed the signs, going up a stairwell that was barely large enough for a single person, then down a hallway, then up another stairwell. It was a maze, with them choosing the wrong hallway once, only to turn around. Eventually they reached another stairwell, this one leading down, and they entered an outdoor terrace, a bar running the length along the building and tables scattered about overlooking the alley below.

Jennifer saw their targets in the corner and pulled Veep to a table on the opposite side, near the stairwell and right up against the balcony wall. They took a seat and Jennifer gave an update, telling Pike where they were and what the targets were doing. He came back with, "Making breach. Keep an eye on them."

Jennifer looked below them and saw another terrace a floor below, this one with dinner tables, making her wonder how on earth they'd missed the entrance to that. She had seen no signs for a restaurant.

Below that was some sort of garden spilling down the hill to the alley below, full of spices and vegetables. Beyond the garden she could see the Oliver Twist pub they'd come from and the entrance to the tiny stairwell/alley they'd used to get here.

The waitress came over and they ordered a couple of soft drinks, saying they were here for the sunset, giving them ample time to sit and watch.

Pike came on, saying they'd found a laptop and were in the process of cloning it, meaning he needed at least ten minutes to complete. Jennifer knew that Knuckles was now carefully going through the apartment inch by inch, not leaving a trace of his presence.

She glanced over at the target table and saw the dark-haired guy staring at the entrance stairwell. She looked that way and saw two swarthy guys in the doorway. They were dressed like Europeans, but they most definitely weren't Croatian.

They walked over to the target's table and sat down. Jennifer could see confusion on the face of the black-haired guy, then fear.

Veep said, "What's up with that? He looks like he was expecting someone else."

Jennifer recognized the tension and said, "Get a picture of those two new guys," then clicked on the net, saying, "Pike, Pike, this is Koko, we have a situation."

"What's up? We're still working here."

"We have a meeting occurring here, but I don't think it's amicable. Just a warning order that I think this is going to go bad."

"What's that mean?"

"I think our targets are someone else's targets and they beat us to the punch."

She heard him say something into the room, then he came back on, saying, "We're almost complete. Keep eyes on them and let me know what happens."

Veep said, "Gun. I see a gun."

Jennifer heard a muffled pop and recognized it for what it was:

a suppressed round. She looked at the table in time to see the red-haired target fall backward out of his chair, then run to the stairwell right behind them, his left leg dragging as if it wasn't working right. She said, "Get on him. Keep him in sight."

Veep took off and Jennifer returned to the target table. The black-haired guy from the surveillance photo held up his hands in supplication, then grabbed a bottle on the table and smashed it into the head of the swarthy man across from him, the glass shattering and knocking him to the ground. The second man leapt up, drawing a knife and blocking his escape to the stairwell.

Jennifer saw the black-haired man look wildly left and right, settling on the balcony wall. He ran to it and leapt over like there was a swimming pool underneath him. Jennifer stood up, seeing him lying on the next terrace, having landed on a table with patrons eating. They were wildly gyrating their arms and shouting, pointing at him on the ground. He rolled left and right, holding his side, then jumped up and vaulted the short fence at the edge of the terrace. He landed in the makeshift garden, then slid down the hill.

Jennifer looked at the two men left behind, seeing one holding his head from the beer bottle shot, the other pulling him upright. The first shook off his hands, waving his pistol around, then realized what he was doing. He glanced back at the bar, seeing patrons all shocked at the fight. He shouted something in a language Jennifer didn't understand, then the two went over the wall themselves, only much more slowly, lowering themselves far enough until they could safely drop to the bottom terrace. Before Jennifer knew it, they were upright and sliding down the garden hill.

Without thinking, she followed them, throwing herself over the wall, holding on for a brief second, her feet seeking purchase in the rough stone. She found it, and she began going hand over hand like a rock climber until she was hanging on the sill at the bottom of the balcony wall, a table below her.

She shouted, "Look out!"

The patrons at the table saw her and leapt back. She dropped, hitting one side of the table and riding it down like she was on a surfboard. Before they could react, she was over the next railing and in the alley running flat out behind the target and the men chasing him.

CHAPTER 27

Branko pointed to a table midway between the wall of the balcony and the bar, wanting to be in the back, away from the entrance. He sat down and Pushka said, "Who is this guy? And why are we meeting him?"

"He's a dude I met at Andrei's place. He was there for something different. We didn't really talk about it because—you know, Andrei. We just bullshitted a little bit, but you know me. Anyone wants to party, and I'll go with them."

Pushka scowled and said, "Every time you bring in some lost puppy you create a risk of compromise."

The waitress came over with a couple of beers, knowing them on sight. Branko thanked her and made a lame joke, which caused her to force a laugh. After she'd left, Branko said, "Come on. Remember those girls from Slovakia? They were lost puppies, too. This guy is a power player. He might help us in our work. It's worth it."

"It's not going to be worth it. It never is. Remember your 'cryptocurrency genius'? All he did was fleece us."

Chagrined, Branko said, "Yeah, well this guy works for Andrei, and he looked like he was powerful, even if he was dressed like a bum. He's someone we may want to know. You were the one talking about getting out from underneath the yoke of Andrei. Maybe this is it."

Pushka took a sip of his beer and said, "I'd rather be working that hot girl over there."

Branko looked where he indicated and saw a woman staring at him, shoulder-length blond hair in a ponytail, wearing what every hiker in Croatia did—Salomon hiking shoes and nylon clothes. She glanced away when he looked at her, leaning over the balcony wall, and he saw her body was like a snake's, solid muscle all the way through.

The man next to her looked years younger, but he was also in shape, like he was about to do a CrossFit competition, his lank muscles rippling whenever he moved. Branko realized that neither he nor Pushka would stand a chance with her. She was someone who would never want his flaccid body, even as he probably made more in a week than that punk she was with did in a year.

He said, "She's a bitch. Look at her. All about the package."

Pushka was about to respond when he saw two men descend the stairwell. Both were obviously not from Croatia. Both had swarthy complexions, with long black hair and full beards. But the most disconcerting thing was that both zeroed in on their table like a couple of wolves after a wounded deer.

Branko saw his face cloud up and said, "What? What's the problem?"

He said, "Them."

The two men stared for a moment longer, and the bigger one seemed to recognize Branko. He came forward, the other trailing behind. They sat down, the bigger man saying, "You're here for Ahmad Khan, yes?"

Branko said, "Yeah, are you friends of his?"

"Let's just say we used to be. He won't be coming tonight.

And both of you will be leaving here with me. We have some questions."

Pushka tensed up and said, "What does that mean?"

"My name is Shakor Hekmatyar. I'm from Afghanistan, and your friend has stolen something of significance, which is now in your hands. We want it back."

Branko bunched his eyes and said, "What the fuck are you talking about? He said he was coming here for a party night. I don't know what you're asking."

Shakor pulled out a pistol, one that was long in the barrel, with most of it looking much larger than necessary to work the action of the gun, something Branko had only seen in the movies.

Shakor said, "You will tell us where the treasure is. Or you will die. It's really that simple. Let's go. Stand up slowly."

Branko said, "Wait, wait, I think you've got us confused with someone else. We don't know anything about any treasure. We only know Ahmad from previous work. Where is he? He can tell you."

"He's dead. And you're the last trace."

Branko's head was spinning. *Treasure? From Afghanistan? What the hell?*

He said, "Hey, man, let's talk about this. We both work for Andrei. Maybe we should call him before we start waving guns. Right?"

Shakor lowered his weapon and pulled the trigger, the sound of the bullet firing a muted spit, soon overwhelmed by Pushka screaming and falling out of his chair. Pushka rolled, and then stood up, hobbling as fast as he could to the stairwell exit.

The scene of him falling over generated a little excitement in the bar, but not a lot. Branko looked around, seeing that nobody was really paying any attention to what had just happened. He raised his hands and said, "Okay, okay, whatever you want."

Shakor put the weapon underneath the table and said, "The treasure. That's what I want. Where is it? I don't want to hurt you. I really don't."

Branko snatched a bottle off the table and smashed it into Shakor's head, knocking him out of the chair. He leapt up to escape out the stairwell like Pushka had just done and found himself facing the other man, now holding a knife. He glanced left and right, saw the wall for the balcony, and ran toward it, jumping over as if it was literally a fence separating him from the earth on the other side at the same level.

But he knew that wasn't true. He fell, the drop longer than he expected, with his mind wondering what the impact would be like.

He hit a table direct center, crushing it and cracking the left ribs of his body. He rolled over on the ground, moaning, hearing the shouting of the people around him. He looked up and saw the second man staring over the balcony wall, fury on his face.

He rolled upright, leapt the small iron railing of the lower terrace, and fell to the earth below. He slid for a few feet in the dirt, saw the alley below, and dove forward, going head over heels until he slid on the street itself. He looked back and saw Shakor and his mate coming over the wall.

He hit the street and began running. He reached the Mlinski Stairs and took them four at a time, crashing into the walls left and right as he barreled down them. He lost his footing and spilled into a courtyard next to the stairs. He rolled over and pulled out his cell phone, dialing Pushka while watching for anyone behind him.

Pushka answered, saying, "What the fuck, man? I've been shot!"

"I know, I know. I'm being chased right now. We need to get back to the apartment and clean it out. We have to run."

"I'm *in* the apartment, man, and someone's been here."

"What's that mean? What do you mean?"

"Two guys were here. They left the apartment when I entered the hallway."

"Is the place turned over? Like it was tossed?"

"No. It's just like we left it. Nothing changed. Man, I'm fucking bleeding out here. I'm fucking shot!"

Even with the world of hurt he was experiencing, Branko knew he needed to get Pushka back into the fold. He couldn't go back to the apartment, but he didn't need to with Pushka.

Even as he didn't believe it, he said, "Pushka, nobody has been into our apartment. There's a first aid pack in the bathroom. Bandage yourself up and get out. Take the computer with you. The rest is no threat, but get that computer."

"Are you fucking serious? We just got shot at. What the fuck is going on?"

Branko heard footsteps coming down the stairs and said, "I don't know, but get out and run."

"Run where? What the fuck do I do? I don't do this, man. Where do I go?"

Branko saw a shadow and leapt up, saying, "I don't know. Jesus. I've got people behind me right now. Just get out."

He took off running again, reaching Radiceva, and thought about turning north to his apartment to meet Pushka, when two men passed him, both hard-looking, but giving him no attention. It spooked him. They already knew where he lived. He turned

south and began jogging, running out of energy, his lungs screaming for air in his dilapidated body, the adrenaline not giving him
the boost he needed.

He heard his name shouted behind him and that was all that
was required, the adrenaline shooting through him like a bolt of
lightning. He ran south until he reached a small archway in a
building right up on the street, darting inside of it and racing
forward.

He entered a concrete tunnel built decades before he was even
born, the dim lights creating shadows throughout, barely illumi-
nating the path ahead, the dampness and moldy smell a familiar
feeling.

He knew where it ended, and hoped the people following him
had no idea.

CHAPTER 28

I got the call from Jennifer and looked at Knuckles, saying, "This is going to go bad. Pick it up."

He said, "Me? What's that clone thing doing?"

I said, "Four minutes left. What do you have?"

"A bunch of brochures for skin clubs here in Zagreb. Nothing yet. This looks like a penthouse for parties, not a headquarters for an elite hacking cell."

We kept working the problem, me wondering about Jennifer's call while the clone device spun along, and then the situation split open like a waterfall.

Veep came on the net saying, "Following Red Head. He's been shot and he's coming to you. You have about a minute and a half."

I said, "What? What did you just say?"

"We had a gunfight here. Red Head's about to penetrate your building. Get out."

Knuckles looked at me with the same expression I knew I held. I said, "Pack it up. Let's go."

I ripped out the clone device before it was finished, getting an angry alert from the computer I was stealing it from. I clicked on the "okay" button, letting the computer know I'd made a mistake, then watched it return to the home screen.

I said, "You haven't fucked anything up, have you?"

Knuckles laughed and said, "No more than you."

"Let's get out."

We left the door and went to the stairs, meeting the redhead target running up with a limp, a glaring bit of blood on his leg. We ignored him and kept moving down, me wondering what the hell was going on. I suppose, as the team leader, I could have cut on the net demanding an answer to the debacle, but I knew with my team that I'd get the answer when it was available to give.

Nothing was worse than hearing from some asshole not in the fight demanding to know the situation. But man, I really wanted to.

We reached the entrance to the building, running into Veep. I said, "What the hell is going on?"

He had wild eyes and looked like he thought he'd screwed up. He said, "I have no idea. There were two guys, then a gunshot, then it just went to shit. Jennifer ordered me on Red Head, and I left her. I don't know what's going on with her."

He shook his head and said, "Maybe I should have stayed with her."

I chuckled and said, "If you had, we'd have been compromised. Red Head would have come in with us still there. Jennifer can take care of herself."

We walked out into the street, me starting to worry despite what I'd told Veep, and then my little protégé finally came on, and I could tell she was running.

"There's been a gunfight, our target dropped off the balcony, the two unsubs followed, and I'm behind them. Entering the stairwell."

She was panting in between the transmissions, telling me without telling me that there was a footrace going on.

I said, "We've just left the target building. Are you saying he's coming here? He's on the stairwell in between the buildings?"

I heard panting, then, "Yes. Two men want to kill him."

Shit.

Now I had a decision. I had the information from the apartment, and Lord knows that computer drain would probably break it all open, but this guy was going to get killed in the meantime.

Did I care?

Maybe we should just go up and jack the guy that we'd passed. The Red Head target. He probably knew as much as the one running. But I didn't have authority for that. We weren't at Omega. We were at Alpha, and I'd accomplished that mission. As far as the guy on the run, I didn't have any authority to interdict him, either. According to my orders, he was on his own.

Those thoughts were running through my head in an analytical sphere, but truthfully, I hated bullies. And the men chasing that guy were bullies. I knew it wasn't the right decision. In fact knew it was the absolute *wrong* decision. He'd clearly done something against some other element and was now going to pay the price, but it just wasn't in me.

I looked at Knuckles. He saw my face and said, "So it's time for the stupid shit?"

I laughed and said, "Leaning that way."

I started walking toward the exit of the stairwell and saw our target come bolting out, running like he was being chased by a pack of wolves. Which he was. He disappeared in the distance, moving at a pace we couldn't match unless we were willing to invite compromise for following him.

I said, "We keep on him. Low and slow."

We started jogging his way and two other men exited, both running flat out, one with a gun in his hand. A suppressed weapon.

Which gave me a little bit of a pause. Using a suppressed

weapon inside Croatia was decidedly unique. Hell, having a handgun here was unique. There was something else going on besides a bad gambling debt. Seeing it made my decision.

We reached the stairwell and Jennifer came out, panting. She ran up and said, "Pike, I have no idea what's going on. What do you want to do?"

That was about the most succinct SITREP I'd ever received.

I watched the clusterfuck go down the street in the dying twilight and said, "We interdict."

We started running down the street in a group, only seeing the back of the hunters, the black-haired guy out of sight. We saw them run into another archway of a building, and I knew we were not going to get to our target in time. No way was I about to attempt clearing a building.

I slowed, saying, "We're done. Whatever is going to happen in that building we don't want to be a part of. Too many witnesses."

Jennifer said, "That's not a building. It's the Gric Tunnel."

"What? What are you talking about?"

"Well, it *is* a building, but he's going into the tunnel."

"What tunnel?"

"It's an old bomb shelter from World War Two. It runs underneath the city. He's trying to escape using it."

I should have known that Jennifer would have done a deep dive on the history of Zagreb before we arrived. It's just what she did, and now it was paying off.

I said, "Where's it exit? Can we meet them there? Going overground?"

I knew it was a risk, given that he could be killed inside, but it was all I had. There was no way we could chase the killers who were chasing our target in a tunnel.

She looked like she was failing me, saying, "I don't know. I just know it exists. I didn't map it out."

I called Brett and said, "I need to know the exits for the Gric Tunnel, and I need it right now. Google it."

I turned to the group and said, "We know it goes from east to west." I pointed to a road past the entrance and said, "Put on your running shoes."

We took off like we were starting a 10K, passing by parks and houses, the road winding up and down, telling me we were losing the race because I knew the tunnel was a straight shot. Luckily, the target didn't look like he worked out much, and I hoped he had become winded and was walking now. Unluckily, that could also mean his death.

Brett finally came back, saying, "It's an old war tunnel. Only been opened since 2016. The tunnel starts at Radiceva and ends at Mesnicka. It's like a comb, though, with the spine going east and west, and some of the tines going south. There are two exits that end in something called the Art Park, right toward the end at Mesnicka. Two other tines are apparently still blocked off, waiting on reconstruction."

I slowed to a walk, saying, "Where is that?"

Jennifer had her phone out, saying "It's right below us. Right here."

I looked at what she'd pulled up and said, "Okay, if he's not dead yet, he's going to exit at one of those places. Jennifer, Veep, you get Mesnicka. Knuckles, we're going to take the Art Park. Call no matter what. The mission is to break the men chasing him."

Knuckles said, "You want to let him get away? We might not get a better chance."

"Yeah, I get that, but we don't have Omega here. We don't even know if he's the ransomware guy yet, but if he is, I don't want him killed by the assholes following him. Just stop the follow and we'll figure it out."

Knuckles grinned and said, "Okay, no Omega, but we're about to execute something here. How are we going to sell this? If it becomes kinetic?"

I said, "I'm pulling the risk-to-life-or-limb card if someone from the Oversight Council bitches. I can't plan a capture, but we can always protect the life or limb of someone, and these guys have clearly showed they want to take one or the other."

Veep said, "ROE?"

I said, "Hostile force. They're definitely hostile. Interdict with least amount of violence, but if they push the issue, escalate. Remember, at least one of them is armed."

Jennifer showed us the map on her phone and I said, "Let's go. Every second means we could miss them."

Jennifer and Veep took off to the east, running to the final exit, while Knuckles and I started slipping down the slope of the upper town, slinking through alleys and backyards until we ended up at an ancient funicular railroad connecting the upper town to the lower. The Art Park was just to the right of it.

The train was running up and down, but we didn't have the time to use it to get to the lower level. We started jogging down the stairs next to the rail line, going about halfway down, then jumped the railing, passing between the buildings next to the funicular and running across the slope to the park.

We reached an open space of grass and I slowed, seeing an entrance in the side of the hill that was painted with graffiti. It looked like an old mining tunnel that some kids had decided to decorate, and I knew that was the exit. I said, "That's the first one. Stage there."

Knuckles took a knee behind a small tree and I kept going through the park, finding another entrance on the other side of a playground. This one had no graffiti and opened out into the park like a miniature train tunnel, with a concrete façade and two doors swung wide left and right.

I kneeled behind some shrubs, drew my Glock, and waited, breathing heavily, wondering if we'd missed them. I didn't have to wait long. My earpiece crackled with a call from Knuckles, saying, "Coming now. Coming now."

I heard shouting over at Knuckles' exit, then the muted spit of suppressed rounds.

I started running that way, hearing the metronome of Knuckles' voice on the radio.

"Contact. I say again contact. Target is running and hostiles are shooting."

He was so calm you'd have thought he was ordering an Uber.

I broke through the playground in time to see the target running by me flat out down the hill, going so fast he lost his footing on the slope, something in his hand flying out as he tumbled. He sprang back up and kept going, disappearing below me. I turned to the threat, seeing two men engaging Knuckles with suppressed weapons, him returning fire. One man dropped and the other raced back into the tunnel, running away.

I reached Knuckles just as he was changing magazines. He jerked to the left when I appeared, whipping his weapon at my head. I said, "Whoa, whoa, it's me."

He lowered the pistol and relaxed, saying, "I was going to take one of them out with a physical attack, but they literally came out shooting. The target was running and ducking, and they both had pistols out, firing. I had to take a shot."

Like I was mad that he'd pulled his weapon.

I said, "No worries. Check the body. The target lost something in the woods when he fell. I'm going for that."

I walked down the hill a little bit and started stomping around, finally seeing a glow in the brush. I went to it and found a late-model iPhone sitting in the dirt. I snatched it up and went back to Knuckles and the body.

He stood up and said, "The guy is from Turkey. Turkish passport. What the hell is that all about?"

I had no idea.

CHAPTER 29

Branko reached a flight of concrete steps leading down and attempted to take them two or three at a time, barely maintaining his balance as his windmilling arms sought to protect him from the forces of gravity. He fell once, bashing his knee and elbow, but sprang back up like a jack-in-the-box, continuing his flight. He reached the road at the base of the Art Park, spilling into the street and putting his hands on his knees. He sucked in great gouts of air and glanced behind him, seeing nobody following. He returned to the pavement, breathing heavily, and saw that his jeans had torn and his left knee was scuffed and bleeding. He hadn't even felt the pain. He straightened up and took a left on the road, starting a shambling jog, his lungs screaming in protest.

Initially winded in the tunnel, he'd been forced to slow to a walk, his sides cramping with the unaccustomed physical effort he'd expended running from the café. He'd thought he was safe when he caught up to a group of teenagers going the same way he was. He'd matched their pace, trying to blend in, and then had heard the footsteps thundering behind him. He'd moved to the inside of the group, pretending to check his phone, ducking his head, hoping the hunters would pass him by.

They did, and he breathed a sigh of relief. He reached the first tunnel for the exit to the Art Park and had begun thinking through what he would do next. First, he had to find Pushka, but his phone had no service in the tunnel. He began a fast walk to the exit, the noise of the teenagers' footsteps fading in the distance, then growing stronger, as if they had decided to return. He'd whipped around and saw the two men from the bar coming at him, both with pistols drawn.

He'd turned and began running as fast as he could down the darkened tube. He heard several sharp reports, but none nearly loud enough for a gunshot in this enclosed space, then saw the concrete chipping with gouges along the walls, the bullets ricocheting out. He had no idea how the noise was muted, but he knew they were shooting at him.

He saw the exit of the tunnel in the stark light of the overhead incandescent lamps and put on a final burst of speed, feeling the men behind him gaining ground. He broke into the park and almost ran into another man holding a pistol, the appearance causing him to lose his balance, the iPhone in his hand flying out as he tucked his arms to break his fall. He'd tumbled head over heels, slid for a second, then sprang back up, finding the stairs and running down them, falling one more time before reaching the street.

He stuttered past a youth hostel called Chillout and paused to look behind him. Nobody was following. He opened the door to the hostel and went inside, finding a lounge area next to the check-in desk with several men and women his age lying about like lizards under the sun. He nodded at them and took a seat next to a bookshelf with a sign saying "leave a book, take a book." Several in the room glanced his way, but nobody showed any specific interest.

He calmed down and began to think through his problem, the first being who on earth was trying to kill him. *Who the hell were those guys? Why would the Afghan man I met in Liechtenstein want to send anyone to kill me? And what was that about a treasure?* It was completely bizarre, but the reasons why were not his immediate problem. Staying alive was the priority, regardless of whatever misunderstanding was playing out. Right now, he needed to avoid them, and he was sure they were still hunting.

His initial thought was to simply get a room at the hostel and spend the night, cleaning himself from any connection in Zagreb. Maybe spend several nights. Hell, an entire week. He was supposed to be in Split tomorrow, but he could get on a computer here and let his team know he was coming later. There was no rush, and letting the hunters simply give up seemed to be the best option. Then he remembered Pushka.

He would be panicking right now and would eventually call Branko's phone—one he no longer had. He needed to find Pushka first, but to do that, he needed another phone, which was a little ironic, because what he really needed was the computer Pushka took from the apartment in order to wipe his *lost* phone. He had to use the features in his MacBook to eliminate and lock the iPhone he'd dropped. No way could he allow that to be found by someone on the street—especially since the AirTag for Andrei's crate was tied to it. If that was found by some stranger, Branko would be wishing the two Afghans tonight had simply exterminated him with a bullet, because Andrei would not be so kind.

He had a burner phone in his car, but it was located in a parking garage in the lower town, near the train station. He'd have to traverse the entire lower town to get to it, with the hunters probably out looking for him en masse. But all they knew about him was he went to a bar in the upper town, and he had a knowledge of all of Zagreb that they did not possess.

He could do it. He told himself that, but it didn't raise his courage. He really wanted to remain in the hostel, in front of others to prevent his killing. He knew he could not. That would only delay his death from another hand. He rose, went to the door, and looked left and right, seeing nothing but an empty alley, the dim glow of lights from windows providing shadows that he envisioned held silent killers.

He steeled himself and slipped out, running into a north–south alley. From there he slinked through darkened streets and rubbish-strewn alleys, using the very ones that he would have avoided on any ordinary night. He figured the dangers potentially lurking inside them far outweighed the killers who were chasing him.

Eventually he made it to King Tomislav Square, the entrance to the Glavni Kolod train station right in front of him, the underground mall known as Importanne Center across the street to his right. It was wide open here, with statues and fountains and cars coming and going in front of the station. He worried about exposing himself, but it would only be for a minute.

The mall was built underneath all the open space, as was the garage where he'd left his car. The shopping area had several access points, stairwells leading down like one was going into a subway, but instead of finding tracks like the train station next door, there were a plethora of shops.

Branko sat on a bench watching people come and go, building his nerve to leave the shadows. He glanced left and right, seeing nothing alarming, then jumped up, running across the street to the nearest stairwell access.

He took them two at a time and entered the mall, now on more solid footing, the crowds giving him comfort. He ran down an escalator to a lower level, and then went to the end, where the garage was located. He opened the entrance door and watched for a moment, wondering if they'd staked out his vehicle, waiting on him to return. He saw nothing. Just blinkering overhead fluorescent lights and rows of cars.

He sprinted through the rows until he reached his vehicle, an old Kia SUV—the same one they'd used to transport the crate. He unlocked it, went to the glove box, and pulled out three old-school flip phones.

He locked the vehicle and raced back to the mall, taking a seat on a bench next to a wine store, the escalator to the upper level in view. He dialed one of the phones, praying Pushka wasn't dead or captured.

Pushka answered on the second ring, warily asking, "Hello?"

Branko sighed and said, "Hey, it's me. Where are you?"

"I'm hiding in a park! With a bullet hole in my leg! What the fuck, man. I've been shot."

"How is the wound? Are you in trouble?"

Pushka backed off, saying, "No, it's not that bad. The bullet grazed my leg, making a gouge, but that's about it. It looks like someone went after my thigh with a garden trowel, but it's not deep. I've already bandaged it up. I'll live."

"Good. Good. I need you to come to me, but make sure you aren't followed. I'm at the Importanne Center. You know that wine store at the bottom level?"

"Yes, I know it, but what's going on? What happened?"

Exasperated, Branko said, "I have no idea. Just listen to me."

"Did this have something to do with that crate we took to the forest?"

"No! Damn it, shut up and listen."

He heard nothing, and continued, "Come down to the wine

store and go to my car. Walk by me to the garage, but don't look at me. Just walk by and go to my car."

"Why not just meet at your car?"

"Because I don't know what's going on! I want to see if someone's following you. Looking for me."

"You mean this is all about you? And you want me to come to you? What am I, bait? You're fucking insane. I'll take my own chances."

"Listen to me, this is about Andrei. It's not about me. You take your own chances and you're dead. I don't know what's going on, but we need to get out of here. Together. I need to call Andrei and we need to get to Split."

He heard nothing but breathing, and then, "I'm on the way."

Branko waited for thirty minutes, then his phone buzzed with a message: **At the entrance. Coming down.**

He typed back, **I'll be watching. If I call your phone, don't answer, just get out.**

He saw Pushka come down the escalator and disappear down the hallway for the parking garage. Nobody followed him. He stood and raced to catch up. Two minutes later they were driving his car out of the city, headed to Split, with Pushka bitching the entire time.

Finally leaving the suburbs, reaching Highway A1 headed south to Split, he turned to Pushka and said, "Shut the fuck up, man. I don't have the answers you want. Let's get to the safehouse and figure it out."

Pushka looked like a whipped dog, settling into the seat and saying, "It's just not how we operate. Nobody comes to us with guns. I always worried about getting put on some U.S. sanctions list or having an arrest warrant, but never someone shooting me. This is getting to be too much."

Branko saw the team breaking up. Saw his primary penetration man scared to continue. Right when they had their biggest score on the horizon. He pulled over to the side of the road and said, "Look, man, you drive. Let me call Andrei. Let me sort this out."

Pushka stared out the window for a moment, then nodded. They switched seats and began going down the road again.

Branko said, "Here goes nothing." He dialed the burner phone and got Nikita, saying, "I need to talk to Andrei."

Nikita said, "What about?"

"Somebody just tried to kill me. Just now. And it was somebody that was in Andrei's house when I was there."

"Stand by."

Andrei came on, saying, "Nikita says you have had a problem. Does it involve my box?"

"No, sir. I don't know what it involves. Two guys tried to kill me tonight, and they were babbling about a treasure. They used the name of the guy who was there when I met you a few days ago."

Andrei said, "Go on. Tell me more."

And Branko did, telling him everything that had happened during the night, leaving nothing out. When he was done, he said, "What do we do now?"

"Where is my box? Is it safe?"

Branko heard the words and realized it wasn't him they were chasing. It was something else. He said, "Yes, yes, of course they didn't get the box. I told you I'd make sure that was safe. Does that have something to do with this?"

"No. Go to Split. Get the team together. We're close to initiation on the final target. When I send the gateway package, I want you to execute. Do you understand?"

Branko knew that wasn't true. The men who tried to kill him kept mentioning a treasure. Andrei's box didn't hold papers, of that Branko was now sure.

He said, "What about the men chasing me? What do I do about them?"

"Nothing. I'm sending Nikita. He'll take care of them. You just worry about two things: my box, and the next target."

CHAPTER 30

Dylan Hobbes followed Alexander Palmer down the hallway, surprised at how the trappings of the White House no longer overwhelmed him. Before, the short walk to the Oval Office had left him in awe. Now it was just another walk in an old building. He wondered how quickly the awe left the regular staff members, like Palmer. Hobbes was just visiting, while Palmer actually worked inside the administration. Did he think this was just another day at Burger King, or did he still feel the weight of the history of the building?

It was barely seven in the morning, and he'd been called last night to give an update on the quest for solving the ransomware. He was told the meeting had to happen early, before the president's official schedule began, in order to protect the fact that it had even occurred, but in truth, *he* was the one who wanted an update. He wanted to know if they'd captured or killed the ransomware team.

They entered the Oval Office and Dylan saw that it was a much smaller crowd today. Only President Hannister, George Wolffe, and the director of the CIA, Kerry Bostwick, were present, all three bent over a desk looking at a tablet.

He heard President Hannister say, "So we know it's them. Now all we need to do is find the cell."

Alexander said, "Sir? Dylan Hobbes is here."

All three looked up. President Hannister said, "Tell me you

have some solution to the ransomware. It's ticking down to zero and George here got another threat."

Hobbes said, "Threat? What else could they do?"

Wolffe smiled and said, "They say they're going to release sensitive documents they've secured. Executives of the organization, their pay, their connections to other companies inside our organization. That sort of thing."

"That doesn't sound so bad. I mean, it's not like you guys are Apple or Sony. What threat could that be?"

Kerry said, "You've been read on. You've worked at TAO in the NSA. What would happen if the commercial infrastructure you used was put out on the open web? Could you do anything again? Even if it wasn't a bombshell?"

Hobbes saw the threat immediately. He'd been thinking like a civilian, not like the spook he had once been. If Blaisdell Consulting—and all of its connections—were put on the web, they'd all have to be burned to the ground. Destroyed, and even that wouldn't protect them from the future, as the names associated with every entity would now be available on the web forever.

And he saw something else: Defeating the ransomware was no longer the problem. Killing the team was now the issue, as they would have the information from the company whether they paid the ransom or not, something that the National Command Authority couldn't allow. He smiled inwardly.

Perfect.

President Hannister said, "So have you made any headway on the ransomware encryption?"

"No, sir. I haven't. It's not an easy thing to break, and might take another week, or up to a month. I realize you don't have that time, but it's just a fact. Although what I just heard means you need to get these guys physically. Get their hard drives. Get everything they have. The ransomware is no longer the big issue, correct? Did my information help?"

Nobody said anything for a moment, then George Wolffe said, "Yeah, that's right. Your information proved to be correct. We penetrated an apartment we found, drained a MacBook laptop, and it was from the ransomware guys. But we've lost control of them."

"How? Why didn't you take them right then?"

"Because we didn't know it was them then. We can't just rip someone off the street in a foreign country based on suspicion. We needed proof, and now we have it. The men in that apartment were involved in this attack, and that laptop is now being tracked. When it settles down, we'll try again. You just keep working the ransomware. That's your mission. We'll work the cell."

Hobbes nodded, happy with the words. It was clear the team would be wiped out, and with it, any evidence of his culpability.

The television inside the Oval Office switched to a breaking news story, and the president turned to it, saying, "At least we have some good news. Finally breaking ourselves from the Russian monopoly for a ride into space."

The screen showed a rocket on platform 39A at the Kennedy Space Center in Florida, the closed captioning on the screen scrolling along.

The first launch to the International Space Station with a compliment of both NASA astronauts and civilians. Also the first NASA manned launch of the Valkyrie rocket from Auriga Systems. A new world of space has opened up.

Wolffe said, "Yeah, a bunch of civilians and a billionaire. What could go wrong?"

President Hannister smiled and said, "I'm with you. It worries me to no end, and I'm not sure if this is good or bad, to be honest, but it's better than relying on the Russians."

Hobbes turned from the screen and said, "I thought that launch was next week?"

"No. Well, it was, but the weather pushed it into the first bit of the launch window. NASA still has oversight of the launchpad, even if Fitch owns the rocket."

Hobbes nodded, now wanting to leave the room. He said, "Is there anything else I can help you with today, sir? I'm sorry I haven't cracked the code, but you must understand, that's expected."

He didn't mention, of course, that he'd done absolutely nothing to crack the code, given that it was his own.

President Hannister said, "No. Thank you for coming. Just keep us informed if you make any headway. You have Wolffe's secure number, correct?"

"Yes, sir."

Palmer led him back to the West Wing entrance and said, "We appreciate what you're doing here. It's like that space launch. American commercial enterprises helping the national security of the United States. The NSA couldn't help us with this problem, and the only ones in the past who could help us with the launch were the damn Russians. Now that's changed."

Hobbes chuckled and said, "I don't think I've been a lot of help, but thanks. And I don't know anything about space launches."

Palmer patted him on the back and said, "You don't need to know about space. Your help here on earth has been invaluable."

Dylan Hobbes walked back to his car without another word. He'd been disingenuous with that answer. While he dealt in the realm of cyberspace, he knew a great deal about Auriga's space ventures. It was the target he'd chosen for his ultimate objective. He'd followed the company's rise and thought it the perfect vehicle—no pun intended—to return America back to what he'd known in his youth.

There had been two things that had united the U.S. in his life. One was the *Challenger* disaster in 1986. The other was 9/11. He'd been a college student in 1986, but had seen how it had coalesced the feelings of patriotism in the United States. Later, much later, he'd seen the same thing when the twin towers fell. And he'd decided to re-create both in a single strike. Remake the partisan bent of the United States into one of unified goals.

He'd watched Skyler Fitch spend his billions on creating a commercial space tourism company, eventually becoming the leader in both government and commercial spaceflight against a host of competitors. Government, in that his rockets resupplied the International Space Station, and commercial in that those same rockets took rich people into space for brief moments solely for the bragging rights of having been there.

This launch was the first combination of both. In a race to beat the Russians yet again—who'd actually sent a civilian camera crew to the space station for a Russian movie—this one was the first fully civilian crew to fly to the space station.

The members included an actual retired NASA astronaut, the billionaire himself, a former fighter pilot who was now a senator on the subcommittee on space and science, and a schoolteacher from Little Rock, Arkansas.

That final person was key. He remembered the *Challenger,* the last time a teacher had been sent into space, only to disintegrate on live TV for all to see. She was key to his plans. If the destruction of the spacecraft could be blamed on an enemy, the entire United

States would forget about their petty political differences and co-alesce around a new feeling of national unity.

The Cold War had been frightening for many reasons, but in Hobbes's mind, it had also provided a unifying theme. No matter how bad the politics got inside the United States, there was always a threat. He wanted to re-create that time.

If it involved a war, so be it. That was the price of saving this democracy. Wars had always saved America. Name one that hadn't. Every single war the United States had entered had caused a rally around the flag that made the people realize they lived in a better country than the petty disagreements seemed to show.

Stock market crash in 1929? World War II took care of that. Splinters at the edge of the reconstruction after? Korea took care of that. Infighting among the political parties over petty differences? 9/11 stopped that in its tracks, at least for a little while. Yeah, there had been some issues with Vietnam, and Iraq had most certainly been a debacle, but that was because nobody had shown the public what was at stake. They had no idea, and he was going to change the calculus.

No longer would people like him, who spent their entire lives protecting the fragile fabric of democracy in the United States, be pilloried by some elected asshole out for points. The entire architecture of the United States would turn to fight, and in so doing, the entire population of the United States would quit its petty political disagreements to join together against a greater threat.

That had been the plan initially, but with the ransomware attack against some top-secret organization inside the U.S. government, Hobbes had decided to protect himself instead of proceed. But now, he might be able to do both.

He drove out of the White House complex, went far enough

away to be clear from whatever electronic devices were monitoring that area, then pulled over to the side of the road, dialing a number he'd promised he would never use again, routing the call through the Bluetooth in the car.

The phone rang and rang. He knew that even with the time change he was within daylight hours, and wondered if he'd been cut free. Like the guy didn't want to talk anymore because he'd heard of the issues from the ransomware cell.

He put his finger over the button on the steering wheel to close out the call, and someone answered, saying, "Hello? What is your business?"

"I need to talk to Andrei. My name is Sphinx. He'll know me."

"Stand by."

Thirty seconds later, he heard Andrei say, "To what do I owe this pleasure? You said you'd never call. You know, because everyone in the United States intelligence apparatus is tracking you. I'm assuming by the fact you're using an open cell line that you're clean?"

"No, I'm not clean, but nobody is tracking me. I'm assuming because you gave me this number for an emergency, that *it's* clean. Is that not the case? If so, I'll hang up now."

He heard Andrei laugh and say, "One-time use. Never been on the cell network. You've just destroyed this number, so it had better be important."

Hobbes toyed with telling him that they'd attacked a classified organization of the United States, but couldn't see how to leverage the information. He decided to go with what he knew, leaving Andrei in the dark.

"The scheduled launch has been moved up a week because of weather. We need to initiate now."

"But you said they'd find the bug if we penetrated early?"

"The launch is going early. They have some weather thing going on. What I want your team to do is penetrate the system and implant the malware, but use a timer. Get into the system and set a time bomb for initiation."

"I'm not sure they can do that. I'm not skilled in the intricacies of this attack. All I'm skilled in is that I will profit from it. Do you understand? I will profit, right?"

Hobbes said, "Of course you're going to get a payday. Just like me. But in order for that to happen, I need them to inject now."

What he didn't say was that the team was about to be wiped out by a killing crew deep in the heart of the United States government, hence the time delay. Or that he intended to use his company to implicate another nation-state for the Auriga attack, and cause a cascading effect.

Hobbes continued, saying, "They need to implant with a countdown. I know how to do this. I need the chat room they operate in to coach them. To tell them how to make it work."

"I don't know what you mean by 'chat room.'"

"Andrei, don't kid me on this. It's my job. I know they talk in a chat room on the dark web because that's what all of them do. I need that access. I'll tell them how to accomplish the mission, and we'll both make money. I send them the gateway access, and they learn how to do a time-delay response."

Andrei paused for a moment, then said, "If I give you the chat, can you access their systems?"

Hobbes laughed and said, "No, come on. The chat is just the chat. I can't access their systems. And nobody is watching me, if that's what you're worried about."

Andrei said, "Okay, I'll send you the dark web chat room. But if you're thinking of screwing me out of money by some backdoor deal, I will find you."

Hobbes lied and said, "I'm not doing that. We both want the same thing. Money."

CHAPTER 31

J ennifer gave me a cup of coffee and leaned into the computer. I said, "Nothing new yet."

She nodded, took a sip of her own coffee, and said, "Any backlash from the Taskforce?"

"None yet, but you know it's coming. That SITREP probably has them changing their diapers."

"You don't have a response?"

"Nope. Not yet."

The computer made an announcement, and we both whipped around to the screen. A blue marble was highlighted inside the old town of Split. Along with it came the same caveat we'd heard before: *Cannot confirm current, but this is the last known location.*

I stood up, saying, "Looks like it's Split. Get everyone ready to go. No telling how long that signal will last. He's already wiped his phone. Hopefully he thinks that computer is clean."

She said, "And the authorization?"

"It'll come. Just get everyone ready to move."

We'd exfiltrated from the kill zone of the so-called Art Park, which had ended up being nothing but graffiti, and had left a dead body behind, along with another live one in the wind, but that couldn't be helped. We had a clear mandate to determine the ransomware, but not one to become Batman, saving every shitbag from an early death. If the guy we'd rescued was involved in our problem set, then we'd done some good. If he wasn't, then we'd just created problems by leaving a dead Turkish guy on the ground.

The team itself was wondering how it would bleed out, not the least because I'd given the call to interdict, but I wasn't worried about their reaction. To a man—or woman—they would always err on the side of saving someone's life. Even if it was a bad guy. But, like them, I *was* worried about my command. If what we'd done didn't pan out as the right decision, I'd be in a world of hurt. The Taskforce didn't take kindly to killing someone on foreign soil without justification.

It was easy being the hero when the bad guy was a known entity, like on an assault in Fallujah, but that wasn't my reality. Sometimes the bad guy was just a normal person using a weapon that wasn't a gun, but he was bad all the same. The problem was figuring that out, and up until Creed's message, I wasn't sure.

We'd linked up after the actions at the Art Park, ran back to our hotel, and then had spent the rest of the night transferring the computer data, shacking up a SITREP and conducting an after-action review. Ordinarily, the purpose of the AAR was to determine what we could do better. In this case, it was simply to try to find out what the hell was going on before I contacted higher.

We had a simple penetration target associated with computer crap—meaning he was an egghead and not a trained killer—and that penetration had led to some sort of shoot-out with guys from Turkey. It was crazy.

We'd batted about what we were dealing with, along with what we should be doing now, but truthfully, the computer would tell the tale. At least I hoped it would, or I'd be in for some serious explaining.

We'd kicked around going back to the apartment but had decided that was a dead end. There wouldn't be anything new at that location after Knuckles and I had penetrated, so why go? Midway through the discussion, I'd messed with the phone I'd found, but it was locked. I'd tossed it onto the table, saying it was no help, and Veep said, "Send that to Creed as well."

"What for? He's got the computer. He can't do anything with this. The phone is locked out. Nobody can crack an iPhone. The FBI can't even do it."

Veep smiled and said, "I think you're wrong."

He got behind the computer and began typing, saying, "You know your Israeli friends can crack an iPhone, right?"

I said, "Who are you contacting?"

"Creed. He's hip-deep with them." He typed, You still working that Israeli thing off the books? iPhone hacks?

He got back, Yeah, but why are you talking about it?

Because we have a phone. You're working the computer?
   Yeah. That's easy. You have a phone?
Yes.
   An iPhone?
Yes.
   The target will wipe it. It's going to be wiped. He can do
   that remotely.
Can you clone?
   Maybe. Plug it in. Let me see.

Veep turned to me and I handed him the phone, saying, "What is this? You've never said anything about it."

Veep said, "It's just a project I was working on with Creed. A way to crack an iPhone using the Cloud. Aaron and Shoshana told me about it, and helped Creed along."

A little miffed, I said, "Why wasn't I told?"

Veep said, "Because it was just a little project that had nothing to do with operations. It might not work, but what he's going to try to do is duplicate the phone through the cloud, then download that to a new iPhone. Which means we need an iPhone."

"What about the passwords? Even if it downloads, it'll still need a password."

"Pike, I'm not an expert on the ins and outs, but the phone will go to a cloud account, and when it comes back to earth, it'll just duplicate on our phone, but act like the phone is brand-new. There won't be a password. Or maybe it'll ask to set a password. Maybe it'll work, maybe it won't, but it's worth a shot."

I nodded and said, "Plug it in," then turned to Brett and said, "Go buy an iPhone. I figure you want out of this hotel room by now."

He laughed and said, "No doubt. Any idea where?"

Jennifer said, "There's a mall right next door, underneath the park, called the Importanne Center."

Brett nodded and left. In between, Creed told us that the computer drain we'd accomplished was healthy, and that these guys were involved in the lockup of GRS. The man we'd saved was, in fact, the ransomware gang.

Should have taken him down.

But I knew that was just wasted breath. I had no idea at the time if he was a bad guy, and I had no authority to do so even if he was. With everything we were working now, we'd get another shot. Maybe.

Creed could tell us what was on the computer, but none of that data had any location we could target. But maybe Veep's work would change that equation.

Brett returned with a brand-new iPhone, saying, "When this is done, do I get to keep it?"

I said, "No. But you can give it to your wife."

He passed the phone, saying, "I don't have a wife."

I took it, plugged it into the VPN on our Taskforce computer, the iPhone I'd found in the grass right next to it, and said, "Oh. Sorry. I guess Jennifer gets it then."

He scowled and said, "Sounds a little bit like nepotism here."

Creed came on saying, "Okay, the phone's good. Downloading to yours now."

When it was complete, I said, "All right, Creed, how does this help us?"

He said, "The phone is tied to that computer you cloned. The same guy owned both. He has the 'Find my Mac' segment on, and I can see his MacBook like he was searching for it."

"You can see where that computer is, right now?"

"Yes."

"Send me a map."

He did, and it was in the heart of the old town of Split, right smack dab in what was known as Diocletian's Palace.

Creed said, "It also has an Apple AirTag tied to the system. I have no idea what it is, but he's tracking something."

"What's that mean?"

"I have no idea. AirTags are used to mark things that are ordinarily lost. Could be his keys, could be a bicycle. Could be anything. But what's odd is the trace is in the middle of a national park. Nothing else around."

I said, "Okay, let's focus on the computer. It's in Split?"

"Yeah, right where that marble shows. You're basically duplicating his phone and they're tied together."

I said, "Okay, good to go, Creed. Good work."

I disconnected the VPN and said, "Let's get some sleep. I'm going to send the SITREP asking for authority to interdict anyone who's associated with that computer, but the first thing I want to know is if it's still in the same place tomorrow. I don't want to do a 'Where's Waldo?' on this thing."

The next morning, I awoke and checked the trace again. It was in the same spot. I picked up the target phone, and sure enough, the guy who owned it had wiped it. The background screen no longer showed some snowboarder doing a jump, and the phone itself showed no apps having been downloaded.

It was now functionally dead, but luckily, our cloned phone was still active. I initiated the VPN and pulled up the answer to our SITREP, worried about what I'd see. I'd asked for Omega authority, but really, I'd left a dead guy from Turkey on the ground in Croatia while operating out of Tajikistan. It was a little bit much, even for me.

Jennifer leaned over me to read what the Taskforce had sent, saying, "Can't wait to see what they thought about last night."

Her wet hair fell in front of my face, and I smelled the shampoo. I turned to her and said, "Do you mind?"

She looked at me like she didn't understand, then said, "Are you hiding something? You don't want me to see what the Taskforce sent?"

I shook my head and said, "No. All I meant was that your shampoo tends to break my concentration."

She smiled and said, "Well, it's good that something can do that, because you never listen to me otherwise."

I stood up and waved my hand, saying, "It's all yours. Must have been the shampoo in your hair last night when I was listening to you telling me what to do."

I heard, "What was that?" then saw Jennifer's face blush.

I turned and saw Knuckles in our suite, which had been converted to our tactical operations center. Incensed, I said, "Do you ever fucking knock?"

He said, "Knock? This is the TOC. Why would I knock? You gave us the keys to enter."

Behind him I saw Brett and Veep and knew I was not going to live down what I'd just said.

Brett said, "So if I wash with her shampoo I won't stay in the hotel? I'll get a shot at doing something worthwhile? Is that it?"

Jennifer was mortified, which is what they wanted. I looked at her and chuckled, saying, "You're getting your shot. The computer is in Split, and the Taskforce has authorized us for Omega. Go pack your shit."

CHAPTER 32

Shakor sat in front of his computer screen trying mightily to find some thread that would allow him to continue. Last night had been an unmitigated disaster, and he didn't want to report back to his Taliban masters without something to show for it. He knew they were as unforgiving as he was.

He heard his door open and saw Din in the entryway. His trusted friend. He walked forward, his limp causing his left arm to swing more than his right.

Din said, "What are we going to do about Abdul Aziz?"

"There's nothing we can do. He's dead. The police are already on the scene."

Din shuffled his feet and said, "I meant what were we going to do about his body. We're now compromised. The authorities in Zagreb will be looking for us."

"They won't be looking for us. They'll be chasing down a passport from Turkey. We're good."

"So that's it for Abdul?"

Shakor turned from the computer and said, "What do you mean?"

"Just that he's been fighting his entire life and now he's going to go away as a Turkish mugger in Croatia."

Shakor said, "We do what we do for the Islamic Emirate of Afghanistan. He died for that very thing, which is something I hope to achieve."

Din nodded, saying, "Me as well. What do we do now? We have no idea where the treasure is."

"I think we might have something."

"What?"

"In the emails I exchanged with Branko. I'm looking at them now. When I first contacted him he said he wanted to party in Split, but didn't know when Ahmad was arriving. He had to go there today."

He turned the computer monitor to Din and said, "See that?"

Din scrolled through the email chain and saw:

It's great to hear from you. I'm surprised you even contacted me, but I'm glad you did. I'll show you a good time. Are you in Zagreb? Or not here yet? I'm headed to Split tomorrow, and that town is much better for partying than Zagreb. I have a house within walking distance of the Game of Thrones castle, with a lot of good pubs around.

Let me know.

Din said, "So? What's that mean?"

"I answered him and told him I was in Zagreb, which is how we got the bar where Abdul and I met him. But he said he was going to Split. Maybe that's a clue."

"What clue? Split is huge."

"He said he had a house next to the *Game of Thrones* palace. I googled that, and it's a place called Klis Fortress, about ten minutes outside of Split proper."

Shakor pulled up a Google map and said, "This is it."

Din said, "That's no help. Look at the roads around it. Unless he lives inside, we'll never be able to find him."

"Look closer. The fortress is on a steep ridge, built right on the mountain. The roads to the south are all below it, and there's only one road coming in from the north."

"So?"

"So he said he was within walking distance to the castle. He wouldn't have said that if his house was on the south side, below the fortress and the ridge. He said that because his place is on the north, where the tourists enter."

Din nodded and said, "Okay, that makes sense, but why does this matter?"

"Because he's gone to Split. That's where he is, I'm sure of it. And his house is on that northern road. As he said, 'within walking distance' to the castle."

Shakor pointed at the screen and drew a circle with his finger, saying, "It's right here. One of these. All we need to do is find it."

"How?"

"There's only one main road that leads to the fortress. He might be living on a side alley, but he's going to use this road to get home. He's within a kilometer of the entrance. We stage surveillance on that road and wait. Sooner or later, he'll show up."

Din squinted and said, "That's pretty thin. He might be anywhere. Are you sure this is the *Game of Thrones* place? Maybe it's somewhere else."

"This is it, I'm sure. They also filmed in the old town of Split, but there's no other castle near Split that would be from the show *Game of Thrones*. It's this fortress, and yes, it's pretty thin, but we have nothing else to go on."

Din looked at Shakor, then back at the computer screen. He said, "Okay, so what now?"

"Now we set up surveillance on that road. Could take three days, might take a week, but eventually, we'll find him. And when we do, we'll find the treasure."

CHAPTER 33

Branko heard glasses clanking in the kitchen, rolled over on the couch, and groaned. He sat up, seeing Rodavan making coffee. Pushka came out of the bedroom, saw him, and said, "Did you sleep okay?"

Branko couldn't tell if he was kidding or not. He said, "No, not at all. I'm not staying here tonight. I'm headed to the safehouse."

Pushka smiled and said, "Not nearly the amenities we have here."

Branko stood up and said, "At least I'll have a bed."

Rodavan brought him a mug and said, "Sorry about that, but you're supposed to be at the safehouse anyway. I wasn't going to give up my bed just because you were too tired to drive north."

Pushka and Branko had finally arrived at Split's old town—known as Diocletian's Palace—and he'd parked the vehicle in a lot just outside the palace walls. He'd planned on only going up to their operational headquarters and using the T1 internet trunk to wipe his iPhone out of existence, but once that was done, he was too tired to walk back to the car and drive the thirty minutes north to the safehouse. He'd simply crashed on the couch.

He went to the window and looked out at the ancient cobblestone streets, seeing the tourists already starting to move about. Pushka was right about one thing: this location had much better amenities than the old house in the middle of the hills.

A long-term Vrbo rental, paid by Andrei, it had been picked

for two reasons: One, it was inside the old town, which meant no vehicles were allowed, with the majority of pathways too narrow for a vehicle to traverse, something that would make escape easier if the authorities ever closed in. They had a network of IP cameras and proximity alerts for early warning, and a plan of escape that involved climbing down a pipe on the outside terrace should the worst ever happen.

Two, this Vrbo was the only one offering high-speed internet in the entire old town, a necessity for the purposes of their work. The whole of the den was blanketed with laptops, all connected via a VPN to the World Wide Web, and all of it designed to be broken down and moved at a moment's notice, with a self-destruct feature wired into the hard drives should packing up become untenable.

It was but one of the operational locations for Dark Star, with others spread throughout Croatia all the way down to Dubrovnik, but Branko only allowed one cell to operate at any one time. The others were dormant while the Split cell was active.

Branko said, "I'm going to head up north to the safehouse and check on the guys. I'll be back later."

"Do you want your laptop?"

Branko thought a moment, then said, "No. I'll be back in the afternoon. First thing I have to do is get another smartphone." He held up his burner phone and said, "These things are shit. I'll contact you once I get it to let you know the number."

Branko left the apartment and went down the narrow stairwell to the street below, winding his way through the alleys until he reached the eastern gate in the city walls. He passed through it, walking by vendors setting up for the day, and continued until he reached his car, wanting to leave before the attendant arrived in the morning and charged him for the night.

He stopped once on the outskirts of the city, buying a new iPhone and paying for service, then headed north out of the city, eventually hitting the foothills, the road winding left and right in hairpin turns with spectacular views of the coastline. Having seen it a thousand times before, he ignored it, solely aggravated to be behind a tour bus going the same way he was. He tried to pass multiple times and was rebuffed by oncoming traffic, increasing his aggravation.

Eventually he came to an intersection with a much smaller road, one that he knew the tour bus wouldn't take. He cut left and wound through a maze of side roads, getting to a house that was within spitting distance of Klis Fortress. He pulled the car into a little concrete pad off the road, the parking area clearly homemade, given the roughshod nature of the work. He exited, locked the car, and stared off the way he'd come, the coast of Split splayed out before him like a map laid on the table. He turned to the house, seeing the Klis Fortress above it, a construct of stone that was imposing even now, in the twenty-first century.

Built on a razor edge of a ridgeline and running for over two football fields, it commanded the entire countryside. It was amazing to him even in his modern world, where skyscrapers touched the heavens. He couldn't imagine what those in the past thought of the fortress. Or how they actually managed to build the damn thing so high in the mountains.

Its past was lost on the world stage, relegated to Croatian local history, but had been given new life with the HBO series *Game of Thrones*. HBO could have built a set in Hollywood, but instead decided to use something real, and the fortress became one of the set pieces of the entire series, creating a magnet for tourists, which Branko found a little disgusting.

A great many people years ago had built the fortress to protect the coast of Dalmatia, and all it was known for now was as a setting for a city that didn't even exist in the real world. He wondered if the people who'd died building it would relish the new tourists who came for no other reason than to see a backdrop they'd already witnessed on their television screen.

He walked up the path to the front door, the house they'd rented built into the side of the hill itself. Pushka had been right: this abode made of rough brick and pine boards was nowhere near as sexy as the operational headquarters in Split, but it didn't need to be. He didn't care if it had high-speed Wi-Fi or whether the satellite dish for the television worked. All he wanted was a functioning toilet and stove for his men.

He banged on the door and it was opened by a man about the same age as him, with the same ratty attire. He said, "Hey, Drago, how's the house?"

"It's better than Zadar, but that's not saying much. Not sure why we make so much money only to sit in shitholes like this."

Branko pushed through the door, saying, "One more week. We're about to hit the mother lode."

"Apparently we're hitting the mother lode right now."

Branko turned around and said, "What's that mean?"

"Pushka texted. We have the gateway and the target. He's implanting now. Apparently the customer in the United States is talking to him over chat."

"Chat? What chat? I just left his ass."

CHAPTER 34

Sitting in a parking lot next to an outdoor café, Shakor was watching one of the many roads that led off the main highway from Split, the Klis Fortress towering over him as if it were upset by the intrusion. He knew this effort was a long shot for success, but it was all he had. He felt his phone vibrate. He pulled it out and saw a simple text:

Target acquired.

He smiled, texting back, Meet me at the fortress parking lot.

CHAPTER 35

S itting in his computer laboratory at Liberty Crossing, Dylan Hobbes saw a new person enter the chat window, the screen alerting him with a mackerel smacking his avatar in the face. Literally, a female in a bikini holding a fish came forward and smacked him on the screen.

He typed, Who is this?

He got back, The man in charge of this entire cell. How did you get in this chat room?

Andrei. I'm the one calling the shots, and I'm talking to Pushka.

Five thousand miles away, in a crumbling safehouse outside of Split, Branko was about to lose his temper. He typed, You don't call any shots.

Pushka came on, aggravating Branko, saying, He's given us the gateway and the target. I'm working it now. It's big. He is, in fact, calling the shots.

Branko typed, I don't know who you are, but best case, you're a customer. Like you assholes in America like to say, I can refuse service for any reason whatsoever.

Branko waited on the bubbles of the chat window to clear, then read, Refuse this and you'll lose an enormous payday. Have you seen the target?

Pushka typed, He's right. It's big. Biggest one ever.

Exasperated, Branko typed, Pushka, I'm coming back now. Shut up.

Then the target package came through, with Pushka saying, Open this. Take a look.

Branko did, and saw a target that would create a world of hurt. It was the private space company Auriga, owned by one of the richest men in the world. A spectacle of greed and celebrity, with the high potential to be the biggest payday ever.

He typed, We don't attack government facilities. We only target private companies. And we don't target anything that has the potential for lethal harm. It's why we don't attack hospitals. This is a no-go.

Pushka typed, This isn't like some stranger attached to a heart-lung machine. It's the prestige of America on the line. They'll have to pay, and pay big.

Branko squeezed his eyes shut, then typed, And then they hunt us to the end of time. They will never forget, and they will never forgive. Eventually, they will come for us. Look at Conti. They now have a ten million dollar bounty on their head. It's why we always go low. Never big enough to piss off the beast.

The Conti group was the biggest player in the ransomware game, attacking bigger targets that would inevitably aggravate nation-states, until they literally strangled the entire country of Costa Rica, which caused the United States to finally sit up and take notice, offering a reward on anyone in the group like they were Al Qaida. Branko wanted none of that, preferring to make a nickel here and a nickel there.

The stranger broke in, saying, After this hit, you can retire to Costa Rica. There won't be another one necessary.

Branko ignored the statement, saying, Are you secure? How do I know who the hell you are? The last thing I need is an FBI sting.

The bubbles went up and down, and then Branko read, I'm Sphinx. I'm on the TOR network, and my IP address has been washed maybe a thousand times.

TOR was a secure encryption program for communication, mostly used in the dark web for selling illicit products. It stood for The Onion Routing project, and was a crowdsourced method of hiding IP addresses, preventing anyone from knowing where your communications originated. It consisted of millions of people around the world allowing their computers to bounce your messages through their systems until it was impossible to find an origin source.

> That's great. I'm glad you used security to contact us, but I don't trust you. How do I know you're even vaguely aware of what I do?
>
> Because that code you're using is mine, you arrogant shit.

And Branko realized he was talking to the real deal. The zero-click inventor. He typed, Okay, what do you want?

> I want access to your penetration. I want control over the ransomware. And I want you to implant the time schedule I just discussed with Pushka. I've given him the code to make it happen. Execute.

Branko felt the hairs on his neck stand up. Why do you want that? We do the ransomware. We've gotten pretty good at it. You're a leak. A stray piece of voltage that could screw everything up.

Because I'm the customer and you're using my code. Make it happen.

Branko typed, What's to prevent you from taking the money? Why would I do that?

I'm not going to take your money from the ransom. I'm the one facilitating the attack. Think about it. If I wanted to steal from you, why would I give you the code? This is personal to me. I just want to make sure it succeeds.

Branko sat for a moment, then decided. Can you do that, Pushka? Is it even possible to allow him access?

Pushka came back, It's already done. Easy to do. Implant is in, with the countdown starting. Zero click worked like a charm. All I need to do is pass him our own gateway.

Branko heard the front doorbell ring, and Drago stood up to check it. Branko typed, Okay, okay. Pushka, I'm leaving the safe-house and coming back to you. Give him the gateway, but don't do anything else until I get there. I want to see the access before we trigger.

Then he heard Drago scream.

CHAPTER 36

Wandering through the small cobblestone alleys of Split's old town, I had to admit, this mission was about the best ever. Humping a rucksack in the Hindu Kush certainly gave you memories, but this was something else. Especially with the gelato. Italy can claim to have invented the frozen treat, but nowhere on earth was it better than in Croatia.

I was on my second cone, walking down an alley full of tourist shops and cafés, when Jennifer elbowed me, saying, "Are you listening?"

I said, "What? What did I do wrong?"

"Other than eating about a pound of gelato? We're walking by the target right now." She showed me her phone, and the marble was directly to our left. The lower level of this building was full of tourist shops and cafés, so the marble had to be on the next floor.

I took a bite of my cone again and said, "You have to admit, this shit is really good."

She smiled and said, "Maybe we should open a shop in Charleston. Then I wouldn't have to spend my time getting shot at."

I licked the cone again and looked at her to see if she was serious. Two tourists bumped by us and I let them get out of earshot before saying, "Okay, okay. No more fun. Where's the alley?"

She pointed over my shoulder and said, "Right there."

I glanced behind me, seeing a narrow little spit of a stone lane going through the buildings. I extended my cone to the front of her face and said, "Brett and Veep found the front?"

She took a lick and said, "Yep. They've already been by it. It's a stairwell in a tunnel leading to a restaurant called Makarun."

I took a huge bite of the gelato cone, then held it out to her again, but she shook her head. I tossed it into a garbage can and said, "Let's go take a look at the back."

We entered the alley, literally small enough that I could almost touch both walls of the buildings just by stretching out my arms, and walked down it, keeping an eye on everything around us.

I said, "Can't get any vehicles in here."

Jennifer said, "This is it. Right here. On the second floor."

I looked above us, seeing a terrace with open-air seating. I saw someone on the terrace and grabbed her arm, leading her away. We got around the corner and I said, "That's their escape route. We hit the front, and they go out the back. With the alleys around here, they'll disappear in seconds. No way for anyone to interdict with vehicles. It'll all be on foot, and I promise they've planned out how that race will work. They want to disappear, and that alley gives them the ability."

Jennifer looked at the terrace from our corner and said, "I agree. What's your point?"

But she knew the point before she even raised the question. I said, "You know why. Look behind you to the alley. Can you get up it to the terrace?"

She did, saw the old brick and cast-iron pipe, and said, "Yeah. No sweat. So, I'm what?"

"You're squirter control, but you have to get up there without anyone knowing. Can you do it?"

She looked again, seeing the windows across the way on the other building, and said, "Yeah. If it's dark, I can do it."

We went back to our hotel, which was an Uber drive from the old town. Called the Radisson Blu, it was a high-rise on the outskirts of the city but gave Jennifer some credited points for her frequent flyer card. She was trying to get platinum status, and constantly picked hotels that would award her points on the government dime. One of these days, I'd take control of planning our hotels, but I hadn't here, and so we were in a tourist hotel a cab ride away from our target.

I alerted everyone to come to my room. We waited for them to show up, and Jennifer said, "We have Omega on this, but it's a little different from what we've done before. Capture alone won't solve the problem."

I said, "I get that. What do you mean?"

"I mean we'll have to lean into whomever we capture to stop the ransomware. That's a little different from just bagging a guy. What are we going to do?"

I studied a picture on the wall of our hotel, a beach scene that looked like the definition of serenity. Something I would never have. I turned back to her, saying, "I'm going to force him to give us the key for the ransomware. That force could just be me looking at him. But it could also be something else."

She nodded, thinking, then said, "Be careful on this."

She knew me better than anyone else on earth, and she was telling me to not get into groupthink with the team or the Taskforce. I understood it, and appreciated the words.

I said, "We get in and he'll comply. I promise I won't break any limbs for this, but I can't promise there won't be any pain."

She circled our room for a moment, not saying anything. I said, "You still don't trust me."

She came to me and leaned forward, kissing me on the lips. She said, "I have always trusted you. Never say that. At the end of the day, our company is not worth your soul."

"Well, that might depend on you. You have the terrace. Who do you want with you?"

She thought a minute, then said, "Brett. He's the only one who can make that climb without me worrying. And he's really good at controlling himself in a firefight. If they try to get out back, I want him there to contain it."

I smiled and said, "As you wish."

The door opened and Knuckles came in with a thumb drive, followed by Brett. He said, "Here's the front of the place. It's off a tunnel that leads to the restaurant Makarun, which is really a courtyard. Right before you reach the entrance to the restaurant there's a single stairwell going up into the building."

I took the drive and plugged it into the computer, seeing exactly what he'd told me. It wasn't that great for an assault, but it was good for locking down the target. Besides the terrace, there was no escape. The only issue was the restaurant.

I said, "Creed's done some work on the place. Turns out it's a Vrbo rental, and the advertisement for it actually includes a floor plan."

Brett said, "You're shitting me."

"Nope."

I clicked to a web page and said, "This is it. A two-bedroom place with a large den and an outside terrace."

Knuckles said, "Doesn't look that hard."

"I agree, but we need to get these guys alive. No killing, even if they have a weapon."

Brett said, "What's that mean?"

"It means they aren't DOA. If you have to protect your life, then do so, but don't shoot just because a guy shows up with a possible gun. Treat it like a hostage rescue. Take him out in other ways."

Brett nodded and said, "That's increasing the risk."

"I know, but they're a bunch of computer geeks. I don't think we'll have to test it. If we do, then kill them. If it comes down to you or him, drop him. Just don't do it as a matter of course."

I went back to the computer, then said, "But you won't have to worry about that. You aren't on the assault."

He bristled and said, "More black man bullshit here? I just did the recce. I blend in with this city. Plenty of men like me."

I turned around and smiled, saying, "No. Jennifer is going up the side of the building to the terrace for squirter control. I asked who she wanted, and she said you."

He looked at her to see if I was lying, and she said, "You're the only one I trust on that wall. The only one who can do it."

He broke into a smile and said, "About time someone appreciates me."

I chuckled and said, "Dig into this thing. We hit it tonight, and I want everyone solid."

CHAPTER 37

B ranko ran to the front of the house and saw a swarthy man standing over Drago with a pistol, Drago on the ground holding his head. He immediately turned and ran back the other way, darting into a bedroom.

He slammed the door shut, locked it, and heard men storming in. He looked around for an escape, saw a window that was basically flush with the ground, and leapt toward it, trying to jerk it open. It had a century of paint on the sill and refused to budge. He heard the men pounding on the door, backed up, put his hands over his face, and dove straight forward, crashing through the glass and hitting the slope outside the building. He rolled upright, saw a man appear in the room, and took off down the slope around the house. He hit the street and saw the Klis castle in front of him. A place with tourists. A place of protection.

He ran toward it, reaching the long, winding road that led to the entrance. He kept going, feeling his lungs begin to cave like they had in Zagreb. He slowed to a fast walk, turned behind him, and saw the men from the house all coming his way.

He felt a bolt of adrenaline and charged up the hill, running past the ticket counter. He heard someone yell but kept going.

He reached the first terrace and stopped, hands on his knees, gasping for breath. The castle was a linear stretch that didn't help his ability to escape, and he wondered why he'd even chosen it.

There was nowhere to run on top of this hill. The entire fortress was built to prevent penetration—which also prevented escape. He was dead.

Except for one thing. One little thing that the fortress had used in medieval times. An entrance that the members of the fortress accessed when they needed to come and go during a siege. A secret entrance.

Because of the location of his safehouse, Branko had spent a fair amount of time at the fortress, drinking wine at the cafés outside and hiking the ancient hills. One thing he'd learned would now help him survive. Underneath the first bastion was a portal, built to resupply the castle should it fall under attack. It led to the valley below, and was known to anyone who bought a ticket for entrance, but he was sure it wasn't known to the men chasing him.

Branko ran to the bastion and heard the men behind him, the granite stones echoing their footsteps. He darted down the stairs to the lower level, underneath the earth, and waited, hoping the men would just pass him by. He went to the small enclosure where the secret entrance was located, seeing the earth fall away from an open hole, a footpath that had been used a millennium ago faintly visible.

The entrance wasn't an easy exit. In fact, it was downright dangerous. Built on the steepest slope of the castle, it was designed to be hidden, and designed to be hard to use.

He heard shouting above him and went to the opening, bashing the iron bars that had been put in place to prevent some stupid tourist from exiting.

They didn't give. He heard a conversation above, someone yelling about people not paying for the entrance, and smashed the bars with his feet, a desperation born of full adrenaline. The iron bars sprang free, tumbling to the earth below.

He dangled out of the gap in the castle wall, the ground twelve feet below. He heard the clapping of footsteps on the stone above and dropped through the gap, hitting the dirt outside the castle walls.

He rolled twice, slid down the slope for about ten feet, then sat upright. He looked behind him and saw the castle rising above him, but nobody following. The secret entrance had just saved his life. He stood up and began slip-sliding down the slope to the highway below.

Shakor tapped the man he'd bludgeoned with his pistol, not showing any animosity, but conveying it with his mere presence. In truth, he was completely surprised by how quickly they'd dominated the place. The man had opened the door, apparently looking for a food delivery, and Shakor had hammered him in the face with his pistol, the skin on his forehead ripping from the front sight post. He'd fallen to the ground and they'd entered with no other resistance. The rest of the assault hadn't gone as smoothly, as their target had literally jumped through a plate-glass window to avoid them.

Shakor said, "Drago, is it? Is that right?"

The man groaned and rolled over, the right side of his face split from the pistol whipping at the front door. He pulled his hand away from his forehead, saw the red, and said, "Help me here. Please."

Shakor tossed him a cloth, and Drago put it to his head. Shakor raised his pistol and bounced it lightly off the man's skull. "Where is the treasure?"

Drago looked at him in fear, saying, "I don't know anything about a treasure. All I know is what I do. I get paid to find places like this. I don't do anything but find places to stay. That's what I do."

Shakor's two men came bursting back into the house, sweating and out of breath.

Shakor said, "And? Where is he?"

"He's gone. We don't know where. We followed him into the castle, but he disappeared. We searched it thoroughly, but we didn't find him. He managed to escape."

Shakor heard the words and became incensed. He turned back to Drago and said, "That's very bad for you. Where is he going?"

Drago recoiled into a wall and said, "I have no idea. We have a place in the old town of Split, and another place in Dubrovnik. He could be going to either."

Shakor leaned back and said, "Where is this place in Split?"

CHAPTER 38

Jennifer watched the sun drop below the buildings next to them and looked at Brett, saying, "It's getting close to hit time."

He took a drink of his Coke and said, "Yep. About time to rock and roll. You ready for this?"

She smiled and said, "Me? I think we should be worrying about you."

He put his glass down and looked at her. She glanced away and he said, "What's this about? I can climb that wall, but I'm not the best at it. Veep and Knuckles are both as good as me."

"So? I wanted you."

"Why? Everyone saw how mad I was about the last thing, even as I understood it. Is this your way of affirmative action?"

She turned her head to him with a little disgust and said, "This isn't about climbing a wall. This is about what happens after we drop."

Brett leaned back in his chair and said, "Okay, what's that mean?"

"It means that I need someone up there who understands the cost of life. The cost of killing. Shoshana told me once that she wanted you on a mission because you understood."

Brett sat forward and said, "Shoshana said that? Understood what?"

Jennifer said, "I have no idea. But Shoshana did. And does. She has a way about things. If she saw something in you, then so do I.

I didn't pick Knuckles because he's on the edge. He's looking to kill to release the pain of Carly. I didn't pick Veep because he's always deferring to me. Wanting me to make a decision that I'm not sure I can, because I also want to kill those fucks. I picked you. You and you alone. I have a whole team here to protect me, but only one who I wanted on top."

The sun dropped below the horizon, and Brett said, "Pike puts a lot of faith in you. I've never seen him defer to anyone, but he does to you. You trust me that much?"

Jennifer tossed some bills on the table and said, "Yeah, I actually do. Pike thinks you're the best thing since sliced bread. Even with your skin color."

He laughed and said, "Good to know I'm wanted."

She looked at him and said, "Shoshana can read people, but so can I. Pike is going in the front, and I'm going to be in the back. I needed someone with me that I trust. Someone who knows when to pull the trigger."

He sat back and said, "Because that's not you?"

She shook her head, like she was trying to rid herself of a thought. She looked at the waitress coming to take their bill and said, "Yeah. Because of that. I don't trust myself. But I trust you."

He looked into her eyes and slowly nodded, saying, "Okay. I'm your man."

She smiled, started to say something, and both of their phones vibrated.

In the courtyard next to the Makarun alley. Waiting on breach.

She looked up and saw Brett's face break into a smile. She said, "Looks like it's showtime."

He said, "As it should be. Let's start some climbing."

She rose and he said, "You know why I stayed on this team?"

They left the café and crossed the street into the alley. She said, "No, I didn't know you guys got a choice."

They started speed-walking down the narrow lane and he chuckled, saying, "Everything is a choice. I've been shot at more times than I can count, but all of it was a choice. I could have been a case officer in Bermuda. I chose Sudan. And then I chose this team."

They reached the back of the wall, the terrace above them, Jennifer honestly curious. She said, "So why?"

He looked at the small iron pipe leading up, the darkness closing in, and he said, "Because of you."

"Me? What's that mean?"

He looked at the wall, surveying the stone for holds, then went back to her, saying, "Because of what we just talked about. You do what's right. You always have. It's why I'm on this team. I could have done anything within the intelligence community. I came here."

Embarrassed, Jennifer said, "I don't know about that. I've had my own problems in this world."

He smiled in the fading twilight and said, "Yeah. Yeah, you have. You got my back?"

She said, "Yes, of course."

He grabbed the pipe and said, "Catch me if I fall?"

It was the same words she'd told Pike years ago right before she began a climb, the statement disconcerting. She said, "What's that mean?"

He said, "Nothing. You think I'm going to wait on a woman to catch me?"

Now doubly confused, she started to retort, and saw him smile in the gloom, showing her the inside joke.

He said, "Race you to the top," and began climbing.

She knew she couldn't beat him using the same iron gutter pipe. It's not like she could climb over him. She looked back down the alley, and then grabbed the rough-hewn stone of the wall. Within seconds, she was past him. She glanced in his direction a single time, seeing him smile, but spent the most of her focus on the holds.

There was no one to catch her if she fell.

She reached the terrace, pulled herself up just enough over the wall until she could view inside the house, and saw no threat. She knew that the lights inside would hamper anyone looking out, and lightly dropped to the floor of the terrace. Brett came over the wall right after her, saying, "Okay. You win."

She smiled and keyed her earpiece, whispering, "Squirter control in place. Cleared to breach."

Rodavan came out of the bathroom, saw Pushka behind one of the four laptop computers arrayed on the dining room table, and said, "You're still working that problem?"

"Yeah. I had to make a call on this. Branko never came back here and I can't get him on the phone."

"So you passed our gateway to that Sphinx guy?"

Staring at the screen, Pushka slowly nodded, saying, "I know that's going to piss off Branko, but I had to make a decision. In my mind it won't even matter because the countdown is fire and forget. He probably won't see it that way, though."

Rodavan came around the table, looking at Branko's computer. Lines of code were scrolling like something out of *The Matrix*. All four of the laptops were daisy-chained together via cables plugged into Thunderbolt ports. The only one standing alone was Branko's MacBook.

The screen to Pushka's right flashed an alert, and Rodavan went to it. He took one look and felt the panic flood. He said, "Someone's coming up the stairwell."

He turned the laptop to Pushka, showing three men sprinting on the stairs, guns drawn. Pushka stood up so fast his chair upended. He stared into the screen, seeing the hard faces and the intent. He said, "Time to go."

"Pack out?"

"No. Destroy."

Rodavan ran back into the bedroom, snatched up a go-bag he'd prepared, then raced to a switch on the floor, a cable leading from it to the first computer. He said, "You sure?"

Pushka, now getting his own bag, said, "Yes. Kill it."

Rodavan hit the switch and smoke started streaming from the first computer, then the second. The front door exploded inward, with three men barreling inside, and Pushka screamed, "Escape plan!"

Rodavan was trapped between the door and the terrace. He tried to run by one of the men but was caught, lifted off the ground, and slammed to the floor. Pushka made it to the terrace, panting in panic. He threw his bag over the wall, leapt on a table next to the iron gutter pipe, and was ripped off it with the force of a hurricane. He slammed into the concrete, rolled over, and found himself staring at the barrel of a gun held by a blond woman. He saw her snarl, then her finger tighten on the trigger.

He held his hands up and said, "No, no, no. Don't."

A black man appeared, touching her shoulder. She relaxed. The black man said, "You speak English?"

Pushka shook his head. The black man said, "Then what was 'No, no, don't'? And why are you shaking your head at the question if you don't understand?"

He punched Pushka in the face, bouncing his head on the concrete. He said again, "Do you speak English?"

Pushka nodded. The black man said, "Good. Let's go inside."

CHAPTER 39

I took one look at the cloistered space and knew that the minute we hit the stairwell to the safehouse we'd alert them. They weren't stupid. They were computer geniuses, after all. So I'd decided to go in hard, like a hit in Fallujah, Iraq. No subtlety, no sneaking around. Just set up squirter control to contain any escape routes, then storm the place full-on, using speed, surprise, and violence of action. Once we broke the plane of the stairwell, I'd assume we were compromised, as I did when cracking a gate in Fallujah.

I'd set things in motion, getting Brett and Jennifer in position, then Veep, Knuckles, and I sat for a little bit at an outdoor café in a courtyard adjacent to the Makarun alley waiting on the squirter team to climb the wall. I was a little bit antsy because if they had some perimeter warning out the back, we might be screwed, but I figured if they realized we were coming up the wall, they'd come running out the front. The stairwell was a choke point that would prevent escape, but it would create problems, as we'd have to take them down right here in the tunnel, with the patrons in the restaurant in full view.

Knuckles twiddled a bread knife in his hands, saying, "Full-on assault here. That's a little bold."

I chuckled and said, "Oversight Council gives us Omega. We determine how to execute. Yeah, full-on assault. We break that stairwell, and you know they're going to run."

He smiled and said, "I'm not complaining. I get a little sick of the 'snoop and poop until we get shot at' scenario. I'd rather be the ones doing the shooting from the outset."

I squinted my eyes, and he held up his hands saying, "Metaphorically speaking. I'm not going to blast away just because."

Our earpieces came alive. "Squirter control in place. Cleared to breach."

I clicked on and said, "No issues?"

"Nope. No compromise. Standing by."

I looked at Veep and Knuckles and said, "Looks like it's showtime."

I glanced around, saw nothing of concern, and went back to the net, saying, "We're on the way."

We sidled up to the tunnel entrance leading to the restaurant and the stairwell. We went down the tunnel, stopping right at the gap of the stairwell and seeing a guy sitting on the bottom steps bouncing a rubber ball. I had no idea if he was early warning, but didn't think so. If they had an alert, it would be through cameras and motion sensors, not some guy on the steps. They were sophisticated in high-tech solutions, not social ones. He was probably just some worker hanging around.

I stopped in front of the man and held out a fifty-kuna note, saying, "Go get yourself some gelato."

He smiled with rotting teeth, took the cash, and walked back up the tunnel. I turned to Veep and Knuckles saying, "Okay, it's on the third floor. Hard breach. Veep, you've got the door. Knuckles, you've got breach."

We stepped into the stairwell, getting out of sight from the restaurant courtyard, and Veep circled his backpack to the front, pulling out a small battering ram that looked like a two-foot iron telephone pole with handles at the front and back. Knuckles withdrew his suppressed Glock, looked at me, and I stacked behind Veep, bringing out my own.

I said, "Execute," and Knuckles took off up the stairwell, leading the way with his Glock, Veep right behind him, all of us running like gazelles being chased by a cheetah. We reached the door in seconds, but knew we'd already been seen, either by a proximity alert or an actual camera. Knuckles put his barrel on the door for security and Veep came from behind him, swinging the ram in a vicious arc, shattering the locks. He spun aside, dropping the ram, and Knuckles raced in, me right behind him.

Knuckles saw one man coming around a table full of computers, immediately focused on his hands, realized he was unarmed, and grabbed him by the throat, slamming him to the floor. I went right, getting around him and trying to reach another man racing with a backpack to the terrace. He made it, but I knew that would be no escape.

Veep came in, running to the bedroom. He came out, said, "It's clear," then, "The computers are smoking."

I looked at the table and saw all four of them daisy-chained together with a computer cable, the first one looking like it was melting, the second showing a great deal of smoke, and the third just starting to puff. I grabbed the fourth and jerked it off the table, separating the cord.

To Veep I said, "Close the door." He did so just as Brett came in frog-marching the man who'd fled, his face showing the start of a shiner. I recognized him from our operations on the bar terrace in Zagreb. He was the one who'd been shot.

I said, "Put them both in a chair. Veep, see if that last computer is still worth a shit."

Veep went to the table and I turned to the men, saying, "You two chuckleheads have caused a lot of problems for me and my friends."

The one from the terrace said, "We have done nothing. You are robbers. You have broken the law."

I pulled up a chair opposite them, close enough for our knees to touch, and Knuckles circled behind their backs, causing them to track him. All designed to make them feel afraid and compliant. I leaned forward and tapped Terrace Guy on the forehead with the barrel of my pistol, saying, "Don't worry about him. Look at me. I'm the one asking the questions. You'll know what he's doing when you answer wrong. You were shot in Zagreb. Now, that wasn't by our hand, but we were there."

His face went slack in shock, but he tried anyway: "I don't know anything about that!"

Knuckles smacked the back of his head, not hard, but enough to show him that he no longer held his own freedom.

I said, "That is a lie. You know it, and I know it. You lie again, there will be no love tap. Now, let's start with names."

The other man blurted out, "I'm Rodavan. I don't do anything but maintain the computers and survey for targets. He's the skill. He's who you want."

I smiled and said, "That's a good start." I turned to Terrace Guy and said, "You?"

He took a breath and let it out, then said, "Pushka. Are you from Russia?"

I said, "No, but we'll get into that in due time. First, there was a man in that bar with you. Where is he?"

Pushka's face grew cagy, and Knuckles smacked Rodavan in the back of the head. Rodavan blurted out, "Branko's in a safehouse about thirty minutes north of here, in the mountains."

"Good. Rodavan, you now know how this is going to go. Pushka lies, and you get smacked."

Rodavan looked at Pushka in fear, saying, "Just tell them what they want to know."

Pushka thought a minute, then slowly nodded, saying, "Who are you? What do you want?"

"First, I want you to give us the key for the ransomware you injected in our systems. You do that, and then we can talk about what happens to you after."

Pushka gave a stunned appearance, as if it was the last thing he expected. Knuckles rabbit-punched Rodavan in the kidney, causing him to fall out of his chair. He stood over his body with a pistol raised and Rodavan screamed.

I held up my hand, ostensibly telling him not to pull the trigger, but it was just an act. This whole thing was an act, and it worked.

Rodavan sat up and said, "It's Pushka's fault. We're Dark Star. We did it. Please don't kill me. Hurt him. He's the liar. All I do is investigate the corporations for attack."

I waved to Knuckles and he pulled him back into his seat. I said, "How did you find Blaisdell Consulting? Where did that come from?"

He rolled his eyes, looking for Knuckles, and I slammed my hand on a table, causing both of them to jump. I snarled, "Where?"

He blurted out, "Just research, man. Just research. I find the fish and Pushka is the one who hooks them."

I looked at Veep and said, "The computer?"

"It appears to be working."

"Still hooked to the Wi-Fi?"

"Yep."

I turned to Pushka and said, "I want that ransomware key, and

I want it right now. You are going to send it over the channel you asked us to use for the ransom. I have a friend on the other end who can make it happen."

He said, "I'm not authorized to do that. I'm not the payment guy. You'll have to wait on Branko to do this."

I leaned into him and pulled out a knife, flicking the blade open. "You fucking think I'm going to pay for this?" I turned to Knuckles and said, "Hold him in place." To Brett and Jennifer I said, "Hold his legs and remove his shoes."

He struggled, but in short order his nasty feet were open to the air. I said, "I'm assuming you'll have to use all five fingers to type, so I'll be taking off a toe for every second you wait."

I saw the sweat break out on his brow, and I placed the edge of the blade next to his big toe, saying, "No sense starting with the little one."

"Okay! Okay! Give me the computer."

I waved at Knuckles and Brett. They jerked his chair behind the computer while I called Creed. He answered, I put him on the line with Pushka, and they began typing together.

As he worked, I turned to Rodavan and said, "Where's Branko? The leader?"

He was now completely compliant, and because of it, I knew he wasn't going to lie to me. He said, "I have no idea. He left here this morning and went up to the safehouse. He called here on his new phone, said he was there, then chatted over the internet with Pushka. Said he was coming right back."

That perked up my interest. "New phone? He used it to call here?"

"Yes."

"Where's the phone that answered?"

He pointed to Pushka and without a word, Pushka held it up while still typing. I said, "Plug that thing into the computer. Let Creed see it as well."

He did so, and I returned Rodavan. "Why did those guys want to kill you in Zagreb? What was that about?"

Rodavan said, "I wasn't there. That was Branko and Pushka. Hell, Pushka got shot. I have no idea about that. The guy came in ranting about some sort of treasure and then shot him. It had nothing to do with this."

Pushka said, "Stop talking, man. You think this guy is going to help you? He's here to hurt you."

I heard *treasure* and made a connection. I said, "So these guys were from Afghanistan?"

"Afghanistan? Like the country?"

I saw complete confusion and figured he had nothing left to give. I turned to Pushka, saying, "Where do we stand?"

He leaned back and said, "You're good to go. Key sent. You're clear." I called Creed and he confirmed, elated, like we'd just solved the problem of world hunger.

Pushka looked at me and said, "So what's that mean for us?"

I said, "What it means is I want the leader. It's not your fault, but you guys fucked with the wrong people here. I want Branko. Where is he?"

He raised his hands and said, "I have no idea. He was supposed to return here today, but never showed. I could call him . . . see if he answers."

I said, "That's not necessary. I have his phone number now. I'll find him myself."

He said, "Who are you? Nobody can do what you say without significant resources. Are you from Andrei? Or Sphinx?"

Now intrigued, I said, "Who's Andrei?"

He turned away and said, "Nobody. Nobody!"

I said, "He's a somebody or you wouldn't have mentioned him."

Knuckles towered over Rodavan, giving him the full weight of his capacity for violence. Rodavan cowered and said, "He's our bankroll. Some Russian guy. We've never met him, but Branko has. Man, all we do is computer shit. I didn't sign up for this."

I tapped him in the head with the barrel of my pistol and said, "Who's Sphinx?"

Rodavan said, "I don't know. He's an American. He helped with the code."

Pushka said, "Rodavan! No more!"

I turned to him and said, "I'm going to get the answers one way or the other. That's a given. What's unknown now is how much pain this will cause."

Then someone knocked on the door.

CHAPTER 40

Shakor walked down the promenade outside the tourist entrance of the old town of Split and punched Drago in the back, saying, "You'd better not be lying to me."

People from all over the world spilling around them, Drago said, "He's here. I'm sure of it."

They continued until they reached the Bronze Gate of the old town, the southern one facing the Adriatic Sea, and walked through the archway. Shakor said, "Where? Where do we go?"

Drago led him past an ancient cellar, walking up a stairwell into the sunshine, passing by multiple table merchants selling local artisan products. They entered the courtyard of the city proper, walking beside buildings that were older than them both by a millennium.

Shakor looked around, saw the crowds swirling about, and said, "Where?"

Drago said, "It was farther in. Near a restaurant called Makarun."

Shakor said, "Keep going. If this is a trick, you'll be the one to lose."

Truthfully, Shakor didn't believe Drago was using subterfuge. After they'd attacked the house, and Branko had escaped, Drago had been as compliant as possible. Almost to the point of obsequiousness. But Shakor still had to keep fear in the guy, if only because he knew the man would attempt escape if given the chance.

Drago pointed right, to the Cathedral of Saint Domnius, the bell tower rising above everything else, saying, "It's this way. I recognize that."

They reached the end of the courtyard and Drago took a left into an alley, walking under an arch. He reached an intersection with alleys going in all directions and turned in a circle, unsure where to go. He looked up, saw an ancient clock behind him, and said, "This way, this way."

He went left, and within seconds the alley opened up into a broad plaza lined with cafés. Confused, he turned in another circle. Shakor's patience growing thin, he pulled Drago up short, saying, "Where are you taking us? Where is this stairwell?"

"It's here. It's here. We must have just passed it."

Shakor jabbed him with a finger and said, "Find it."

Drago said, "I'm trying, I'm trying. I didn't spend a lot of time here. I just picked it out and paid."

Drago went back down the alley and saw the tunnel leading to the restaurant. He exhaled and said, "That's it. It's a stairwell right before the entrance to the restaurant."

He led them down the tunnel and Shakor saw the courtyard to the Makarun restaurant, full of packed tables with white linen and trees. He knew that if Drago ran through into it, he'd be free. Drago stopped and Shakor grabbed his shirt, saying, "You'd better not be tricking me."

Drago pointed to a stairwell to the right and Shakor said, "That's the operational cell? Right up those steps?"

"Yeah. It's a Vrbo we found with high-speed internet. The only one around."

Shakor turned to the other men and said, "Same thing as before. These guys don't like to fight, but they do like to run. They probably have a plan of escape out of this place just like they did in the other one. We get in, show them some violence, and dominate the place. Drago, you lead. You knock on the door, get them to open it, and we'll do the rest."

Now scared, Drago said, "If they come out shooting, they'll shoot me first."

"Shooting? Do they have guns?"

Drago looked from Shakor to the other men, then hung his head, saying, "No. They have no guns."

Shakor said, "Good. You go first because they'll recognize you. That's our edge. The only thing you need to worry about is if Branko isn't there. If he is, you go free. If not, you come with us to the other safehouses you've arranged. Now get moving."

Drago hesitantly walked up the stairs, winding around the landings until he reached the top, seeing the door lock had been smashed and was slightly ajar. He pointed at it with wide eyes, and Shakor simply shook his head, indicating he should knock and call out.

Drago did, heard Rodavan answer, and calmed down. Rodavan cracked the door, saying, "We've had some issues. Where is Branko?"

Shakor slammed him in the head with his pistol, just like he'd done successfully to Drago in the safehouse earlier, then shoved his body past the threshold. He had a quick glimpse of a man behind a computer—the same one he'd shot in the leg in Zagreb— and four other people in the room. None of whom were computer geeks.

A man to his right immediately locked up the wrist holding his pistol, slamming it into the doorjamb. It went off, the bullet ricocheting from the stone and hitting the man behind the computer.

He fell out of the chair while two other men rushed forward with their own guns drawn. Drago screamed and began racing back down the stairs as Shakor's other two men bounced against him trying to get inside.

Shakor fought for his pistol only to have his elbow torqued in a joint lock, the pistol falling to the ground. The man swung in a tight circle, using the joint lock of Shakor's wrist and elbow to force him to follow or else have his joints splinter. He felt the pain and screamed, diving in the air to try to relieve the pain. Just before it shattered, his attacker released him, flinging him against the two men trying to enter and throwing all of them back into the stairwell.

Shakor felt his head smack stone, untangled himself from his own men, and looked back at the doorway. He saw two men with pistols drawn staring down at him, but so far they hadn't fired.

He said, "Back! Go back!"

He and his men rolled and stumbled down the stairwell, spilling in a heap into the tunnel of the restaurant, the patrons in the court-yard noticing their arrival. Shakor gave a split-second thought about charging back up, but knew that was a dead end. With them holding the door frame and the high ground, they'd be killed quickly. He'd learned that lesson long ago in Afghanistan.

He said, "Hide your weapons. Let's get out of here. Where's Drago?"

The three other men looked left and right, like it was the first time they realized he was missing. Din said, "He ran past us when we tried to enter the room."

Ghulam said, "He escaped."

Shakor saw the crowds staring and said, "Let's go. Get back to the main area."

They returned to the intersection by the clock and Shakor held up, searching behind them. Nobody was coming for them. He said, "Okay, Drago's trying to get out of the city. He's our last link to Branko."

"But what about that room? He might be in it."

"He's not. There were only two like him in that room, both captured. One I'd shot before and another I haven't seen. Branko wasn't there. Let's go back to the courtyard with the cathedral at the south gate. By the way he led us in, he's not familiar with this city, and he'll return to an area he knows."

They began jogging that way, their heads on a swivel, when Ghulam said, "What about the other men upstairs? They might be the killers from Zagreb. Maybe we need to focus on them."

"No, not unless they want a fight. They still don't know who we are. If they did, they would have killed us in the stairwell. They chose not to shoot because they're in that room on other business, and they don't want trouble any more than we do. They're not after the treasure. Our priority is to find Drago. He is the key because he knows all the safehouses Branko will run to."

They threaded through the cobblestones, searching left and right for any sign of their quarry, but eventually reached the stairwell leading down to the south gate having seen no sign of Drago. Shakor wasn't surprised. The entire city was a rat maze of alleys and he could have been hiding in a dumpster right next to them, waiting to slink out after darkness fell, but Shakor didn't think so. The guy was panicking, which meant he wouldn't be thinking two steps ahead. Shakor was sure he was trying to escape the gates of the old town as fast as his treasonous legs could take him.

They went down the stairs to the merchants underground, milling through the tourists, but didn't see him. Maybe they'd beat him to the gate. Or maybe he'd simply run blindly until he found another gate, which meant he was long gone.

He was mulling over options when Din pointed first left, then right, saying, "Cellar tours. Apparently they filmed that *Game of Thrones* show here as well. It's a hidden maze of rooms underneath the city."

Shakor said, "Why on earth would he run into those when the gate is right here?"

"Because he thinks we're on the street outside, where the vehicles are allowed to run."

"Then why come here at all? He could have hidden in any number of alleys."

"Because he wants to be close to the gate. Maybe he's just going to kill off time until he feels safe."

Shakor said, "That's just stupid. He'd have to be an idiot to do that."

Ghulam said, "He is, in fact, an idiot. And it can't hurt to look. We have nothing else."

Shakor thought, *Maybe he did. Maybe he's watching us right now. Ghulam's right. Can't hurt to try to flush him out.*

He saw an entrance on the left and an exit on the right, the dungeon making a circle for the tourists underneath the city itself. He said, "Okay, Ghulam and I will buy two tickets. Din and Karim stay out here, one at the entrance, and one at the exit."

They nodded and split up. Ghulam came back with the tickets and a map, and Shakor led the way, walking past the tourists into a deep underground room that smelled of time and mold. Shakor looked at the map and saw it was but one room of many, the cellar sprawling out underneath the old town above.

He motioned to Ghulam and began exploring one chamber after another.

He was surprised to find that there really wasn't anything to see other than the rooms themselves, stone floors damp with seawater and unadorned walls. They made quick work of each area, not spending the normal time tourists did reading the plaques and iconography in the chambers. All they did was study the people. They'd made it about two-thirds through when he saw sunlight to his right—something different than the moldy, wet rooms they'd searched before.

He followed the light, crouching down and walking through a small portal in the stone, finding himself in a courtyard right next to the walls of the city, the roof of this section long gone, and the original exits blocked by iron doors with signs saying "no farther" in about fourteen languages. He looked up and saw Drago hanging from a layer of brick, desperately trying to get over the wall to the modern city beyond.

He smiled and said, "Watch the entrance to this courtyard. Don't let anyone come in." Ghulam nodded and went to the small portal with his pistol, then saw an orange cone with a sign in Croatian. He placed it in front of the portal, assuming it said, "Closed." Or "Cleaning in progress." Or something that meant *do not enter.*

Shakor went below the wall Drago was on and said, "Come down here."

Drago saw him for the first time and began to panic, scrabbling up the bars of a window to get over the top. Shakor fired one round next to his fist, causing it to release. He hung by a single hand wrapped in the bars and Shakor said, "Next one will be in your body."

Drago let go, dropping in a heap at Shakor's feet. He rubbed his elbow, shook his head, then looked up, resigned to his fate. He said, "I suppose you'll kill me now."

"Oh, no. You have much more information to give me. This safehouse didn't work out, but there are others. Where would Branko go if not here?"

CHAPTER 41

The room was vividly quiet, the front door still open. Veep said, "What the hell just happened?" I looked at Knuckles and Brett in the doorway, still with their pistols out, and they were just as confused as I was. I said, "Anyone hit? Everyone okay?"

I got an okay from the team, then Jennifer said, "Pushka's down." Brett, our medic, ran to him. I said, "Close the door. Veep, get on Rodavan. He moves, drop him. Knuckles, stay on the front."

I went to Pushka's body, seeing Brett working on him, but knew it would do no good. He'd been hit right above the heart, through the lung. His breath was making frothy red bubbles and his eyes were glazed. Brett did what he could, rolling him to check for an exit wound and finding none. He flipped him back over and ripped open his shirt, exposing the entrance wound and the blood coming from it. He slapped his hand over the top of it and said, "His lung is punctured, and it's sucking. He doesn't have long."

I crouched down next to Pushka's head and opened his airway, clearing his tongue from the back of his esophagus, doing what I could to get life-breathing oxygen to his brain. Brett looked around the room, seeing Jennifer at the kitchen island. He shouted, "Jennifer, find some ziplocks or cellophane."

She began ripping through drawers, then came running back with a gallon plastic freezer bag. He tore it in half and slapped it over the wound, yelling at me to hold the seal. I tried, my hands slipping in the blood, pressing to get his lung to reinflate. Brett fought the slippery bag himself and said, "This is like putting a Band-Aid on an amputation. That bullet hit something big next to his heart. He's bleeding out."

And like that, he died. I was over his head, pressing down on the freezer bag, and saw his eyes go slack in that way I've seen too many times. He gave me a last rattling breath right into my face, and then his lungs quit working to get air. His heart stopped. And his soul fled his body.

I looked at Brett, and he shook his head.

I raised my hands, now coated in Pushka's blood. I unconsciously shook them, like I was wringing out some nastiness I didn't want, then stood up, holding them in the air like a surgeon about to save someone's life instead of one who'd just killed.

I went to the sink and said, "Knuckles, get Creed on the line. Brett, get cleaned up. Veep, stay on Rodavan. Jennifer, go downstairs and see if we have a threat coming."

They all started moving, except Jennifer. She came my way, saying, "You okay?"

"Okay? I just had a detainee killed under my control. I could have prevented that. I didn't."

"You did what you could."

She watched the red running down the sink and I said, "I know. Doesn't make his death any better."

She looked at the team running around the room doing what I commanded and said, "You know, at the end of the day it's a lot easier being the clown than the guy in charge of the circus."

I gave a stilted laugh and said, "Go make sure we aren't compromised."

She turned to leave and I said, "Jennifer."

She turned back around, and I said, "I appreciate it. Thank you."

She smiled and left the building.

I dried my hands and said, "Knuckles, you got Creed?"

A phone to his ear, he nodded and said, "Right here."

He handed me the phone and I saw Pushka's eyes still staring at the ceiling. Brett came out of the bathroom, and I took the phone, saying, "Brett, cover that guy."

He nodded, knowing exactly what I meant.

I put the phone to my ear and said, "Creed, are we good?"

"Yeah, we are. I don't know how you did it, but we're clean, like it never even happened. The only issue now is that they might have our data somewhere."

I looked at the table of smoking computers and said, "I don't think that's going to be a problem. It looks like all of their hardware is melted, and these guys don't use the cloud. If it's somewhere else, we'll have to deal with it just like we did here."

He replied with a little excitement, saying, "Man, I don't know how you always pull this out. You're a miracle worker. That commando shit is pure gold."

I saw Brett putting a jacket over Pushka's face and bit back my initial response, saying, "Are you back up and running?"

"Not completely. It'll take probably a day to get the systems here going again."

"What about that phone we just sent you? Can you get anything out of it?"

"I have the data, but I can't do anything yet. Why?"

"Because it's tied to the leader of this whole enterprise."

"Give me a day to get the systems back and operational."

"Okay. Okay. Is Wolffe there?"

"Stand by."

On the floor, Rodavan said, "What are you going to do with me?"

I said, "I honestly don't know. Maybe you'll end up like your buddy here. Maybe not."

I then realized he had heard everything I said on the phone. Up until this point, it was something he already knew, but the next part of my conversation would be with my command. I said, "Veep, take him to the bathroom, close the door, and turn on the shower."

Veep nodded and told Rodavan to stand. He led him to the back of the Vrbo and closed the bedroom door. I didn't have noise-canceling earphones, but the bathroom should do.

Wolffe came on the phone and said, "Pike, thank you for the work. The Oversight Council will be kissing your ass. I don't want to sound like I'm unappreciative, but I have a live operation going on in Dubai right now. What do you need?"

I have to admit, I was a little bit miffed that I wasn't the only game in town. Although I was sure with this operation, I was the only game that mattered.

I said, "How is that working out? Now that you have control of our computer assets? Is it going okay?"

He laughed and said, "Okay, Pike, touché. What do you need from me?"

"I have one guy dead and another alive. What do you want me to do with the breathing one?"

I heard him inhale, then, "You have a dead guy? Pike, I told you this wasn't sanctioned as DOA. No killing."

"I didn't kill him. We were attacked after we'd locked down the place. Our entry was clean. We were clean. But he's dead nonetheless. It was the same assholes from Zagreb. I'm sure of it."

"You got attacked after you locked the place down?"

"Yeah. Same guys. They aren't from Turkey. They're from Afghanistan."

"Wait, wait. The guy killed in Zagreb had a Turkish passport. How are you making this leap of logic?"

"Remember I told you about the two teams running around? One was after Jahn, the other was after the treasure that was stolen. These ransomware guys have something to do with the Bactrian Treasure, and those assholes from the Badr Battalion are still hunting it. I think they're looking for the leader of this whole gang. Branko."

He said nothing for a moment, then said, "You have a live guy and a dead guy?"

"Yes."

"Let the live guy go. Give him the fear of God about doing ransomware again, and let him go. Let him spread the word that our reach is great and their business model has changed. It's no longer just losing money from the FBI stealing their bitcoin. It's now life or death."

I heard that and thought it was stupid. I said, "You want me to let him go? How about we bring him back to the United States and wring him out? Then go after everyone else he knows?"

He said, "That's not from me. That's from POTUS. He wants to send a signal, and he might be right about that. Do what I'm asking. Scare the shit out of him, then let him go."

I said, "Okay. I can do that, but these guys were working for a Russian. I don't think we'll be putting the fear of God in him."

"He can't do anything if he doesn't have people willing to risk their lives. That's the point. That's precisely the point. Sanctioning the Russians doing this stuff hasn't worked. POTUS wants to send a signal to the men working the keyboards."

Which actually made a little bit of sense. I said, "What about the leader of this whole gang? You want me to hunt him?"

"No. We're clear of the ransomware. Let the leader hear about it and wonder if we're hunting him. He won't start up again after this hit."

"And the Afghans running around? What about them?"

"Whatever they're doing has nothing to do with U.S. national security. They want to hunt a treasure and kill that guy in the process, fine by me."

"Maybe we should ask the old Afghan national security advisor about that. See what he thinks."

I heard Wolffe sigh, then "Pike, he's dead. Assassinated in Switzerland."

I wanted to throw the phone into the wall. I shouted, "He's dead? After I told you guys he was under threat? Seriously? The guys that were shooting at me tonight were the ones who did it, and you want me to let that go?"

"Pike, we don't make policy. We are the instrument of policy. Don't go there. You were right, but honestly, there was nothing we could have done differently."

"Bullshit. There was plenty we could have done differently. Just look at Afghanistan right now. Don't give me some political crap."

"Pike, I hear you. Now you hear me: Put the fear of God in that guy and let him go, then you pack up and come home. You stopped the ransomware and you saved Jahn and his niece. Call it a win."

Anyone else, and I would have told him to go fuck himself, but George Wolffe had seen the beast from the inside out, and I believed in him. Something he knew. Sometimes you just had to swallow the sour milk, knowing another fresh quart was coming.

I said, "Okay, sir. I'll execute. But this is really not the right thing here. Those bastards deserve to die."

He said, "I know, I know. I'm sorry."

I hung up and said, "Tell Veep to get that guy back out here."

Knuckles said, "What are we doing?"

"Scaring the shit out of him, then letting him go. You want to play bad cop?"

He said, "Oh, yeah. I'm good at that."

CHAPTER 42

Branko saw a man giving him a little bit more attention than he felt he deserved, making him skittish. He left his seat in the main room of the ferry and went outside, going up to the top deck. The wind began whipping as he climbed the stairs, threatening to blow off the ballcap he was wearing. He clamped it on his head and glanced behind him, seeing nobody. He walked to the outside bar on the aft of the ship and bought a large Heineken, then continued to the very back of the boat, the sun warm against his face, seeing the blue water churned up by the propellers. He glanced behind him, but saw nobody paying him any attention, and took a long pull of the beer.

Last night had been trying, to say the least. He'd managed to flee from the men chasing him by dropping through the ancient secret entrance to Klis Fortress, but the fall had left him bruised. He'd tumbled down the hill and then had flagged a car on the lower road, claiming some calamity that the people in the car seemed to believe. The driver had taken him to the city proper and dropped him off just outside the ferry terminal. He'd had nowhere to stay, and thought about going to the operational cell like he had the day before, but didn't dare. If they'd found him in the hills, they most assuredly knew about the house in the old town.

He'd bought a ticket on the ferry to Korcula, and then had spent the night inside the ferry station, lounging on chairs like dozens of other patrons, only snapping awake whenever someone new entered the area. At six in the morning the ferry had boarded, and he'd walked aboard mixed in with every other person doing a day job on the island. He'd been convinced that they'd followed him even here, his eyes darting left and right looking for swarthy men—but he really had no idea who "they" were. The entire event was disconcerting, not the least because he had no allies to help him. He was being hunted by predators and had no idea why.

He took another pull of his beer, keeping a wary eye on the people around him, and then felt his phone vibrate with a call. He pulled it out of his pocket, didn't recognize the number, and thought about just shunting it to voice mail. He didn't.

"Hello?"

"This is Nikita. Where are you?"

Branko felt relief and trepidation at the same time. He said, "I'm on a ferry to Korcula. They attacked our safehouse. I barely made it out alive."

"The box?"

"It's safe. I didn't have it there. It's safe, I promise."

"I need more than your word. Make no mistake, I'm here to protect you, but only because of what's in that box. If it's gone, I'll kill you myself."

"Nikita, it's well hidden, but the next attack is in play. Andrei needs to know that. Pushka put it operational with Sphinx before I was attacked, and I can't get in touch with him. I'm on the run and there will be no way for them to turn it off without me. No payment, no relief. And it's a big one."

"I don't give a shit about any ransomware. Where are you going?"

"I told you. I have an apartment in Korcula. I'm going there. I needed to get out of Split because everyone is trying to kill me. I don't know who they are, but they keep talking about a treasure. First in Zagreb, now here. I've lost control of my ransomware cell. Pushka is still there as far as I know. He won't answer his phone, but he embedded the next attack."

"This attack is happening now?"

"No. It's on a timer. He talked to Sphinx—the guy who gave us the code. I never got a chance to confirm because someone was trying to kill me."

"Honestly, I don't care. I have my orders. I'm here for one thing: the treasure. When does your ferry dock?"

"Wait, what? *You* said treasure now. That box is full of diamonds or something?"

Nikita said, "Shut the fuck up and answer my question. When does the ferry dock?"

Branko smiled, knowing Nikita had just slipped up. He said, "Another hour or so. But that attack is going to trigger soon, and I have no way to turn it off."

"Don't worry about that. Get in the apartment and hunker down. I'll give you contact information to break free of the men chasing you. And then you'll take me to the box."

"I don't think you're listening to me. This attack is going to make worldwide news. Andrei needs to know, because when it hits, it's going to cause America to go nuts."

"Not my problem. Get to the apartment and bed down. I'll see you tomorrow."

CHAPTER 43

G ordon Dillard paced about behind the Auriga launch control crew like a nervous father waiting on a birth. As the NASA lead for the launch, he had some sway, but ultimately, he had no ability to alter anything the company was doing. Auriga had rented the space and paid for the launch. It was the first such lift-off the United States had ever done. A solely civilian crew headed to the International Space Station.

To be sure, the Russians had been doing such a thing for years, with various oligarchs paying to head to the space station as tourists, and other U.S. billionaires had launched people into space only to fall right back to earth, but the United States had never sanctioned a civilian flight to the space station—and even when the Russians did it, it was the Russian equivalent of NASA doing the launch. Not an entirely civilian company. Today was a first of firsts. While they'd be using NASA's launch facilities, nobody from NASA was in charge. It was completely in the hands of the company, which was both good and bad. Good, in that NASA wouldn't be blamed if something went wrong, but bad in that NASA couldn't seem to duplicate what the private sector did. They were losing their luster as the preeminent space agency, becoming nothing more than a facilitator of the launches. It aggravated Gordon, not the least because NASA's chosen successor was Boeing, and they'd had three failed launches in the time that Auriga had managed to not only test, but actually resupply the space station and send up astronauts.

He went to one of the screens, seeing the giant rocket stationed on launch complex 39 of the Kennedy Space Center. The same launchpad the *Challenger* used, NASA's first attempt to put civilians in space.

Gordon remembered that day vividly, the disaster burned into his brain, but today wasn't the same. Auriga's rocket systems had traveled to the space station multiple times, all successfully. Today should be routine, even if the entire crew were a bunch of dilettantes paying their way into space. It amazed him that they thought money could buy them safety, as if the schoolteacher in 1986 would have lived if she had been rich enough.

It was a cloudless morning, with little wind. At 1107 the countdown began, and he held his breath, praying for a successful launch. The number hit zero and thousands of pounds of thrust blasted out of the vectors of the rocket. It slowly rose into the air, gaining speed as the arms holding it swung away. Within seconds it was hypersonic, traveling into space at five times the speed of sound.

The rocket reached the outer atmosphere, and the second stage broke free, just as it was supposed to do. The Auriga crew cheered, all sitting behind desktop computers—a far cry from the original launch control facilities of the Johnson Space Center. Gordon wasn't as old as the Apollo series of launches, but he could still remember when the computers were custom made for space travel, not Windows machines with extra RAM. It was definitely a new world.

The second stage fell away, now on its return to earth as a reusable rocket, and the first stage with the capsule began flying into position for its first orbit around the earth. All as planned.

Unlike every single other NASA launch in the past, this one

was completely executed by the ground teams. The men inside the capsule had no control over how or when they would dock with the space station—and truthfully they had no reason to. The rocket had docked with mundane supplies for the space station several times in the past. No human had been inside, and it had worked flawlessly. But Gordon had worked the Boeing launches when the only thing that had screwed up docking was that the computer on board had somehow decided it was twelve hours in front of the current time, and then had decided on drastic measures to realign itself where it should be twelve hours later.

Boeing had to abort, the launch a failure, something that Gordon was sure could have been fixed had there been a human on board with the ability to correct. He'd learned about Neil Armstrong and his extraordinary override flying to the surface of the moon, and knew if it had only been computers on that landing, it would have failed.

Sometime later, the flight lead said, "Starting first orbit. All systems go."

Gordon knew the capsule would slingshot around the earth for two and a half days before attempting to dock on the space station, something that was part of the "experience package" the space tourists were paying for. After that, they'd spend five days on the International Space Station—probably aggravating the real astronauts on board—before returning to earth.

He looked at his watch, saw it was past noon, and decided to leave them to it to get some lunch.

He went over to the flight lead, congratulated him on the launch, then said, "Gravy from here, right?"

"Yeah. Hard part's over. We'll dock just like we've done a dozen times before."

"Hey, just between us, you ever think about the waste of time it is to launch those civilians? I mean, a senator up for reelection, a billionaire, and another schoolteacher? What are they going to do when they get to the station besides get in the way?"

The flight lead laughed and said, "It makes great press, and because of it, great money. That's why the owner is on board."

Just then a flight engineer at the end of the room shouted, his hands in the air, staring at his screen. Like dominoes, one after another technician began shouting, all of them waving their hands as if it would stop the destruction.

Gordon looked at the flight lead's computer and saw a laughing skull. He was pretty sure that wasn't from the company.

In flight aboard Air Force One, President Hannister received a flash override message: The celebrated launch between private industry and NASA government systems had been hijacked. The computers were corrupted with ransomware and the ship was going to crash unless the systems were cleaned.

Meaning paying the ransom.

President Hannister read the message, then stood up, shaking in rage. He said, "Is it Russia? Did they do this because we're not using their Soyuz spacecraft anymore? Tell me it wasn't them, because if it is, we're going to war."

The man who brought the message said, "It's not Russia. The intelligence community has already looked, and we know the group. They have ties to Russia, but they're just criminals. No geopolitical stuff at all. They found an ability to penetrate Auriga and took it. We have about sixty hours before that spacecraft slams into the space station. It's operating on its last instructions, and we can't feed it any more unless the system gets cleaned."

"Can't the astronaut inside take over?"

"No. It's all automated. He can't do anything but ride at this point. He has the ability to emergency-abort the entire trip on board, but apparently that's been corrupted as well. Auriga is in contact with the capsule over radio, and the lone astronaut on board is stating that the computer is refusing his commands, like HAL in *2001: A Space Odyssey.*"

"Just great. Who the hell are these guys that did it? Do we know?"

"A group called Dark Star. They've been hacking companies for a couple of years, but it's always been small-time attacks. They've never attacked a government system."

Hannister looked at him and said, "Dark Star? Is that what you said?"

"Yes, sir. We have a dossier if you want to see it."

"I don't need it. Tell Alexander Palmer to come in."

Palmer entered, rubbing his face from sleep and saying, "What's the crisis of the day?"

Palmer saw the president's expression and said, "What is it?"

"Get George Wolffe on the phone. I want Pike Logan operational right now."

CHAPTER 44

I was all set to head up to the outdoor swimming pool for dinner and a beer, one more successful mission under my belt, when my phone dinged with the tone reserved for the Taskforce. I checked the message and saw a command to connect via our encrypted VPN.

Jennifer came out of the bathroom wearing a robe over a swimsuit, saying, "Do they have pool towels, or do we take our own?"

I showed her the phone and said, "I don't think I'm going to the pool."

We'd spent most of the night executing the mission as commanded, completing the search of the apartment and putting the fear of God in Rodavan. We'd let him go and then had exfilled the crisis site, returning to the Radisson Blu hotel on the outskirts of town just as dawn was arriving. I'd told everyone to get some rack time, then sent a detailed SITREP of the mission back to the Taskforce. It had hit their servers at midnight their time, but that was over twelve hours ago. It was just after one o'clock in DC now, and Wolffe would have read that thing as soon as he showed up to work, so while I hoped mightily, I didn't think this had anything to do with the report.

This was something else.

I said, "Why don't you head on up with the rest of the guys. I'll take this and meet you when it's over, but you'd better lay off the rum and Cokes just in case."

She laughed and said, "No way. I'm not leaving until I see what the call is about. But the pool bar closes in two hours. Just sayin'."

I turned on my laptop and started the intricate authentication dance for our Taskforce encryption, saying, "Well, if you're staying, don't get on camera. The last thing I need is Wolffe questioning me on why you're running around in a bikini and a bathrobe."

She grinned and I saw the link beginning to do its handshake, showing me our systems were up and running again. I said, "Do me a favor and let the team know what I said about the alcohol, in case this is some emergency."

She nodded, and the screen cleared, showing me Blaine Alexander. I said, "Hey, sir. What's up? Did you not get the SITREP?"

He said, "We did. Stand by for George Wolffe."

Which was a little ominous. I was hoping I'd just forgotten to cross a *t* or dot an *i* in the situation report. Maybe get a question or two, then relax by the pool with the team.

Wolffe sat down behind the computer and said, "Read the SITREP. You guys are clean?"

"Yes, sir. No drama on exfil, and I think we sent the message POTUS wanted."

"Well, that message clearly didn't get through. Dark Star has hit again, only this time they're attacking the Auriga space company."

"So what's that mean for us? I let Rodavan go, and Pushka, the guy who does the actual penetrations, is dead. Let them sort it out on their own. Is President Hannister really going to start using us in a game of Whac-A-Mole every time someone is hit with ransomware?"

"It's a little bit worse than that. They didn't penetrate corporate headquarters. They hit the launch systems for a spacecraft—after the thing had left earth."

"You mean that civilian launch this afternoon? Well, I guess morning for you guys? It was on the television a couple of hours ago."

"That's the one. It's going to be catastrophic if we can't fix those computers, and the problem we have is that we just hit the very people who would be collecting the ransom. The ones who *could* fix it. In other words, there's nobody to pay now, and we need to stop it the hard way."

"Can't you tell the Maverick inside the capsule to start doing some pilot shit? Abort the flight and come back home?"

"No. The geniuses at Auriga tied everything into their launch facility. Without those computers, the thing is just free-flying without any commands."

"I find that hard to believe. Surely someone can do something."

"Well, believe it. The spacecraft they're using has been to the International Space Station a half dozen times, but fully half of those were unmanned—meaning they were controlled from the ground. They had backups to the backups, but every single one of those systems has been hit, just like all the Blaisdell Consulting connections. The astronaut on board had the ability to abort, but apparently that's also been corrupted. They're trying to rebuild the infrastructure as we speak, but it's literally like trying to build an aircraft while it's flying."

"How'd they do it? I mean, how did this happen after we took out the cell?"

"We don't know how they penetrated, because Auriga has a pretty robust protective infrastructure, but they managed to do it.

Apparently on some sort of time-delay Trojan horse. I think Blaisdell Consulting was a test, and Dark Star invaded Auriga's systems on a time delay, based on the launch. Auriga systems would have been on high alert the day of the launch, but not so much before. And then we destroyed the cell that did it before it initiated."

"How much time do we have?"

"They'll be orbiting two and a half days, apparently just sightseeing, then the capsule will attempt to execute its last commands and line up for docking, but that's the last thing it knows. Without the ability to control it, it's going to fly into the space station at Mach five or six, killing everyone on it, including the people in the capsule."

"I'm not a rocket scientist, but can't you move the space station? Let those guys in the capsule miss it and just go off into space?"

"Maybe. I don't know, but that's not the answer President Hannister wants to hear. It's a little coldblooded, even for you."

"Well, it's the price you pay for space tourism. A little karmic justice if you ask me."

Wolffe chuckled, then said, "I'd agree with most of the people on board, but one is just a teacher from Arkansas. The owner gave her a seat. She isn't rich and certainly didn't ask for this."

That made me feel a little slimy. He was right. She didn't deserve any of this. He asked, "Can you get to Rodavan again?"

"No. That guy is probably out of the country by now, and anyway, he doesn't do the penetrations. Pushka did that. Pushka handled the keys for the ransomware encryption, and he's dead."

Then a thought occurred to me. "Hey, did you try the key we got from Pushka last night? The one that unlocked our computers?"

Wolffe sighed and said, "Yeah, we did. It didn't work. It's a new key, and without someone who knows how it was created, we're dead in the water."

I said, "Branko is the keymaster, and the leader of this whole thing. We have their last functioning computer here with us. If I get his ass behind the keyboard, he can remove the ransomware."

"That's more like it. Do you know where he is? We only have about two days to solve this. Maybe a little more, but that's cutting it close. They're making those orbits of the earth because they paid for the flight and want the full monty."

"I don't know where he is, but Creed can find him. Are we back up and operational?"

"Yes. All of our systems are now working. How will Creed know?"

"Branko bought a new smartphone and called Pushka on it. Creed has the information. Get me a geolocation of that phone and I'll go hunt his ass. His last known location was here, in Split. Might be easy."

Wolffe gave some commands to Blaine, and I saw Blaine leave the room. Wolffe returned to the screen and said, "This is all being kept under wraps for now, but it's going to get out. They had so much publicity for this launch that someone's going to leak, and the end state isn't going to be good. The first commercial United States space launch ends up destroying the International Space Station, killing all aboard, to include three Russians, three Americans, and a Japanese scientist? And that's not even talking about the dilettantes who paid a fortune for this tourist trip in the capsule. Everybody is shitting bricks on this one. We need to find that guy."

"What about putting him in Interpol? Put the word out and just get him arrested."

"That would mean telling the world we couldn't protect our own space systems. It's something we might end up doing, especially if it leaks, but right now, that's not an option. President Hannister wants him taken down quietly, and he has some obscene faith in you. Especially after you solved the Blaisdell Consulting problem. Your team is the closest to this issue."

I said, "Speaking of that, this whole cell is fronted by a Russian named Andrei, and there's some guy named Sphinx who gave them the code to penetrate our systems. He's an American."

"Any idea who he is?"

"None. I didn't get a chance to finish the interrogation because we were attacked by those damn Afghans. Rodavan didn't know who Sphinx was, and Pushka was dead. But that Russian should be someone we could find because we have a real name instead of a code word."

"Can he help stop this, or is he just the payroll? We don't have time to mess around."

I thought about that, and realized he was right. Getting the Russian would only be a linkage to finding Branko, the only guy who could stop this, and thus would be wasting time. I could find Branko without him.

I said, "Good point. I need Branko's location."

Blaine returned and said, "Creed's got a geolocation. It's in a town called Korcula. He has the bed-down location."

Wolffe said, "That mean anything to you?"

"Yeah, it's an island south of here. The quickest way to get there is by ferry out of Split, but we've missed all the ferries for today." I looked at my watch and said, "I could drive to Orebic and try to catch the ferry there—they run a lot later—but I'm not sure I'd even make that one."

"Can't you fly there?"

"No airports. The closest one is right here in Split, where the Rock Star bird is sitting right now. People fly into Split and then take the ferry."

"Looks like you're driving. I'll send you the information. Get on it."

"So I'm not going to get a meal and a beer by the pool after a shoot-out and saving Blaisdell Consulting from compromise? Story of my life."

"You get this guy and I'll buy the beer."

I said, "Will do." I disconnected and found that Jennifer had changed back into her operational clothes, her bag by the door, having known where this was headed.

She said, "Saddle up?"

I sighed and said, "Yep. Get the team ready to move. I want to leave in twenty minutes."

She pulled out her phone and I leaned back in the chair, saying, "One of these days, I'm going to get to use the hotel pool."

CHAPTER 45

Dylan Hobbes sat on a bench in the entranceway of the West Wing, his "visitor/escort required" badge around his neck, feeling the sweat start to pour out from under his arms and the back of his neck, an uncontrollable stream he hated but could not control.

He was horrible at this game, and always had been, even with his time in the Tailored Access Organization of the NSA. Certain men did the actual reconnaissance pretending to be telephone repairmen or something else, but that wasn't him. He was the technical component, and knew that anyone who looked at him pretending to be something he wasn't would suspect him and his anxiety immediately. But he knew he had to put on a performance here. Pretend the news he was about to learn was a complete surprise.

Alexander Palmer approached and said, "Sorry to call you back in, but you're the only expertise that's been read on to this specific problem set. Follow me."

He started walking, Hobbes behind him saying, "What is it? Is it Dark Star again? So soon? I thought you stopped them?"

Palmer turned around as he walked, saying, "So did we, but we have an issue. Let's wait until we get inside the Oval."

Hobbes nodded and Palmer did a little bit of a double take, saying, "You okay? You don't look that great."

Hobbes mopped his brow and said, "Yes, yes, I'm fine. I just sweat a lot."

"Okay, no issues." He opened the door to the Oval Office and announced Hobbes's arrival. Hobbes entered and found the same four people around the table from the meeting the day before. The president, the secretary of defense, the director of the CIA, and the man he knew as George Wolffe.

He hesitated, not sure what to do, and President Hannister said, "Come grab a seat. I'm sure this call comes as a bit of a shock."

He said, "Yes, sir, it did. As I understood it, you'd found the cell who'd hacked your computers and had solved the ransomware problem. I'm sorry I was little help."

Yesterday, before his Trojan horse had triggered, he'd had one final meeting with those whom he called the "Secret Squirrels." He still didn't know what the men George Wolffe represented did, but after TAO, he knew it was something beyond the scope of top secret. To his delight, he'd found out the man who worked his code had been killed, and the other was no threat. He'd left, knowing his attack on Auriga would work, mainly because there was nobody to stop it now.

Well, almost nobody. There was still Branko, but Hobbes was pretty sure he was in the wind and on the run.

President Hannister said, "I hope you kept working on the encryption scheme, because we have another problem. You do that, right? As a part of your business?"

"Yes, sir, of course. My company has a database of over two dozen different ransomware codes, most just variations of Fancy Bear or some other encryption attack, but we haven't gotten anywhere with the Dark Star code. It's something new. What's going on? I thought the cell was destroyed."

President Hannister said, "So did we." He went through the Auriga launch and the current problems, ending with, "They're telling us we have about sixty hours. That's it."

Hobbes hoped his shocked face was suitably authentic. "This just happened? After the cell was taken down?"

"Yes. We're still trying to figure out how, after we took out the primary cell."

Hobbes realized now was the time to plant the seed. The destruction he wanted was designed to galvanize the nation against a common foe, and a simple bunch of criminals wouldn't suffice. He said, "Are you sure it's the same Dark Star and not someone stealing their name to deflect? After all, they've publicly said they wouldn't ever attack something involving life support, like a hospital or power plant, and this is most definitely a life support risk."

"No, we're not sure. We do know that the key we used for our systems did not work, which leans into your theory. That's why you're here. We want you to take a look at this new code like you did for the last one."

Hobbes, of course, did not say the code was running on his computer in his laboratory right this minute, or that he'd made sure that Pushka had changed the key precisely to prevent them from overriding the system from their other operation. He'd been tracking the attack since it had initiated, and he could turn it off in less time than this meeting took.

"Sir, yes, I can do that, but I'm telling you, this is a nation-state. No criminal gang would take such a high risk. This is an enemy of the United States flexing their muscles. I saw it all the time when I worked at the NSA and Cyber Command."

President Hannister nodded and said, "We're looking into

that, which is why we want you to take a look at the code. Find us an origination point—and crack it if you can."

"I'll give it my best shot, but the timeline is not conducive to success. I'm just being honest here, but it typically takes my crew about two weeks to a month to crack a code. A single day is asking for too much. Why not just pay the ransom?"

Kerry Bostwick, the director of the CIA, said, "We tried. Nobody's answering on the other end. The procedures they sent don't go anywhere anymore—which is why I think it's the same crew. We short-circuited their ability to operate, and now we have nobody to pay."

Hobbes nodded, thinking, *That won't do*. He said, "Perhaps, or perhaps it's because they don't really care about a ransom. Maybe it's like I said: a nation-state bent on an attack."

Nobody said anything to that, and he continued: "At least within a day I can give you an assessment of the origination, even if I can't crack it. That might help."

He hadn't really decided whom he would pin the attack on yet. The most likely candidates were Iran and North Korea, both with robust hacking abilities, and both having used those skills against the United States.

Hannister said, "Evidence of a perpetrator with an origin point will help with the retaliation, but it's not going to do anything to prevent a catastrophe."

Hobbes liked those words. It would be just as he envisioned—a combination of the *Challenger* disaster and 9/11. And reunification of the United States' national purpose.

CHAPTER 46

B ranko was awakened at the crack of dawn by his phone bleat-
ing. He picked it up and saw a text from Nikita, complete
with a map as an attachment picture.

Get up and meet me here. Follow the route I sent.

He rubbed his eyes, then texted, I just woke up.

I don't give a shit. Get moving. Before the sun rises and people
start coming out.
    Okay, okay, let me get cleaned up and I'll be on the way.
Be here in thirty minutes. And don't deviate from that route.

Branko dropped the phone, a little aggravated that he had to
put up with Nikita's commands. But also a little scared.

He decided he'd take his sweet time showering and packing
what little he had, mainly because the room he was in was out-
rageously expensive and opulent, and he hadn't had any time to
really enjoy it.

Called the "China Room," it was on the third floor of a boutique apartment/hotel known as the Lesic Dimitri Palace, in the
heart of old town Korcula. Built within a restored ancient stone
building, it only had five rooms, all available for long-term rental,

and all with a different worldly flavor to celebrate the esteemed explorer Marco Polo, who, according to local tradition, was from Korcula. The Arabia Room, the Venice Room, the India Room, all were distinctly different, and distinctly expensive to rent, but since it was on Andrei's dime, Branko had paid for the China Room for close to a year.

Branko cleaned up, taking his time, and heard his phone ding again. He'd missed his thirty-minute window. He'd done it on purpose to show Nikita that he wasn't Branko's boss, but seeing the text asking where he was made him regret the decision. Nikita wasn't a man to trifle with.

Maybe the delay wasn't that smart.

He threw on his clothes, grabbed his backpack, and texted he was on the way. He looked at his watch, seeing it was just past six in the morning—way too early for him in his normal life. He finally looked at the map, confused by the directions.

The apartment was located at the end of the island, the water to the north across the street, and a maze of stone alleys to the south, but the location of the meet was at the supposed house of Marco Polo. It was now a museum and a stone's throw from the apartment, a mere hundred meters away, but Nikita's route took him away from the meet location, on a circuitous route that wound throughout the alleyways before coming back the way he'd left. He could cut his time to nothing if he just went straight to it, making his delay much less.

He decided to ignore the map and get there as quickly as he could to defuse any anger from Nikita. Nikita would have no way of knowing if he'd walked the ridiculous route around the old town.

He exited the lobby into an alley, looked left and right, saw no one, and cut away from the ocean shore of the island, moving deeper into the heart of the old town. He slipped through one alley, then another, reaching a small courtyard with an overhanging arch, a set of stone stairs leading up to the purported house of Marco Polo. He went to the stairs and saw that the place didn't even open until 9 A.M. *How is this going to work?*

He mounted the stairs, went to the front door and thought about knocking, then heard footsteps behind him. Not wanting to look like he was breaking in, he refused to glance behind him, instead trying the knob, finding it unlocked. He turned it, pushed the door in a half inch, and it was jerked open, causing him to fall forward. Someone grabbed him by the hair and flung him into the room. He hit the floor, rolled upright, and saw Nikita in the doorway with a suppressed pistol, shooting down the stairwell into the alley. He saw gouges appear in the stone of the door frame, Nikita slam against the wall, then lean out again, returning fire.

Nikita paused, took a breath, glanced out, then slammed the door shut and said, "You fucking idiot. The time schedule is because we have a ferry to catch. The route was to see if you were followed. You were."

Confused, he said, "What?"

Nikita snatched him by the hair again and said, "The route was to take out anyone following you. It's why I designed it so early in the morning. You chose not to use it and were almost caught. Now we have no escape because I know there are men in the alley with weapons. Get the fuck up."

Branko rose on unsteady feet and said, "Afghans? Were they Afghans?"

Running to a room at the back of the house, Nikita shouted, "No. One was white, the other black. They were coming for you, dumb-ass."

Nikita returned to the main room and said, "What do you mean, Afghans?"

"They've tried to kill me before. It's why I called Andrei. It's why you're here. They're looking for the treasure."

"Well, you'd better hope they don't find it, because you're dead if they do. Follow me."

He went to the back of the house again, shoved a display case full of artifacts aside, and opened a window. He pulled out his phone, dialing it and saying, "Get out."

"What?"

Nikita spoke into the phone for thirty seconds, hung up, and said, "Get your ass out onto that ledge, then drop to the ground. We're going to have to run to beat them. They're probably circling this place right now. This house cuts the alleys in half, but that won't stop them for long."

"I can't do that!"

Nikita put the barrel of his pistol into Branko's face and said, "You get the fuck out of this window or I'm going to split your head open."

Branko flinched, then crawled out of the window onto a ledge that was barely an inch wide. Nikita said, "Jump. Get off the ledge. We need to go."

Branko looked below him, saw the stone fifteen feet away, closed his eyes, and dropped, hitting hard enough to slam his skull into the ground. He rolled over holding his head and Nikita dropped like a cat next to him, jerking him to his feet and saying, "Let's go. Stick close to me. We have maybe a minute to get out of the kill box, and if you cause me to fail, I'll slaughter you myself."

They took off running, Nikita dragging him through one alley after another, Branko barely maintaining his balance on the narrow stairway, until they reached the road that circled the island next to the water. Nikita jerked Branko to the left, running north up the blacktop, until they reached the upper end of the town, an ancient bastion that used to guard the harbor towering over them. Nikita glanced around, then ran to two Land Rovers parked in a loading zone, one full of men and the other with only a driver. He opened the door to the empty one and said, "Get your ass in."

Branko did, and the vehicle left at a high rate of speed, exiting the old town and entering a highway leading to the ferry port. Branko put his hand to the bruise forming on his forehead and said, "What was that all about?"

Nikita leaned around from the front and said, "It's about try-ing to save your life. When I give you instructions, you follow them. Who were those men?"

"I have no idea."

"How did they find you?"

"I . . . I don't know. I honestly don't. Nobody knew about that apartment. Nobody. Not even my men."

"We're going to another spot and see what happens. You pay attention to what I say, and you might live to see the sun set."

CHAPTER 47

By the time we'd finished the reconnaissance of the bed-down site it was after midnight, and it looked like we were going to spend another night without sleep. It had taken us close to three hours to drive from Split to Orebic, and we'd missed the last vehicle ferry to the island. There was one more passenger-only ferry, forcing us to leave the vehicles in long-term parking and hoof it on foot. Not the best thing, but there was nothing I could do about it.

Like all great commando formations, we took a couple of Ubers to the old town of Korcula and started hunting for the phone's location. I'd found out immediately that the center of old town Korcula was more cloistered than Diocletian's Palace in Split, with a single paved road circling the village next to the coast and a rat maze of tiny alleys and stairs—lots of stairs. If I'd learned anything at all about Croatia, it was this: if you're walking, you're climbing stairs.

I was hoping for another single-entrance Vrbo like we'd hit in Split, but it wasn't to be. The bed-down was some fancy small hotel crammed between two alleys right on the ring road, with only five rooms, which meant trying to penetrate the lobby and capture Branko was a nonstarter. The phone was still inside, but the geolocation feature had a plus or minus of anywhere from thirty to a hundred feet, meaning we couldn't precisely pinpoint which room he was in, and no way did I want to crack more than one.

If it had been a large hotel, with four stories and hundreds of rooms, we could have spent a few hours trying to determine the precise location on the inside, as there would be plenty of people coming and going. Once that was done, we'd enter and bash that guy on the head, putting him behind a computer. With only five, and the expense of the stay—guaranteeing concierge services at all hours—it was a good bet that the front desk knew every person staying there and would question us trying to enter. They probably had a dedicated person for every room.

So we were going to have to do it the hard way—box the exits to the hotel and wait on him to leave.

I'd dispatched Jennifer to get us a hotel on the north side of town, a place where we could rack out as we rotated, and possibly take our suspect once we got him. Then we'd started surveillance of the site.

The problem with our technology and the geolocation feature of the phone was that we had to ping it to get a location. It wasn't like an Uber or Lyft ride, where we could track the driver—or in this case, the phone. All we could get was a geolocation on each ping. So far it was still inside the building, so we knew he was in there, but now we'd have to physically watch until he left.

The hotel was sandwiched between two small alleys left and right of the building, with the lobby entrance on one and a service entrance on the other. There was a terrace restaurant on one end overlooking the ocean, but I didn't think he'd leap over that unless he was chased, so we set up on the two exits and waited.

It got harder as the night went on, as the crowds of tourists grew less and less, leaving us vulnerable to compromise. We resorted to putting a Bluetooth button camera on the doors, with the surveillance bumper positions finding a spot to sit that was close enough to see the feed. I stationed myself on the beach wall with a fishing pole I'd found on the ground, hoping to look like I was just a fisherman out early in the morning. I'd left Jennifer in the hotel to coordinate the rotation of the teams and keep in constant contact with the Taskforce, and then we'd begun the painfully boring work of watching and waiting for a chance to bag his ass.

By 5 A.M., acting as the surveillance chief, I'd rotated everyone through the two sites once, letting the folks get a little shut-eye in the hotel room before pulling them back in. I was getting groggy, but knew time was precious. It would've been perfect if we could have taken him in the night, but that hadn't happened, and because of it, I wouldn't be getting a rotation. I wanted to be on the ground when he left.

At 0605, right before the sun crested the horizon, I had Brett on the lobby entrance and Veep on the service one, Jennifer on the net for control, and Knuckles getting some rack time.

Jennifer called me direct and said, "How's it going?"

I said, "So far, all quiet. What's up?"

"Nothing. Just trying to stay awake."

"You want to switch out with Knuckles?"

"No. He just got here. I had some sleep when you switched out Brett."

My earpiece was overridden with Brett saying, "Contact. Target is leaving the building. I have him."

I told Jennifer, "Gotta go," then switched to the team net saying, "Direction and distance?"

"Out the lobby door, headed north in the alley. Veep, Veep, can you back me up?"

"On the way."

I stood up, laid the fishing pole where I'd found it, and said,

"I'm on trailer. Give me a call if you need some help, but the minute you get him in a secure area, take his ass down."

I jogged across the road and went up the stairs into the old town, entering the narrow stone alley next to the boutique hotel. The bad thing about the alleys here was that it was impossible to follow someone for more than a few turns until they knew you were behind them. The good thing was that we could take this guy down without anyone seeing, if we got him in the right spot. And at this time of day, everything would be the right spot. I slowed to a fast walk, not wanting to step on the surveillance effort.

"This is Blood, still on five-five. He's entered a courtyard and there's nobody around. He's going to know I'm following if I continue."

Veep said, "I circled around to the alley leading out. Hold back. He'll walk right past me."

I called, "Location?"

Veep said, "Next to a stairwell for something called the Marco Polo House. Stand by. I see him. He's looking around. Appears to be hesitant."

"From us?"

"No. We're clean. Don't know why."

"Brett, can you close?"

"Yeah, I'm right outside the courtyard."

"Are we clean?"

Veep said, "This is Veep. Nothing on my side."

Brett came on, saying, "This is Blood. I'm clean here."

Veep said, "He's climbing the stairs."

Running up the alley, I said, "Take him. Now. Get him on the ground, get a barrel in the face, and let's exfil to the hotel."

Brett said, "Roger that."

The next thing I heard was the unmistakable sound of a suppressed weapon. Hollywood will have you believe the weapon is almost silent, but it's not. It's just not as loud as a gunshot. Even with a suppressor, the report reverberated against the stone walls. I drew my Glock and began sprinting. By the time I saw the courtyard entrance, Brett and Veep were rounding the corner back into my alley, weapons drawn but unhurt.

I reached them and said, "What happened?"

Veep glanced around the corner and said, "He reached the top of the stairs and someone stuck a gun out, shooting at us."

"Someone in that museum has a suppressed pistol?"

Brett said, "Yep. No idea who, and I don't think Branko did, either. He was jerked off his feet and thrown inside."

"The Afghans? Is it them?"

Veep said, "No way. The guy was a tall Caucasian, dressed like he was on a security contract. Definitely not the Afghans."

"So someone's helping him. We need to get a box on this building right now. Don't let them out. I got the front door. Find the back."

They took off through the alleys and I called Jennifer, saying, "Koko, we're at a place called the Marco Polo House and we've made contact. Give me what you know."

I heard nothing for a second while she worked the computer, then she came back, saying, "It's a museum, but it's not open now. Doesn't open until nine A.M. It's supposedly the house Marco Polo lived in."

I said, "I don't care about its pedigree; the target is inside and we have the front door locked down. How can he get out?"

"Stand by, checking. Knuckles is coming."

I called the team, "Blood, Veep, status?"

"Trying to find the back of the building. The house itself cuts the alleys in half, and the ones we are on are running parallel. Trying to find a cutoff."

I said, "Koko, anything?"

"They can get out over the roofs from the third floor, but they'll be trapped and unable to get down after a few buildings. They can jump out the window on the second floor to a courtyard, and they have a clean run to the end of the island."

I said, "All elements, all elements, it's the window. Get to the back. They're probably jumping now."

Veep came back, saying, "We can't find a perpendicular alley."

I heard a noise behind me and saw Knuckles running up. He said, "You were going to let me sleep through the high adventure?"

I said, "No. Get ready."

On the net, I said, "I'm going in."

Jennifer said, "Wait for backup, Pike."

"Knuckles just showed up. They aren't coming out the front, and going in that way would be the last thing they would expect. Veep, Blood, continue to the back."

I turned to Knuckles and said, "You ready?"

"What are we up against?"

"At least one guy with a suppressed pistol"—meaning the people inside had some skill—"maybe more, but I don't think so. He took a few shots at Blood and Veep, but didn't continue the fight. He's here for Branko just like we are, and he's trying to run."

He glanced around the corner and said, "Stairwell to the second floor?"

"Yep."

He shook his head and said, "Man, I hate stairwells. Get on them, and you're committed."

"You can have low."

He racked a round into his own suppressed Glock and said, "Won't get any arguments from me."

We took off running with him in the front. He knelt down behind the stone banister on the right, his weapon trained on the entrance of the door, and I went up the stairs on the left, running flat out, knowing he was my protection. I reached the top, rolled to the left of the frame where the knob was, and took a knee, now with my barrel on the door.

In seconds he was on the landing, his own barrel out on the right side of the frame. I looked at him, he nodded, and I reached forward, turning the knob and flinging open the door. He flowed in with me right behind him, he went left and I went right, but there was nobody there. It was an empty room with plaques on the wall and display cases circling the area.

Knuckles nodded to a room off the back and we flowed that way, clearing the same way as before. It was empty yet again, but this one had a display case overturned and an open window, the curtains blowing in the wind.

I went to it and looked out, seeing Brett and Veep rounding the corner into the courtyard. They looked up at me, weapons aimed, and I waved them off, saying, "Shit. They're gone."

I got on the net and said, "Jennifer, pack our stuff. Everyone else, return to the hotel. They're on the run and trying to get off this island."

CHAPTER 48

Crossing the Franjo Tudjman Bridge, which spanned a spit of water running into the Adriatic Sea, the outskirts of Dubrovnik on the other side, Shakor saw people attached to harnesses and standing on a ledge. His first thought was that they were being executed for something heinous that they'd done. Public executions were something he was very familiar with. The Taliban hadn't done something like this yet, but it was only because they didn't have a bridge such as this on which to execute the people who defied their beliefs.

He said, "What is that? Are they criminals?"

Driving the vehicle, Drago laughed, then saw Shakor's scowl. He hurriedly said, "No, no. They're bungee jumping. They're tourists."

"What does that mean?"

"They attach what's really a giant rubber band to their legs, and the tourists jump over the bridge, the harness slowing them before they hit the water. It's a thrill thing."

Shakor shook his head, unable to assimilate the stupidity of someone putting their own life at risk while only protected by a rubber band. But even given what Drago said, he wasn't sure he believed him. After the Bosnia crossing, he knew he had to keep a close eye on his escort. Drago would do whatever it took to get away.

After forcing Drago out of the cellars in the old town of Split, they'd reached the road to the ferry terminal where Shakor's car was parked, and Drago had made a scene, hoping to escape with the help of the tourists.

As soon as he'd seen Shakor's men unlocking the doors to two rental cars, he knew he was done, and had taken off running, thinking nobody would shoot him in broad daylight. He'd shouted in Russian, Serbian, and English, begging for help, threading through the cars, hoping to make it to the security guard at the gate.

Shakor was on him in an instant, punching his kidney hard enough to cause him to collapse between the vehicles. Shakor stood up over his body, looked around, and saw some curious stares, but nobody came to investigate. He'd leaned over Drago and said, "You do something like that again, and I'll bash your head in. Do you understand?"

Wheezing, Drago nodded.

They'd loaded up and traveled south to the next safehouse that Drago knew, on the outskirts of Dubrovnik. He'd told Shakor that it was a straight shot down the coast, and then they'd hit a queue of cars at a border crossing, causing Shakor enormous concern.

He'd said, "What is this?"

"It's the Bosnian crossing. We have to pass it to get to Dubrovnik."

"We have to pass through another country? And you knew this?"

Now afraid, seeing the anger, Drago had said, "Yes. Everyone knows this. Bosnia owns a spit of land that splits Croatia in two. It's been that way for centuries."

Shakor said, "Could we have taken a ferry and avoided it?"

Drago inched the car forward and nodded, the fear growing. Shakor said, "What's it take to cross? We don't have a visa for Bosnia."

"Nothing, I promise. You're supposed to have a visa, but everyone uses this road. They won't ask."

Shakor saw they were next in line, pulled out his pistol, and jammed it into Drago's side, saying, "You do anything to cause us trouble, and you'll be dead. Do you understand?"

Drago nodded again, and the next thing Shakor knew, they were through the crossing. Drago had been right, but Shakor was sure he'd had something else planned. Now on the outskirts of Dubrovnik, he wasn't giving him any leverage.

They finished crossing the bridge and Drago took the first exit, looping around and heading toward the Adriatic Sea. Shakor felt his antennae rise again and said, "Where are we going? I thought it was in Dubrovnik?"

"Well, Dubrovnik is the closest city, so we say it's there. It's in Lapad, on the coast right here. Dubrovnik is like ten minutes away."

Shakor gave him the death stare, and Drago said, "I'm not lying! This is the house."

The road looped around under the bridge, passing by a marina, and then entered a peninsula, Drago saying, "This is Lapad."

He started driving down narrow two-lane roads, the steep slope to the ocean on the left and the hills rising on the right. Eventually he pulled over into a small parking area with about ten slots for cars, most already taken. He found one and said, "We walk from here."

"Walk?"

"The house is down the hill, on the coast. It doesn't have a road. Branko was always adamant not to get a house where a car could drive up to the front door. He always wanted a way out."

Shakor looked down the hill, seeing a staircase disappearing into the vegetation, the twinkling waters of the Adriatic off in the distance. He could just barely see the roof of a building.

He said, "Is that it?"

Drago nodded. Shakor looked back up the hill, to the houses higher that had car access. He said, "Why would having road access matter? Why no cars?"

"He wanted early warning before someone showed up to crash us. That's all. It's the reason he had the place in Split. No way for a car to roll right up."

Shakor opened the door and got out, seeing the slope with the staircase spilling down the hill. He thought a moment, then said, "Because you could control anyone coming on foot?"

Shakor saw Drago's reaction and knew. "You have early warning for people coming, don't you? The people in that house can see us coming down?"

"No, no. It's not that. Branko just didn't like cars."

Shakor bashed his head into the door frame and said, "I should kill you right now, but I'm not. Call them. Tell them you're coming with friends of Branko."

Drago looked left and right, then said, "I . . . I can't call them. I don't even know who's there. We should just walk down and knock on the door."

Shakor pulled out his pistol and slammed it into Drago's cheek, ripping the skin, then grabbed his skull by the hair and bashed his head into the car door again. He said, "I'm sick of you trying to trick me. Call them."

Drago cowered, a hand to his cheek. He felt the blood, and nodded, saying, "Okay, okay, okay. I'll try."

He dialed the phone, said something in a language that Shakor didn't understand, and then hung up, saying, "We're good."

"What did you say?"

"What you wanted me to!"

Shakor didn't believe him for a minute, but it was too late now. He should have specified the language before the call. But then again, the people in the house would have been on high alert if Drago had spoken in English instead of his native language.

A problem set he didn't predict and now couldn't stop.

He poked Drago's back and said, "Let's go. You first. I honestly don't care if any one of them run from me, but if they alert Branko, I'll hunt all of you down."

His hands up, Drago said, "Nobody's heard from Branko in two days. He's probably not here."

Shakor pushed him down the stairs and said, "That won't work out well for you."

They went past another building on the hill, the stairs snaking through the foliage, and then the upper deck of the house appeared below them, the stairs continuing to the coastline.

Shakor said, "Go ahead and knock. Let them know we're here."

Drago swallowed and went to the door, knowing what was going to happen. He rang the bell, and the door opened wide, the man behind it saying, "Come on in!" With a huge smile on his face.

Shakor pushed Drago to the side and smacked the man in the temple with his weapon, knocking him to the floor. His men entered, running through the place looking for Branko. An unknown man tried to flee down a stairwell and was shot in the back, his body falling forward like a doll, smashing into the stairs and rolling to the bottom. In short order, they found that Branko was not there.

Shakor found Drago cowering in a corner and said, "Where's Branko?"

"I don't know! I told you that. He lost his phone and has a new one. I don't have his number anymore. He'll come here. I promise he'll come here."

"You'd better hope so. Your life depends on it. Who is this fuck?"

Drago looked at his friend held by the man called Ghulam and said, "His name is Bogdan. He's just the caretaker. He's the guy who does the contract for our places. I scout them and he pays for them, coordinating for Wi-Fi and other things. We let him live here. He knows nothing."

Shakor pointed at the body down the stairs and said, "Who's he?"

"He's a coder. Or was a coder. He built stuff for Pushka to use. When he designed the code, he was done. Pushka and Branko did the work after that."

Shakor said, "Okay, then who can contact Branko?"

Drago shrank against a wall and said, "None of us. He contacts us, not the other way around. He pays our way, and we do what he says. We can't contact him."

Then a phone rang.

Shakor heard it and said, "Whose cell is that?"

Drago looked at Bogdan, and they both shook their head. Shakor went to the stairwell and the sound got louder. He ran down it, flopped the body over, and found a smartphone. He ran back up the stairs, held it in Drago's face, and said, "Answer this."

Drago took it, but before he could hit the talk button, Shakor snatched it away from him, saying, "Wait a minute. You're supposed to be in Split."

He turned to Bogdan and said, "You talk."

Bogdan hit the call button and began speaking in Serbian. Shakor smacked him in the head, then snatched the phone, putting his hand over the microphone, saying, "Speak English."

"You want me to speak English? He'll know something's going on."

Shakor paced a bit, then said, "Is it Branko?"

Bogdan hesitated, then said, "Yes, it's him, and the longer you hold that phone, the more he's going to wonder what's going on."

Shakor handed the phone back and said, "You'd better not tell him what's waiting here."

Bogdan nodded, but Shakor realized he had no control now. No idea what he was saying, and he knew that Bogdan would do whatever it took to live.

Then he had an idea. Yes, he was Taliban, but he'd also lived in the West. He understood technology.

Bogdan started talking and Shakor put a gun to his head, saying, "Tell him to hold on, because someone is at the door. Tell him that now."

Bogdan did, then put the phone on mute, looking at Shakor, saying, "What is this about?"

Shakor pulled out his own smartphone, put it on a voice recording, and said, "Keep talking, but when it's done, I'm going to translate it. If you scare him off, I will skin you alive."

CHAPTER 49

We reconsolidated at the hotel and did a quick after-action review. The bottom line was that nobody knew anything more than what we'd seen. There was a guy with a suppressed weapon in a country that didn't even allow firearms, which meant he was something other than just a friend helping a friend. Something else was going on, but I'll be damned if I knew what it was. All I knew was that the longer we stayed, the farther away he got.

We packed up and I called the Taskforce for a ping, getting one right in the middle of the Adriatic Sea, telling me they were on a ferry. Which was fine with me. He could run, but he couldn't hide.

We fled the hotel as fast as we could, going down to the ferry terminal. I spent thirty minutes tapping my foot, knowing that those guys were on the boat before ours, feeling like I was on *The Amazing Race.* Eventually our ferry appeared, and we headed across the water, running to our cars when it docked just like a contestant on the TV show.

We started driving to the mainland, and I called the Taskforce to ping the phone again. Creed was probably in bed, but someone was monitoring the phone, because Taskforce operations were 24/7. I got a guy I didn't know, saying things that would cause him to die a slow death.

"Pike, I've been told to hold up on the next ping."

Incredulous, I said, "Who is this?"

"Hey, I'm just the guy manning the net right now. I have my orders just like you do."

I gritted my teeth, saying, "Where's Creed?"

"He's asleep. I was given my orders after he left."

"By who?"

"George Wolffe."

I looked at my watch and knew it was closing in on two in the morning there. Wolffe wasn't around to fix this.

I said, "You had better give me that ping right now or pray that I die in a plane crash coming home."

Jennifer glanced at me in alarm, and I shook my head, telling her to keep driving. A new voice came on, and I recognized it. Why George Wolffe was inside Taskforce headquarters at this hour was beyond me.

"Pike, this is Wolffe. The thinking has changed here."

"Sir? What's that mean?"

"The president is leaning toward this being a nation-state attack, and that keeping you in the field is a risk that's not worth the reward. He's turned off Omega authority."

That was a head-spinner. I said, "What?"

"You heard me. We have a guy working this for us, grew up in the NSA TAO, then went to the new Cyber Command. He's saying it's not Dark Star, and that their declaration is a smoke screen to protect the country. He's going to find out who did this, giving the president some evidence for retaliation."

That didn't smell right to me. I said, "Why is one guy dictating policy? He 'used' to work for the NSA and Cyber. What is NSA and Cyber saying?"

"They don't know. They're way behind the eight ball on this.

They might have some assessment in a week or two, but they're risk averse. The president is deferring to this guy."

I said, "Does that sound right to you? You want me to stand down?"

I heard nothing, then said, "The Russian guy Andrei only wants money. He wouldn't do this. It's too big, inviting someone to come for him."

"That's what our expert says. You're proving his point."

I could tell he wasn't sold on the president's assessment and wanted me to convince him to continue. I threw everything against the wall, saying, "But there's someone else in the mix. The American code-named Sphinx. And there's the Badr Battalion running around here."

"Badr Battalion? Who cares about them? And all you've got on the American is a code name. No help."

"Sir, Branko can answer for both. Maybe he's not involved anymore, but maybe he is. We're running out of time to stop this thing. Do you want to just roll over and find out it was from the same group, when you could have stopped it? Fuck the president."

I heard a breath on the phone, expecting a rebuke at my statement. What I heard was, "Can you operate without your usual signature?"

"What's that mean?"

"It means I don't want a bunch of dead bodies every time you go somewhere."

That was a little aggravating. I said, "Hey, sir, I haven't done anything like that on this mission. The bodies were from someone else. *You* sent me on this mission. It's not my fault people are dead."

"Answer the question."

I smacked my fist into the dash of our car, causing Jennifer to snap her head toward me. She had no idea what was being said on the other end, but even behind the steering wheel, she knew it wasn't good. She shook her head, telling me to let it go.

I said, "Yes, sir, I can do that."

"Then get on it."

I looked at Jennifer, and she saw my grin. Into the phone I said, "So I'm on my own on this one?"

Wolffe laughed and said, "No, it'll be my ass on the chopping block this time. Just don't put it there."

I said, "You got it. Give me the geolocation."

He passed the phone to the computer guy, and I got a ping. It was now at a restaurant in a place called Mali Ston, a small town on the water about twenty minutes away. Really close.

I passed the grid to the team as Jennifer drove, saying, on the net, "Here's the last known location. We're going to close in and assess."

Jennifer passed the town called Ston, with a giant wall made of rock encircling it, something from medieval times, and we continued for another few minutes, reaching Mali Ston—meaning little Ston, like a sister village—with the wall following us the entire way.

Knowing Jennifer had already done the research, I said, "What's up with that wall?"

She said, "It's the largest fortification still in existence here. Basically, back in the day, they were afraid of getting attacked, so they built a wall, like China did. It reaches from the town of Ston to Mali Ston, protecting the harbors of both. And it's pretty cool. Want to walk it?"

I laughed and said, "I don't think they'd let us."

She said, "No, that's the whole point of its upkeep. You can walk from Mali Ston to Ston. All the way from one to the other, along a fortification steeped in history, but like everything here, it's full of stairs. Not sure you want to follow me up them."

I looked to see if she was kidding, but she wasn't. She just loved old shit. I said, "I'd love to *follow* you up the stairs, but maybe later. Let's get our guy first."

She gave me her death stare at my twisting her words, and we pulled into a small parking lot next to the water, with only a single Land Rover in it, which had to be our target. A decrepit stone bastion was to the front, looking like it still wanted to fight but had long ago lost the ability. A map at the edge of the parking lot gave us the historical background, with restaurants stretching out along the intercoastal waterway. This place was older than our entire country.

I studied the stone crumbling from the bastion, wondering who'd built it. I pretended I wasn't really turned on by ancient stuff like Jennifer, but I was. Seeing the bastion made me wonder, as a military guy, who'd used it and how they'd faired. How many men had died defending this port?

And how many more might today.

CHAPTER 50

I exited the car and saw Knuckles approaching. I had the team gather around me, saying, "Okay, here we go. This is our last chance. Brett and Veep are burned from the gunfight earlier. I'm not. Neither are Knuckles and Koko. Brett, Veep, I want you out here in case they leave. You're the vehicle follow."

I pointed at the Land Rover and said, "That's got to be their vehicle. Get a beacon on it. Knuckles, you go long beyond the restaurant. Koko and I are going in. If I sight him, I'll call. From there, we'll work it out."

Veep said, "What if he comes back out here to the parking lot and we get a chance at him? If he's clean?"

"Take his ass down."

Brett said, "We have sanction for that?"

I turned to him and said, "No, we don't. Well, we do, but it's because George Wolffe is hanging his butt out on a sling. The National Command Authority no longer thinks this guy is worth the effort. I convinced Wolffe that he was because I believe he is. We have about a day and a half before those people die in space. And this guy can solve it, so take him down, no matter what."

Brett said, "The NCA doesn't believe in this mission? And you want to continue?"

I glanced at Jennifer, then at him and said, "Yeah, that about sums it up."

He said, "Why?"

"Because there are Americans about to die. I don't give a shit that they've paid to be there. I don't care that they're all rich fucksticks—which they are. At the end of the day, they're Americans. That's why."

He smiled and said, "Well, they paid for the trip. Sounds like they're reaping what they sowed. Not sure that's worth our team."

I said, "One of them didn't. One of them is just a small-town schoolteacher from Arkansas. Her flight was paid by the owner of the company for his own bullshit sense of worth, but she's not going to die on my watch. She's up there right now, and she's coming home."

I said it more forcefully than I should have. Brett saw my commitment and said, "Okay, Pike. I'm in."

I glanced at Jennifer, then Veep. They were both looking back at me like I had a screw loose. If the National Command Authority didn't believe in the mission, why were we doing it? But Knuckles knew why. The men in the NCA put their pants on one leg at a time, just like we did, and sometimes they were wrong.

He stepped in, saying, "You have the assignments. Let's execute. This is for Carly. She sacrificed her life for Jahn. The least we can do is sacrifice our career for the schoolteacher."

That meant more than anything I could have said. I nodded at him, and we broke up, Knuckles heading to a stairwell to get above our location. Jennifer and I went down low, next to the water and the last known location of the phone. We found three restaurants right next to each other, all with outside dining that was ubiquitous here in Croatia. We passed the first one slowly, looking, and didn't see our target. We hit the second one, and Jennifer pinched my arm.

There he was. Branko, otherwise known as Doctor Evil in my book. He was sitting with two men who looked like they'd just come from a safari, with loose-fitting shirts and pants full of pockets. Both were hard men, and I instinctively knew one of them had held the pistol in Korcula. Unlike Branko, they most definitely weren't computer geeks. The man across from Branko locked eyes with me and I glanced away. But he'd seen me. Seen something.

I pulled Jennifer to the menu as if we were wondering where to eat, and said on the net, "Target acquired. Stand by." I gave the team the restaurant we were in and waited on the hostess to give us a seat.

We were led to a two-seat table on the other side of the patio. Jennifer ordered a giant bowl of mussels, which was apparently the thing in Mali Ston, and we settled in to see what would happen. We didn't have to wait long.

Before our food was even brought out, Branko and the other two men stood up. On the net, I said, "Veep, Blood, get ready. They're on the move."

Only they didn't head back to the parking lot. They went to a stairwell on the left of the restaurant, heading deeper into the little village. I said, "Knuckles, Knuckles, they're coming to you on foot. They aren't going to the car. Track them and if we get a shot, let's take Branko."

"ROE?"

Which was a big question. Wolffe was putting his neck in a noose to allow me to operate, which meant I couldn't just start a gunfight then claim self-defense, although I was sure that would work. Both of the guys shadowing Branko were definitely pipe hitters.

I reversed course, saying, "Just track them. No overt acts. See where they go. Find a bed-down location and we'll take it from there."

Veep came on, saying, "Want us to come in?"

"No. We'll handle it. Keep your position. I'm pretty sure they'll be headed back to their car."

Knuckles said, "They're walking to the wall. They aren't going to another place here."

I said, "Wall? You mean the wall that's a tourist attraction?"

"Yeah. They just bought tickets and they're headed up it. Should I follow?"

I smiled at Jennifer and said, "Looks like you get your wish."

On the net, I said, "No, don't burn yourself. That thing is a straight linear target. Jennifer and I will take it. A couple on a date, not some strange hippy all by himself."

I heard him laugh, then, "Better get here soon. They're moving out."

I threw some money on the table, gave our waitress an excuse, and we left the restaurant, threading up the ancient stairs into the village. We found a sign pointing the way to the fortification, continuing higher. We met Knuckles right outside the ticket counter.

He said, "No idea what they're doing, but they're moving out with a purpose."

If I'd had any sense, I would have thought through the problem set. Instead I said, "We'll keep an eye on them. Get some chow and rotate Veep and Blood through a restaurant. When they come back, we want to be able to move."

He nodded, and I went to the counter, paying something like ten bucks to walk my ass off on a giant set of stairs. Jennifer and I started climbing, and I muttered under my breath, causing her to laugh. I said, "Just stay in front of me. That'll keep me moving."

That shut her humor down.

The wall was exactly like you'd expect: a stone hunk of stairways leading up and over the mountain between Mali Ston and Ston. Within seconds I was sweating like I was in a gym, wondering why anyone would do this. More importantly wondering why our targets would be walking the route.

Mali Ston disappeared behind us before I finally saw our quarry. They were about a hundred meters ahead of us and steadily trudging uphill. I could see the break-off for the Ston portion of the wall about a half kilometer away. I hoped they were sweating like me. The only good thing was there was nowhere for them to deviate. They were on this wall just like I was, and there was no reason to suspect us, as plenty of tourists were doing the same thing.

They kept climbing and Jennifer said, "What do you suppose this is all about? Why take him on a walk?"

"I don't know. If I were to guess, they're going to meet someone on the wall for some reason. Either way, it'll be worth our effort to see. We locate another target and it just opens up opportunity."

We threaded higher and higher, reaching a turnoff to a fortress at the crest of the ridge, but our targets ignored it, heading downhill to the village of Ston.

I said, "Shit. Guess I was wrong. Must be something in this town."

We finally hit the downhill portion and I picked up the pace, saying, "We've got to be on them when they exit."

We closed the gap, a family of four in between us and them. I saw them disappear into the modern building that controlled access to the wall. Two stories tall, it was made of burnished metal and stained wood, looking like a miniature ski chalet in Switzerland. I gave them a chance to get to the lower level, then scooted past the family, dragging Jennifer behind me. I entered the top floor, seeing a ticket office, the air-conditioning immediately making me feel my sweat. I held up, letting them exit and looking down the stairwell as they did so. When they were gone, I motioned to Jennifer and we went down the stairs.

We exited on the streets of Ston, a small village full of cafés and tourist kiosks. I rapidly surveyed the area, but didn't see our targets. Jennifer pulled my arm and nodded to the left. They were disappearing into an alley. We went behind them, me saying, "Okay, they're going to meet someone. Let's see who it is."

They met no one. They walked straight to the exit of the town, and like a lightning bolt striking me in the head, I realized why they'd used the wall. When they went through the arch at the entrance of the town, crossing a stone bridge to a parking area, I said, "Jesus Christ. These guys just played us."

Jennifer said, "What?"

"They wanted to break themselves from the surveillance, and they just did."

They were standing together across a small bridge, waiting. We kept eyes on them, but I knew it was worthless.

Jennifer said, "What do you mean?"

"Just watch."

Sure enough, a car pulled into the parking area, and all three loaded. Within seconds, they were gone, with no way for us to follow.

They thought they were smart, but they didn't have the might of the United States behind them. I let them leave, waiting for a few minutes to allow them to commit to a road that would give me some indication of where they were going. I called the Taskforce and asked for a ping on the phone.

It came back to Mali Ston. I said, "That's impossible. Do it again."

They did and got the same result.

I called Knuckles and said, "Go to the restaurant. Is his phone there?"

Eight minutes later, he said, "Yeah. It's here. They left it here."

CHAPTER 51

Nikita saw the man looking at the menu and recognized him for what he was. He was with an attractive woman, but there was no hiding his skill no matter how he tried to act like a tourist. A little over six feet, with close-cropped hair, he had ice-blue eyes and a scar on his cheek that radiated controlled violence. He most certainly wasn't a tourist.

Nikita said, "Put your fork down and get ready to leave."

Branko said, "What?"

"They're here."

Branko looked around and only saw a couple staring at the menu. He said, "What are you talking about?"

Nikita purposely avoided looking at the couple a second time. He said, "Get the waiter and pay the bill. Leave your phone here, on the table, underneath a menu."

Branko started to say something else but saw Nikita's visage and thought better of it. He waved at the waiter, then slid his phone under a menu, saying, "Why am I leaving my cell?"

"Because we broke from the men chasing you in Korcula, and yet here they are. They're tracking your phone."

Now a little scared, Branko said, "How are we going to get away from them? If they're here, they'll just follow our car."

"The car is probably already bugged with a GPS. We're not

going back to it. I chose this location for a reason. We're going to get them to follow us, then leave from the other side, in Ston."

The waiter brought the bill and Branko said, "Am I paying?"

Nikita stood, saying, "No, Andrei is. Doesn't he fund your credit card?"

Branko handed the card to the waiter without another word. When he was done, Nikita said, "Follow me."

They walked up a narrow stairwell, following a sign proclaiming "Entrance to the old city walls." Nikita stopped at a ticket booth, purchased passage, then gave each of them a ticket. Branko said, "Where are we going?"

"To the other side. Let's move."

Thirty minutes later, they reached the top of the ridge where the junction of the wall offered a path to the right, going higher to a small fortress, or straight, heading into the town. Branko wiped the sweat off his brow, panting from the climb. Nikita and his other man showed no apparent effects.

Branko said, "What now?"

Nikita glanced back the way they'd come, then pointed down the hill, making Branko smile. *Thank heavens.* Nikita said, "We reach the bottom and go straight out the portal to the city. Let's move. Our car is waiting."

"What about the other car?"

Nikita started walking, saying, "What about it? Let the people chasing you keep an eye on it."

Branko glanced back, seeing a family of four, and beyond them, a man and woman walking the same way as every other tourist on this wall. He said, "Who is chasing us? That family?"

Nikita said, "Just get down the hill."

Within ten minutes, they were through the modern-day ticket

office and on the streets of Ston, heading toward the bridge and stone arch that marked the entrance to the village. They crossed it, with Nikita on the phone. Seconds later, a car appeared, and Nikita said, "Get in."

Branko did, and the vehicle returned to the main highway, heading to the mainland. Nikita said, "So we're now clean. Where can we go? Where is a safehouse?"

"Outside Dubrovnik is the closest." They reached the main coastal highway and the driver took a right, heading south. Nikita said, "Call them. Tell them we'll be there in an hour."

Branko said, "I don't have a phone."

Nikita gave him his and said, "Don't tell them we're with you. Just tell them you're going to spend the night."

Branko did as he asked, with Bogdan answering the phone, confusing him. He'd called Pushka's coder, not Bogdan. Then Bogdan told him to wait a minute, that someone was at the door, and Branko knew something was wrong. He thought about asking pertinent questions but had no way of knowing if Nikita or the driver spoke Serbian. He didn't want to give Nikita any reason to think he was trying to do something against the wishes of Andrei. He let it go.

Nikita said, "So, are we set?"

"Yes. They have room." He made no mention of the strangeness of the call.

"Okay. We spend one night there, and then you can take me to the treasure."

An hour later they were winding through the narrow roads on the ridgeline above Lapad Beach. Branko directed them to a parking area overlooking the ocean, but still on the top of the ridge, and Nikita said, "What's this? Where's the safehouse?"

"It's down the hill. The house doesn't have parking. I never pick a safehouse that has access to cars. It keeps me from being arrested."

Nikita looked at him with a small bit of respect and said, "Okay. Let's go. You lead."

The four of them walked down the narrow concrete staircase, threading by another house, and reached the one that Bogdan had rented. Branko said, "They've seen us on the cameras. Let me knock on the door."

Nikita said, "That's fine. Just get us inside."

Branko went to the door and rang the bell. Bogdan opened it and said, "We have the beds ready. What's going on? Why are you here?"

He was sweating profusely, his eyes wide open and darting around.

Branko hesitated, then Nikita pushed him past the entrance. Branko pointed behind him, saying, "They're with Andrei. We're only staying the night."

Nikita followed behind him with the two other men and said, "Don't ask any questions. Just show us the beds."

He took one more step and a bullet hit him in the head, splitting it open. He collapsed like the bones in his body had turned to rubber, hitting the floor with his eyes wide open, staring out at nothing, a gaping hole in his forehead. The two men with him dove behind cover, and a gunfight began, the bullets splitting the air.

Branko saw Drago running from the kitchen, then heard Bogdan scream and they both dove to the ground, scrambling to get out of the fire on their hands and knees. Drago ran to the stairwell in the back of the living room and was hit twice in the chest, his body toppling like a felled tree. One minute he was running, the next he fell forward like he'd been put asleep midstride. He collapsed at the front of the stairwell. Branko saw the blood flow, and knew who was here. It was the Afghans.

If he didn't get out, he was dead.

Branko leapt up and ran forward through the fire, hands over his head, dodging the bullets like a man trying to avoid the raindrops in a storm. He reached the stairwell leading to the lower floor, leapt over Drago, and raced down it, hearing the fire going on above him. Halfway to the bottom, he lost his balance, and went the rest of the way rolling down head over heels. He hit the landing on top of a body. He recognized the coder, saw the pool of blood around him, and crawled across his form in a panic, reaching another stairwell.

He stood up and took them two at a time, then ran down a hallway that led to the exit for the coastal walking path.

He sprinted through the garden spilling out below the house, trying to reach the walking path that snaked along the coast. He came to a gate, but had no key to open it. He saw the walking path beyond and vaulted over the gate with sheer adrenaline. He hit the path and rolled on the ground. He saw a couple of tourists staring at him and took off running, getting away from the death above him.

He jogged for about a hundred meters, and as had happened in Zagreb, his body began to fail him, his lungs screaming for air. He stopped, hands on his knees, and looked around him. Nobody from the house was following, but plenty of people were looking.

He stood up and began walking as if nothing had happened. He reached a hotel called More and glanced behind him. Still, nobody behind him. The hotel split the walking path, with the rooms above him and a deck built on the coast below. He knew that deck led to a unique bar—one the people hunting him wouldn't know.

He jogged down the concrete stairs to the deck, ignoring the chairs, umbrellas, and tourists lounging next to the ocean, instead circling around them to an entrance of a rough-hewn natural tunnel that went straight into the rock wall of the cliff.

It was a bar built inside a limestone cave, and he'd been there many times when he'd stayed at the Dubrovnik safehouse. He went down the tunnel, the air turning musty from the moisture seeping out of the rock. He reached the main chamber and saw there were no seats. The lower level of the cave wasn't that large, and there weren't many tables, each one situated on any available rock outcropping, with all already taken by hotel patrons and other tourists. There was a smaller tunnel leading to a space with a glass floor where one could see the water sluicing below, but that wasn't any help.

He glanced around, seeing a stairwell that led up to tables on another level. Built long after anyone had discovered the cave, the stairs were incongruously modern, with planks of polished wood and a railing made of stainless steel. He took them and found a small table empty, barely larger than the trunk of a tree, crammed into a corner off the stairwell. He saw it had a view of the tunnel entrance and sat down, his mouth open and panting like a puppy hearing fireworks for the first time.

A waitress came over and he ordered a beer, saying he was waiting on his wife. She looked at him with a little bit of curiosity, clearly wondering about his disheveled appearance, but took the order. He wondered if she would call the police, but then realized that would never happen.

The Cave Bar was a tourist attraction for anyone coming to

Lapad Beach. His dress and agitation wouldn't trigger an alarm. She wanted a tip, and she would get it, if only to keep her from remembering he'd been there.

She brought his drink and he paid handsomely, saying he didn't know where his wife was, but she'd be there soon. The waitress nodded, now relaxed, and he knew he was good.

He glanced back to the stairs he'd come up and saw an elevator leading to the hotel above. He'd never used it before, but he might now.

He focused back to the tunnel entrance, waiting. After five minutes he began to relax, and then the light was blocked by someone coming down.

He saw Shakor enter the main chamber and snapped back into the corner, his spine against the rock, getting out of view. But now he couldn't see what Shakor was doing. Was he coming up the stairs? If he did, he'd walk right by Branko's table.

He panicked, running to the elevator, jamming the button over and over. The elevator opened and he entered, hitting the button for the lobby level, a full seven floors above.

He crammed his body into the corner of the elevator, next to the buttons, jamming his finger into the close-door one. It finally slid shut, and he rode up to the top. He exited, walked into the lobby, and went to the concierge, saying, "Could you get me a cab? I'd Uber, but I don't have my phone."

"Where would you like to go?"

"The old town. The quicker the better."

CHAPTER 52

Shakor came back to the house in a rage. He ran up the steps, saw Ghulam and Karim standing over the dead body of Din, and shouted, his anger spilling out.

Ghulam said, "Where is he?"

"I don't know. He got away. Din is gone?"

"Yes. He's gone."

Shakor looked around the carnage and said, "Who are these people, and how did they do this?"

"It's the Americans. It's always the Americans."

Shakor took a breath, calming down. They'd lost Din, but had killed all three of the intruders. That was something. He walked to Nikita's body and said, "It's not the Americans. These men aren't American."

Ghulam said, "Whoever they are, they deserved to die. They were protecting the man who has the treasure."

Shakor said, "They were after the treasure as well." He glanced around the room and realized he'd fixated on the results of the gunfight, not on their next moves.

He said, "Get some security on this house. Karim, go out front. Make sure we aren't about to get attacked."

He left and Ghulam said, "We need to avenge Din."

Shakor said, "How do you expect to do that? Look around you. We killed all three men. What we need to do is find the treasure."

Ghulam nodded, but said nothing, and Shakor began to think

he didn't believe in the mission. All he wanted to do was lash out. Shakor knew what had happened to Ghulam at the hands of the Americans, and understood his pain, but that wouldn't help here.

He said, "Ghulam, look at me. I'm sorry about Din, but we need to find the treasure, and I need to trust you. You and your skill. This isn't a blood vengeance thing. There are no more men to kill. There is only one to find."

Ghulam nodded and said, "Okay. But this is an American thing. I just know it."

"Maybe it is, maybe it's not. But we need to find Branko. Today."

Ghulam said, "How? How are we going to do that? We don't have the resources of the United States. We can't track a beacon that we've shoved up his ass. He's gone."

And then there was a scratching behind the couch. Both men whipped around, putting the barrel of their guns on the sound. Bogdan stood up with his hands raised, one streaked with blood. He said, "Don't shoot. Please don't shoot. All I do is get places to stay. I have nothing to do with this."

Shakor had forgotten about Branko's other men. He said, "Where's Drago?"

Bogdan pointed to the stairwell and said, "He's there. He's dead."

Shakor went to the landing and saw Drago's body. He said, "Come out from behind the couch."

Bogdan did, saying, "Please don't shoot. I don't know anything. All I do is purchase the places to stay."

Ghulam said, "He's lying."

"I'm not! I don't do anything with ransomware. I just rent stuff."

Ghulam aimed the barrel of his gun between Bogdan's eyes and said, "Let's just kill him and get out of here."

Shakor thought a minute, then had an idea. He said, "You use Branko's credit card to rent these places?"

Bogdan nodded his head so fast, Shakor thought it would snap, saying, "Yes, yes. That's what I do. That's all I do."

"Who's paying the bills?"

"I don't know. A Russian, but I don't know who he is."

"Does Branko have the same card? Same number?"

Bogdan nodded. Shakor said, "Can you see when that card is used?"

He nodded again, now thinking he might live because he had something to offer.

Shakor said, "Get on a computer and pull up that account. Right now."

Bogdan did, typing like he was late for a deadline.

The account showed the card had been used earlier at a restaurant in Mali Ston, and a recent charge for a cab company, the destination the old town of Dubrovnik. Which wasn't a lot of help, but it wasn't nothing.

Shakor said, "Where would he go in the old town? Is there another safehouse?"

Bogdan shrank back and said, "No. This is the only house."

Shakor raised his weapon and said, "You'd better come up with something better than that, because it's the only thing keeping you alive."

Bogdan reloaded the page with shaking fingers, and another purchase magically appeared. It was at a place called the Caffe Bar Buza, which meant nothing to the Afghans in the room.

Shakor looked at the screen, then at Bogdan, saying, "Where is this?"

"The old town. At the top. It's a bar at the top of the old town."

CHAPTER 53

We gathered back at the restaurant in Mali Ston, sitting around the table and silently chuckling about what had just happened. We had been suckered in a big way, and while it made me angry, it was our fault for not seeing the layout connection between the two towns of Ston and Mali Ston. Hell, I'd even quizzed Jennifer about the damn fortifications.

Knuckles said, "So the ransomware geek has some skill on his side."

I said, "Yeah, but we knew that the minute he took a shot at us with a suppressed pistol. If I were to guess, I'd say they're Russians working for that Andrei guy, protecting the investment. And they're long gone."

Knuckles said, "What are we going to do? Call it a day?"

I sighed and said, "That'll depend on Wolffe, but if I were a betting man, I'd say yes. Last time I talked to him, he said POTUS was looking at a nation-state and didn't think the risk of us continuing in a foreign country was worth what we'd get out of it even if we did capture Branko."

Veep said, "What do you think?"

"I think Wolffe believes that POTUS is being risk averse, and because of it he's only increasing the danger. Ignoring Branko is asking for potential failure against the Valkyrie crew, just like ig-noring the clear signs we had before 9/11. And I absolutely agree with him, but it's a moot point. We couldn't get to Branko now if we wanted because we were stupid."

I slapped the table in disgust, the humor of the situation dissipating. I said, "I *knew* that guy was skilled. I should have predicted he wasn't just coming here for lunch. I got tunnel focused on some mythical meeting and missed the signs."

Knuckles said, "We all missed it." He pulled out the phone he'd found on the table and handed it to me. I took it and said, "I'm starting to build a collection of Branko's phones. Maybe I'll open a shop here in Croatia selling used iPhones."

Veep said, "Hey, we still have his original cloned iPhone, don't we? I mean he wiped the primary, but we cloned it, right?"

I said, "Yeah?"

"Well, we can't do a real-time geolocation track, but we can find historical patterns of that phone here in the country. It's not optimal, and we'll probably see a bunch of bars or clubs he frequents, but we might also see a historical cluster at another safehouse."

"That won't tell us he's there."

"I know, but we've got nothing else. If you want to continue on this guy, that's what we've got."

Brett said, "That might work if we had a single date where we knew he was somewhere and wanted to know that location, but looking at a date range is going to be information overload. His cell has been all over this country."

I picked up my Taskforce phone, looked at my watch, and said, "You're right, but Veep's got a damn good idea, and the information overload is Creed's problem. It's nine in the morning there. He'll be at work."

I dialed and was surprised when I got a switchboard operator instead of the network operation's cell. A woman said, "Blaisdell Consulting, how can I direct your call?"

I stuttered for a moment, then said, "Hang on." I muted the phone and said, "What's this month's code to tell them to go secure and that I'm not under duress?"

Knuckles said, "Why? We have a direct secure line for this operation."

"I don't know. I got Marge at the front desk."

Marge was about two hundred years old and had been working as our "receptionist" since the Taskforce had been created. She loved me, but there was no way I was getting behind her firewall. Either I knew the code, or she'd tell me to pack sand.

Jennifer said, "Tell her, 'I'm calling about your team-building services.' She'll ask how you found out about them, and you say, 'I was given a brochure at a conference by Xavier Barclay.'"

I said, "You're shitting me." Honestly, I never bothered to memorize the bullshit the Taskforce put out about these things because I was always on the forefront of any operation, but now I wasn't, and I was happy that Jennifer never ignored them.

She smiled and said, "Nope."

I unmuted and said, "Hey, you still there?"

"Yes. How may I direct your call?"

"I'm calling about your team-building services."

"Okay. How did you hear about us?"

"I was given a brochure from Xavier Barclay at a conference."

She said, "Let me transfer your call," and the encryption protocols began. I waited, saying, "This secret spy stuff is really getting ridiculous. Xavier Barclay? Who came up with that damn name?"

I understood the reason why in that we had no idea who was listening in on our phone calls, meaning we needed to sound innocuous before we encrypted, and the Taskforce had to make sure that I wasn't calling with a gun to my head. If I had been, it would have been a different name I'd supposedly met.

Knuckles said, "The bigger question is why are we cut off."

Marge came back, the encryption making her sound a little like she was speaking in a tube. "How can I direct your call?"

"Hey, Marge, it's Pike. I need Creed in the network operations center."

She said, "Well, at least you remembered the protocol this time. Stand by."

Reminding me I'd used the switchboard line a few times without remembering what I was supposed to say . . .

The phone rang through and Creed answered, saying, "Sorry about that redirect, Pike, but we've been shut down on the Branko mission. No more phone pings or other work."

"What? Why?"

"I don't know. I'm just the computer guy. Something to do with the threat. George Wolffe is headed to a briefing at the White House right now."

I rolled my eyes to the team and said, "Okay, well, I don't need an active ping on a phone, just some historical data drawn from the phone itself. Can you do that?"

"What do you have?"

"I've got the original Branko cell phone. Well, at least the clone we made."

"What do you want?"

"I want to know where this phone has been in the past. That's it."

"Do you have a date? Something to zero in on?"

"Uh, no. I need a couple of months, but you can skip anything that involves a store, bar, or other establishments. Focus solely on bed-down locations. And you can skip Zagreb, Split, and Korcula. We know them, so it's unnecessary. Focus on new cities, but only here in Croatia. If he's got a safehouse in Serbia or Bosnia, that's out of my reach."

"Pike, I don't know about this. I just told you we were called off."

"Creed, I'm not asking you to do any manipulation of the cell network. Just look at this phone. Any direct action will come from me."

He said, "Plug in the phone." I looked at Jennifer, and she already had it slaved to her computer, the laptop itself tied into her own Taskforce phone's VPN. I said, "Jennifer's sending linkup now."

He said, "Okay, I see it. Give me a little time," then, "Shit. Don't say I'm doing anything."

"What?"

I heard him say, "Hey, sir, it's Pike. I just told him we'd been turned off."

I heard the phone shuffle, then Blaine Alexander came on, saying, "Hey, Pike."

Taken aback, I said, "Sir, what's going on back there? I tried to call Creed and our line was redirected. I got Marge."

I heard him sigh, then, "Yeah, your op has been turned off. Wolffe was given a direct order to pull you. Honestly, we were sort of hoping another phone ping wasn't necessary and you'd have this guy in a bag before we could tell you to back off. We delayed telling you for that reason. I was supposed to release a message at noon today, six P.M. your time. I'm assuming by the call you have no joy?"

I ignored that question, saying, "What's POTUS thinking?"

"Apparently, the expert we used to find Branko in the first place is coming in today with proof of who's doing the attack, and it's not the original ransomware team Dark Star. They're just using the name."

"That's bullshit. Too much of a coincidence. Too many things that don't add up for a completely new team to do this. Especially since they're using the Dark Star name. What's Wolffe think?"

"He thinks like you. Well, he thinks that pursuing Branko can't hurt. If it ends up being a nation-state, so be it, but letting Branko go might be like missing the flight training in Florida before 9/11."

"Couldn't agree more. What do the others think? What about the NSA and Cyber? They've had a day to look at it."

"They're chickenshits. So far they're just nodding their heads at what Dylan Hobbes says. He has a lot of referent firepower because he worked at both places. He's apparently a genius and they know it. If he's wrong, they're happy to let him take the fall. If he's right, they're agreeable to saying they concurred."

"And Kerry Bostwick? What's CIA saying?"

"He thinks it's bullshit. But he's on his own with that."

"Well, that's something. Did you get anything on the Afghans? They're a wild card in this whole thing."

"Afghans? What could they do with this? They can barely work a computer. Why do you keep bringing them up?"

"Because they're running around here chasing Branko, and they killed the Afghan national security advisor, all for some treasure. If you had something on them, it might lead me to Branko. It's another thread."

"Forget about them, Pike. Trust me, I know how you feel.

We've all lost a little bit of our life over there, and I know you want some vengeance, but they aren't doing any of this. Let them go."

"I'm *not* doing this for vengeance. Jesus, sir, they're at the heart of this and they don't even know it. They're running around blind chasing Branko and don't even know the threat that he's created. You give me a thread on those guys and I'll find Branko. They're tracking him right now, I promise."

"Pike, far be it from me to say you're crazy, but you're crazy. Now, if you'd found some Iranians or North Koreans chasing Branko, that might be a different story."

I gave up. "Okay, okay. One final question—if I hang up right now, and don't check my messages until I bed down tonight, can I take the day?"

"What do you have?"

"Nothing yet, but I have some things working. I think you should be aware I'm probably going to go kinetic here."

He said nothing for a moment, then, "We're running under twenty-four hours until that Valkyrie capsule creates mass murder. And when that happens, someone's going to pay. It won't be Dark Star. Hannister is going to be forced to react to whatever proof is presented today. You and I both know how that will work out. No matter who wins the fight, our men will die. If you can prevent that, yeah, you got your day."

"Don't let the president do anything stupid until I can prove it isn't Branko. Don't let him take the word of a single egghead, no matter how smart he is."

"Pike, you do what you do, but I can't prevent the president from doing anything based on Branko, because this conversation never took place."

"Understood, sir. Before I go, can you put Creed back on the line?"

"What for?"

"Sir . . ."

"Never mind . . . I'll expect a confirmation of your marching orders to come home sometime tonight."

CHAPTER 54

Wolffe walked into the White House Situation Room with the meeting already in progress. He'd been called forward for this, but clearly it wasn't because he was needed, as they'd started without him. It didn't bother him, because the stakes of this mission had clearly eclipsed his mandate. The Taskforce scalpel was no longer the tool to use here.

He softly closed the door and went to the back of the room, taking a seat against the wall next to a scrum of other low-level advisors. The president was at the head of the table—the same one seen in every famous photograph of a president in crisis—with the important people flowing down each side of the table from his location. Behind them, on chairs along the walls, were the aides.

Nobody in this room had any idea what Wolffe did for the nation, and he preferred to keep it that way. At the opposite end of the room was Dylan Hobbes. He stood in front of a Power-Point presentation, and apparently was in the middle of his briefing. Wolffe surveyed the table and saw a few Oversight Council members, like the SECDEF, the D/CIA, and the SECSTATE, but most were from somewhere else in the behemoth that was the United States government.

Wolffe returned to Hobbes and saw he was sweating profusely. Wolffe thought he looked like a character from *Breaking Bad*, the sweat rolling off his face as if he was being interrogated. *What's up with that?*

Hobbes was conducting a synopsis of his research, and in so doing spouting off a plethora of cybersecurity terms, showing the depth of his investigation. DNS, malware, Zero Day threat, rootkit, phishing, IP addresses, TOR network, you name it, it was a cornucopia of buzzwords complete with inscrutable graphs that only one or two people in the room could even decipher. The rest just took him at his word.

When he was done, he said, "Given the evidence, I think I've managed to locate the origin of this current threat. It's not a bunch of ransomware guys from Serbia. It's a nation-state."

He paused for dramatic effect, and President Hannister rolled his hand forward, saying, "Spare me the theatrics and just give it to us. Do you know where it came from?"

"Yes, sir."

Everyone took a breath, and he flicked to the next slide, saying, "It's Iran."

The room erupted in murmurs of sidebar conversations, and President Hannister held up his hand, quelling the chatter. He said, "How do you know that?"

Hobbes pointed to the next slide, saying, "Honestly, I thought it would be North Korea, but the fingerprints didn't match. Remember when the Iranians took out the casinos in Las Vegas in 2014? They managed to penetrate Sheldon Adelson's entire network and cause enormous damage, but in so doing, they left a lot of fingerprints behind in the code and in the contact routing back to the person doing the work. They were good, but not that good."

"Okay, but is this a guess, or you *know*?"

"Sir, I used the fingerprint analogy for a reason. When you do a fingerprint comparison, you're basically finding points of intersection from one print to another, until the points become so great that the fingerprint in question is unlikely to be the fingerprint of someone else. It's the same way here. I have found multiple points of intersection that lead nowhere else."

President Hannister sat back and said, "So you don't *know*. You're just saying in your best estimation, it's the Iranians. I mean, you didn't find an Iranian flag embedded in the code or anything."

"No, sir, but none of this is absolute. The reason they chose a cyberattack is precisely to give them plausible deniability. Short of having a video of someone working a keyboard, or an Iranian attacker going on CNN to brag, we're never going to have absolute proof. But like a fingerprint, the trace doesn't lie."

President Hannister sighed and said, "But it's not enough to give us a Cuban Missile Crisis moment, either. If I took all this to the United Nations and demanded they turn off the ransomware, would your evidence matter? Is it like Adlai Stevenson showing satellite photos of missiles in Cuba, or like Colin Powell showing hand-drawn pictures of supposed biological weapon vans in Iraq?"

Hobbes said, "To the initiated, it would be a slam dunk, but for the United Nations, it wouldn't be what you want. There is no way to educate them on the fingerprints, and there is no way to get an actual smoking gun out of cyber. It just doesn't happen."

"So what am I supposed to do with that?"

Hobbes said, "Sir, I don't know. Policy is your realm. I'm just giving you the facts."

Kerry Bostwick, the CIA director, said, "I'd like to know what the NSA and Cyber Command think of this. What's your assessment?"

General Franco Baggetti, dual hatted as both the commander of the NSA and of Cyber Command, said, "We've looked as well, and while we haven't gotten nearly as far into our analysis as Dylan, his outcome is something we wouldn't disagree with at this stage in our investigation."

Wolffe thought, *What a mealy-mouthed answer. None of his men will face any shots fired in anger.*

Kerry said, "That's it? With the entire power of the United States government paying for your capabilities, you don't have an opinion?"

General Baggetti took offense and said, "This isn't like taking a car engine apart, where you have a manual and just follow it. We're looking, but we want to be precise. We've found nothing so far to disprove Dylan's projections. That's all I'm saying."

"So you can't disprove it? That's your level of success? We're about to pin a catastrophic attack on a foreign country. Don't you think a little bit more introspection is required here?"

President Hannister held up his hand and said, "Okay, let's deal in specifics. What's the clock on this? Where do we stand?"

The head of NASA said, "We have less than twenty-four hours. We've managed to get the abort protocol in play from inside the capsule, but we're worried about corruption. We can use it as a last resort."

"What's that mean?"

"It means we can more than likely prevent a collision with the space station, but we'll probably lose the capsule in the process. Once he initiates abort, the fall from orbit is going to need to be controlled from the ground as a failsafe. We think we've managed to get the abort code to work in the capsule using firewalled systems, but once he pulls the trigger, without the ability to control from the ground, he'll probably burn up in the atmosphere like a meteor."

President Hannister shook his head and said, "This is the best we've got? This is it?"

Everyone remained quiet, as if they were stone statues. He continued: "I'm living that Bruce Willis movie *Armageddon*. Do I need to go find some oil drillers to solve this problem?"

The NASA man took a breath, then said, "Sir, I'm just telling you what we have. This isn't a NASA launch. If it were, I might be able to give you more options, but it's not. Auriga oversees this thing, and they're working twenty-four seven on solutions, but all NASA can do is provide advice and support."

Wolffe thought, *Meaning don't look at cutting our budget when this goes to shit.*

Wolffe felt his phone vibrate and pulled it out, seeing a text message from Blaine.

> Pike is hunting. Says don't do anything stupid. He doesn't think the egghead is right.

That caused Wolffe to smile. He'd been given a direct order from Alexander Palmer to pull Pike off, and he'd done so—with a little bit of a delay. He texted back, What's he have? Does he have Branko?

No. No Branko, but maybe soon. Pike says not to do anything until he can prove it isn't Branko. And that makes sense to me.

Might not have the time for that. What's he chasing?

I don't know. He didn't tell me because I ordered him off the chase, and then we agreed that the phone call hadn't happened. He's got the Afghans in mind.

Wolffe rolled his eyes at that and texted, Afghans? What is it with him and the Afghans? Does he have anything real?

He does. Let him work. I know it sounds strange, but that guy is never wrong.

CHAPTER 55

After the second lap without finding any parking, Shakor decided to take just Ghulam, leaving Karim with the car. He turned to the backseat and said, "Where is the nearest gate to the city?"

Bogdan, sitting next to Ghulam, said, "Just up here on the left. See that ramp going down? That leads to the gate."

Shakor said, "Karim, drop us off and stay with the car. We'll call when we're done."

Karim nodded and pulled over next to the sidewalk. Shakor said, "Bogdan, if you attempt to run, I'll kill you in the street."

Bogdan didn't get a chance to respond, being forced out of the car by Ghulam. They walked down the stone ramp, going lower and lower, the towering walls surrounding the Dubrovnik old town rising above them. Bogdan led them through multiple stone arches, passing tour groups and street artists, eventually reaching a plaza connected to a wide thoroughfare running the length of the city, an ancient church on the left and a row of stores on the right. He started walking up the left side of the church, saying, "This is the main street, but the bar is up high, near the top of the walls."

He took a right behind the church and reached another plaza lined with cafés, a wide, ornate staircase beyond the umbrellas. He stopped and pointed, saying, "We need to go up the shame stairs, then cut through a few alleys and more stairs."

Confused, Shakor said, "Shame stairs? Why are they called that?"

"They filmed the *Game of Thrones* here. They made one of the characters walk down those stairs naked in the show as an act of shame. It's just something our group used when we were trying to link up after drinking."

Shakor shook his head, wondering how that television show had permeated the entirety of this country. There was a reason Islam forbade such corrosion. He said, "What about the other bar? The low one? Mala Buza?"

"I don't know where that is. That's something you found."

In Pashto, Shakor turned to Ghulam and said, "Go find it. You know it's on the water, just outside the walls. Be waiting on my call."

Ghulam nodded and set out trying to find the location. Bogdan said, "Why are you sending them there? I don't get it. The credit card was used at the upper bar, Caffe Buza."

Before leaving the house, Shakor had used the Wi-Fi to research the location of the Caffe Bar Buza and was concerned by what he'd found. Like Bogdan said, it was just below the top of the city walls, built into the cliffs overlooking the Adriatic Sea. It had a single entrance, a small portal in the stone of the wall, leading to layers of decks on the cliffs outside. In other words, it was a complete dead end.

Shakor had chased Branko enough to have some grudging respect for his ability to escape, and it was always predicated on never stopping in a place without a back door. There was no way he would put himself in a position like the cliff bar. Everything he had shown up until this point was that security came first. No cars allowed near his houses, secret drops out of castles, World War II tunnels, pedestrian gates to a coastal walkway, terrace balconies within reach of the ground—there was always a backdoor escape.

And that was Shakor's concern, as this place was the absolute opposite of having an escape route. Branko was trapped there as surely as if he'd entered a limestone cave, and he would know that, so why choose to go there?

One picture on the website gallery gave Shakor a clue. Below the decks he could see a rope line in the water making a square about seventy meters wide and connected to the rocks below.

Shakor ignored Bogdan's question and said, "Just take me to the upper bar."

Bogdan led him up the wide staircase, then right down an alley, then up another flight of stairs, this one much narrower, almost like a tunnel. They passed art galleries, houses, and cafés, the process repeating itself until they were on an alley running right next to the city wall itself. Shakor kept his eyes open, scanning the tourists coming and going in case Branko popped out of the crowds. It had been close to an hour since the credit card had been used, and Branko might have decided to leave.

He didn't appear, and Bogdan finally stopped outside a small square in the wall, just over five feet in height and looking like a portal for a cannon, which it well may have been eons ago. Beyond it was a stone stairwell leading down. He said, "This is it. What do we do now?"

"We go in. You lead."

They waited for a couple to exit, the man saying, "Great view, but it's a little crowded."

Shakor nodded and said, "Any seats at all?"

"At the upper level. Nothing on the lower. But you'll want to go down there anyway to check out the idiots jumping."

And Shakor knew his instincts were right.

Bogdan went through the portal and then began down the stairs. Shakor followed, seeing the bar spilling out below him, tables crammed on multiple levels down the cliff. Bogdan stopped on the upper level, the actual bar area covered with thatching of bamboo to ward off the sun, a few tables scattered about in front. Shakor surveyed the area and saw no sign of Branko. Bogdan pointed at an empty table and Shakor shook his head, saying, "Go lower."

Bogdan did, Shakor right behind him, the rough concrete steps winding back and forth. They made a final turn to the deck, and then Shakor saw Branko on the other end, next to a second stairwell leading to another level. He yanked Bogdan's shirt, getting him to stop, then looked around for a way to approach so Branko wouldn't see them. Shakor wanted to surprise him before he had a chance to run, but there wasn't a way to get to him without simply walking through all the other tables with tourists.

Shakor thought about sending Bogdan, using him to lull Branko with a story of escape or something else, but knew Bogdan wouldn't comply. He looked back at Branko as he debated, and they locked eyes.

Branko sprang up, knocking over his chair, then leapt to the stairwell. He began skipping down the steps and Shakor gave chase, the crowds at the table looking up as he went past. He reached the second set of stairs, turned around, and saw Bogdan running back to the top. Shakor ignored him, focusing on Branko.

He started down and saw Branko jump the railing to the rocks adjacent to the stairs, then begin scuttling across them. Shakor stopped at the railing, knowing what was going to happen.

Branko looked back at him, then ran forward, leaping off the rock face, windmilling his arms from forty feet above the water. He dropped straight down, hitting the water with a splash and causing the tourists on the deck to stand up to see, some cheering, but all of them chattering. Branko surfaced, looked back to Shakor, then raised his middle finger before stroking toward the rope line meant to delineate the end of the swimming area. He crossed it and kept going, paralleling the city walls on the shore.

Shakor only smiled in return. When he'd seen the rope line in the bar's galley pictures, he'd realized there was a swimming area below, but couldn't see any way to get there short of jumping. Then he'd seen a single picture of a man doing just that, and thought he'd found Branko's back door. Now, standing on the railing, he could see a ladder bolted into the stone forty feet below him, then a narrow set of stairs leading back to the rock shelf, but that would have been much too slow for Branko to use.

All in all, it was smart, because there was no way to get down to the bottom level of the city before Branko was out of the water and running, and no way any of his men could follow him into the water wearing boots and strapped with weapons—even if they had the nerve to do so. But like any strategy built on surprise, once the secret was known, the plan was worthless. In fact, worse than worthless, because the plan itself could be used against the planner.

Shakor had researched the rocky shore away from the cliff bar, searching for an exit point Branko could use to get back into the city, and had found another bar, this one at sea level, with another rope-lined swimming area. It was the bar where he'd sent Ghulam.

Shakor pulled out his phone and called Ghulam, saying, "He's coming to you. Don't let him see you. Let him get out and back inside the walls before you pounce."

CHAPTER 56

Inside the Situation Room, Wolffe texted Blaine Alexander one final time, saying, Okay, delay the termination order to Pike as long as possible. Let's see what he can come up with, then put his phone away when President Hannister said, "Okay, options. What are our options?"

Amanda Croft, the secretary of state, said, "We can take this evidence to the Swiss. Bypass the Security Council and go straight to Iran. Tell the Iranians we know it's them, they've made their point, but if it comes to fruition, there are going to be repercussions."

Kerry Bostwick said, "All that will do is engender a bunch of 'we didn't do this—the Great Satan is looking for ways to attack us.' They're going to say they have no idea what this is about, and we're trying to start a fight. You do that, and they'll be the ones to leak it to the press in a preemptive bid to show, A, we suck at space exploration, and B, we're picking on them. That won't work."

Croft said, "So do nothing? I mean, what else is there?"

Alexander Palmer said, "We could go to the Swiss with a message basically saying, 'If this spacecraft crashes, we're doing regime change.' That would get their attention."

President Hannister nodded, rubbing his face, thinking.

Kerry Bostwick spoke up, saying, "And if it's not them? What do you think they're going to do? We just threatened their very existence over an event they do not control. They aren't going to sit back and wait for the buildup of forces like Saddam did. He had no weapons of mass destruction and let us prepare to invade anyway. Iran has seen that playbook. If they have nothing to do with this, they're going to attack us with all they have preemptively, which is formidable in an asymmetric way. I'm talking Israel, troops in Iraq, suicide bombers here at home, more cyberattacks, you name it. That, in turn, will guarantee a response from us, but won't do a damn thing for the space station."

He looked around the room and said, "In short, if you send that message, and it's them doing this, we might be able to save that capsule. If you send it and it's not them, we're going to war."

President Hannister said, "Dylan, how sure are you on this?"

"Sir, there are no absolutes, but if I were still working in Cyber Command, I would tell you that this is Iran just like I did when they penetrated the casinos in Las Vegas. It *is* Iran."

President Hannister turned to the NASA engineer and said, "How long do I have before I have to send that message? If they turn off the ransomware, how long does it take to obtain control again?"

"If they turn it off, it's pretty much instantaneous. We're talking minutes, maybe an hour for complete control."

"So I have what, twenty-two more hours to figure out more proof it's Iran?"

Amanda Croft said, "No. Not really. We have no direct diplomatic relations with Iran, so there is no way to send them the message immediately. If we go through the Swiss, that alone will take time—first convincing them to send the message, then letting them send the message, then time for the Iranians to deliberate before giving a response, which the Swiss will then relay to us. It's not a quick process."

"So what are you saying?"

"I'm saying you have about six hours. Total."

Nobody in the room spoke, and then President Hannister said, "Send the message. Tell them we know it's them, and that we won't tolerate it. Do it now."

The secretary of defense said, "Sir, like Kerry, I must caution you that the message you're sending may engender the very thing we want to avoid. They might not even respond with diplomatic words. You're basically telling them we're finally an existential threat. They've thought it for years, but they've never heard it from a sitting president."

President Hannister slapped the table and said, "I understand that!" He calmed down a little bit, then said, "I understand that, but what else can I do? They're holding our people hostage in a spacecraft just like they did in the embassy in 1979."

Kerry Bostwick said, "Unless it's not them."

Nobody replied to that statement. President Hannister said, "Just get it done. Amanda, give me a readout on the Swiss in the next hour. General Oglethorpe, get everyone on alert that you need to — 82nd Airborne, Fifth Fleet, whoever. Kerry, give me the chatter this causes. Let me know if this is real or something else."

He looked around the room and said, "Any questions?"

When none came, he said, "Meeting adjourned."

President Hannister stood up and left the room, the principals of the Oversight Council right behind him. The rest of the minions broke up into small cliques, talking about what had just occurred, as if they were discussing how to get more votes for an ethanol subsidy.

Wolffe saw Kerry Bostwick still in the room and went to him, saying, "This is a war of choice. We don't know it's them."

Kerry sighed and said, "Yeah, we don't. But we also don't know it *isn't* them."

"You know Pike is on the hunt, right?"

Kerry looked at him in confusion, then said, "We turned him off. He is *not* on the hunt. Right?"

"I turned him off, but the message isn't going until tonight. I need some help here. If Dylan Hobbes is right, then so be it. But if he's wrong, we're going to war for the dumbest of reasons. I need some help."

"I can't turn off the president. What help?"

"CIA help. You can do that. You have much more leeway than I do."

Kerry glanced around the room, then said, "We're stepping over a dangerous line here. I can't cross Taskforce activities with CIA ones."

"And I can't bring the men who get killed in a misguided war back to life. Think, man. Give Pike a chance."

"What, specifically, do you want?"

"Specifically? I have no idea, but I'm sure Pike will."

CHAPTER 57

My car was starting to heat up even with the windows down and the sun setting. I looked at my watch, wanting my surveillance rotation to begin just to get out of this seat. Actually, I was leaning toward just hitting the place. If we startled some German tourists renting the Vrbo, then we'd apologize and leave, holstering our weapons.

At least that's what I wanted to do.

My earpiece came alive with another SITREP, this time from Veep. "Still no activity. I say again, no activity."

We'd been outside the target house for two hours now, and hadn't seen any movement at all, which, given our evidence that it even *was* a target house, didn't mean anything at all.

Creed had managed to download the GPS file in Branko's phone—well, our cloned phone—and had plotted all the points for the last month. Two months was just too great of an ask.

The problem set was the opposite of what one usually did with this sort of data. For instance, in 2003, the CIA snatched a bad guy named Abu Omar off the streets of Milan, Italy, using what they considered good tradecraft at the time. Unfortunately, the times had leapfrogged beyond the Cold War.

The Italian police had taken the snapshot from the moment of capture and analyzed every cell phone in the square, focusing on each one to determine who owned it. They'd come up with about a dozen that didn't fit, and eventually used that data to trace the path of the owners until twenty-three Americans were convicted in absentia of kidnapping on Italian soil. Those twenty-three still have warrants for their arrests, including the chief of station in Milan, even as the CIA to this day disavows all knowledge of the operation.

Our problem was the inverse. Unlike the Italians, we knew the cell number, but we had no specific point in time to analyze. Creed had started on areas with more than one visit, which eliminated an enormous amount of data, but still left a universe's worth. From there, he'd axed bars, restaurants, train stations, and the like, focusing on places to stay—houses, hotels, youth hostels, whatever. He'd found the ones we'd already assaulted in Zagreb, Korcula, and Split, eliminating them, then narrowed the list to three.

One was in Liechtenstein, which he'd only visited twice and wasn't worth my effort. Another was in Zadar, with at least thirty hits, so that was something. The final was in Dubrovnik and also had about thirty hits. So, I had a choice. Since Zadar was up the coast, beyond Split, and Branko had consistently moved south, down the coast, I'd chosen the Dubrovnik location. It was on a hill in an area known as Lapad, without any access to vehicles, which was a clue in our favor. It seemed Branko never wanted a place where a car could pull up right outside, disgorging men before he could get away. He always built a little surveillance box to catch you coming on foot. And he'd done so here.

We'd found the cameras in the trees and bushes and had avoided them, settling down to wait until we saw someone leave. If it had been a little old lady, we would have reassessed. If it was some guy wearing Birkenstocks with skinny legs and a pasty complexion from staring at computers all day, we'd assault.

So far, we'd found nothing at all, and I was running out of time. Blaine wanted my acknowledgment of his termination order "tonight," which I understood meant my time, but I was going to use "tonight" as in his time, meaning I had an extra six hours to work with. Even so, the clock was running, because the sun was starting to set.

I glanced at Jennifer in the driver's seat and said, "I'm thinking about cracking it, right now."

She said, "We don't have any evidence one way or the other."

I nodded, then said, "We get to the door and radarscope it. If we find life behind the door, we back off. If we don't, we crack it."

"What about the early warning net? You'll trigger."

"Only if we get in front of the cameras. We found three. I'm pretty sure they haven't wired the woods like it's Fort Knox."

"But they might have some motion detectors, heat sensors, or something else we haven't seen."

I nodded and said, "Yeah, they might, but there's a space capsule about to crash and I'm sick of waiting around. My bet is the place is empty and we're wasting our time here watching."

She smiled and said, "And you'll have to quit once the sun sets." She reached behind the seat and pulled up her backpack, saying, "I'm sick of sweating in this car as well. Let's do it."

That brought out a grin. I called in the team, gave them my assessment, then said, "Jennifer's got the lock. Brett, you've got security of the breach, and you're lead. Take us through the cameras. Veep, radarscope. Knuckles, you and I in after initial breach. But only if we get a negative on the scope. If we get a live body inside, we pull back and wait. I don't want to scare some couple from France if they've rented the place."

We spent about three minutes kitting up, then got in order of march, with Brett in the lead. He went down the stairs until he reached a landing, then climbed the rail, circling around in the woods. We got parallel to the edge of the building, about thirty feet into the woods on the side of the hill, and he said, "Last camera is just above the overhang for the door. I'll take Veep for the radar check and alert you. If you see us coming back, it's no joy."

I nodded, feeling the familiar trace of adrenaline rising. I said, "Execute."

I watched them slink through the woods, then hug the wall past the porch overhang, avoiding the last camera. Brett put his weapon on the door and Veep went to work. After about three minutes, I was going to call and ask him if he had the damn batteries in the device or needed a class on how to work it, because he was taking forever. Thirty seconds later, I heard, "Cleared to breach. I say again, cleared to breach."

Jennifer took the lead, her lock-pick kit out and ready, no weapons in her hands. That was Brett's job. Knuckles and I raced across the slope right behind her, until we were stacked in the small alcove. Brett shifted his position to allow him to cover the door without putting his barrel over Jennifer, Veep came up to the rear of our formation, and she went to work. Twenty seconds later, she turned back to me, telling me the door was clear.

I nodded, and she swung it open, with me leading the way. I went right, Knuckles went left, Veep followed me to the right, then Brett went left.

I smelled it as soon as I entered. The sickly sweet odor of blood. I saw a body on the ground, but ignored it, continuing to clear. Jennifer entered, now with her Glock out, and I said, "Cover the door." She rotated around, took a knee, and we split up into two-man teams, each clearing rooms. I took the stairs with Veep behind me, and we reached the bottom, finding another body. I went right, saw a door, and waited on Veep's squeeze. He rubbed my shoulder, and I entered a laundry room, nothing else inside.

We returned up the stairs, and the place was clear, Knuckles and Brett searching bodies while Jennifer maintained eyes on the door.

I said, "What do we have?"

"Three dead Russians, a dead Serbian, and some guy without any identification."

Knuckles handed me a passport, and Brett looked at it, saying, "That's the guy who took the shots at us in Korcula."

I said, "Great. Well, it looks like someone else was better with a gun than you guys."

Brett chuckled and said, "Anything down below?"

"An exit to the shore and another body. Veep, check that guy at the bottom of the stairs."

He left and I surveyed the damage, saying, "I'm so proud. We found the next safehouse. A little late, but at least we can say we were right."

Knuckles said, "Too bad we wasted our timeline staring at a house full of dead guys."

"I know." I went to the guy without identification and rolled him over. He was swarthy, with black hair and a face tan that didn't fit, like he'd just shaved off his beard.

I said, "This one had nothing?"

"Nope. His pockets are completely empty."

I went to the Russian, his face obliterated, and said, "This one?"

"Had all sorts of shit, including a bunch of receipts from Zagreb, Korcula, and Liechtenstein."

"Liechtenstein? As in the country?"

"Yeah. Just pocket litter, but it was there. He's also got visas in the passport from the same place. Just like the other Russian over there."

One of Creed's hits on Branko had been in that country, and this guy was Russian. Not too hard to figure out who he worked for, but it was good to know where Andrei was located.

I looked at the picture in the passport Knuckles had given me, since the face on the body was beyond recognition. It was the man from Mali Ston. The one who'd tricked us with the surveillance detection route.

Veep came back up and said, "Serbian passport, but nothing else."

"So, we have two dead Serbians, three dead Russians, and one unknown?"

Knuckles said, "Yeah, looks that way."

I shook my head and paced a bit, then said, "The fucking Afghans have Branko."

Knuckles said, "What? Where did that come from?"

I pointed at the unknown and said, "He's Badr 313. He's Afghan. They ambushed the Russians here and took Branko." I circled, still thinking, saying, "They must really, really want that treasure."

Knuckles looked first at Brett, then Veep, then Jennifer to see if anyone else in the room could make sense of what I was saying. He finally said, "You're going to have to connect those dots here."

I said, "Those two Serbians are part of Dark Star. Computer geeks. They were here in the safehouse. We know for a fact that"—I checked the passport—"Nikita here had Branko under control in Mali Ston. We saw him take him away. Now, they're all dead, and we have a guy in here without any identification, which means someone was left alive after the fact to clean his body. His alone. Who would do that? Not any Russians or Serbs, because they would have cleaned *all* the bodies."

I paced a bit, now convinced. I said, "No, the Afghans found this safehouse somehow, just like we did, and they waited for the Russians to show up with Branko, and when they did, they ambushed the team, killing all of them. Since Branko's body isn't here, and every swinging dick in this adventure is chasing him, he's the key. And it's the Afghans, I'm sure."

Jennifer looked amazed at my analysis, saying, "Wow. That was impressive. Why can't you do that when the air-conditioning breaks in our house? Instead of making things worse by bashing everything with a hammer?"

Brett said, "I have to say, that was Perry Mason impressive. You've convinced me, but so what? The sun's setting and we're about to turn into pumpkins soon."

I said, "Veep, you got that cloned phone from Branko?"

He nodded and brought it over. I said, "You know how AirTags work? I've never used one."

He said, "Yeah, you mean that tag Creed found early on?"

I said, "Yep. I originally thought Branko knew something about this Bactrian Treasure that the Afghans could use to find it, which is why they were chasing him. Now I think he actually *had* the treasure and did something with it. He hid it and put that tag on it."

Veep ran the Find My app, went to items, and saw one labeled "Demon Seed." He said, "Look at the name. Clearly, Branko didn't want much to do with that thing."

"Where is it?"

Veep worked the app a little bit, then said, "Believe it or not, it's in the middle of a national park. Someplace called Plitvice Lakes. It's back to the north."

"How far?"

"About five hours away."

I said, "Pack it up, we have to go. They might be on the way to the treasure right now, and when they find it, they're going to kill Branko. Leave the bodies where they lay. Veep, you've got lead. Take us to that tag."

Knuckles said, "What are we doing?"

"I'm sick of chasing those guys. They have Branko, but they want something else, and I want to own that something. Like they're fond of saying, I'm going to make the mountain come to Muhammed."

Jennifer glanced out the window of the door, saw we were clear, and opened it, saying, "That's not the quote. You butchered it."

We raced back up the stairs with me saying, "Maybe I've invented a new quote. Ever think of that?"

CHAPTER 58

Driving the car full of Afghans, Branko saw headlights through the rain and recognized the turnout he was going to use. He pulled over to the side of the road, cutting the lights, the windshield wipers still beating time inside the car.

Shakor said, "What are you doing? Why did we stop?"

"There's a car in my parking location. I don't know who it is, but they can't see us. Going in behind them is asking for questions. We're basically breaking into the park."

"Who are they? Police?"

Branko turned around and said, "How in the hell would I know? All I see are headlights."

Shakor slapped him in the mouth, and Branko regretted letting the words escape his lips. He already had a black eye from the goon named Ghulam. The guy was a sadist who wanted nothing more than to torture any infidel he came across.

After he'd evaded Shakor in the Cave Bar, Branko had slipped the net once again, this time going to the Dubrovnik old town, to a bar he knew had Wi-Fi and an escape route. He'd had the taxi drop him off at the eastern gate and then had sprinted up the various stairs until he was sitting next to the cliff. His plan was to wait about eight hours, until the bar closed, giving the Afghans plenty of time to search, and then leave the area. He hadn't thought there was one chance in a million they'd find him at the bar, but just in case, this was a perfect location.

The shock of seeing Shakor coming toward him was absolute, something he couldn't at first reconcile in his brain. When he did, he immediately went into fight-or-flight mode, focusing on the flight part. He couldn't fathom how they'd found him, and as he ran down the stairs, he saw Bogdan going the other way, up the stairs to the entrance. From that, he assumed it had just been a wild guess, with the Afghans torturing Bogdan to tell them where he liked to visit in the city.

They might have found him, but they wouldn't capture him.

He'd leapt off the top wearing shorts, a T-shirt, and Teva sandals, hitting the water and surfacing, completely confident that he'd escaped. So much so he'd taken the time to tell Shakor to fuck off with his finger, and then had stroked as fast as he could to the landing around the point. He'd reached it, climbed out of the water, blending in with the rest of the people in the water and on the rocks, then jogged inside, chuckling to himself at his own genius for escape. This had been what? The third time? The fourth?

He'd gone through the bar area and entered the old town through the city walls, thinking about his next moves. He could call Andrei, but wasn't sure how to tell him that his entire team had been killed. Andrei might not take kindly to that.

He'd decided to flee back to Serbia, using the credit card Andrei had given him until it was cut off. Which meant he'd need to purchase tickets within the next few hours. Along with clothes and a new phone. He'd been running through the next steps, walking fast down a narrow alley that was more like a tunnel, when something had slammed into his head with the force of a pickax.

He'd hit the ground, rolled over, and saw Ghulam standing above him.

How? How did they keep finding him?

He'd been forced out of the old town at the end of a barrel and had met Shakor on the street. Shakor had simply smiled, saying, "Waiting on a car. Good of you to join us."

Branko had said nothing, glancing back at Ghulam, who he was sure wanted to kill him just for being an infidel. A vehicle had arrived and he'd been told to take the wheel. He did so, with Ghulam in the passenger seat and Shakor directly behind him. Shakor had said, "Take us to the treasure, right now."

He'd said, "Okay, okay, okay. But if I do, you'll let me go? I don't care about that treasure. I'm sorry I ever brought it here."

Shakor had leaned forward and whispered in his ear, saying, "If you don't, your death will be very, very painful. That's what you should be thinking about."

Branko had gulped and started driving. That had been over five hours ago, and since that time the sun had long since set and a steady rain had begun to fall, making it hard to see the road.

Eventually they'd reached the outskirts of Plitvice Lakes National Park and he'd begun to think about escape. He was sure if he led them to the treasure they'd just trade his body for the box, each kilometer ratcheting up the tension. He recognized the turn-off he'd used to hide the box and saw headlights with bodies moving around the vehicle. He'd pulled over, regretting it instantly. He should have parked right behind them and exited. He didn't know what they were doing, but any help at this stage would be welcome.

Shakor said, "They're getting back in the car. Wait until they leave."

Branko did, breathing through an open mouth, the adrenaline rocketing. He knew he was close to dying. The vehicle left and he stayed where he was. Shakor tapped him on the head with the barrel of his weapon and said, "Go."

Branko parked in the same spot he'd used with Pushka and killed the engine. Shakor said, "What now?"

He turned around and said, "We have to go into the park. It's not an easy walk, especially with the rain. Do you guys have lights? Headlamps or something else?"

Shakor looked at Karim and Ghulam. Both shook their heads. He said, "We have the lights on our phones. Let's go."

They exited the vehicle in the rain, the narrow strobes of the smartphone lights doing more harm than good. They jumped the railing to the park and Branko led them to the narrow stairwell leading down to the caves, the lights from the phone strobing the area like an alien landing. They began climbing down, the Afghans cursing as they went, sometimes slipping on the wet stone. They reached the bottom, all of them panting, and Shakor said, "Where?"

Branko crawled over a railing and led them to the large cave chamber. Shakor shined his cell phone light about, the beam not strong enough to penetrate, and said, "Where is it?"

Branko said, "Follow me. The light isn't strong enough." Shakor did so, and Branko walked to the edge of the cave, circling it in the feeble light. His light hit a hole at ground level and he said, "This is it. You have to worm your way in, but on the other side you'll find a Pelican case. That's where I put it."

Shakor motioned for Ghulam to enter and Branko said, "It'll take more than one to get it out. It might take all three. It's heavy."

Shakor smiled and said, "Let's see if it's there first before I leave you alone in here."

Ghulam went through the hole and then Branko heard him curse. He came back out with a Pelican case, but it was small, about the size for a pistol. He exited the hole, now covered in grime, and said, "What is this?"

Branko was shocked. He said, "That . . . that isn't it."

Ghulam raised his pistol and pointed it at his head, saying, "You have tricked us for the last time, infidel."

Shakor shouted, "Wait! Stop!"

Ghulam glowered at him and said, "Let's kill him now. I'm sick of this."

Shakor said, "We kill no one until we get the treasure. Open that case."

Ghulam knelt down and snapped the latches. They gathered around and saw a small iPad inside. Shakor said, "What is that? Did you leave it here?"

Completely confused, Branko said, "I have no idea. I swear that's where I left the box. It was in there, but that case was not."

Ghulam pushed the home button on the iPad and it sprang to life, showing a note in full screen.

It read, I have your treasure and you have mine. I want to exchange one for the other. If you want to see yours again, Branko stays alive. He is my treasure. And this is yours.

Beneath the text was a harsh photo taken in this very cave, showing the Bactrian Treasure inside a large Pelican case.

Underneath that was a phone number, with the words, Call if you want it back, but if Branko is dead, the treasure is gone.

Shakor looked at Branko and said, "What is going on? Is it the Russian? Does he care about you that much?"

With wide eyes, Branko said, "I have no idea."

CHAPTER 59

George Wolffe had never been to a National Security Council meeting in the middle of the night, but then again, he'd never been in the upper echelons of the United States government. He remembered the picture of President Obama and his staff sitting around this very table when Osama bin Laden had been killed, and supposed it happened from time to time for significant events. Which this was.

The national security advisor, Alexander Palmer, was chairing the meeting, and he was not allowing any cross talk. It was after midnight, and they'd almost run out of time to prevent a catastrophe. All that remained after was to determine the response.

He said, "Okay, let's start with State. What's the response from the Iranians? It's been close to twelve hours now. What are they saying?"

Secretary of State Amanda Croft said, "Just what we predicted. They're saying they have no idea what we're accusing them of, and are professing confusion about the entire event."

"Your take?"

"Well, I obviously wasn't in the room, but the Swiss seem to think it's genuine. According to the Swiss proconsul, they were genuinely taken aback, first by the demand for a meeting, then by what the meeting was about. According to him, they didn't even know we'd launched a rocket to the space station. Had no idea. But once he relayed the message, they went into overdrive."

"What's that mean?"

"According to him, they took the threat seriously. He said they assumed the regime change comment was real, and this was the end."

Palmer said, "Good. Do we still have access to the Swiss, if they decide to send something else?"

"Yes. They're standing by, but I'll tell you, even *they* think this is a trumped-up thing to depose the mullahs. They aren't buying it."

"Well, when that Valkyrie capsule either destroys the space station or comes home to earth in a flaming mass, they'll see it wasn't trumped up. It's real."

"I'm just relaying what they said."

"Do you mean they believe we'd kill our own people just to start a war?"

"I don't know. All I know is they don't believe the Iranians are behind it, and aren't even sure it's real, because we've kept a lid on the entire problem set. It's not like Apollo 13, where the entire world was watching. We've kept it secret."

"Okay, okay, that was by design. General Oglethorpe?"

The SECDEF said, "I've got the Fifth Fleet notified, with all ships in the Hormuz Strait on alert for attacks, with the USS *Nimitz* carrier strike group taking the lead. The 2nd Bomb Wing at Barksdale has a warning order, as do the B-2 bombers at Whiteman. The 82nd Airborne is on alert, as are two Ranger Battalions and the 3rd Infantry Division. The 173rd in Italy is mobilized, and we have a slew of assets in Europe prepositioned because of Ukraine that we can use, but our main problem is staging.

"We gave up Bagram Airfield, and Iraq won't let us in without significantly tipping our hand. In other words, I have them ready to go, but there's no way to pre-stage without telling Iran we're coming for them. We need to put something out officially, letting the world know what's going on, because the minute we start moving, Iran will assume it's for hostile reasons."

President Hannister said, "We will, if we have to, but now's not the time. We do that publicly, and I believe we'll have crossed the Rubicon. It'll be a self-fulfilling prophecy." He looked at Palmer and said, "Continue."

Palmer said, "Yes, sir." He turned to the Director of National Intelligence and said, "What's the assessment from the intelligence community?"

The DNI said, "I'd like each component to talk directly, starting with General Kirby from the National Reconnaissance Office."

Wolffe knew that the NRO controlled the U.S. arsenal of spy satellites, and was interested in his response.

General Kirby said, "We're seeing significant movement from all of the key players in the region. Hezbollah in the Bekaa Valley is showing abnormal activity, the Iraqi Popular Mobilization Units—the militias under the sway of Iran—are creating new signatures we haven't seen before, and the IRGC in Iran itself looks like someone kicked over an anthill. Basically, we're seeing massive displacement of irregular forces, but none of it is indicative of a pending attack. Or at least pointing to a single attack."

Palmer said, "So we know they're taking the threat seriously. NSA? What are you seeing?"

General Baggetti said, "For Dark Star, it's a little strange. It's all confusion inside the IRGC, with elements blaming each other for starting a war, and nobody admitting they've conducted the operation. Basically, it's a bunch of higher-ups trying to pin down who did the hit. Because we said it, they believe they did it, but they can't figure out who is responsible in their network cells."

President Hannister rolled his eyes and said, "That's just great. Are you saying it's some rogue element that hacked us and they don't know who it is? So they can't actually turn it off?"

"Maybe, maybe not. If they find the cell, I'm confident they'll turn it off. They don't want to die any more than we want to go to war. The question is whether this really is a rogue element, or if it's so compartmented that only a select few know about it, and the rest are now running around in the dark. Given the stakes of the attack, that's possible. They know our ability to listen, and would want plausible deniability, which is what they're getting with the SIGINT reflections. Could be either one."

D/CIA Kerry Bostwick cut in at that point, saying, "Or maybe they aren't behind it. Jesus Christ, do you hear yourself? We have SIGINT reflections showing the Iranian command is dumbfounded at what's going on, and you turn that around to mean that's precisely what they intended to happen, and proof they're behind it?"

Palmer said, "Hang on, Kerry. We'll get to the CIA." He turned back to Baggetti and said, "Continue."

"Well, outside of the Dark Star component, everything else backs up what General Kirby said. Hezbollah is talking about attacking Israel and the PMUs are talking about attacking United States assets in Iraq. The IRGC is doing the same, discussing fastboat operations in the strait."

"Is that something new? Don't they always say that?"

"Yes, it's nothing we haven't heard on a daily basis, but the sheer scale of the SIGINT reflections is what's compelling. It's exponentially greater than normal, and it's precise. Not like we usually hear. In addition, Cyber Command is seeing an increase in attempted penetrations of energy and telecom assets here in the United States. We assume that's also coming from Iran."

Palmer nodded and said, "Okay, Kerry, what are you getting at CIA?"

"Mainly it's coming from Israel. They're seeing the same threat stream we are and are bashing us in the head as to why. They want to know if the activity and chatter they're seeing is because of something we did, or if it means Israel is in the crosshairs. So far, we've just shrugged our shoulders, but if we keep this up, Israel may preempt both us and Iran in a hard strike that drags everyone in. They can't afford to ignore the signs, because it's an existential threat. They did that once in '73, and trust me, they aren't going to again."

Palmer said, "What's your point?"

Kerry turned away from Palmer and faced President Hannister, saying, "My point is we can't do this in secret. It has second- and third-order effects that we can't control. If Iran did this, we need to publicly say so, then publicly state the repercussions before it's too late. Let them publicly say it's not them, and then, when the spacecraft crashes—either into the space station or here on earth—we have something to stand on. Because make no mistake, that disaster is most definitely going to be public. There's no hiding it."

President Hannister said, "I know, and I agree. I was just hoping to do this without all the political bullshit that comes with a public statement. It puts Iran's back to the wall and stiffens their will to stand by their story. If we can do it back-channel, that's the way I want to proceed. I understand there is a time limit."

He turned to the NASA engineer and said, "How much longer do we have?"

Looking like he wanted to be anywhere but in that room, the engineer said, "We have about five hours before they leave orbit and attempt to dock with the space station. We need to execute the abort before that time. After that, they'll most likely die with the abort, and we might not be able to spare the space station."

"Why is that?"

"Sir, it's too complicated to explain, but basically, if we abort while in orbit, we stand a chance of them coming home. Once they've left orbit on the preprogrammed trajectory to the space station, we assess about a five percent chance of success, and a fifty percent chance of collision with the space station, because the Valkyrie capsule will be executing its last known orders, and I'm not sure Auriga can override those systems with the assets in place."

Hannister said, "Five hours. That's it?"

"That's it."

George Wolffe heard the words and thought, *Come on, Pike. This is cutting it close even for you.*

CHAPTER 60

The rain hadn't let up throughout the night, and now at six in the morning, it had turned into a slow drizzle that was absolutely miserable. Although it kept the tourists away, which worked in our favor.

We'd left Plitvice Lakes National Park right after midnight, lugging the treasure back up the stairs in the rain, which had been a hell of a lot harder to do than I'd thought it would be. The stairs were slicker than whale snot, and narrower than the box itself, causing us to have to hoist it in the air over the railing as we went. It had most certainly been easier carrying down my little Easter egg we left in lieu of the treasure. Eventually we'd made it back to our vehicle and had loaded up, calling Jennifer for our next location.

I'd tasked her and Veep to find a place for us to bed down and conduct planning, then find a site to conduct the transfer if that came to fruition.

What I wanted was a public place, but not in a downtown city, because I wanted to stage an overwatch element for protection. It sounded like an impossible task, but she'd found a location that not only had a hotel—more like a rustic farmhouse—but also facilitated both the security of the transfer site and the transfer itself.

Called Rastoke, it was a quaint little village situated at the juncture of the Korana and Slunjcica Rivers about thirty minutes north of the park. The water from the rivers split up around the site, forming waterfalls and little streams all over the place, which segregated one area from another. Only about ten acres, it had four distinct pieces of land connected by small wooden bridges, and was wooded, with old water mills and other ethnographic displays scattered about, surrounded on all sides by rushing water. The best part was they had a café and hotel—although calling the place where we stayed a hotel was stretching it a bit. The site catered to tourists, but reminded me of the old roadside attractions in the United States back in the day, where one could see Indian bones, a snake farm, Egyptian mummies, or the largest ball of mud.

It was perfect for us, and with the rain, even better, as the few tourists who'd stayed at the hotel and were up this early were all in the café drinking coffee instead of roaming about through the grass to see the sunrise over the various waterfall lookouts.

Jennifer looked at her watch and said, "They're late. We're going to look a little weird standing out here in the rain for an hour."

I said, "Yeah, you're probably right." I glanced behind me, seeing a shed labeled "Point 11," and motioned to it, saying, "I told him to come to eleven, so I guess hiding inside isn't really off the instructions."

While we'd found the treasure, nobody was sure our little iPad trick would do anything, least of all me. I was sure they wanted it, but if they waited a day or two to come get it, it would do us no good because the space capsule would have already turned into ash, either against the side of the space station, or in earth's atmosphere.

Late last night I'd set up a roster to monitor the phone, not wanting to risk trusting the ringer waking me up, and before I could even start the first shift, at 2 A.M., it had rung.

We'd jumped at the noise, and then I'd recognized that it was the Taskforce by the ringtone. I'd answered, gone encrypted, and given Wolffe a rundown of what I was doing. He was incredulous at the plan, but never once asked about the stand-down order he'd sent. I'd hurriedly gotten him off the phone so as not to miss our call, and no sooner had I hung up than it rang again.

It was the Afghans. And boy, were they pissed. I'd introduced myself, saying I didn't want the treasure, but that Branko was near and dear to my heart. The man who'd dialed was called Shakor, and I didn't tell him why I wanted Branko, letting him think whatever he wanted. He'd ranted for a bit, threatening to kill Branko while I listened and other stupid shit involving him cutting off my head, but none of that mattered, because I had the treasure.

I interrupted him, saying, "You're from the Badr 313 Battalion, aren't you?"

That caused a pause in the conversation. He said, "Who are you?"

"I'm the guy who used to slaughter your asses. You killed a friend of mine in Tajikistan, and I'm trying mightily not to let that interfere with my mission. If you want this treasure, you need to listen to what I say, because I'm sick of hearing your shit."

He started ranting about killing me again, and I hung up the phone.

Knuckles said, "What happened?"

"He was pissing me off."

Incredulous, Jennifer said, "You hung up on him?"

"Yeah, I did. All I could see was Carly's face. I'm not sure I can do this. I'd rather kill those fucks than give them the treasure."

Knuckles, who'd felt the pain of Carly's death more than any-one, got me refocused on the mission. He said, "This isn't the time for revenge. We can't bring Carly back, but we can save those people in space. It's what she would have wanted. We killed the assholes in Tajikistan. Let it go."

The phone rang again, and I answered, saying, "Do you want the instructions, or do you want to rant some more?"

Shakor said, "Give them to me."

I did, telling him the location and the time. I'd made it at dawn to prevent him from doing any sort of reconnaissance of the area—something we'd already done—and because we were running out of time. He agreed, saying, "No weapons."

I said, "Yes. No weapons. You bring Branko, and I'll bring the treasure."

CHAPTER 61

The entrance to the site was a wooden bridge across a stream, accessed from a blacktop road that dead-ended at a farmhouse. The bridge provided a natural choke point for surveillance, which I had positioned in depth. At 0615 Veep called to say the Afghans had arrived and were studying the map at the entrance. At 0621 Knuckles called to say they'd moved past the café and into the park.

Jennifer and I left the old shed we were in and reentered the grassy area out front. I called Brett, saying, "You have them?"

He said, "I got 'em. Branko and three Afghans. I have them stone cold."

I said, "Don't fire unless we're threatened. If I want some lead, I'll call."

"Roger all."

I waited in the rain, Jennifer by my side, and they came across the little wooden bridge separating the old water mill from our area. They marched across three abreast with Branko in front of them. We just waited.

They came within ten feet of us and stopped. The one on the right glowered at me like he wanted to gut me. He looked positively evil, and I was sure he had some American blood on his hands. One day, I'd love to wipe that snarl off his face with my fist, but that wouldn't be today.

The one in the middle, behind Branko, said, "We're here. Where's the treasure?"

I said, "Shakor, I presume?"

He nodded, and I tossed him a ring I'd brought from the Pelican case. I said, "Just to prove I wasn't lying."

He studied it, then said, "You don't have the treasure here?"

I said, "I do."

I tossed him a key fob to one of our Land Rovers, saying, "It's in the trunk of that car. Now let Branko go."

He said, "How do I know you aren't tricking me?"

"Where would I go if I was? There is no reason for me to trick you. If I'd wanted the treasure, I could have just flown home with it. I want Branko."

He said, "The treasure is in this car?"

"Yes."

He pushed Branko forward, and the man on the right had some sort of mental breakdown, snatching Branko by the collar and pulling out a pistol. He shoved Branko to his knees and screamed something in Pashto. I held out my hands, saying, "What the fuck are you doing?"

Shakor shouted back at the man with the weapon, and they had a heated discussion. I saw the face of the man holding Branko and knew he wanted to kill him. Wanted to kill all of us. I knew it, because I felt the same way about them.

The man looked at me with hatred and, in English, snarled, "We have our treasure now, you American dog. Watch your treasure die."

He jammed the pistol into Branko's temple, and I said, "Take the shot."

There was a crack, and the man's head exploded all over Branko. The body collapsed on the ground. Shakor looked at the bloody corpse in shock, then at me, saying, "You said no weapons. You said this was a pure exchange."

"Are you shitting me? After your guy just pulled out a weapon? If either one of you moves your hands, you're dead. Stand still."

They did, and I said, "Branko, get over here."

He crawled to me on his hands and knees, almost catatonic from the events. I said, "Jennifer, get him out of here."

She stood him up and took a wide berth around the Afghans, avoiding blocking Brett's shot. Shakor said, "So I suppose you think you'll get Branko and the treasure. Just like an American to lie. You can kill me, but make no mistake, the Badr Battalion will hunt you all over the earth."

I said, "Shut the fuck up. I should slaughter both of you where you stand, especially after that stupid stunt your man pulled. Just be still for a few minutes longer."

Shakor said, "Ghulam lost his family in an American air strike. He was a little heated. I did not authorize that action, and do not fault you for killing him."

My earpiece came alive with Jennifer saying, "We're in the vehicle. Branko is secure."

I said, "Roger," then went back to Shakor, saying, "You dumbasses didn't even ask where the vehicle for those keys is located. How were you going to find the treasure?"

Shakor said, "I assumed you would tell me."

I laughed and said, "You mean after your buddy put a bullet in my head?"

"I told you, I didn't authorize that. He acted on his own."

I have to admit, he was pretty damn calm considering his predicament. I said, "I really should kill your ass for breaking the rules, but against my better judgment, I won't."

I pulled out Branko's cloned cell phone and put it on the ground, saying, "There's a thing called Find My on this phone. It's tied to an Apple AirTag that's in the trunk with your treasure. You follow it to the vehicle. Understood?"

"No, I don't. I don't know how to use 'find me.'"

"That's not my problem. Maybe you can find a child here to show you, but you're not going to do it for fifteen minutes."

"What do you mean?"

"If you move at all in the next fifteen minutes, your head will explode like your friend. After that, you've got your treasure."

He glowered at me. I walked past him, and he said, "Maybe one day we'll meet again, and I'll be the one with a weapon."

I stopped, turned around, and punched him as hard as I could in the face, knocking him to the ground. He rolled over, but didn't try to retaliate, showing remarkable control. His friend jumped forward, and I pointed at him, causing him to stop as he remembered the reticle on his forehead.

I said, "That was for my friend in Tajikistan. You want to meet me again, and I won't use a gun. I'll beat you to death purely for the pleasure."

I jogged out of the park, saying on the net, "All clear, all clear. Meet at the vehicle. Brett, go ahead and break down the hide site."

"You sure?"

"Yeah, they aren't moving for fifteen minutes. I'm sure."

We collapsed on the remaining Land Rover, cramming Branko in the back bench between Veep and Knuckles. Jennifer took the wheel, and I turned around from the passenger seat while we waited on Brett to return from his hide site, tossing Branko a pack of wet-wipes to clean off the blood and saying, "Branko, you are one hard man to find, I'll give you that."

He wiped his face with trembling hands and said, "What do you want with me?"

"Want? What does anyone want with you? I want you to turn off the ransomware you initiated. Only the payment is going to be allowing you to live."

CHAPTER 62

Inside the Valkyrie capsule, Abigail Raintree watched the sun rise yet again as they circled the earth five times faster than the speed of sound. It only took about ninety minutes to complete a rotation, and given their current predicament, she'd long since quit marveling over the view.

She knew she'd been billed as a small-time high school physics teacher, which she was, but her pedigree was more than the press releases indicated. At one time all she'd wanted was to be an astronaut. She'd obtained an appointment to the U.S. Air Force Academy with a goal of becoming a fighter pilot, the first step to achieving her dream. Much to her surprise, she'd learned that she was red-green color-blind. She'd thought it was a mistake, because genetically that condition was passed to the male side of the family and she'd had no trouble in life. She could see just fine, but she couldn't complete the plate test. She was one plate short of a passing score, meaning her condition was extremely mild, but that one plate shattered her dream of becoming an astronaut.

She'd graduated from the academy with a degree in aeronautics and then had joined the Air Force, working on the ground and watching others fly. She thought she'd make a career out of the Air Force, looking for the lemonade in the lemons, but it wasn't satisfying. She'd reached the limit of her payback for the academy and had resigned her commission. She'd wandered about in life, doing one job after another at the big defense contractors—Raytheon, Northrop Grumman, Boeing—but none of it helped her self-actualize. She'd earned her teaching certificate and had taken a job as a physics instructor at a high school in Little Rock, Arkansas.

She found she enjoyed the work. Opening the minds of high school seniors to a world beyond what they could smell and touch had given her a sense of self-worth. And then the call came for a teacher to join the first civilian flight up to the space station.

She was well aware of the *Challenger* disaster and the fate of Christa McAuliffe, but that hadn't dissuaded her at all. She'd competed, and then won the coveted slot, spending sixty days with the other men of the crew learning the ins and outs for their trip. It had been her dream come true, but now it had turned into a nightmare.

The camaraderie they'd built during training was proving to be nothing but a veneer, with the egos inside the capsule each determined to take charge.

The supposed commander of the mission was a retired NASA astronaut named Clay Hutmacher. Even at sixty, he looked like a Hollywood poster boy for a fighter pilot, with chiseled features and a thick shock of salt-and-pepper hair, earning him the callsign "Fabio." He'd been their lead instructor, and had earned the respect of everyone on board, but apparently not to the point of actually being in command.

Skyler Fitch, the billionaire owner of Auriga, had taken to giving orders to the ground from inside the capsule, showing a crack in the planning for the flight. Fabio was ostensibly the final word, but it was Skyler's company, and technically, Fabio was just an employee. Skyler hadn't gotten to where he was in life by being subservient to the minions he'd hired.

Not to be outdone, Allan Laughlin considered himself a voting member as well. The chair of the Senate subcommittee on space and science, he was also a former fighter pilot, the final cog in the wheel turning their glorious spaceflight into a carload of squabbling kids in a station wagon headed to the Grand Canyon.

She felt like screaming, "If you guys don't quit fighting, I'm turning this spacecraft around and heading home!"

The thought brought a small smile to her face, the first one she'd had since they'd learned of the ransomware disaster. Of course, she couldn't do that, which was precisely why the men were bickering back and forth.

For the second time, speaking with more force, Fabio said, "Skyler, we need to hit the abort in the beginning of the window. We wait until the end, and we don't leave ourselves any room to react if it doesn't work."

Skyler said, "The window is two hours. I'd rather give my men on the ground that time to work a complete solution. The odds are better for our survival."

"Sir, if it doesn't work, the odds are zero. We'll shoot off into space toward the station."

The debate had been going on for the last three hours, right up until they'd entered the abort window. Honestly, Abigail had long since given up any hope of returning alive. She knew that without control from the ground, they were going to be a spectacular shooting star, splitting apart into flaming chunks once they hit the earth's atmosphere.

Senator Laughlin said, "I'm agreeing with Skyler on this. If you abort and it *does* initiate, and they don't have control systems from the ground, we're dead. Give them more time to work the problem."

Fabio said, "The abort sequence is inside the computers here. If it initiates, then it should follow protocols. The problem is whether their override will work. If it doesn't, we need time to fix it."

Skyler said, "You're hoping the system works. I'm waiting on a backup. Didn't you tell us in training, 'Two is one and one is none'?"

Fabio said, "Okay, let's split the difference. We initiate at one hour, giving them an hour and us an hour."

Skyler said, "An hour and a half, and that's as far as I'm going."

Fabio shook his head but said nothing to Skyler, instead relaying their plans to the ground.

They sat in silence, each with their own thoughts about what was to come. An hour and a half later, Fabio said, "Buckle up. Here we go."

There was no sequence of events, no flipping of switches or Apollo 13–ish "main bus breakers" to manipulate. There was only a single button protected underneath a Plexiglas shield.

Fabio flipped the Plexiglas up, looked around the capsule one last time, then pressed the button. Nothing happened. No thrusters, no rotation of the capsule, nothing. He hit it again.

Nothing.

He shook his head, looked at Skyler calmly, and said, "You're an idiot."

CHAPTER 63

We were three hours into our nine-hour flight back to the United States and Branko was having trouble turning off the ransomware. I would have thought he was screwing with me, but after talking to him, I believed his story.

It had taken us an hour and a half to drive from Rastoke to the Zagreb airfield to link up with our aircraft, and during that time I'd told him what we needed him to do. He'd looked astounded when he found out that he'd attacked systems controlling a spacecraft in flight, saying, "No, no. We hit Auriga corporate. That's what we attacked. It was to be our biggest ransom ever, but we don't attack things that involve life support. It's our creed."

I'd smacked him in the head, saying, "Bullshit. You hit the spacecraft, and now it's about to destroy the International Space Station, killing everyone on board."

He shook his head, saying, "No, no, no. That's not what we attacked. I know, because I did the exploration after getting the gateway."

"Who gave you the gateway? The Russian?"

"Yes. Well, he passed it to me. He got it from Sphinx."

"Who is this Sphinx?"

"I don't know. He's an American hacker. He gave us a Zero Day, no-click exploit and then gave us the gateway."

Which was interesting. I leaned into him and said, "Who is he?"

He'd recoiled, saying, "I don't know! I'd tell you if I did. I want no part of killing people."

I thought about it, realizing that Sphinx was the hundred-meter target, and I needed to take care of the five-meter one first. I said, "Okay, look, you just get rid of the ransomware. We have about four hours left before they abort that spacecraft and it burns up in the sky."

He said, "How? I need something to work with."

Brett handed him the single laptop we'd taken from Split—the one that we'd saved from burning up—and he said, "I need an internet connection. And all four computers. Not just this one."

I'd already thought about the Wi-Fi problem, and decided that our aircraft was the best bet. It had a communications architecture that rivaled Air Force One, with satellite internet just like that aircraft used, including a bandwidth that would make Google proud. It would take some time to get airborne, but I thought that was a better choice than pulling over to the nearest hotel and taking a gamble that the Wi-Fi wasn't crappy. And it would allow us to get out of Croatia before someone started connecting the dots to all the dead bodies scattered around the country.

The computers, however, were another problem.

I'd said, "You'll get the Wi-Fi, but your buddy burned up the other three computers with some self-destruct device."

He'd nodded, not liking the answer, saying, "I don't know if this will be enough."

Three hours into the flight, and his statement was proving true. He was on a chat with Creed in the rear, and they were both trying to duplicate the other computers that had burned up, using Creed's systems, but so far it hadn't worked.

My whole team stood around him, watching him work, all of

us feeling helpless because we couldn't do anything. I said, "How are we looking?"

He rattled off a bunch of geek code crap to me that made no sense. I said, "Just tell me if you're making progress."

He said, "Working with this system, Creed has managed to duplicate some of the protocols, so we're moving forward. That's all I can say."

He went back to the chat, typing furiously, and I called Wolffe to give him an update.

He answered and I said, "We're still working the issue, making progress, but I don't know if it'll be quick enough. How's it going back there?"

"Not well. Not well at all. The PMUs in Iraq have started lobbing rockets into the Green Zone, targeting our embassy, and Hezbollah has launched a swarm of drones across the Lebanese border into Israel. And the IRGC are using their fast boats all over the Hormuz Strait, threatening our ships. Luckily, so far they haven't done anything kinetic."

"What the hell are you talking about? I meant with the space capsule."

"POTUS sent a crystal-clear message to Iran that if the capsule crashes, either here on earth or into the space station, he was going to hold Iran responsible. And Iran is reacting to that."

"I told you it wasn't the damn Iranians! Who's the adult in the room back there? You guys are going to start a war for something they have no control over."

"Look, Pike, I understand your thinking, and that was presented to the president, but we have proof it's the Iranians, and that's what took precedence. We're just one opinion of many. The president had to weigh them and make a decision."

"And he made it based on *one* opinion from some computer geek?"

"Unfortunately, yes. With some lukewarm concurrence of NSA and Cyber Command."

I shook my head, amazed that one guy could use some computer gobbledygook to sway the entire national security architecture of the United States. I said, "How long do we have?"

"The abort didn't work. We have about thirty minutes before the capsule leaves orbit and begins flying to the space station. After that, it's over."

I hung up and looked at Branko, saying, "You have less than thirty minutes. If you don't solve this problem, I'll kill you myself."

CHAPTER 64

The NASA liaison Gordon Dillard listened to the crescendo of shouting in the room and thought, *We'd never panic like this.*

Auriga mission control was in absolute chaos, with every person behind a computer arguing with someone else or pounding the keyboard in a futile attempt to get something—anything—to work.

There had been a debate over when to attempt the abort, and Gordon was surprised to see the captain of the ship, Clay Hutmacher, overruled by Skyler Fitch. He'd known Clay when he was an actual NASA astronaut, and thought he was one of the coolest pilots under pressure he'd ever seen—and Gordon had seen a lot. He'd thought the callsign of Fabio was ridiculous because there was nothing whimsical about the man. He was pure business, and if he wanted to initiate at the beginning of the abort window, then Gordon thought they should have.

Gordon walked over to the lead Auriga engineer, ignoring all the panic and saying, "What happened? Why didn't it go?"

The engineer had told Gordon he believed he'd found a firewalled workaround for the abort sequence, as that protocol was shielded from the other systems precisely to avoid it being corrupted or accidentally initiated, and he was sure that his workaround was valid.

The engineer said, "The protocol is fine; we just can't get to it.

Believe it or not, the initiator—and I literally mean the button that's pushed—is tied into the primary system."

"You mean into the system being hijacked by the ransomware?"

"Yeah. Tripping the switch sends a signal along the primary system to the abort protocol, so right now it's the damn button that's preventing us from aborting."

"What's next? What else can you try?"

"We're doing everything we can to get that abort signal to trip." He looked up at a giant digital clock on the wall, the numbers rolling down through ten minutes, then said, "Unfortunately, I don't think we'll fix it while they're in orbit, which means even if we can get it to abort later, we'll only be saving the space station. The people on the capsule are dead."

Gordon nodded, realizing Auriga was about to have their own *Challenger* moment. He felt sorry for them and for NASA, as this would set back space exploration for decades, leaving China as the undisputed leader. He felt a pang of guilt, realizing that there were four souls on board that spacecraft who were about to die.

He heard someone shout from the other side of the room. He turned, seeing a man standing up and pointing at his computer. He said, "Hey, my screen's clearing. I have control. I say again, I have control."

Then another engineer said the same thing. Then one after another began cheering, like they'd just watched the capsule splash down. Gordon looked at the time and said, "Send them around again. Send them around again. Don't let them break orbit. Give yourself time to make sure all systems are go."

He looked at the clock, saw it pass through three minutes, and screamed, "Send them around again!"

The lead engineer began shouting commands as the clock

ticked through zero. He called up to the capsule, saying, "Valkyrie One, Valkyrie One, what is your status? Have you broken orbit?"

Through the speakers in the walls, the entire room heard Fabio calmly say, "Nope. Looks like we're looping the earth again."

This time the cheers were a crescendo.

Wanting to see the real-time results of his handywork, Dylan Hobbes was mesmerized by the live stream video Gordon had established from mission control. When he heard the cheering, then the latest exchange from the spacecraft, he threw the laptop against the wall, shattering it.

How in the hell had they cracked the code? They had no skill at his level of expertise—and even he couldn't have cracked that encryption in the timeline they'd had available. Somehow, they'd either gotten lucky, or Branko was trying to erase his tracks from having had anything to do with the attack.

That must be it. He learned of the true target, saw his friends getting killed, and decided to check out completely.

In the end, it didn't really matter how. It was done, along with his mission. They'd think it was the Iranians who had backed down, and the entire situation would be defused.

Unless he reinitiated. He still had the original ransomware computer in the lab, and it still had the wormhole into the gateway of Auriga. The question was when to initiate.

He looked at the smashed laptop, then went to a locker and pulled out another one, loading the live stream from mission control. The screen cleared and he saw the celebration still going, the relief clearly evident on everyone's faces.

In the corner he saw Gordon Dillard arguing with the lead engineer. He couldn't hear what was being said, but he could clearly see Gordon wasn't happy. He waited until the conversation was over and Gordon had gone back to his desk at the top of the room. He pulled out his cell phone.

"Gordon! Looks like the Iranians backed off. Good news!"

"Yeah, it's good news. We have control of the capsule now and can bring it down safely, but these idiots want to continue."

"What do you mean?"

"Skyler is saying he wants to continue the mission."

"You're kidding. Bring the damn thing home right now. You have no idea what that malware corrupted. If you have control right now, you need to use it."

"That's exactly what the astronaut said, the one in charge of the mission inside the capsule."

"And? What happened?"

"Skyler Fitch overruled him, saying it would be a public relations disaster for his company. He's basically saying this is just a reset, and that we're all systems go."

"But the astronaut's in charge, right? Skyler's just a paying passenger."

Gordon laughed and said, "Yeah, sure. A paying passenger who happens to own the company that's doing the launch. At the end of the day, this isn't like a government thing, like NASA or the military. The astronaut is an employee of Fitch."

"So what are they going to do?"

"Circle the globe until they're sure the systems are clean, then attempt to link up with the space station as intended."

"That is insane. They should spend a month going through those systems before ever attempting to use them again on a live launch."

"I know, I know. At least I got them to agree to firewall the entire abort procedure. The initiation is tied off from the main systems now so if these idiots proceed with the lunacy, and some latent corruption occurs, we can always initiate."

"What's the timeline?"

"Probably going to try to leave orbit in six hours. From there, the docking will take another four."

"Well, good luck with that."

He hung up and tapped his lips, wondering if the plan could be salvaged. One thing from the last NSC meeting stuck out to him: one of the men in that room had said that maybe the attack had been compartmented from even the hierarchy within the IRGC. And that gave him an idea. The U.S. government was already primed to blame Iran, and if "they" attacked the systems again, there would be arguments back and forth, but the war would come. After Americans began to die, the country would coalesce around a common enemy.

The key would be to initiate after the Valkyrie left orbit and started on the final trajectory to the space station. At that point, an abort would kill all aboard.

CHAPTER 65

Six hours after we'd single-handedly saved the United States from a ridiculous war, we landed at the FBO on Reagan National Airport, the sun rising slowly over the runway. We'd been going on no sleep for over twenty-four hours, and I was looking forward to a bed and a beer, not necessarily in that order. While it was dawn here, I figured it was past noon where I had just come from, so it was justifiable.

It would have been appropriate to have a marching band and a bunch of civilians waving flags, but all we got were a couple of federal agents to take Branko into custody. I didn't tell them who we were, and they didn't ask. All they wanted was Branko.

While the Iranians were being blamed for this latest catastrophe, he was still wanted for a massive number of ransomware attacks in the United States. I'd told George Wolffe about his help, and that would hold sway in his ultimate sentence, but he was still a criminal, and the Department of Justice was making a case against him for all of the Dark Star attacks over the past couple of years.

I appreciated his work helping us and felt a little sorry for him. The Russian Andrei and whoever this Sphinx guy was would escape justice, while the minions would bear the brunt of the punishment. But Branko had still harmed many, many people's lives here in the States and very well might have been complicit in Carly's death. If he hadn't shut down Blaisdell Consulting, maybe we'd have executed that mission a little differently.

Hard to tell, but my sympathy only went so far.

We'd left the plane for the pilots to take care of—they had to work sometimes, too—and drove over to Blaisdell Consulting headquarters in Clarendon, right next to Arlington National Cemetery. Technically, Grolier Recovery Services personnel shouldn't ever come to the HQ, because if someone was watching the comings and goings at the facility, they might make a connection they shouldn't, but I figured this was a special occasion, and I wanted to talk to George Wolffe face-to-face.

We entered through the parking garage in the back instead of the official one in the front, ringing the bell outside a glass door leading to a small anteroom about the size of a service elevator, with a steel door beyond. We waited, then heard Marge coming through the speaker mounted in the cement of the garage wall. I looked at the camera, convincing her to let us in, and she did. But she refused to open the second steel door.

The glass door closed shut and locked, leaving us trapped in the anteroom. Marge really took her job seriously. The anteroom was an initial trap for anyone wishing the Taskforce harm. Once in, you weren't getting out, with the glass of the first door being bulletproof, and the second door being reinforced steel. I looked up at the camera and said, "Come on, Marge. It's me!"

I got nothing. Two minutes later the steel door opened and I saw Blaine Alexander. I huffed, "This secret spy shit is getting to be a bit much."

Blaine laughed and said, "She's just doing her job. She's convinced that if you don't have a badge to get in, you're going to kill everyone inside like that movie *Three Days of the Condor*."

We walked upstairs, me saying, "Yeah, well, it gets a little old."

We entered the Taskforce conference room and took a seat, Blaine saying, "George will be here in just a second. He's on a call with Alexander Palmer."

Knuckles and Brett put their arms on the table and cradled their heads, immediately falling asleep like soldiers anywhere. Veep took a seat in a chair against the wall, leaning his head back and doing the same thing. Jennifer and I stayed awake, wanting to know what had happened.

I said, "So everything's okay now? Billionaire space pirate saved?"

Blaine grinned and said, "Yeah, and it worked out well for us. Nobody knows it was the Taskforce that solved the ransomware problem. They all think it was Iran backing down, which helps us both ways—nobody in the U.S. government is wondering what assets were used to stop the attack, meaning we don't have to worry about any questions, and Iran might just think twice before attacking us for real because they know we're serious."

"Well, I'm glad to be of service, but please tell me that POTUS doesn't believe that shit about the Iranians. He needs to know that was hogwash."

"I don't know what he believes. I'll leave that up to Wolffe to tell you. In the meantime, while we wait, you can have a front-row seat for your most favorite space tourist heading up to the International Space Station."

"What? What do you mean? Are you saying they didn't bring the capsule home?"

"Nope. Esteemed billionaire and international space expert Skyler Fitch overrode everyone at NASA and the commander of the capsule himself to say they were going forward with the mission."

"And we let them do that?"

"Not a lot we could say. It's the first purely civilian flight. He owns the capsule, the rocket, the control systems, you name it. NASA owns the launchpad, and that was used days ago—after he paid to rent it."

"He doesn't own the damn space station."

"Yeah, well, someone had to give concurrence to allow him to dock, I'll give you that, but it's not our problem."

"He's an idiot."

Blaine turned on an overhead monitor and said, "No argument there. They left orbit about forty minutes ago and are now headed toward the space station."

The live stream began feeding, and the control room looked like a bad zombie movie where the surveillance camera is showing everyone inside turning into monsters. Instead of seeing calm men working behind a computer, everyone was running around the room like they were trying to escape something.

I said, "What the hell is going on?"

George Wolffe burst through the door, waking up the team. We all looked at him expectantly and he said, "Where's Branko?"

"With the federal agents you sent. Why?"

"The computers just locked up again with new ransomware, right after they left orbit."

CHAPTER 66

Inside Valkyrie One, Fabio was apoplectic about the new turn of events, although his placid demeanor belied that fact. He keyed his radio, speaking calmly. "Say again, mission control?"

"We've been hit again. We've lost all control of the capsule. They hit us again."

He broke radio protocol, saying, "You've gotta be shitting me."

"Unfortunately, no. You're headed to the space station at Mach five, and we can't do anything about it."

Skyler Fitch cut in, saying, "But you firewalled the abort, right? We can abort?"

The engineer said, "Yes, sir. We can still abort. That would save the station."

"What's that mean?"

Nothing came over the net.

Skyler repeated, "What's that mean?"

Finally, a new voice came on the net. "Sir, this is the lead engineer of mission control. We can abort, but we believe you'll have about a fifty percent chance of survival from the attitude and trajectory you're currently on. The abort protocol is designed for orbit. After that, once you've left orbit, the abort protocol is controlled by us. We're supposed to safely bring you home."

"And if we don't?"

The capsule heard nothing. He repeated, "And if we don't abort? What then?"

"You're going to smash into the space station."

Fabio cut in, saying, "How long do we have to solve this problem?"

"Two hours, give or take."

"Is someone working it on the ground?"

"We're all working it."

"I mean someone who can actually do something."

The Situation Room at the White House was not much better than Auriga mission control, with everyone arguing back and forth at the new turn of events, all trying to assess what the attack meant.

President Hannister entered the room, quieting the scrum. He took his seat at the head of the table and said, "Okay, what the hell is going on?"

General Baggetti, the commander of both the NSA and Cyber Command, said, "Sir, my opinion is just what I said earlier. There is a rogue element within Iran that's doing this. The IRGC or the mullahs found the original cell and shut it off because they don't want to go to war, but somehow, that same cell is now initiating again. There's a fight going on within the Iranian government over who is the true leader against the Great Satan."

President Hannister said, "Okay, so they know it's been initiated again. Even if it's a rogue cell, they'd have to prepare the regime for our response. That's the whole point. What are we seeing for posturing? We sent the back-channel message saying they chose the right path by turning it off, and told them we were standing down. The rockets stopped, the Hezbollah activity ceased. Are they ramping back up again?"

General Baggetti rubbed his hands and said, "No. We've heard no chatter about mobilization. In fact, the only thing we've heard is that their posturing caused us to back down. They're bragging about it to each other."

Kerry Bostwick, the D/CIA, said, "Meaning they don't know what the hell is going on and are taking this as a victory of deterring the Great Satan. Sir, they aren't doing this."

"Then who is?"

"I don't know. I wish I did, but I don't."

President Hannister said, "How much time do we have?"

The hapless NASA liaison said, "About three hours before they impact the space station."

"And can we abort?"

"Yes, sir, but if we do, the spacecraft has about a fifty percent chance of survival. Without the ground control, it's a flip of the coin whether they survive."

President Hannister rubbed his face, then looked around the room, going face to face. He said, "This is my call. We abort. I'll take responsibility for the disaster if it occurs. I can't have that ship destroying the International Space Station."

The NASA liaison looked pained at the statement. President Hannister said, "You don't agree?"

"No, sir. It's not that. We don't own the capsule. We have no legal ability to order Auriga to abort. It's not our ship."

That caused President Hannister to chuckle. He said, "The space station is a government thing, not private. We own the right for them to go there. Tell them they no longer have permission to dock. Let them figure it out."

The NASA liaison nodded, looking sick.

President Hannister said, "That won't work?"

"Sir, they're headed to that space station at Mach five. They aren't going to dock. They're going to bring it down."

President Hannister said, "Get me the CEO of Auriga. I'll order him to abort."

The NASA liaison said, "Sir, he's on the capsule."

President Hannister looked around the room, supposedly the greatest minds of the finest country on earth. He said, "Is there anyone here with a solution?"

CHAPTER 67

I saw the people on the screen doing their zombie dance, running back and forth, and said, "Branko's no help. This isn't him."

Wolffe said, "Well, somebody's doing it. And either it's the Iranians, or it's Dark Star. One thing's for sure, if this thing goes bad, we're blaming Iran."

I said, "Creed's got everything Branko had. Tell him to start working it, but I'll bet Branko's codes are no longer valid. It's not Dark Star, and it's not the Iranians."

"Then who?"

"It's Sphinx. It's the American. He's at the heart of this thing."

"Who is he?"

"I have no idea, but I know how to find him. Can you get Kerry Bostwick to do some work? I have a linkage, but it's not in our problem set. It's CIA."

Wolffe smiled and said, "Yeah, I think I can."

"What's the smile for?"

He went to the gray phone on his desk—a secure, encrypted line directly into the CIA—and dialed, saying, "Nothing. I told him you might need some help."

The phone rang through and Wolffe got a flunky telling him Kerry was at the White House for an update. Wolffe told him in no uncertain terms to get Kerry to a gray line immediately and call.

While we waited, I told Wolffe everything I knew about

Sphinx. He was here, in the United States, had given the Auriga gateway to Dark Star, had tricked Branko about the target, and had also supplied the malware code to penetrate. I'd thought Branko was Doctor Evil, but it was Sphinx, and I was sure I could find him. If I had enough time.

The phone rang and it was Kerry. Wolffe passed the handset to me and I said, "I need someone to squeeze a Russian oligarch, and I need it in the next hour."

"Russian oligarch? Why?"

I explained the connection to Sphinx as quickly as I could, and he said, "Okay, given that, how am I going to find him? I need more than the name Andrei."

I said, "I have his house. It's in Liechtenstein, but I don't know who he is. You guys keep track of that stuff, right? Being the CIA and all?"

"Yeah, if you can give me something to go on."

I snapped my fingers off the phone, holding my hand over the receiver, saying, "Get Creed's ass up here with a computer. One networked to the CIA."

To Kerry I said, "I'm sending all I know. He's the key to Sphinx. He knows who he is."

Creed showed up with a laptop and I motioned to Jennifer, knowing she would have already read my mind. She started talking to Creed, and he started pounding the keyboard. On the phone I said, "It's coming to your counterterrorism mission center now."

Kerry said, "Give me a minute," and hung up.

Literally one minute later, the gray phone rang again. I answered, and he said, "It's Andrei Obrenovic. He's a tech sector guy, large-scale computer systems and database management, made his money after the fall of the Wall. He does a lot of black market stuff, but he's not into geopolitics. He lives in Liechtenstein because he doesn't want to deal with Putin in Russia. He's an unlikely guy to be doing this."

"He's not doing it. He was bankrolling Dark Star, and now he's hip-deep in this mess even if he doesn't know it. Sphinx gave him the gateway and a zero-click malware attack that allowed the penetration. Sphinx is some computer guy on this side of the pond, but he knows who he is."

"I can't squeeze him in person. We don't have any assets in Liechtenstein with the requisite skill set. They're in Switzerland."

Shit.

"Get me a number to him. Some way to talk to him. We have about two hours to find out who Sphinx is."

"I think you have less time than that. POTUS is going to order them to abort."

"Abort? They'll be killed."

"Better them than the entire space station."

"Just get me that number."

I hung up and turned to Wolffe saying, "POTUS has ordered them to abort. We need to turn that off, immediately."

George Wolffe called Alexander Palmer in the Situation Room, putting it on speaker. Palmer answered saying, "George, I don't have time right now."

Wolffe said, "Tell POTUS to turn off the abort. We might have a way to stop this."

"What? How? You have some line on the Iranians?"

"I don't have time to explain right now, but it's not the Iranians. Don't let them abort."

"The president has already given the order to their mission control."

I said, "Then tell him to countermand it!"

"Who is this?"

Wolffe glowered at me and said, "It's Pike Logan. Sorry, you're on speaker."

"So this is his idea?"

"No, it's mine. Look, we can save that capsule but we need more time."

"The president isn't available right now. He's in a prescheduled meeting with the president of Lebanon. They have a state dinner tonight."

"Get him out of the meeting!"

"I can't. Not without alerting everyone that something's amiss."

I said, "Then you make the call. Contact their mission control and countermand the order."

"I don't have that authority."

What is it with these people afraid to make a decision? No wonder they're always wetting their pants when I'm on the ground.

I said, "Look, sir, this isn't hard. Just countermand the order for time. Tell them to hold off until the last moment, then abort."

He said, "How do I know you've actually got anything?"

"You don't, but you do know something."

"What?"

"You sit on your ass and the deaths of those four people are on your head."

CHAPTER 68

Gordon Dillard watched the debate inside mission control intently. As NASA liaison, he could give his opinion, but he wasn't involved in the ultimate decision.

The lead engineer from Auriga said, "I can't believe I just got a call from the president of the United States ordering us to abort. He can't tell us what to do with our company."

A female engineer said, "But he has a point. The farther the capsule gets from the orbital plane, the less are their chances of survival."

"The chances are less than fifty percent as it is. Waiting a bit isn't going to make that much of a difference."

Gordon felt his phone vibrate and stepped away.

"Hello?"

"Gordon Dillard, from NASA?"

"Yes. Who is this?"

"It's Alexander Palmer. I'm the national security advisor to the president. I know he just called to tell Auriga to abort. I need you to tell them not to."

"What? Why?"

"Things have changed. We think we have a lead on the ransomware. We think we can turn it off."

"Are you sure?"

"No, but it's worth a wait."

"Not really. They're debating the issue right now. The problem is the farther they leave from the orbital plane, the less the chance of survival."

Palmer didn't respond. Gordon said, "Hello? Did you hear me?"

"Yeah, I heard you. Look, it's your call, but we have a greater chance of saving that capsule than they have if they abort. That's all I'm saying."

"Sir, it's not my call. I have no authority here."

"Do you agree with what I just said?"

"Yes, it makes sense. If you have even a sixty percent chance of success, that beats the odds of them aborting."

"Then figure out a way to convey that."

Gordon saw the group of Auriga engineers huddle around a computer and said, "I gotta go."

He hung up and went to the computer, pulling the lead engineer away. He said, "What's going on?"

"We decided to punt. Let Skyler make the decision."

"I just talked to the White House. The thinking has changed. They no longer want an abort."

"Well, no offense, but it's not the White House's call. It's ours, which means it's Skyler's. Not only is he CEO, but it's his ass on the line."

"You don't understand. They think they can clear the ransomware."

"They think? The longer we sit here, the less chance that capsule has for coming home."

"It has less of a chance right now than the odds of clearing the ransomware. Don't let them abort."

One of the engineers pulled the lead away, handing him a headset. He put it on, and Gordon grabbed one from an adjacent computer. He heard "Mission control, this is Valkyrie One. More precisely, this is Skyler Fitch. I've decided to abort. We will initiate shortly."

Gordon keyed the mike, saying, "Sir, this is Gordon Dillard from NASA. We believe that's premature. We recommend waiting until being forced to do so due to time constraints."

"That's great, NASA, but you aren't running this show. My people have told me the pluses and minuses and I've made my decision."

The Auriga lead engineer tried to pull off Gordon's headset, but he batted the hands away, keying the mike again. "What's the mission commander say?"

Skyler came back with "I'm the mission commander."

Gordon said, "Fabio, Fabio, this is NASA, are you on the net?"

On board the capsule, Fabio looked at Skyler, then keyed his mike. "This is Fabio, go ahead."

"Don't abort. I say again, do not abort until I say so."

Skyler said, "Mission control, get that man off the net."

They heard nothing for a few seconds, then the lead engineer came back on, saying, "He's gone. If he gives us any more trouble, I'll call security."

Skyler said, "Okay, we're proceeding with the abort. Prepare to receive."

Fabio did nothing. Off the net, Skyler said, "Push that button."

"No. We're not aborting. I'm the mission commander."

"And I'm your boss. Push that button or you're fired!"

Fabio looked at him and said, "Fuck off."

Skyler's eyes grew wide and Fabio wondered if this was the first time someone had ever told him no.

Skyler began to work the buckles on his harness and Fabio said, "If you leave that seat, you'll spend the rest of this journey unconscious. We aren't aborting."

CHAPTER 69

A ndrei Obrenovic felt his phone vibrate and thought, *Finally*. He looked at the number and saw it wasn't Nikita. It was an unknown. He thought about declining it, but then recognized the area code as Washington, DC. He accepted the call.

"Is this Andrei Obrenovic? The Russian oligarch?"

"It is, but I don't like that term. I'd prefer 'the Russian business-man.'"

"Businessman? What's your business? I mean besides bankroll-ing hackers to take money from U.S. corporations?"

That got Andrei's attention. He said, "Who is this?"

"Who I am doesn't matter. What I represent does. My reach is long, and your protection right now is poor."

Andrei laughed and said, "I promise my protection is adequate. You'll have to do better than phone threats."

"You mean Nikita? And his pack of pipe hitters? They're dead. I killed them in Croatia. And I'm coming for you unless you an-swer one simple question."

Andrei turned in a circle, not wanting to believe the words, but how else would he know the name of his head of security? *And* that he was in Croatia?

Andrei hadn't had contact with Nikita in days, which also bol-stered the story. He said, "What do you want?"

"I'm not after you. Yet. I'm after a man I know as Sphinx. I only know his code name, but I know you know his identity. He's an American and of no consequence to you."

"I know of no such name. I have no idea what you're talking about."

"Andrei, listen to me closely. Nothing this man says will come back to you. I have bigger fish to fry than to chase you down, but make no mistake, I'm going to find Sphinx. If I do it the hard way, it'll be through you. I'm going to find you. And I'm going to kill you."

"I can't give you what I don't know."

"Then enjoy what's left of your life living like a pauper."

"What's that mean?"

"It means the only way you're going to extend how long you walk this earth is to disappear, meaning no more yachts, no more villas in the mountains, no more caviar. It'll let you live a few months longer, but you'll still die. It's what I do. You do ransomware, and I hunt men for a living."

Andrei considered for a moment, then said, "So if I give you the name, you leave me alone?"

"Yes. With one caveat: you no longer bankroll ransomware gangs. I've already destroyed Dark Star. Don't give me a reason to regret today's decision."

The mention of Dark Star made up Andrei's mind. The man was telling the truth, and if he'd killed Nikita and the rest of Andrei's security, he was skilled.

He said, "His name is Dylan. I don't know his last name, but he runs a cybersecurity firm in the United States. He's some sort of computer genius."

"That's it? That's all you know?"

"Yes. Well, when I talked to him on the phone he had a DC

area code just like you. I don't know if that's where he lives, but that was his cell phone."

"Give me his number."

"It won't do any good. It was a burner phone. Each time he called me, it was from a different number, but the area code was always DC. He only used each SIM card once, and that's all I know."

"That's enough. You just earned the right to keep eating caviar. Don't forget what I said."

Andrei started to answer, but the line went dead.

CHAPTER 70

I hung up the phone and said, "What was the name of that guy that helped us with our ransomware and then helped the NSC? Wasn't it Dylan?"

Wolffe said, "Yeah, Dylan Hobbes. Why?"

I looked at Knuckles and said, "Head upstairs to the team rooms. Get a low-vis package for the team." I turned to Blaine, saying, "Show him what we can steal."

Blaine led the team out of the room and I said, "What's his company? Where is it? It's here in DC, isn't it?"

"It's called Second Day Solutions and yeah, it's here in DC. Why?"

I turned to the computer on the desk and googled the name, saying, "The Russian said his first name was Dylan, he was a computer genius, and he had a DC area code. That's our target. That's Sphinx."

"Dylan Hobbes? That's insane. He has a security clearance higher than God. He worked for both the NSA and Cyber Command. He's been briefing the president of the United States, for Christ's sake."

I saw the address in Tysons Corner, about twenty minutes away. I said, "And what's he been briefing? He's the one that's been talking about Iran. All the proof of the so-called Iranian penetration came from him. He's the reason we're about to be at war."

I stood up and Wolffe said, "Wait a minute. Wait just a minute. You can't conduct an assault on United States soil. It's against the charter and might very well compromise the Taskforce. Let me call the DC police. Get a SWAT team on it."

I looked at my watch and said, "It took Kerry Bostwick an hour to track down that number. It's going to take me twenty minutes just to get there. It'll take you at least an hour to get through the red tape, and we don't have that sort of time."

I hollered down the hall, "Creed, get your ass in here!"

"Creed? What's he going to do?"

"He's going to help me stop the ransomware."

Fabio looked at his watch and called mission control, his eyes on the abort button. "Mission control, mission control, how are we looking?"

"The PONR is in thirty minutes," meaning point of no return.

Skyler heard the transmission and said, "Hit it now, just in case we're in the same boat we were before. Give us some time to fix it if it doesn't fire."

Fabio said, "No. Let them work the problem."

Skyler lost his calm demeanor, saying, "Press that damn button! If we wait and it doesn't work, we're going into the space station!"

Fabio turned to him and said, "I'm not pressing that button until NASA instructs me to do so."

Skyler got on the radio and said, "Mission control, mission control, this is Skyler."

"This is mission control, go."

"Get that NASA guy on the net. Tell him to tell this asshole to press the button."

We went racing out of the parking garage in two cars, getting on Interstate 66 toward Tysons Corner, me talking on the radio the whole way.

"Okay, we're going to get there with about five minutes to spare. We go in hard, no knock and wait. If the door to the office is locked, we breach it explosively. You all have Dylan's picture. Just control anyone else. Get them on the floor and move on. There are no hostiles here."

I got head nods in my vehicle and a "roger" from the one following.

We reached the 495 loop and I said, "Five minutes out. Anyone who gets jackpot call Creed forward. Creed, you wait at the breach with Jennifer until we call."

I turned around and looked at him. He nodded, childlike glee on his face from being involved in an operation on the ground instead of staring at a computer screen.

Behind the wheel, Jennifer exited 495, passed the National Counterterrorism Center, then said, "That's it. That's the building."

I looked at the structure, seeing what appeared to be a warehouse instead of some sleek, modern building housing a cutting-edge computer company. I said, "You sure? That's not what I thought it would look like."

"That's the address."

"Pull up front. Knuckles, you have breach. Jennifer, stay with Creed until we call. Your other duty is going to be security for the people we find inside who aren't Dylan. You have enough flex-ties?"

She nodded, and I said, "Veep, Brett, stack with me."

We screeched to a stop, everyone bailing out on the run. There was no door at ground level that we could see. We found a flight of stairs and raced up them to the second level. There was a steel door with a small sign stating, "Second Day Solutions. Ring the bell for service."

Knuckles tried the handle, shook his head, and slapped a charge on the frame right next to the lockset. We scooted together behind him, getting out of the blast radius and drawing our weapons. He crouched, I cleared the radius, making sure everyone was behind me, then rubbed his shoulder.

The door lock shattered in a blinding flash, the overpressure slamming into us, the noise splitting the air, and I was moving, running around Knuckles and kicking the door open on its twisted frame.

I entered an anteroom with two people in it, neither of them Dylan Hobbes. I pointed my weapon at them and shouted, "Down, down. Get the fuck on the ground."

They did so, and I went forward to an office, saying on the net, "That's the holding area. Koko, flex-tie them and don't let them use a phone." I stopped at the door, felt a squeeze, and entered, seeing a man behind a computer looking at me in shock.

I jerked him to his feet and flung him into the anteroom, letting Jennifer take over. I didn't even wait for him to hit the ground, racing to the next office, Veep behind me. I saw Knuckles and Brett on the other side of the room doing the same thing, going into one office and extracting people before moving to the next. I reached the last office, finding yet another man behind a computer, and instead of jerking him out, I pointed my gun at him and said, "Where's Dylan Hobbes?"

He raised his hands in the air and said, "In the SCIF. In the lab SCIF."

"Where is that?"

"Downstairs. It's downstairs."

I broke out of the office, saying on the net, "All elements, all elements, downstairs. Koko, get those last two on the ground, get their cells, then bring Creed."

Knuckles was first in the stairwell, me right behind him. We took the steps two at a time, leapt over a landing, and continued on to the bottom. Knuckles jerked the door handle and we met Dylan Hobbes, his hand out like he was trying to open it.

He said, "What was that explosion?" Then he saw us with our guns and said, "What—"

Knuckles stunned him with a jab to the face and grabbed his arm, planting a hip into his body and rotating. Hobbes flipped over Knuckles' back and slammed into the ground, hard. Knuckles rolled him to his stomach, then flex-tied his hands together, Hobbes screaming the whole time.

Knuckles jerked him to his feet and I leaned into him, pointing my weapon at his nose. I said, "You have about five minutes to live. Where is the ransomware computer?"

"Wh . . . what?"

I theatrically racked my slide, a round flipping through the air, then shoved it into his temple.

He pointed with his head, saying, "In there. In there."

CHAPTER 71

Gordan Dillard looked at his watch, saw they were out of time, and pressed the mike, resigned to the fact that he was about to kill four people. But four was better than the entire space station.

"Fabio, Fabio, this is NASA, do you copy?"

"This is Fabio, go."

He took a deep breath, then said, "We're out of time. I'm sorry. It didn't work out. Go ahead and abort."

Sounding as if he were ordering a pizza, Fabio said, "Roger. Copy abort. Confirm?"

"This is NASA. I confirm."

Inside the capsule, Fabio looked at his fellow travelers and said, "It's been good to know you. Everyone take fifteen seconds to pray or do whatever you need to do."

The time elapsed and he reached for the button, flipping up the Plexiglas shield. He glanced once more around the capsule and put his finger on the button.

His helmet came alive, someone shouting, "Stop! Stop! Stop!"

He pulled his hand back, saying, "Mission control, this is Valkyrie One. What's the situation?"

"The screens are clearing. I say again, the screens are clearing. The point of no return is irrelevant now. Don't abort. I say again, do not abort. Let us get control."

Fabio exhaled and said, "Roger all, mission control. Valkyrie One standing by."

They floated through space for another thirty minutes, the space station finally visible in the distance, when mission control came on, saying, "Valkyrie One, Valkyrie One, we have control. I say again, we have control."

Skyler keyed his mike, saying, "You have all systems up and running? All systems are green?"

"Roger that."

"Then let's dock. I can see the space station. We're almost there."

"Uhh . . . this is mission control. We recommend an abort to get you home. I think we've had enough adventure on this trip."

Skyler said, "That's a complete waste of money and time. We're within an hour before we dock."

"Yes, sir. Your call."

Fabio looked at Skyler, then the other two, stopping on Abigail. She slowly shook her head left and right.

He returned to Skyler, said, "Fuck you, asshole," and slammed his fist into the abort button.

CHAPTER 72

I walked into the Four Courts Irish pub about five minutes before it opened, right at 4 P.M. I saw a scrum of people all working to get the place ready and a man came forward, saying, "We
aren't open yet."

I said, "You are for me. Get me Bryce."

He started to say something else, and Bryce came through the
kitchen door. A rangy man with salt-and-pepper hair, he was the
manager and an Army veteran. He took one look at me and shook
his head.

He came forward and told the waiter, "I'll handle this." The
waiter walked away and he said, "You lost someone."

"Yeah, we did. And the men involved are coming here today.
Sorry."

He smiled and said, "Don't be sorry. It's the least I can do."

The Four Courts Irish pub was where we held all our memori-
als. It had a unique place in my heart because a bunch of assassins
had tried to kill me inside the place a long time ago. Bryce wasn't
read into our program, but he believed in what we did, even if
he didn't know what that was. We'd shown up one day toast-
ing a fallen soldier, and then we'd kept showing up, until he'd
pulled me aside one afternoon. He'd seen us keeping to ourselves,
knowing we didn't want to be disturbed, and had told me if we
wanted privacy the next time, the bar was ours. He'd never asked

any questions, and being located so close to the CIA, I'm sure he thought that was where we worked, and I didn't disabuse him of the notion.

All I knew was that when I showed up, he shut down the bar.

He flipped the sign on the door to closed and said, "I'll be serving the drinks."

"I appreciate that. I really do." I'd initially tried to pay to rent the place, but he was having none of it. He didn't even let us pay for our drinks.

He chuckled and said, "Don't worry about it. Last year this time we were closed permanently because of COVID. One night is nothing. Rum and Coke?"

I said, "Sure," and moved to a table. He brought the drink, then ushered the waitstaff out of the bar. I sat in silence for a moment, then the door opened. George Wolffe and Blaine Alexander came in, looked around, then walked to my table.

They took a seat, Blaine saying, "You like cutting it close, but yesterday was damn near a record."

I laughed and said, "I saw the capsule landed safely."

"Yeah. A little bit of drama afterwards for the network shows, but everyone's safe."

"What happened?"

"The mission commander got out of the capsule and decked the owner, Skyler Fitch. He was waving to the cameras all smiles one second, then sitting on his ass rubbing his face the next. Pretty sure that astronaut won't be taking up the next flight."

Wolffe said, "Where's Jennifer?"

"At Reagan National picking up Amena. I had Kylie fly her up here."

"Really? You're going home tomorrow."

"I know, but when we talked to her last night she begged."

He smiled, saying, "And you can't tell her no."

I took a sip of my drink and said, "Nope. That's the truth."

Bryce came over and took their orders. When he left, I said, "So what's going on with Dylan Hobbes?"

Wolffe said, "That's a sticky one. President Hannister wants to keep the Iran narrative alive. If Dylan's actions hit the light of day, it'll be a debacle. Iran will use it as leverage any time we say they're doing something wrong."

"Just like the WMD thing from Iraq."

"Exactly. If we say they're starting up new centrifuges, they'll say, 'You mean like when you said we hacked your spacecraft?'"

"So, what's going to happen?"

"Well, as far as Iran knows, we fervently believe they did it— and our actions against them may very well give them pause if they're planning on any cyberattacks in the future."

"I meant with Dylan. Tell me he's just been labeled DOA."

Wolffe chuckled and said, "We don't do that to American civilians."

"We have before." A long time ago, on the same mission where I'd almost been killed in this very bar, I'd uncovered a cancer inside the National Security Council. A man who was Ollie North times ten. He'd almost started a war, and when I'd prevented it, he'd met his just rewards.

Wolffe said, "Standish wasn't a civilian, and we didn't kill him."

I laughed and said, "Only because he was already dead when we arrived."

Wolffe waved his hand and said, "Old history. Either way, Dylan isn't DOA."

"So, he just skates? Keeps raking in the money with his corporation like nothing happened?"

"He thinks he's a patriot. He believed he was bringing the country together, trying to fuse the partisan divide by focusing our attention on a common enemy."

"Off the backs of people he murdered? Who cares what he thinks? We're giving him a pass because he thought he was doing good?"

Blaine held up a hand and said, "Keep it down. He's not getting off. He's going to jail for murder."

"Murder? How?"

"Last week one of his guys fell down the stairwell, bashing his head into the concrete. The fall killed him and was ruled an accident."

"Now?"

"Now the authorities are taking a harder look. And Dylan, because he doesn't want to be DOA, has agreed to plead guilty to murdering him."

"Did he?"

"Not as far as I know, but it works."

I leaned back and said, "I guess that's the best we'll get."

Blaine said, "Shit, you're just lucky your entire team wasn't thrown in jail from the assault."

After we'd solved the ransomware problem, we'd secured the crisis site, then I'd thrown the entire mess into Wolffe's lap, letting him figure out how to conduct extraction. He'd pulled some strings, and we'd given control of the site to Department of Homeland Security guys from the National Counterterrorism Center down the road. Their agents processed the people we'd tied up while we fled the scene, dragging Dylan Hobbes with us.

I had no idea if they even had the authority to assume control, but we'd gotten out clean—although Wolffe was still dealing with the fallout. Luckily, he had the president of the United States on his side. They were calling it a "national security exercise conducted by DHS," basically "admitting" that the exercise had gone awry, and the "DHS" team had hit the wrong target. Instead of a bunch of role players in a rented building, they'd attacked a live office. It made the DHS boys look like buffoons, but it worked. The press became bored quickly.

The door to the bar opened and Veep, Brett, and Knuckles came in. Bryce waved at them, Knuckles did a twirl with his hand, telling him to bring over some drinks, and they sat down.

Wolffe said, "Only missing the females."

Knuckles said, "They're on the way." He turned to Wolffe and said, "What's the deal with Carly and her star?"

Wolffe technically still worked for the CIA, same as Carly, but because she was sheep-dipped into the Taskforce, her star on the CIA memorial wall was an open question.

Wolffe said, "Kerry Bostwick is making it happen. I don't know how, but she'll get her star."

Knuckles nodded and said, "Good. Good man."

The door opened again, and I looked up with expectation. Instead of Jennifer and Amena, it was Johnny and Axe, from another Taskforce team. I was surprised to see them, since we hadn't advertised we were doing this.

Wolffe saw my expression and said, "I told them. They did some work with her in Colombia. They wanted to be here."

I nodded, saying, "I'm impressed. Axe doesn't do these things."

Johnny was lanky, full of ropy muscles like a cowpuncher. Axe looked like a *Call of Duty* character. About six feet four, with a clean-shaven head and a full beard, he wore the muscles on his body like a display. He wasn't body-builder large, but he was most definitely intimidating.

I stood up, shook Johnny's hand, and said, "Thanks for coming."

He said, "Wouldn't miss it. Free drinks and all."

I laughed, and the door opened again. I saw Jennifer, wearing a sundress and sandals, her hair a tousled mess in a clip, looking like a surfer just off the beach. I smiled at her, and from behind her Amena came running.

She wrapped her arms around my waist and buried her head into my belly, saying, "I missed you."

I squeezed back, saying, "I've only been gone a few days. But I missed you, too."

She smiled and I let her free, saying, "Okay, the gang's all here."

I waved to Bryce and he came over. To the group, I said, "Anyone know what Carly drank?"

Knuckles said, "Bourbon."

I squinted, because I knew that's what he drank, and he said, "I'm not making that up. In fact, she drinks Bardstown. The Prisoner." He turned to Bryce and said, "You have that?"

"I do. It's in the back."

Knuckles said, "All the way around."

Bryce delivered the drinks, and everyone looked at me. I said, "Knuckles, it's your show."

He turned to Jennifer and said, "You do the honors."

She nodded and said, "For Carly."

We all said, "For Carly."

She said, "May she rest in peace."

In unison, we said, "Peace is an illusion. May she continue to fight."

We downed the whiskey and I saw a tear in Jennifer's eye. I put my glass down and went to her, wrapping my arms around her and kissing her forehead. Amena stood next to us awkwardly, not sure what to do. I brought her into the embrace.

We broke and I said, "It'll be good to get back to Charleston. I could use some sleep."

Amena said, "Jennifer told me you'd take me to the Air and Space Museum before we go."

I looked at Jennifer and she wiped her eyes, smiling. She said, "As long as we're here. Kylie is staying because of Veep. I figured it couldn't hurt."

I chuckled and said, "As long as I don't have to sleep in a tent."

Amena said, "Me either."

We drifted apart, talking to the others there, dusk starting to fall, and I found myself with Axe.

He said, "I heard you had those Badr guys dead to rights, in the crosshairs, and didn't take the shot. That true?"

I'd thought about that decision a lot in the last few days, wondering if it had been right. I knew that Shakor and his friends had American blood on their hands, and they deserved to be planted, but killing a man takes something out of you. It's like a chip in the armor of your soul each and every time. Killing in self-defense was one thing, but putting a bullet in their heads that day was something else.

I said, "It's true. I let them walk."

"Even after Carly?"

I said, "We slaughtered the men who hit her. They're dead. This wasn't them."

He said, "You're a better man than I am. I'd have smoked them no matter who they were. Badr 313 aren't good guys. In fact, I'll probably end up doing that very thing someday. Cleaning up your leftovers."

And that was the crux of the argument. Had I let Shakor go only to have him kill some other Americans? But you can't see the future. You can't put a bullet into somebody's head just because you think he *might* be dangerous. Because of that, I hadn't taken the shot. By all rights, they should have been dead for what Ghulam had tried to do against Branko, and I'd let them live. It would haunt me.

I said, "Maybe you will, Axe. Maybe you will. But I have to look in the mirror each morning, and I want to like what's looking back."

He nodded and said, "I hear you. I know."

His eyes held a sense of loss, and I realized he'd been in a similar situation before and had gone the other way. I didn't know what to say to that. He clinked my glass and said, "To Carly," then wandered away, joining Knuckles and Brett.

I sat down in a chair and saw Amena hovering near the bar. She'd heard the conversation. She came over and said, "This is because someone died, isn't it?"

I hadn't explained anything to her, just letting her run around the bar figuring she wouldn't understand, but I should have known that was dumb.

I said, "It is."

"Carly was a friend?"

"Yes. A friend."

"And you had the ability to avenge her death and didn't take it, like you did with me?'

She'd heard the exchange between me and Axe, and now I was going to listen to my adopted daughter tell me how I'd screwed up. Amena had lost her entire family to a sociopathic Chechen, her father and brother killed right before her eyes. She had a little bit of a vengeance streak because of it, and I'd satisfied that streak, killing the man hunting her.

I said, "Honey, this was a little different. It wasn't the same thing. The men weren't trying to kill me. It was a meeting we'd agreed to have."

She stared into my eyes, then said, "But you regret it."

I said, "I don't know. Maybe I do. It's not that simple."

She crawled into my lap, saying, "My father used to tell us to do the right thing. Even when I was stealing from the tourists in Monaco, he would say that. I kept what I did hidden, because he would never understand, but we needed money for food. I'd come home and get a lecture about how it was easy to do wrong, but sometimes hard to do the right thing."

She laid her head into my chest and said, "I think what you did was the hard thing. But it was the right thing."

And that was all the absolution I needed.

ACKNOWLEDGMENTS

I will tell you this up front—Croatian gelato is the secret to life. I've had gelato in Italy, and here in the United States, but that stuff in Croatia is on another planet. If I could have written an entire book centered on that, I would have.

For the first time since COVID, I had the opportunity to travel for book research, but the options were limited. Most countries still had massive restrictions, but Croatia said, "bring it on." Truthfully, I had an entire book research trip planned for the country for my previous novel, *End of Days*, but COVID sidelined it. When the world started to reopen, my wife, the DCOE, said, "Where are we going?" I'd already done the planning for Croatia a year before, and said, "No brainer."

Our first stop was Zagreb, the capital of Croatia, and I'm indebted to our guide for setting the tone for the rest of our research. In Zagreb alone he showed me the Gric Tunnel, and when I asked for a local's only speakeasy, he told me how to find the Café A'è. He asked where we were headed, and suggested the Makarun restaurant in Split, along with an underground airfield Tito had during the Cold War. (I really wanted to use that, but it was surrounded by old minefields and off limits.)

As is our want, we decided to rent a car and drive down the coast through the entire country, figuring that it can't be that hard. Of course, that didn't work out. Not that the country was hard, just that my GPS was a little pathetic at directions. Every day was an adventure. For instance, if you ever visit the Plitvice National Park, be sure and get a map, because the posted signs are absolutely worthless. We took what we thought was the "2 hour" hiking route, and then found ourselves in the middle of the woods inside a driving rainstorm. Eight hours later—EIGHT HOURS LATER—we made it out. Only a part of that made it into the book. The cave where the treasure is buried. That place is real, and we saw it within thirty minutes. The rest of that? Just something for the history books and my wife.

We hit many towns along the coast, and some of the stories are hilarious. At one point, we were waiting in the car line to get on a ferry and it was completely full. The guy at the terminal waved us forward, and I said to Elaine, "What's he trying to tell us? Park somewhere until the next ferry?"

He was standing there in his yellow vest and furiously waving. Elaine said, "I think he wants us to board." I said, "Where? The entire boat is full." She pressed the gas (because I *always* make her drive) and he parked us sideways on the ramp of the ferry. I couldn't even open my door to get out. I said, "I'm not sure this is legal." Elaine said, "Who cares? We made it onboard!" My own personal Jennifer.

An hour later we were in Korcula, which, of course, made the book. Marco Polo, according to legend, was from there. The boutique hotel in the book is real, but I wasn't going to spend the money to stay there. (Well, I wanted to, but couldn't justify it. The only thing available was the China Room, and it was really on the edge of being rockstar stupid.) The DCOE found our digs, and that's what the Taskforce uses in the book.

There's a reason *Game of Thrones* is mentioned several times in the story, and it's because it was referenced everywhere we went, to the point it got to be a little ridiculous. Klis Fortress was majestic, but it had now become a *GOT* pilgrimage site. The old town of Split is one of the coolest places I've ever visited—and the cellars in the book exist, but once again, with a *GOT* twist (okay, if you have to know, it's where Daenerys kept her dragons). In fact, the old town now includes a *GOT* museum. Speaking of Split, our guide in Zagreb had been right—the Makarun restaurant was stellar—and he didn't know it, but the setting was perfect for Branko's safehouse.

I'm also indebted to my next-door neighbor Lana for telling us to get some lunch at Mali Ston on our way to Dubrovnik. She's from Bosnia, and was really just giving us some restaurant ideas, but when I saw the wall between Ston and Mali Ston, I immediately had a scene in my head, which played out in the book. We stopped in Ston and stomped around it long enough to get a feel, then got a huge plate of mussels in Mali Ston.

We found the Caffe Bar Buza in the old town of Dubrovnik all on our own, purely by accident (after walking up the *GOT* "shame stairs," of course). As soon as I saw it, I knew I was going to use it, but this required a little bit of literary license. Yes, it's exactly as described, and daredevils were jumping off the cliff to the water below—but it's cash only. They don't take credit cards, so save your emails on that. The Cave Bar, on the other hand, I sought out because I'd read about it.

Dylan Hobbes is a real person. I donated a character to the Special Operations Warrior Foundation for a fundraising auction, and the person who won provided the name. I've never met Dylan or the person who bid, but hope he doesn't mind being the bad guy . . .

Elaine and I are ambassadors for SOWF because of their mission of providing education support to the children of fallen Special Operations warriors. Check them out at www.specialops.org if you'd like to support them. The CEO is a personal friend of mine, a retired Major General who used to fly for TF 160 SOAR. One day he said, "When do I get in a book? I want to be flying with long hair like Fabio." His name is Clayton Hutmacher, and he's real as well. Clay, hope you like your callsign in the book.

The plot of this book came from some research I was conducting about the Israeli company NRO and its Pegasus malware surveillance tool. I learned the UAE was using the tool to keep track of journalists, dissidents, and even U.S. citizens. Bad enough, but the men actually using the tool on behalf of the UAE were United States ex-intelligence personnel working for something called Project Raven. While NRO claims they only license Pegasus to vetted nation states, the tool is scary in its ability to be misused, and the fact that former U.S. intel operatives were executing the action became a germ of a story. As I conducted the research on malware in general, learning about zero-click and cyber vulnerabilities, I hit on the massive and growing problem of ransomware. In the last couple of years, ransomware gangs have shut down our pipelines, taken the world's largest supplier of meat offline on two different continents, held numerous hospitals hostage, and literally caused the entire country of Costa Rica to grind to a halt. The groups are all shadowy and it's impossible to determine if they're operating on their own or being bankrolled by another nation-state. In the end, it was a better story, so I went that way with *The Devil's Ransom*.

I'm deeply indebted to my agent, John Talbot, and my team at Morrow, from Tavia in marketing to Danielle in publicity to the sales team who work tirelessly to support my efforts. Without them, my books would be sitting on my nightstand being read only by my family. A special thanks to my editor, David Highfill, who reached a point in his life where he wanted something different. This is my final book with him, and I feel like I've lost a part of my writing brain. He will be sorely missed, and I treasured our time together. I wish him the best of luck! Luckily, my new editor, Lyssa Keusch, has picked up the reins without a pause, and I'm looking forward to working together as we continue to expand the Pike Logan universe.